KEEP CALM

KEEP CALM

A THRILLER

MIKE BINDER

HENRY HOLT AND COMPANY   NEW YORK

Henry Holt and Company, LLC
Publishers since 1866
175 Fifth Avenue
New York, New York 10010
www.henryholt.com

Henry Holt ® and 🏛® are registered trademarks of
Henry Holt and Company, LLC.

Library of Congress Cataloging-in-Publication Data

Binder, Mike, 1958–
    Keep calm : a thriller / Mike Binder. — First edition.
        pages cm
    ISBN 978-1-62779-347-6 (hardback) — ISBN 978-1-62779-348-3 (electronic book)
    1. Ex-police officers—Fiction.   2. Bombings—Fiction.   3. Conspiracy—Fiction.   4. Great
Britain—Fiction.   I. Title.
    PS3602.I53K44 2015
    813'.6—dc23   2014047765

Henry Holt books are available for special promotions and
premiums. For details contact: Director, Special Markets.

First Edition 2015

Designed by Kelly S. Too

Printed in the United States of America
1 3 5 7 9 10 8 6 4 2

This is a work of fiction. All of the characters, organizations, and events portrayed in
this novel either are products of the author's imagination or are used fictitiously.

For Diane, Molly, and Burt . . . as always

One ought never to turn one's back on a threatened danger and try to run away from it. If you do that, you will double the danger. But if you meet it promptly and without flinching, you will reduce the danger by half.

—WINSTON CHURCHILL

KEEP CALM

AFTER

BEFORE

AFTER THE BOMBING ▪ 1

The bomb went off at 10 Downing Street just after six p.m. Georgia had been in the small private bathroom off her office at Number 11, trying once again, as usual, to make some sense of her hair before she met with Alistair Stephenson, the minister of education. She had just taken her third pain pill of the day. The ache in her leg was a distant irritant most times now, sporadically troublesome in the morning or after a long day of travel, but the pills made the tumult of her life easier to deal with, so she ate them gladly, like bright red rock candy.

It was a loud, booming roar of a blast that shook the walls, made the building roll, and even, Georgia thought later, lifted it as if it were just a small cardboard mock-up of Downing Street. The explosion was shadowed by an eerie moment of quiet, a confused sea of silence that washed over the building and cascaded down the halls of both Numbers 10 and 11. Georgia, the chancellor of the exchequer, stood alone for several stunned seconds. Jack Early, her private secretary, broke the hush when he ran down the hall just as alarm bells began to ring and voices could be heard shouting down the back corridors.

"Madam, are you all right?"

"Yes, of course, that was devastating. Please tell me everyone's all right. What was it?"

She was dizzy, spinning, or maybe the room was; maybe Early was spinning and not her. She grabbed the side of her large wooden desk to stay upright.

"I believe it was a bomb. It must've been. In Number 10." Early was even paler then he normally was. The palest, driest-skinned man she had ever known was somehow even whiter and drier now than usual. He was shaking. Others were now gathering in the hallway outside. The two perky blondes who worked in Early's office whispered quietly to him about plans on where and how to evacuate Georgia.

A Metropolitan Police officer, from the Diplomatic Protection Group, a tall man with a thick shock of white hair and a stern, worried look on his face, came into the room speaking in a hushed, determined tone. He spoke quickly to Early in the outer office, then turned to Georgia.

"You'll need to come with me, Chancellor. Straight off, please."

"What is it? What's happened?"

"There's been a bomb. An explosion. Seems to have gone off on the second floor of Number 10. We need to move you at once."

"What about the prime minister? Where is he?"

"It appears that the PM's been hit, ma'am. He's being attended to now."

"Hit? How? Is he going to be . . ."

"Ma'am, all that I've been told is that we need to get you out of the building. Right now."

"Others?"

"No. Just the PM. We need to go, Madam Chancellor."

The Second Lord of the Treasury, or the chancellor of the exchequer, has with time become the most powerful office in the British government, next to the prime minister. Georgia Turnbull was the first woman to ever hold the post. She was Prime Minister Roland Lassiter's longest-running trench mate in politics. Brilliant, steel-willed, and confident to a fault, her relationship with Lassiter was complicated and intricate. It ran hot and cold, was deeply important to both, and confusing to all others. She was Lloyd George to his Asquith or, more to the point, Brown to his Blair. They had gone to university together, had come up through the rough and tumble of party politics, won a bitter election, cobbled together a government, helped the country climb out of a prolonged triple-dip recession, twisted and tugged new life out of a broken civil service, and had even, two years earlier, survived a horrific helicopter crash together. The relationship was so intense that quite a few friends had quietly always suspected that Ms. Turnbull had secretly been in love with the extremely photogenic and very married Roland Lassiter.

Physically, Georgia possessed a brand of beauty that was all her own. The word "striking" had always been used in any description of her. She was tall, with a commanding presence and dark penetrating eyes on a radiant face blanketed with creamy alabaster skin. She had wild hair that ran afoul of any sense of direction or obedience to grooming. Even as a young woman, her drive, candor, and razor-sharp intellect had all combined to make an extremely attractive, if not run-of-the-mill, kind of beauty. She had a slight stoop that was only exaggerated with the fallout from the helicopter accident, her gait now stilted with the constant need of a cane.

People outside were running around Number 10 and Number 11 in what seemed like every direction. There was panic in the wind, sirens bouncing up Whitehall in a pack now, forming together into a single war whoop, coating the air with a blanket of fright. Georgia reached the street outside the buildings just as armored cars and SUVs screeched to a desperate stop. Men in bulletproof police uniforms hunkered down with rifles and communications gear. The entire area was transformed with lightning speed into a locked-down armored military theater. She and Jack Early were quickly and carefully ushered into an army-outfitted SUV and driven out of Downing Street past a never-ending line of arriving squad cars and a short, sturdy row of tanks that were set up in the middle of the main road. A hazmat truck barreled up to the front gate and was flagged in past all of the other vehicles. Helicopters circled overhead, both army and police. An overeager news copter was instantly forced away. As if a switch had been flipped on, a parallel chaotic universe instantly came into existence. Georgia looked back at the rush of manic movement as her vehicle hustled away up Whitehall, smoke billowing toward the sky from a fire in Number 10, her thoughts only on Roland Lassiter, not even daring to think the worst.

A FEW HOURS later, the world had been told—not in the way they had all wanted the world to be told; not in the way Georgia wanted to see it unfold; not to the liking of Kirsty Lassiter, Roland's beloved, permanently put-upon wife, or Sir Melvin Burnlee, the home secretary, and least of all not to the satisfaction of Alan Munroe, Lassiter's long-hovering director of communications and strategy. They hadn't even had the chance to inform anyone at Buckingham Palace. The word was out to the world before any of them really had a clue themselves as to exactly what had transpired.

The entire government was frozen in a shell-shocked daze for more than two hours. In the vacuum, the press took the ball and ran with it. The news was leaked out in a typically tawdry modern way: a patchwork quilt of guesswork and innuendo that belittled everything about the situation, the integrity of the government, the life of Roland Lassiter, and the emotions of the British people. There was no waiting out of courtesy, no checking of facts. The press just tripped over themselves to be the first to report on the tragedy: an explosion at Number 10, Roland Lassiter on his deathbed. He hadn't even reached the hospital when Sky News broke the story with helicopter shots of the Metropolitan Police shutting down and evacuating Downing Street, front and back.

In lieu of any substantiated information, these were the images that the entire world watched, over and over on a continuous loop for several hours. Blurry video from a God's-eye view showed police, government workers, and military figures running to and fro in odd confusion-driven circles, like worker bees whose hive had been shot through with a shotgun blast. Number 10 was utter chaos.

LATE IN THE evening, Georgia and Early were more or less hidden in a secure COBRA conference room somewhere in Whitehall. They were with Sir Melvin Burnlee, whose brief included MI5, the Met police, the Diplomatic Protection Group, and all of the police and investigation services in matters of interior, and Felix Holmby, the deputy prime minister. Georgia had just hung up with the palace and was told she would be getting a call from His Royal Highness, the king, in a short time. She also took a call from the American president and the newly elected president of France.

Finally a call came in from Louise Bloomfield, the prime minister's private secretary. She had traveled with Mrs. Lassiter to the hospital behind the ambulance. The only news she offered was that the PM was still unconscious and that the bomb had done serious, yet not necessarily life-threatening, damage to his midsection.

Lassiter may well survive this one, Georgia thought to herself in the form of a silent prayer. *Maybe he truly does live some kind of magically dusted life, just as he always claimed he did.*

"The gods are on my side, Georgia. I predict we will take South Ribble, Stafford, Ilford North, and even Elmet and Rothwell tonight. They may have history, them, but I'm one charmed bastard on a whale of a run lately, and they'll all have to just deal with it up there."

She thought back on that night of their first general election, the night they came to power, the night the world changed. She also remembered the morning three years later when they crashed to the sea in a giant metal army helicopter, her leg shattering into fifteen pieces, her collarbone breaking in half like a holiday wishbone, two soldiers dead from the crash, another drowned during the rescue, and Lassiter without a scratch. He walked away more or less unharmed. Maybe he was right; maybe he was of a special breed. Maybe he could survive this awful blow. *Dear God, please let it be so.*

BEFORE LONG IT had fallen to Georgia to make the first official public statement, to address the press on behalf of her government, her party, her country, and Roland Lassiter. She dreaded it. It wasn't that she was press shy—she wasn't—and it wasn't that the press disliked her, as she felt they always had. It came with the job, and she lived with it. This was different: she was too gutted, too emotional to make a calm statement.

She normally enjoyed public speaking, got a quiet kick out of the limelight, whether she was addressing the press, the annual party convention, the G20, the Trades Union Congress, or even when she took prime minister's questions at Commons for Lassiter. She reveled in it when she had a point of view, when she argued ways into or out of an issue. In those moments, on the stage or at the podium, she thought of herself proudly as a conviction politician, a soldier with a cause, and it lifted her above anything as petty as stage fright.

The press platform was placed out in front of the Whitehall gate on the far side of the security booths. Downing Street was shut down tight until it was made sure there weren't additional bombs still to go off. The press camped along the front sidewalk and the lip of the driveway. Georgia, Early, and Munroe came up Whitehall in the army SUV and tucked in right behind the platform. As she disembarked from the SUV she thought that maybe she would do without the cane. It obviously spoke of infirmity, an image she wasn't the least bit eager to put forward. In the end she decided she needed it, and the fallout if she couldn't make it, if she needed to be walked back in after, would have been much worse than people seeing her with the cane she'd already been married to for almost two years.

She hobbled out slowly, facing the overflowing crowd of cameras, reporters, sound technicians, and segment producers. It was the biggest gathering of its kind she had ever witnessed at Downing Street or, for that matter, anywhere else. She did her best to settle at the portable podium and meet the crowd out on the avenue there with a brave resolute stance.

"Good evening. As you may already know, we have had a most cowardly act visited upon our house. We are all in a state of shock, to say the least. Our hearts and minds are steadfastly alongside Roland Lassiter and his brave family today. Our prime minister, our friend, our leader, has suffered greatly . . . yet I am pleased to say that though he may be slightly weary from the events of today, his gentle smile and his renowned faculties are all intact and will soon be ready to once again be put to service by us all."

Her speech went on, giving details where she could, in as plainly personal a way as she felt comfortable. She reminded herself that she was there to calm. She tried desperately not to show the fear and the dread she felt, so she spoke clearly, looking into each of the different cameras, hoping not to transmit the doubt she was choking on.

It was the final line of her statement that both she and Munroe knew would get the largest share of ink, would stir the most emotion: a bellicose warning, wrapped in her sharp Scottish accent—a shot across the bow to the perpetrators of the act.

"In short time, as the dust settles, we will piece together the events of this dark day and then, with the warm light of a clear morning, we will come for you, we will find you, and I promise, on behalf of our United Kingdom, there will be hell to pay."

Her statement read, she turned and burrowed her way back inside the SUV. As the press shouted a barrage of questions to her, she ignored them all. She just kept moving into the truck where once inside she slumped into her seat, settled her body in, and then, as they pulled away from view, quickly and energetically, she began to weep.

The best thing about living in Wilmette, Illinois, was how easily Adam Tatum could get to the train station and then to downtown Chicago to his office at Heaton Global Investments, or HGI as it was known in the eleven nations where it had offices. This job, the first he'd ever held that had required him to wear a jacket and tie, still baffled him. How he had gotten it, what they saw in him, what he was supposed to do, and if he was going to be any good at it were still unanswered questions, even after he'd been there for eight months. The only things that made any sense to him were the forty-minute train ride into Chicago and the moments every morning when Kate, his wife, and Trudy and Billy, his two children, all dropped him off at the little redbrick Wilmette train station.

They had previously lived in Michigan before being uprooted by this new job. He had been born and raised in Michigan. He and Kate had met in Ann Arbor when she was a student at the University of Michigan. The gods had somehow sent her to him from London. He was a first-year member of the Ann Arbor police force, three years older than her, nice-looking, quick-witted, and charismatic. He was a cop; he started as a patrolman and had gone on to quickly climb the ranks of the police department and had been made detective in record time. He had spent his life overcoming every obstacle en route to every single thing he wanted to achieve.

In truth, he never really loved being a cop. He became one because his father and his father's five brothers were either cops or reps for the policemen's union. He had floated along in the wake of his family, happy to just do what had been done, to excel in the arena that Tatums had always excelled in—until he met Kate. Kate changed everything.

She was in Michigan studying art and running away from either someone in Britain or Britain in general. She was an answer to a dream he hadn't remembered having, a prayer that had been granted before it had even been solicited. They dated, fell in love, started a family, and built a life—a life that just two years earlier he had stupidly done his best to smash against the rocks.

HE KISSED HIS wife and kids good-bye and settled into a seat on the second level of the aging passenger train. He watched as Kate's Jeep Wagoneer tucked into the morning traffic going out of Wilmette Village, into a line of nice cars driven by all the other moms who looked like they'd been pulled straight out of the background of one of those old John Hughes films: all pretty and relatively thin with bobbing hair and brightly colored Banana Republic wool sweaters, smiling wearily in the morning light as they dutifully dropped their husbands at the train station.

Not Kate. She was no background character. She was the exception. She had star billing in whatever it was she did. She was one of a kind, his Kate: blond, buxom, and sturdy; British to the tee; a stunner; thirty-seven years old, with bold blue eyes and hardened opinions that could bend solid steel.

Adam's sight was locked onto her and the Jeep as the train pulled away, the village traffic letting up at the same time. They drove along side by side, just for a moment, until the road forked off. She didn't feel him staring; she was too busy arguing with Trudy, their perpetually heart-broken sixteen-year-old, to notice her husband watching her lovingly and longingly from the second story of the old Amtrak runner. She couldn't see the want in his eyes, the desperate wish he was making that he could somehow will it all to be better for them, to somehow make her understand that the hell he'd put them through these last two years was truly over.

As the train barreled south and the quiet commuters read their papers, watched their iPads, and sipped their travel cups, he thought again about his job, toiling away at the biggest financial services company on the planet, just one of the many things he'd said yes to Kate about during these last tumultuous two years. He would do anything to make things right. Even take a job in a city and a state in which he knew no one, and in a business which he knew nothing about. Every day he put on the pants, jacket, and tie, boarded the train, went downtown to Heaton Global Investments off the Dearborn Street Bridge, and tried like hell to fit in and to learn—all for Kate and the kids.

In actuality he wasn't doing badly. Not for a neophyte. Not for someone who had never sold a thing in his life. Least of all institutional retirement packages. He'd had a lot of jobs; aside from being a cop, he'd done construction, even been a set carpenter in a movie studio in Pontiac, Michigan, a few years back. He'd done a lot, but he knew nothing about setting up annuities for group retirements and saving plans. This was all a foreign language to Adam, but he was doing it, showing up every day and sometimes, some of those days, people even said he had something of a knack for it.

Kate had gotten him the job. Not Kate actually, but Kate's father, Gordon. Gordon Thompson, who, at least in Adam's mind, never liked Adam and never forgave him for brainwashing his daughter and settling her permanently in Michigan. In America. Yet with all the alleged animosity, it was Gordon, the distant father-in-law, who, after Adam had had his troubles, once they seemed to have finally ended, when he had no work, no idea what to do next, called from thousands of miles away, coming to the rescue with a job at Heaton Global Investments.

Gordon Thompson had been alone in London after the death of his wife from cancer thirty years before. He missed his only child with a hunger that, at least from the other side of the ocean, had made him seem bitter. Kate's father wasn't one to travel. He had left England only once as a young man, when in the service in the Far East. Kate and Adam had only gone to see him three times in the eighteen years since they were married. Gordon and Kate spoke regularly, even talked over Skype, but the decades and the distance had done their damage. Over the years the two of them had grown into something more or less resembling strangers. Gordon's heart was broken.

Two men, Gordon and Adam, each with a deep, endless, aching supply of love for Kate, both did what they could for her. Gordon stuck his neck out and approached his childhood friend and current boss Sir David Heaton, the British billionaire CEO of Heaton Global Investments, and got his ne'er-do-well son-in-law a job; and Adam showed up every morning in an unfamiliar suit, week after week, trying desperately to make sense of a new set of obstacles. Both of them doing it all for Kate.

Kate, who dropped the kids off, picked them up, got the dry cleaning, did the shopping and the laundry and paid the bills as she wondered if it had all slipped away. If she could ever feel like she once felt before. If she could ever laugh and play and coo and pet with her big bear of a handsome husband whom she once thought the very sun rose and set upon. She took the dog for a walk every morning when the kids were at school and every day, like clockwork, she wondered whether she'd ever get over the three months he spent in jail, the charges he faced that could have had him in a federal prison for over twenty years, the shame he brought to his family. Would she ever excuse him for doing something as stupid as he'd done, for putting all of what they'd built and held holy at such silly risk?

She blamed him for everything: for losing their home in Royal Oak, for her friends abandoning her during his incarceration, for the emotional roller coaster on which he had taken their two children. She even found the moral high ground to blame him for the hours she spent staring at photos of Richard Lyle, her high school boyfriend, on Facebook. She blamed him for the afternoons wasted ruminating over Richard and the life she could have had, for combing over his posts, for marveling about what great shape he was in all these years later. It was even Adam's fault she'd been desperate enough to send several messages to Richard's Facebook account. This was all emotional weight that he had dropped onto her when he shattered their lives almost two years ago.

So yes, Adam went off to his strange new job every day on the old clanging commuter train, but the real learning curve belonged to Kate: figuring out from nine to five, day after day, how to get to the next chapter of their story; how to forgive; how to let go; how to get herself home to Adam.

ADAM MADE HIS way down the back hallway of the tenth story of the HGI building. It was a big, modern, metal-and-mirror thing that had been designed and built during the last raging bull market and plopped down onto the river along West Wacker Drive, facing north. The building never seemed to blend in with the other Chicago skyscrapers and it more or less sat there, away from the pack, its own towering entity.

As he ambled through the gauntlet of offices, more than one of the secretaries gave him a sweet smile. He was a regular fixture around the floor by then, and was well liked. The younger women saw him as cute, humble, fun to look at, and safe. He was a married man who knew how to smile and maybe flirt friendly, but not one to send out any signals other than that he headed home every night to Kate and the kids.

Retirement Services had the whole tenth floor, and Adam was headed toward the office of his boss, the head of the Chicago unit, Barry Saffron. Saffron, an ambitious forty-four-year-old transplant to Illinois from Boston's Back Bay and a lifer in the financial services world, had had Adam plopped into his lap ten months earlier in the same way that the Chicago River had landed the HGI building. Needless to say, Saffron wasn't the least bit happy when he got the call from Betty Roytan in the London office.

"Shit, I get it, Betty. This comes from the big man himself, but why Chicago? Send the little fucker to New York or to Dallas! I got way too much on my hands as it is."

"I don't understand it, either, love. This is very out of character for Sir David," replied the very dry and very British Roytan, who headed the London Pensions Package office. "All I can tell you is this young fellow's wife is the daughter of one of Sir David's security men, who also just happens to be one of his best boyhood mates. Give it your best. That's what I would do had Sir David sent me a handful. Give it my all."

With that the phone went dead, she was gone, and Barry was stuck with a new man who for some reason was handed a damn good job and a fat starting salary with absolutely no experience. Zero. Nothing.

When he got to his boss's office, Adam could see that Saffron was not in anything close to a good mood. Saffron waved him in and told him to close the door. Adam did as he was told and sat down in the contemporary leather black greeter chair. The office was stunning. No expense had been spared in interior design and furniture—modern, crisp, and clean. There were three large flat-screen TVs on two different walls so that Saffron could watch sports, world news, and business news, all simultaneously.

Adam noticed immediately that Saffron was plunked deep into his chair, all three screens dark.

"What should I make of you, Tatum? Huh? What are you, Forrest Gump or something?"

"I don't know what you mean?" He was being sincere; he had no idea where Saffron was going with this.

"I've worked my ass off for this company—for thirteen years, Tatum. I worked my way up in this business, since I was just out of college. First one in my family to ever even go to fucking college." Adam nodded. He more or less knew Saffron's history. He also knew it wasn't easy having a new guy just dropped into his world, as Adam had been. He always tried to be respectful, though, and went out of his way to be grateful for all that Saffron did for him, so he truly didn't know where this was going.

"They've put together a delegation on the fucking magnitude of this civil service pitch in London next month, and they cherry-pick from all the offices, and they didn't pick me. I know, I could trust that it was an oversight, I could give them the benefit of the doubt, but they picked you, fucking you, Tatum, and I'm sorry, but that sucks to me. They picked a friend of the boss's son-in-law, and it just kind of makes me want to take a steaming shit right here on my desk and walk right the fuck out."

"I really don't know what you're talking about, Barry. I swear I don't."

"Ah, please."

"I don't. What is it again?"

"A few of the New York group that does all government union services, employee pension specialists, some of them down in Texas that did the whole deal with the Texas government workers program we did, and a bunch of that team in Paris that always gets written up in the company newsletter are going to London next week. They're going to a round table with Sir David himself, and guess where it is? Guess where?"

"Where?"

"At 10 fucking Downing Street. You know what that is?"

"Yeah sure, I mean, it's the White House of England. Right?"

"Good. You're not a total moron. Now guess who they're meeting with, this group? Who they're gonna put the big squeeze on for taking over the investment services on the pension program for the entire British civil service? It's landmark if it happens. Guess who they're meeting with?"

"Who?"

"Roland Lassiter. The prime fucking minister. Among others. And guess who's going from the motherfucking Chicago office. Guess!"

There was silence, for a long moment. Adam didn't want to guess, and Saffron couldn't get the bile from his throat. Finally he did.

"You! Adam Fucking Tatum! That's who. They picked you to be part of the delegation and I swear to God I want to go postal in this damn place. That's how pissed off I am, Tatum."

Adam just stared across the giant glass desk. He shrugged in confusion.

"I swear to you, Barry, I have no idea what you're talking about." He sat back in Barry's expensive chair as Saffron's eyes beamed death rays at him. He started to boil now, too. This was Gordon, his father-in-law. This was a setup of some kind, to get Kate home to England. That was what this was: a setup to get Kate and the kids in London with him, and to somehow use the trip to get her to move back home permanently, with or without Adam. He was being set up. He was sure of it, and now he was just as mad as Saffron. They sat there staring at each other.

"I'm sorry, Barry. That's all I can say."

"I'll bet you're sorry. Go on. Get to work. Ellen Doyle over there in travel's gonna come see you with the details. Pretend like you don't know what she's talking about."

"I don't."

"Okay, fine. Get the fuck out."

————

ADAM DIDN'T IN fact know about the London trip. He was being straight with his boss. Kate did, though. She was in on it. Whatever this plan was, she was well aware of the details.

He was playing tetherball in the backyard of their two-story rented white-brick colonial on Birchwood Avenue up in Wilmette with his son when she finally just came out and admitted it. On the ride home from the train station she had played dumb. She pretended the London trip was all new information to her. Pretended that she didn't know that the overly friendly lady in travel would offer up four business-class tickets and a hotel suite in Mayfair so that all four of them could go. Now, there in the yard, she was finally ready to admit the truth.

"Yes, I knew. Okay? You want me to admit it? Fine. I'll admit it. My father rang me last week and told me he had overheard talk of having you going along in the delegation, and he twisted some arms at the company to have myself, Trudy, and Billy come as well."

Little eight-year-old Billy, with the crazy head of red hair and his father's big brown eyes, stopped his side of the tetherball game at once.

"Go where, Mom? Where are we all going?" Kate looked to Adam for permission to make it public but then decided she didn't need the consent and turned back to Billy.

"London. We're going to visit London. And your grandfather."

"Really? This is true? I'm going to really meet my grandfather? This is true?" He looked to his father, but didn't wait for an answer either. He jumped into the air with childish ebullience and ran toward the house to tell his sister. Halfway to the house he stopped dead in his tracks and turned back to his parents.

"How come I've never met him until now, besides on computer? How come I've never met him in person if he's my grandfather, my only one?" Neither of his parents was quick to respond, each of them sure the answer would either be wrong or bring on more questions. Kate decided to take charge with a reply.

"He lives a long way away, sweetie. London's very, very far from here. It's not so easy for your grandfather to travel all this way."

"Oh. Okay, but now I'm gonna finally meet him, right?"

"That's right, love. You are going to meet him. Finally."

"I can't wait. I'm gonna bring a lot of my soldiers and my sticker collections to show him. And my Portable Play Station." He turned and purposefully headed into the house to finish his mission to inform his older sister of their trip. Kate looked back to Adam, now playing himself in a feeble version of tetherball.

"Yes, okay, Adam. I knew. My father had called. Explained the trip to me. Yes. He did pull strings. He's just trying to get to meet his grandkids. Find some way to be with us. He's lonely, Adam. Very lonely. For me." Then, with those awesome blue eyes trained on him, she barreled down.

"As am I, lonely for him. I need this. For me. For my father and for my children and, Adam, I just can't come up with a good reason that it doesn't thrill you to no end. I cannot understand for the life of me how you would see this as some kind of plot staged against you."

He stopped smacking the big rubber ball on the string and came over to his wife. He wanted to explain to her that he was just being stupidly paranoid. Afraid to lose her. Lose her to her father. Lose her to London, to old friends, lovers, favorite street corners and songs on the radio, things and memories that weren't about him. Afraid that once there, she'd never want to come home. That she would want to reset her life all over, back where she belonged, without her husband. Without the jailbird American wacko who had pathetically lost everything they had ever had. Everything they had built.

He didn't, though. He couldn't find the words, so he gently stroked the side of her face and quietly ended the argument.

"It looks to me like we're all going to London."

AFTER ▪ 2

They met in the Cabinet Room at Number 10 the first thing the next morning. Investigators from the Diplomatic Protection Group and the Met's antiterrorism unit, SO15, worked all night to collect as many clues and forensic samples as they could from the White Room, where it had been determined that the blast did the most damage, and the cupboard from which the explosion had originated. They had also taken extreme precautions to make sure other explosive devices weren't still set to go off.

Georgia, running point on all matters for the hopefully small interregnum that the bombing had brought on, chaired the session with Lucy Barnathanson, the cabinet secretary, who was taking notes and keeping pace. Sir Donald Darling, the head of SO15, and Hardy Milligan, the director general of MI5, were both there, seated directly across the table from Georgia. To their left was the secretary of defense, then the foreign secretary, Elena Dowl-Curtiss. The commissioner of the Metropolitan Police was present, along with her boss, Sir Melvin Burnlee. The remaining seats were filled behind them with ministers, civil servants, COBRA directors, emergency planning experts, senior Met police detectives, and all of their top staff. Many, in fact most of them, had been working nonstop throughout the night.

Georgia hadn't slept either. She had taken too many of her pills, she knew, but she was on edge, taking several calls an hour from Lassiter's worried relatives, foreign leaders, secretaries, and ministers. At one point, as the home secretary was reading another list of questions that had been drawn up regarding ways to move forward, Georgia fell fast asleep while upright in her seat. She had rapidly dreamt she was asleep upstairs at Number 11 in her four-poster bed. When Early, seated behind her, quietly passed her a ballpoint pen to surreptitiously wake her as the room waited for an answer, she was, for a brief second, unsure how she had gotten down and into the Cabinet Room from her bed.

Burnlee, older than most of the others, was weary and impatient with Georgia, as always. He repeated his question with a bit of a growl.

"Does the chancellor agree that SO15 should be given the oversight on this entire investigation? Are we going to go ahead and classify this as a terrorist act?"

Georgia steadied herself nicely. She got back in the game so fast that only a few saw that she had momentarily left the court.

"If that's the consensus, yes. Although I will say that no one so far has mentioned any theories on who or what we are dealing with. I do suppose SO15 is the right horse to lead, though." She nodded to Darling, the Counter Terrorism Command's head, seated to her right.

Sir Darling, the major general, was famously a man of few words. Six and a half feet tall and nearly half as thick, he sat steely eyed, poker faced. A former member of the Special Air Service and Special Reconnaissance Regiment, he was a lifelong intelligence operative. Georgia gently patted his arm on the table, prodding him to give a summation of where they were so far.

"Thank you, Madam Chancellor. At this point I must say we have few leads as to the perpetrators. We are actively speaking to several sources and liaising abroad with all the channels one would think we'd be contacting, but as of now there's nothing yet to put a pin in. We expect to have at least a direction before much longer."

"Let's please hope so," Georgia said as a wish more than a directive. "Is it ISIL, the Islamic State? Do we have any reason to look that way?"

"None yet, ma'am, although that's a tree we're obviously going to be shaking. My guess is that we'll probably find it to be them or an offshoot of them."

"It wouldn't be a homegrown Islamic terror group, would it?"

"I personally don't see that as a possibility, Chancellor. Our ears are pretty good right now on that front, but we are combing through that possibility as well."

Then Sir Darling turned, looked over at the home secretary to give Burnlee one more chance to stop a direction that he was about to go in, and, once getting a nod to move forward, drew attention to a young woman who was sitting in the back row in one of the chairs up against the wall.

"I'd like to turn the floor to someone that I am hoping, with the chancellor's approval, can take the minute-by-minute lead on the investigation. Inspector Davina Steel."

Steel was young, twenty-seven. A pixie, too, so at five foot five she looked even younger, almost like a teen. She was cute, with velvet skin and thick brown hair that fell naturally to a flick, just below both her ears. She had an almost perfect figure. She wished she were taller, but who at her height didn't? Everything else that was God given, she was okay with, including her mind, which since she'd been a young girl had been her very own secret weapon.

She had an uncanny ability to look at things, events, pictures, photos, tapes, depositions, and eventually crime scenes and, seeing them as broken figures, reconstruct them between her ears, remembering details from other scenarios, considering options, dropped leads, or questions in a way few others ever did. She was as keen an observer of people, places, and things that those in that world had ever seen. It was a talent that in three short years had earned her the sobriquet at the nation's top anti-terrorism unit: "Darling's darling." She had risen with incredible speed from out of nowhere to quickly become one of SO15's top investigators. If she weren't so good, others in the Special Branch would resent her, but it was obviously about her talent and nothing more, so she was applauded and protected by her seniors. In fact, her humble humanity in the face of what was almost a freak-of-nature talent, her pleasant looks, and her tireless work ethic made her a much-loved figure in the large investigative department. She could sometimes have a cranky, irritable side, but in light of her many successes, others found it easy to look past those bits when it reared its head.

Sitting directly behind the mountain of a man that was Major General Darling, having been told in advance that she was going to be up on her feet with a pitch, Steel was far more nervous than she thought she'd be, especially with Georgia Turnbull there, two feet away. She had met Ms. Turnbull before, here in the Cabinet Room. She and many of the cabinet secretaries, along with Prime Minister Lassiter, were here when Steel gave the lead report on the arrest last year at Heathrow that had thwarted a bombing at the Syrian embassy. She had run that file and worked it to great success.

In truth, she idolized Georgia Turnbull. She knew every detail and most of the footnotes in Georgia's rise to power, the road she took from Glasgow as a young girl, to Finchley, to Cambridge, and up through the back channels of New Labour. Steel also was from poor Scottish parents who had moved south to run a small business in London, so it made sense that Georgia, whose father had a pharmacy in Finchley, was one of the young woman's heroes. Being here now, about to address her in this most calamitous moment, to be given this responsibility to work, if not alongside of her, then directly under her, was the opportunity of a young lifetime.

Davina rose, looking around the packed yellow-walled hall, across the large, oblong, finely polished mahogany table and the delicate bone-china coffee mugs with the coats of royal arms. It didn't seem real to be here now, or ever. Her home in her parents' musty two-bedroom flat in Bloomsbury, her upbringing as counter staff in their tiny breakfast-and-lunch bar didn't prepare her for this. She had grown up poor. A quiet face in the back row of any crowd, she continued to find this proximity to power to be both foreign and unsettling.

The only consolation was her awareness that none of these power players would find this normal, either. No one in that room could ever have been prepared for a turn such as the one the government had taken yesterday evening.

"Let me begin by saying good morning, and that I wish to extend my deepest sympathies to the family of the prime minister, and my warmest thoughts for his return to health; also to you here in this room, many of whom I'm sure call Mr. Lassiter a close friend."

Georgia liked her already. She had a sweet trace and lilt of a Scottish accent that Georgia found appealing. She remembered her from last year and the attempted Syrian embassy bombing, and of course Sir Melvin had tipped her off in a private moment before the start of the meeting that Darling wanted to use the young Scottish gal on this most urgent matter. She had an inviting face, Georgia thought to herself, a face that could set your defenses down, get a person relaxed and on informal footing very quickly. At the same time, she thought, there was a haze of sadness about Steel's eyes, a sense of knowing too much too well about human nature and about the way things tend to work in a world too often bent toward madness.

"Analysis of the crime scene at this point gives us the very little we have as a first blush. We have the security cameras in the hallways and commons areas here and outside of Number 10, but cameras aren't installed in the White Room, where the bomb went off. We haven't yet been able to ascertain as to why the PM had gone into that cupboard in that room to begin with. We know that earlier he was in the room, during a trades delegation with Sir David Heaton and members of his staff at Heaton Global, a roundtable that Ms. Turnbull and several other ministers took part in. According to the logs, it ended without incident over two hours before the bomb went off. We'll explore if there's a connection to that or not. It wouldn't seem so, but we'll dive into it once we're steady."

"What do we know about the bomb, about its makeup? How did it get into the damn building?" asked Burnlee, always impatient.

"We know that the bomb was made with a highly efficient brand of plastique explosives which for the most part we've not seen used in this form from ISIL or any of the offshoot jihadist groups. We'll have first-round testing done within the hour and we'll know more about its makeup then. We'll also have gone over the logs and cameras in all of the security systems outside and inside 10, 11, and 12 Downing Street for the day, the week, and most likely the month prior."

The home secretary barked across the table at the small young thing trying desperately not to show her shake to the room full of the country's most powerful men and women.

"So in a sense what you are saying, Inspector Steel, is that you have nothing?"

"Yes sir, at this time, I'm sorry, but that is correct. At this point, at this first lap, we've nothing."

With that she sat down in her chair, nodding to Major General Darling to please take back the reins. Georgia, sitting below the famous portrait of Walpole, looked across the table and over to the row of chairs behind the vaunted ministers and made sure to catch Steel's eye. She gave her a warm nod, a bit of a wink, and a sweet half smile. Steel nearly melted in her chair. Her skin caught a slight red flash of heat that for her came alongside moments of embarrassment and pride. She bowed her head softly in respect.

LATER IN THE day Georgia took a call from Kirsty Lassiter. The situation at the hospital was still incredibly grim. The prime minister had initially lost a lot of blood and had many shattered ribs and a ruptured spleen. On top of it all, the blast had broken his left arm.

There was a previously scheduled planning meeting with the parliamentary secretary, and a quick sit-down in her office at 11 that Sir Alan had set up with the editor of the *Guardian*, just to get some kind of press out there that they could control. Georgia agreed with Munroe on the meeting's importance. She wanted to start a conversation that "spoke of the ship not tipping." This was obviously the object of the bombers and she refused to let them see points put up on the board. This wasn't a win, she told the journalist.

"This was a sick attack on innocent people. It will change nothing, profit them nothing, and bring not one soul toward whatever is their 'cause.'" She did little to hide her disgust. It was obvious to the paper's newbie editor, Arnold Lavington, that Ms. Turnbull was taking this "incredibly personally."

AT FOUR P.M. she was up in her room above 11, and exhausted. She took another couple of pills, even though she knew she shouldn't. She was

going to slot in a quick nap, but was called down to an impromptu meeting with Donald Stanhope, the opposition leader of the Conservative
Party. Early forced her to take the meeting, claiming that not reaching
out to the opposition would be "dire." For the life of her, she didn't think
she had the energy to see the man, but somehow she summoned it up.
She hobbled downstairs, through the back hallway into Number 10, and
upstairs into the State Room, a finely decorated drawing room that was
one of Tony Blair's favorite spots in all of Downing Street. Margaret
Thatcher had spent a silly amount of money to have it redone in the style
of an eighteenth-century aristocrat's parlor. Munroe had scheduled the
meeting to take place in Roland's den downstairs, but Georgia wasn't
ready to have a meet there just yet, least of all with the opposition
leader.

Either way, regardless, Stanhope promised to be brief.

Forty-five minutes later the man still hadn't made his point.

Stanhope was rotund, unkempt, and famously flappable. Georgia had
never cared for him. At one point, as he went on about the pain he was
in for "poor Lassiter," she nodded out again and had the instant dream
about being asleep up in her bed. Luckily Stanhope didn't see her eyes
close, or even catch Early poking her back awake. He was too busy pointing, pacing, and pontificating. He was trying to tie these events through
to the years past, through the struggles with the Irish Republican Army
and World War II, the history of the country in facing adversity. *History?* Georgia thought. *He's here to give me a history lesson? Today? Let
me check the other cupboards. Maybe there's a bomb to blow me up as well.
Anything to take leave of this ass.*

Finally, Stanhope, after seeing Georgia shift in her seat one too many
times, came to his point. His visit had to do with the young investigator.
Steel.

"I understand that someone's got to have the tiller until we see what
the next day or so brings, and I'm of course happy to leave it all to you,
but allowing Sir Melvin and Major Darling and that group there to put
this young Scottish girl at the head of the investigation—the image alone,
a girl that age, so little experience, it speaks to the crowd of a wobbly
wheel, doesn't it?"

"Well, obviously you're not all that happy to leave it to me then, are you?" The opposition leader, as usual, didn't have much of an answer. He just glared over at her.

"Then whom would we leave it to, Mr. Stanhope? Should I call the PM in the hospital? Run it by him?"

"No, of course not. Don't be absurd."

Georgia stood. She needed her cane to make the full trip, which irritated her even more. She was angry anyway, and he was upsetting her, this large wooly bull of a man, but truthfully, all out of context. Early, hovering helplessly behind the couch, could see the axle about to come out from under the wagon as her voice slowly raised.

"If my nod's not good enough, if Major General Darling or the home secretary can't make the call, then who should make the call, Mr. Stanhope? You? Should I have rung up for your expertise?"

"No, no, I'm not suggesting anything—"

She cut him off, her voice now bellowing, "Of course, no! It's best that SO15 staffs this out! Clearly."

"Yes, but do they truly need to put a young thing like this out on the curb? What kind of confidence is it going to give the people? We are in uncharted waters here, Chancellor. We need to show them that we are in charge and—"

"We are not in charge here! Not even close!" She had had enough; suddenly she was interrupting, yelling out at the top of her voice, "Darling is in charge here, Burnlee is in charge here! The Met is in charge here. This will be left to the professionals! Not you, Mr. Stanhope!"

Without warning, she slammed her cane down across the coffee table between them. She sent cups and saucers into the air; a dish of cream jumped overboard and threw itself across the priceless rug. The cane made a whoosh and a whack that had Stanhope frozen in place for a full ten seconds. It was seconds that Georgia needed to check herself and realize what she had done—time enough for her to see Early at her side, sweat beading up on his balding forehead.

She stopped, sat back down on the couch. Let the room settle. She looked over to Stanhope, who was still stunned into silence, not sure if he'd really seen what he'd just seen.

"You must forgive me, Mr. Stanhope, please. I'm not myself today."

Stanhope backed off full throttle. The last thing he wanted was for the flames to erupt again.

"Obviously, but who could expect you to be?"

"Is there something else you want to speak to me about?"

"No, Ms. Turnbull. I think we've touched on all my bullet points."

The 258-pound opposition leader was up and out of the building before Georgia had another chance to blink. She turned to Early as two perky blond staffers began to clean up the mess.

"Are there any other 'dire meetings' for me to take today, or can I please go somewhere and shut my eyes?"

BEFORE ▪ 2

Adam carried Billy through Heathrow hoisted across his chest, wrapped onto his shoulders. The little boy's legs twisted around his midsection, fast asleep, a plastic toy airplane clutched tightly in one hand, the wing digging into the skin on the back of Adam's neck. The walk from the plane to the arrival hall of UK Customs seemed to go on forever, and Adam wanted to wake his son and tell him that he was officially too old to be carried like this. He truly felt he wasn't going to make it. The boy was deep in slumber, though, contentedly embedded on his daddy's torso, so Adam trudged forward.

Kate had her hands full with a mountain of carry-ons, and Trudy was in her own world a hundred yards back, desperately trying to get a cell phone signal so she could text the boy back in Wilmette who had most recently broken her heart. Kate and Adam hadn't spoken too much on the plane. She had cocooned herself off in a business-class module and watched a long chain of British television from her youth. The flight seemed like it had gone on and on, for days, not hours. Billy had peppered Adam with endless questions about London and the grandfather he was finally going to meet. Now this slow, interminable walk through the airport was making the flying time seem easy. It was one hallway after another, early morning on a sleepy Sunday. The long trek through the colorless, advertising-lined terminal halls and the numbing jet lag made Britain already seem cold and incessantly foggy even before they'd stepped outside.

On the far side of customs, Gordon Thompson lingered patiently to meet them. He had waited and paced like a father awaiting birth all over again. He craned his neck down the hall, looking for his family, wondering if he could even truly refer to them that way. It had been so long since he'd seen his daughter, her reckless husband, his tiny little granddaughter, or the ginger grandson he'd only a few times said hello to during a series of Internet chats.

He was solid, Gordon—muscular and firm, especially for a man of his age; tall and self-contained to a fault. He had few friends. His job in Sir David's security detail was the last stage in a long, uneventful career of watching and waiting for someone to act up or act out. He spent years in the military police, then the Metro police, finally settling into his now-famous boyhood friend's orbit, basically taking up a post outside his Kensington Park mansion, making sure no one upset Sir David's mornings, running items up to his farmhouse, feeding the farm dogs when the caretakers were at Heaton's home in Switzerland. That's what it had all come down to; his was basically a daily vigil to protect David Heaton from unwanted neighborhood soliciting.

Adam spotted Gordon first, just as they made it through customs with four carts full of luggage. He was there at the top of the ramp, waiting behind the crowd: the tall, gray soldier, shoulders back, chest out, slowly bouncing on his toes. He could read Gordon as either nervous or impatient from thirty yards back. Kate saw him next. Her face lit up.

"Hello Daddy!" She ran ahead with Billy, now wide-awake, on the top of a loaded cart, having the time of his life. She threw herself into the old man's arms, burrowing her face into his chest as he gently kissed the top of her scalp.

Adam let the two trolleys he was pushing go clumsy on him so that he could hang back and let them all have a moment in the crowded terminal. He let Trudy pass him too, let her join the hugfest, gave them all the moment they needed. He was the spoiler; there was no doubt about it. He was fine with that. He wanted to give Gordon a beat. Allow little Billy a chance to have the meeting he had been longing for.

The boy just gaped at the big man with the long arms coiled around his mother. He watched his grandfather's every move as if he were some folklore mountain beast that had stumbled down from the woods. Gordon let Kate partially free and turned to the tiny eight-year-old, smiling as Billy looked up to him from knee high to Gordon's frame.

"Hello there, little one. It's so nice to meet you."

"You're my grandfather?"

"I am." Billy just continued to stare at him, not sure what to say to his mother's father that he had come so far to meet. "You look different in person. Skinnier."

"What can I say lad? I'm getting old. Maybe while you're here we can go out for some ice cream and fatten me up. Do you like the idea of that? You and your Poppa? Getting off for some ice cream?" Billy nodded. Words weren't coming to him. He had put the mystery of the old man in the faraway world of London so high and mighty in his head. Like the ring in the Tolkien tales, this was the holy grail for him for some reason, to see his granddad, and here he was in the flesh, and the boy was tongue-tied. The old man just laughed and pulled him in with his long hairy arms for an energetic hug.

When he could no longer fake bad trolley wheels, Adam pushed to the top of the ramp and said hello. Gordon, happy as could be with young Billy in his wrap, was polite. Almost even warm.

"It's nice to see you, boy. Welcome to England." He let go of Billy and pulled Adam in, gave him a solid hug, so happy to see his daughter, grandson, and granddaughter, that he even had a genuine spillover of affection for Adam.

"The people here at the company are excited to have you, Adam. I've been instructed to make you plenty comfortable. We've got you at the Millennium right there in Mayfair, on Grosvenor Square. You couldn't do better. We've got two interns with two people movers out at the arrivals curb. One of us will go with the luggage and the helpers, and the other will go with Kate and the kids. Makes no difference to me."

"Don't be silly, Gordon. I'll go with the luggage. You can ride with Kate and the kids."

Gordon didn't waste a breath signing off on that version of the plan. "Classic idea! Like the way you're thinking. Let's put a move on."

SOMEWHERE AROUND THE time the two Heaton Global–owned Mercedes vans snaked their way off the highway, as the A4 became Cromwell Road, Gordon decided he had wrung all of the conversation it was possible to get out of an eight-year-old and a seventeen-year-old and let it lie, making a conscious decision to give them the peace to lose themselves to their own thoughts. In Trudy's case, that meant her iPad. Billy sat happily up on his lap, looking out the window to fresh shapes, colors, and images of the brand-new world of London floating by. They passed the museums on Cromwell Road, and the busy mansion flats once they made it to Brompton Road. Gordon pointed out Harrods, the world-famous department store.

Gordon and Kate had a nice chat as they circled around Hyde Park Corner. He reminded her of visits to the park as a little girl that she had no recollection of. It felt good to see him. Though he may have been making all of these little anecdotes up as far as Kate knew, if he was, she didn't mind. She liked the detail he was giving each little story. She thought he was being sweet; she wanted to enjoy it, regardless of the level of veracity.

It was as they came into Mayfair, up Park Lane, that he hit his first sour note.

"Have you heard from Richard Lyle, Kate? I see him a bit, you know? He calls now and then. In fact, we met up for breakfast in a little café off of Hanover Square not long ago. I told him you were coming round."

He checked her eyes for traces of sentiment from the time he mentioned Richard's name. The fact that he did it, the amount of energy he was putting into a search for emotion, agitated her in a way that he probably didn't imagine it would. She just stared at him—for several blocks, it seemed.

"What's wrong, doll? Have I upset you?" She clocked her peripheral view to make sure that the kids weren't focused in on the dialogue, and then she finally answered.

"No. All you've done is to confirm to me that you haven't changed in the slightest."

"Don't be that way. I was being nice."

"I'm sure on some level you believe that, Daddy. But the truth is you are not being nice at all when you play a game like that. Not in the state that you know we're in at this point in my life. My marriage."

"I was just saying that Richard was doing well, I thought . . ."

"I know what you thought, Daddy. It's clear. Don't you think I'm smart enough to know why you're asking?"

The van pulled up Brook Street to the south side of Grosvenor Square and to the front door of the Millennium, just east of the former American embassy. The trip in from Heathrow was over, and so was the conversation.

As Adam hopped out of the other coach with the bags and the HGI interns, Kate made a point to give her husband a sweet kiss and take in the view of the "American Square" in front of the hotel with him. He gladly took her hand and just as sweetly led the children and her inside the charming flag-draped brick building that looked more like an embassy than the now-closed American embassy on the far side of the square ever had. Gordon dutifully followed along behind the helpers, bellboys, and baggage carts.

INSIDE, AS THEY checked in, Trudy saw a young French boy, also at the counter, who was with his mother, a woman who Gordon said was part of the Heaton Global delegation going to Number 10 later in the week. Adam and Kate both slyly watched as Trudy and the very handsome boy flirted briefly in the reception line. They caught each other watching and quietly laughed together about their little girl. It never took Trudy long to rebound. It was a good sign, Adam thought; maybe this trip would help things get back to normal for all of them.

As they settled into their two-bedroom suite, Adam got a call that Sir David would like to say hello. It was surprising, to be sure, but the HGI representative on the phone said that Heaton wanted Adam to walk a block over toward Berkeley Square and have a drink with him in the hotel bar at the Connaught.

Gordon was waiting to meet him in the lobby of the Millennium, having already known of the summons. Adam was wearing a rumpled sweater and blue jeans, looking like he'd just flown across the world. Gordon took one look at him and immediately sent him right back up to his room.

"You put a jacket and tie on when you see this man, son. I'm not sure what's on your mind, but this is the first thing you need to do."

Adam reluctantly went back up to change. Kate got a kick out of it, thought it was cute that Adam hadn't expected that reaction. Once appropriately attired, he reunited with Gordon downstairs and they walked the short block over to the Connaught together. Gordon left him at the front door and waited on the sidewalk.

"I think it's best for you to see him alone. I'm sure it's what he has on his mind."

"What is this about, Gordon? I mean, there's something like, what, eight, ten people on the delegation? Why does he want to see me, the one who knows next to nothing about the business?"

"You're asking the wrong fellow, sport. I never know why this fellow does a damn thing. Never have. Known him my whole life, haven't figured him out yet. I just know he's keen for a sit-down, so get in there and shine up your smile. That's good advice I'm giving you."

Adam silently agreed, turned, and made his way into the hotel's stately lobby.

The Connaught, named after Queen Victoria's seventh child, Arthur, the Duke of Connaught, is a princely building seated proudly in the middle of an open-air courtyard formed by the merging of Carlos Place and Mount Street smack in the middle of Mayfair. Churchill, de Gaulle, and Eisenhower often had dinner in the Connaught's wood-paneled dining room during World War II. What it had become in the present day was a throwback, a holdout, a high-end watering hole and world-class "five star" for the Mayfair-bound jet set.

Sir David Heaton was waiting alone at a table for five in the crowded, smoky bar. He was dressed immaculately: a Kiton K-5 bespoke suit, shoes that glistened as if they were diamonds, and fingernails that were smoothed and polished on a regular basis. Sir David was a good-looking man who had put a lot of time, energy, and money into his appearance. He was smoking a long, thick Cohiba cigar, sipping a fifty-year-old Glenfiddich. He knew Adam the minute he walked in. He stood and offered his hand with a big, ruddy, open smile.

"Adam Tatum. It's a pleasure to meet you, boy. Sincerely. Have a seat here, and let me order you up a scotch."

Adam hadn't been drinking. It wasn't that he wasn't allowed to. It wasn't one of the several stipulations on the settlement of his court case back in Michigan, but it was more or less a promise that he had made to Kate that he was trying his best to keep. Still, this was Sir David Heaton. There was no way he was going to turn him down, so he accepted.

"I hear good things about you, Tatum. From the Chicago office. What's your man's name there? Your department head?"

"Saffron. Barry Saffron."

"Right. Says you can close a deal, Tatum. Is that true?"

"It is, sir, so far, I guess." Adam answered him, nervously. This was just the way Heaton wanted him answering him. Everything about Heaton's game was to make you nervous talking to him. He liked a man to be careful with his words around him, liked his employees always just a little bit off stride.

"Well, we have a very, very big deal here within our grasp now, Tatum. We're gonna need all the help we can get to close it."

Adam's drink came. It quickly became a second and a cigar was soon lit for him. Heaton comically told Adam stories of his life, of his years in business, of his father the wealthy banker and MP in Parliament, of his uncle Edmund Heaton, the former home secretary, of his own time as a member of Parliament representing Hampstead and Highgate, his years as a minister for the European Union, and a brief synopsis of how he then went back into business and built Heaton Global Investments. Of how he almost single-handedly turned it into the largest retirement services organization in the world.

"At any one time we are investing the pension funds for over two thousand organizations and one hundred thousand private individuals, for a grand total of over two hundred ten billion dollars. That's much more than bags of bauble, Tatum. Am I right?"

As Adam's third scotch was brought over, as Heaton lit a second Churchill-sized cigar, he easily signaled for his fourth or even fifth drink. He was a famous man, David Heaton, with a well-documented, outsized appetite for life. Aside from Heaton Global he also owned an airline, a movie theater chain, and several large five-star hotel lines. In fact, he owned the Connaught. He dated models, film stars, and other business magnates—powerful women. He had even, for a short time, years back, dated Georgia Turnbull, the chancellor.

Sir David was confident and cocksure. He was as warm as each situation needed him to be, yet there was also a darkness about Heaton, a mysteriously mischievous cloud above him that Adam could see from afar while reading about him in magazine profiles. An evil glint to his eyes that in person was even more identifiable.

"Tell me about you, Adam. I want to know everything. About your growing up outside of Detroit, your days as a police officer in Ann Arbor . . . and I want to know about this trouble you got yourself into two years ago. It interests me. I've googled up on it, just as I'm sure you've googled up on me. Gordon has filled me in on the big strokes, but I wonder about the details. I want the 'behind the scenes.'"

Adam sat there for a while, puffed on his cigar, and stared at Heaton, not the least bit nervous at this point. The scotch had settled in his belly; the strong Cuban nicotine had calmed and soothed his mind; the smell of the pretty women's perfume that floated through the air from the surrounding tables was giving his spirit a gentle lift. He leaned in closer to Heaton—his new friend. He got inches from his face and declared quietly, but boldly: "I fucked up. Big time."

Heaton let out a bellow of a laugh and whisked an ash from his finely clad knee. "I bet you did. From what I've heard it was a doozy. Tell me about it."

"I lost everything. Every penny I had in the world. I lost my home, my job, and my friends. More important, I almost lost my wife." He leaned back now, puffed the cigar again, hit the scotch. "I got carried away, David. Carried away by political forces, bigger than I was. Bigger by far. A moment in time, the music of the mob. It just happened. I wasn't a political man. That's important to know. Very key to it all. I was a union man, to a point. Had union men in my family. Union in my blood. Always sided with the worker, but the sad truth, why I did what I did, was that I got whipped up by the crowd. Taken by a passion for what I thought was right. We were liquored up, and we thought we had come upon an easy answer to a complicated problem. I wish I had a better story than that. I wish my motives were more intelligible, but they weren't. I was playing a bit part, but I played it to the hilt. Does that make any sense?"

Heaton leaned in, put his arm on the shoulder of his new drinking buddy, and got right into his face now.

"It doesn't make the slightest bit of sense, Tatum. Not one single ounce of it. But let me tell you something else." He flashed his brightest smile now. "I like you. I like you a lot." With that, he started laughing, a big, throaty, arm-slapping gust of mirth. As the laugh subsided, he gently slapped Adam on the side of the face and ordered them each another round.

GORDON WAS WAITING outside of the Connaught when his son-in-law finally stumbled out. It was a solid four hours later. Adam was surprised to see the old man, rigidly standing there on duty as if he were Heaton's own portable porch jockey.

"You're still here?" His speech was slurred, his voice scratchy from three very strong cigars.

"I'm on until he hits the pillow and even after that. C'mon, let's get you over to the Millennium so I can get back here again before he leaves."

"Are you his driver, Gordon?"

"No, of course not. He has a driver."

"Are you his bodyguard?"

"Not me. He has a team of them. Two of them were in the bar watching you all night. I'm surprised you didn't notice 'em."

Adam had in fact spotted two men in cheap, well-worn suits at the bar all night long. He had realized through the course of the night that they were watching Heaton and him quite a bit. He figured them for off-duty cops, maybe hotel security.

"So what are you, then, Gordon? What do you do for Heaton?"

"I'm a helper. I assist with whatever he needs help with. Sometimes I look after his house; sometimes I'm up at his farm feeding the dogs. Tonight he wanted to get to know you better. I helped. It seems to me you two got along nicely."

"Yeah, we did get along. But why? I can't figure it out. I mean, at first,

I thought it was all about you. You making it happen, doing this for Kate. But it isn't, is it, Gordon? This isn't coming from you, is it?"

Gordon looked into his eyes and came to the conclusion that Adam was too drunk and worn out to go into any detail tonight. There was explaining to do, but not at the end of a day this long. He did his best to put both the subject and Adam to bed.

"Let me just say that dealing with Sir David can be tricky. It takes a strong sense of self-navigation. But if you stay sharp, if you come out on top here, with what he has in store for you, you'll be a well-taken-care-of man. Understood?"

"No. Gordon, no. I don't understand a thing about any of this. Seriously? What does he 'have in store' for me? None of it makes any sense."

"Then maybe that's best, lad." They had arrived back at the Millennium. "Go on; go upstairs to your family. There'll be time to fill you in."

The two men said good night and Gordon headed back to meet his mercurial boss at the Connaught.

IN THE MORNING, Adam had a serious hangover. Luckily he more or less got away with blaming it on jet lag. Kate and the kids were on Chicago time and were wide-awake at five a.m. They wanted Adam to come look at the view over Grosvenor Square, out onto the FDR statue and the 9/11 memorial. The bright morning light thundered in when Kate threw the curtains open, slapping him wide-awake, as if it were a jolt of electricity.

Later in the day, when he finally woke, he called the only person he knew in London to tell him they were in town and to make dinner plans. Beauregard McCalister and his wife, Tiffany, were Kate and Adam's good friends from Michigan. A London boy born and bred, Beauregard, a movie producer, had lived in Michigan several years back when the state had a hefty tax incentive. He filmed his movies, mostly Colin Firth–type, frilly necked, Jane Austen–era stuff, out in Pontiac at the Michigan Motion Pictures Studios, which is where they met when Adam was working construction at the facility.

Adam and Kate had loved to spend time with Beau and Tiffany when they were all in Michigan. They had other friends, but none that were as cozy a fit as the McCalisters, and ever since Adam's criminal adventures, most of their "friends" weren't all that high on dinners out. In fact, even when they got to Chicago, they had found themselves with no social life.

It was for this reason that Adam and Kate both were excited to reconnect with the McCalisters and their kids. When Adam had called, he was greeted with nothing but excitement. Beau and Tiffany were well aware of Adam's recent adventures in severe felony, but it wasn't in their nature to judge people harshly for mistakes they had made. They were true friends. A promise was made to get together. It was one of the first times in a long time that Adam had seen Kate smile.

WITH HIS WIFE and kids on a double-decker bus tour of London, Adam spent the afternoon pulling himself together. Late that afternoon Adam, Kate, and their kids had a meal with Gordon at the Millennium's restaurant. Trudy and the handsome French boy had met once again in an elevator and headed down and into the lobby together, giving them the opportunity to have their first conversation. Trudy was happy to learn that he spoke almost perfect, if somewhat broken, English, and was already wondering how that would be—for her to marry a Frenchman. Where would they live? What would their kids be, French? English? Once again, the only thing Adam and Kate could do was stifle their laughter.

After the early dinner, the family, and Gordon, all walked over to Hyde Park, to the Serpentine. Gordon played with Billy as the boy chased a flock of geese to the point where he almost ran into the water. When the sun went down, at not yet seven p.m., the family was exhausted, their bodies' clocks still playing tricks on them, so they headed back to Grosvenor Square, said good night to "Poppa," and went back to their room. Trudy and Billy were in bed by eight.

Kate was in as good a mood as she'd been in years. She took a long shower and came out to the bedroom smelling like a warm blast of spring air. Adam thought it was going to be a nice night. She had that glint in her eyes and was paying that telltale level of attention to him that she did on nights when the drawbridge was down, laughing at everything he said. Kate got into bed next to Adam. He kissed her softly and rolled on top of her as she wrapped her pajama legs around his bearlike body.

The hotel phone rang. It had that European clang to it. It didn't ring like a hotel phone rings in America—it was more mechanical, more staid, one grinding obnoxious blast after another. Another representative from HGI was on the line. Sir David and the others in the delegation were downstairs in two limos, waiting for Adam to come down and join them for "dinner and drinks."

"When? Now? Right now?"

Kate understood, maybe more than Adam did. As he quickly dressed, she helped him pick a tie. The kids were fast asleep. He made her promise that they could pick up right where they had left off when he returned. She made a solemn, if comical, oath and kissed him good-bye at the door as he hustled down the six flights of stairs.

Gordon was waiting in the lobby. With a nod, he motioned Adam to join Heaton and several other HGI employees who were jammed into two Mercedes limos. Gordon escorted Adam to the limo containing Sir David. The French woman, the mother of Trudy's future husband, was in the car as well. There was a stocky redheaded man nestled into the front passenger seat. Adam recognized him and the tall thin bald man in the back of the limo as the two men watching from the bar at the Connaught the night before.

The whole group had dinner in a private room at Nobu, just off Berkeley Square. Heaton toasted "the deal." They talked shop, discussing the figures around managing the pension packages of the entire British civil service's employees—staggering figures. Adam just listened. He knew enough of what they were saying to know that he had no idea what it all entailed, so he shut up and ate sushi.

With the herd thinned to more or less just men, they ended up at Annabel's, a trendy nightclub on the opposite side of the square for a long session of drinking, more business talk, and another toast from Heaton, this time custom-tailored toward Adam. Adam wasn't going to drink but Heaton of course insisted, so there wasn't too much of a fight.

Later, when the talk moved on to sports and movies and women and war, Adam was the center of attention, amusing Heaton with his easy style of banter, making him laugh and at one point even choking Heaton up with a story of his first sexual adventure as a boy in Michigan, with a twenty-year-old babysitter.

The group was later culled to just Heaton, Adam, two HGI men—one from France and the other from Texas—and, of course, Harris and Peet, the two ever-present bodyguards. They all drove in one limo to St. John's Wood and pulled up to a large, Victorian-era mansion that sat on the backside of Primrose Hill. Adam wasn't sure where they were going, but the others were all happy to follow the energetic Sir David into the house. Adam, now feeling zero pain, happily, almost giddily, took up the rear.

Inside there was a party going on. The house was warm and familial, decorated with a subtle, cozy, pedigreed style. It was a catered affair with waiters and waitresses taking and bringing drink orders and hors d'oeuvres. A round of cocktails was brought over. Several men were talking to what Adam finally, woozily, noticed were some of the best-looking women he had ever seen—seriously beautiful women from all walks of the world: Asian, Russian, Indian, and even just good old-fashioned, well-dressed British beauties, one stunner after the other. It was actually, he thought, a bit of a freak show: these women were all so perfect.

There was some dancing in a large room off the main hall. A gorgeous Jamaican woman was mixing records, and the room pulsated with elegantly sexual energy. A buxom, tiny blonde with an adorable pageboy haircut dragged Adam, at that point truly inebriated, onto the dance floor.

A short time later, Heaton had rounded two of the best-looking of the group, a brunette and the blonde whom Adam had earlier been dancing with, away from the party and headed up toward the staircase at the center of the house. He motioned for Adam to follow. Adam hesitated, but Peet quietly urged him to follow along. Adam finally realized at that moment that he was at one of the highest-end whorehouses on planet Earth. A combination of being drunk out of his mind and basically a naive guy from Michigan caused his ability to assess the situation to take a while. He wised up by the time he and Heaton and the two women had reached the top of the stairs. He hustled up to Heaton and caught him right before he went into a bedroom with the brunette.

"Wait, David, hold up. Hold up. I need to speak with you. Wait." Adam grabbed Heaton's arm and pulled him aside. He talked low in a drunken whisper as Peet watched from the bottom of the hall.

"I can't do this, David. I can't. It's not me. I'm married. I mean, the one I'm with—not with, but that I'd be with—she's unbelievable, but I can't. Okay? I can't. I can't do this. Trust me, I appreciate it, but it's not me. I'm not that guy. I have other problems. Sadly, I'm too in love with my wife. I have to get out of here."

He took a deep breath while waiting for Heaton to comprehend the situation he'd put Adam into. He was also hoping to take a beat and stop the floor from spinning underneath him. Heaton went into his room with his brunette, as planned. He looked back at Adam before he shut the door and gave him a snarky, yet friendly, conspiratorial smile.

"Something tells me you're a man that knows how to get himself out of a fix, Tatum. I'll leave it to you to sort this one out." With that he was gone. Adam was on his own.

The blonde tugged his arm with a jerk and pulled him across the hall, opened the door to a candlelit bedroom laid out with fluffy shag carpeting and a plush queen-size bed with thousand-count Egyptian sheets and a quilt, already turned down. There was a bottle of champagne on ice on the sideboard, and an old Duke Ellington album was playing on a Bose stereo system, *Piano in the Foreground*. Before he could get a word out of his mouth, the blonde shut the door, with only the two of them in, the rest of the world out. She gently pinned Adam against the wall.

The soft piano tinkled, the candles flickered, and the rose petals on the bureau gave the room an aromatically erotic lilt. She rubbed her cute little nose against his, giggled, then stepped back and let him look at her in the fractured light. Expertly, she let him have a moment to reflect on the fact that she was all his, that it was just the two of them alone with Duke Ellington and that big playpen of a bed behind her.

With another expert turn she unsnapped her skirt and stood there in a pair of soft white panties. She did a cute spin and served up another perfectly adorable giggle. Adam thought that she looked like a young Lady Diana if Lady Diana had been a high-end call girl. He had always had a thing for Lady Diana. It was probably one of the reasons he fell so hard for a British girl.

He was drunk, good and drunk. That could even be his excuse. But he didn't take it. He fought himself, fought the silky shine coming off of her bare thighs.

"I can't do this. Just so you know. There's no way."

She laughed. "There's always a way."

She pulled her top off. She was built perfectly, with two ample, natural breasts, and a tiny toned and tanned little bottom. She came over and kissed him. Her lips were moist and clean, wet with an inviting liquid lightness. Her breath smelled like honey. He lost himself in the kiss. It seemed to go on and on, the two of them almost floating there in the darkened room. Finally, he pushed away and tried to get his mind to come to a stop; he tried to bring some sanity to the moment.

He just stared at her. Words weren't coming to his mouth. He was drunk, he knew it, but something else was overpowering him. She came close. He tried to push her away again as she unbuttoned his pants. She wouldn't take no for an answer. He saw a white light and he angrily pushed her away yet again. Hard.

She fell back, landed on the bed, and did a cute backward somersault to the middle of the bed that let him know she thought the force he had used was in the service of foreplay. It didn't faze her a bit. She maybe even wanted a little more from that column. She motioned him over with a sneaky forefinger, seductively. It was time.

He burrowed his back into the wall behind him, tried to catch his breath, tried to form words and an escape plan, but it didn't work. His breath wasn't to be caught. His mind and his senses weren't playing along.

WHEN HE WOKE up, there was a dizzying amount of energy in the room. Two of the other girls, the one whom Heaton was with and another from downstairs, were on the bed trying to wake the little blonde up. She was limp and disheveled, lying flat on her back, draped across the bed like a used bath towel. Blood was coming out of her mouth and her nose as they tried desperately to wake her. Her face was swollen and bruised; the sheets were red and black: it looked like the back room of a butcher's market.

Men in suits thundered in. Adam struggled to get to his feet as he noticed his hands and shirt also covered in blood, his knuckles swollen and sore, the skin scraped up as if he'd been hitting the side of a wall somewhere. The men in suits rustled him to a stand. He tried to speak, but the same inability he'd been struck with before was back, only worse. It was as if he were under the influence of some drug that had shut down his motor nerves. He'd never had alcohol affect him like this.

The men in suits pulled him from the room, manhandling him as much as they could. They were mad and obviously doing everything they could not to kill him right then and there. He tried to explain that he had no idea what had happened, but once again his faculties failed him.

The last thing he saw as he left the room was the two women unsuccessfully begging the broken, battered, formerly beautiful blonde on the bed to speak to them. He started yelling for Heaton but was told with a kick that Heaton had left hours ago. The last thing he remembered as he was forcefully dragged and dropped down the long stairwell through the now-empty party house was someone saying that the police were already on their way.

The other thing he remembered was the bald bodyguard Peet, standing quietly, watching the whole thing go down with a slight grin on his face.

WHEN HE WOKE next, several hours later, he was in a jail cell—a steel gray, cold cell. An older, balding, scared little man, maybe sixty-five, in a woman's dress, with fist-blotched lipstick on his face, was sitting on the bench across from him, clutching a small sequined handbag to his chest, a long flowing brunette wig on the seat beside him.

For the longest time Adam said nothing. He finally sat up. Every muscle in his body was on fire.

"Where am I? Do you know where this is?"

The broken little man answered with an accent straight out of *Oliver Twist*. "West End Central Police Station is where you is. Savile Row. They been in and out of here all morning, waiting for you to wake up."

"Why am I here? Do you have any idea? Did they say anything?"

The artful dodger of a drag queen responded ever so carefully, not wanting to elicit a violent reaction.

"All's I know is that I heard them talking about you. About you beating on a young lady. Beat her an inch from the end of her life, they says. Says you busted up her fireman's hose."

He was talking in rhyming slang, "fireman's hose" meaning "nose." Adam had no idea what he was saying, but the soiled little man in the sinfully out-of-season dress was letting loose now, enjoying the role he had as the bearer of bad news.

"Had all kinds of suits and hats come round in here for a butcher's hook of you. Heard 'em says they want to make you pay up good, too, guv. Say they wants to put you in the box, put you away for a long, long time."

Adam leaned back against an unforgiving wall. Here it was, for some unknown, unexplained, unfathomable reason, all happening again. A different town, different country, different circumstances, and a new set of colloquialisms, yet somehow he was back at square one. Back inside a prison cell.

Only one thought came into his broken, frazzled mind. "Kate." It was painfully obvious, he thought; there was no way Kate wouldn't leave him this time. The truth just sat there, plain as the tip on his fireman's hose.

AFTER ■ 3

Davina Steel sat at a table in the front of the family's breakfast/lunch whistle-stop. Her father was diligently preparing the next day's supply of tuna, chicken, turkey, and egg salad; her mother was cleaning the remains of the afternoon rush. The little café on Vernon Place, right across from Bloomsbury Square, had several office buildings, small colleges, and even the British Museum within spitting distance. Foot traffic was a constant. As a child, Steel would gaze out the window just as she was doing now, looking and observing. She'd noticed things, noticed people, training her mind to find little details, to suss out differences, day after day, to watch for patterns, to see who people were, what they were doing, and why. It helped. It took her mind off her life and the fact that she was at work ten hours a day on the weekends, even as an eleven-year-old child.

Today was different. Today she sat, looking out the window, trying to figure out who would go to the trouble of planting a bomb inside 10 Downing Street.

She wanted to know as badly as when, as a teenager, she puzzled over why a Pakistani-born cabdriver she observed out the shop window every day for four months had to spend so much time consulting his map. Why? Didn't he have "the knowledge"? Didn't he take the test like all the other cabbies? Didn't he know the streets like the back of his hand?

Why was he always so lost? It bothered her, angered her, so she watched and made notes, followed him once, watched him and another cabbie both trying, almost comically, to figure out a simple London map. She petitioned the Information Ministry for copies of both applications of their licenses and found out that they and three other Pakistani nationals had all applied for their taxi permits the very same day, all five with cashier's checks from the very same bank, purchased by the very same foreign bank's overseas desk.

Further watching and digging brought her to the facts that she had already guessed: none of them took the intensive two-year test that was required. The same civil servant in the Ministry of Transportation had signed off on all of them on the very same morning. Somehow they had skirted the system. Why? Who had gone to the trouble to get five men taxi licenses? Why didn't they take the same two-year tests that the other cabbies did?

Those on duty the morning the precocious sixteen-year-old Steel marched into the lobby of Scotland Yard with the layman's evidence of a plot to use five London taxis as bombs at the Queen's Diamond Jubilee were, as they liked to say, "gobsmacked." She was quickly ushered around to MI5's antiterrorism desk. The inspectors and the detectives were beside themselves when the young prodigy laid out, with simplicity and detail, the precise particulars of the plot. They were further dumbstruck when it turned out to be true and arrests were eventually made. "Thank God she's on our side" was a common refrain, and before long preparations were made, with her parents' consent, to put the young virtuoso into special university classes on forensic examination and crime scene analysis as soon as possible.

The cars, buses, tour coaches, and museum-visiting pedestrians floated by the little Bloomsbury sandwich shop window on what seemed to be a continuous loop. Steel sat with her ever-present pad of paper and made out lists. It had been twenty-four hours now since the bomb had ripped into the prime minister's midsection. She expected more test results on the blast's residue by the early evening. Since the meeting in the Cabinet Room, she had been combing security camera trails and visitor logs. The home secretary was correct: they had nothing, which was not alarming for a crime this fresh. This was big, though. She wanted to be ahead of the ball. She wanted to be ready when some inevitable group took credit or threatened more violence. She wanted to be poised to have SO15 and Darling and the thirty full-time investigators on her team at her disposal ready to pounce.

She wanted to will herself the answer to who had done this. Desperately wanted to win this one. She wanted to make Georgia Turnbull proud. Her mother didn't like Georgia. There was something about the powerful chancellor she didn't trust. Her mother didn't trust any women, especially rich ones—rich ones and politicians. She didn't trust Londoners, either. She wouldn't listen when Steel tried to tell her that Georgia was Scottish. From Glasgow. It didn't matter. Mother didn't care for her, which most likely made Steel look up to her even more.

THE FIRST THING Steel did the following morning was to go up to North London to have a meal with a friend who worked at the Finsbury Park Mosque. Aviala Farouk was a nice-looking if slightly chubby twenty-eight-year-old Jordanian exile whom she had met three years earlier while working a case involving jihadists who were blackmailing employees of the mosque, forcing them to let traveling jihadists stay in their homes. Aviala was brave, emphatically nonviolent, pro-Western, honest, and dependable. He also had a noticeable crush on Steel. Aviala knew the minute she called why she wanted to see him.

They met at Harput Best Kebab, a small kebab and burger grill nestled by a rusty train overpass on Seven Sisters Road, steps from the Underground station. He had arrived with his hair still wet at ten thirty. She assumed by the harried way he ordered and drank his coffee that it was the first of the day. From what she knew of Aviala, he wasn't a late sleeper. She wondered if the hurried shower and the need for caffeine meant that he had had a sleepless night. Wondered if something in particular had caused it.

"You want to discuss the bombing at Number 10. Am I right, Davina?"

She nodded as she unwrapped a kebab she thought looked completely unappetizing.

"I knew they would put you on this incident. Knew you would be investigating."

"Why do you say that, Aviala?"

"Because they are going to blame it on Islamists no matter who has done it, and you are the best there is at tracking down jihadist activity in London."

She smiled and assumed he was once again overblowing her importance, a trait common to all of her dealings with him since their first case together, the underground terrorists' lodgings, was written up extensively in the *Telegraph*. Sometimes he would talk about her as if she were some kind of a superhero. She chalked it up to his crush, a crush that would remain forever unrequited, not only because Steel didn't see Aviala that way but also because in past conversations his observations about his parents led her to believe that they would never allow him to date a non-Muslim.

"Were they Islamists, Aviala? Is the attack on Lassiter related to any of these groups?"

"This one, I don't think so. I have heard nothing. You know I would tell you if I had, but this is not something that people are talking about. They are only sad. Sad and convinced it will bring people such as yourself around asking questions."

"Well, they're correct, because here I am. With you. Having a kebab for breakfast. You know how I hate Middle Eastern food, so what does that tell you?"

"It tells me you are desperate for something to go on. I wish I had it for you, Davina, mostly so that I could make your struggle easier. Truthfully, I have nothing."

After some small talk and a promise to have him up soon to her parents' café for a "decent meal," she took the Piccadilly line to Euston station, where she transferred to the Northern line to Old Street and walked the four blocks to the offices of Heaton Global on Farringdon Street. She could have easily been driven by a Met patrol car, but she liked the Tube. She liked to wander London on her own, outside and underground, bathed in the sea of faces, scents, and sounds that washed over her on the go. She was at her most productive then, thinking through the questions she needed to answer in her daily work.

She was reasonably sure the conference meeting with the Heaton Global officers at Number 10, two hours before the blast, was unrelated.

Sir David Heaton, the chairman of the company, was as high up and connected in British moneyed society and government circles as one could get and it was he, according to the logs, who had led the meeting, bringing in nine of his company officers.

Heaton was nearly a national institution. He had even cameoed in a series of travel ads abroad, extolling reasons to come visit London. If one were into creepy rich white men who had spent their lives stepping over the less fortunate, Steel would suggest that Heaton could be your idea of a perfect man. In short, she found him repulsive. Nonetheless, she needed to speak with him, if only to get his measure on the mood and movements at Number 10 just before the blast.

The HGI complex on Farringdon Street is a twelve-story modern showpiece that sits flat and firm on an entire city block. Davina was surprised at how quickly, once having showed her badge and announced herself, she was whisked through the three-story atrium lobby, across the back side of the building, and then up into what seemed like a private elevator to the top floor and the suites that she assumed were Heaton's private offices.

A sharply dressed, nice-looking young woman with beautiful hair right out of a shampoo commercial led Steel down the hall into a cushy den with overstuffed chairs and a small sofa. The den connected to a large, sleek office that wrapped around the back of the building, offering a nice view of the Thames a quarter mile south. The woman also smelled like a shampoo commercial, Steel decided. She also noticed that her shoes, while highly polished and cleaned, were of a slightly dated style, and the heels had been redone several times, judging by the way they sat under the body of the shoe. Maybe having an executive job like this came with pressure to dress much wealthier than one was. Obviously it took a certain resourcefulness to keep up with Sir David's expectations.

After a short wait, Heaton came bounding into the den. He had a fake tan and wore an incredibly expensive suit, a custom-fitted tight shirt, and a smartly woven silk tie. He had an oxygenated glow to his skin, and the back of his hair was still wet, which made Steel assume he had just come from the gym—he probably spent a lot of time there, she thought, the gym and the tanning salon. He had a near-perfect set of veneers and perfect fake teeth. She knew they were fake only because she had read online that he had flown his private jet to Beverly Hills to have his teeth done by Dr. Kevin Sands, the world-renowned dentist to the stars. It was an amazing smile, but the idea of all that time and expense to have your teeth fixed left an odd taste in her mouth.

"So I figured you'd be round to see me once I had heard they'd settled on you for the lead spot on the investigation, but I didn't suspect you'd be this quick."

"Who did you hear that from? That they had 'settled' on me?"

"Oh, surely you're not so naive as to think that I don't have friends who were inside of the Cabinet Room yesterday?"

"What made you think I'd be round?"

"We were there, in the very room the bomb went off, a good hour or two before. Why wouldn't you come around with some questions? Especially someone as good at what she does as you are, Ms. Steel."

He sat down next to her, got closer than she wanted him to get. He smiled in a way that was meant to be charming, clubby. Steel had no interest in getting "clubby" with Sir David Heaton.

"Did you notice anything suspicious going on at the time you were at Number 10?"

"Of course not. If I had, I would have said something straight up. This whole thing is devastating to me. I've known Roland Lassiter going on thirty years."

"What was the business of your meeting? Why was it held in the White Room?"

"I would think for the sake of the size. There were a handful of us, more than a good ten or so from the civil service side, the chancellor, the cabinet secretary. The PM just popped in for a few minutes, but there were too many for one of the offices, and I don't think it was of a nature that was right for us to meet in the Cabinet Room."

"What was the meeting's nature?"

"Civil service's pension program. We were pitching a plan to privatize. A scheme to make the pensions more valuable, to give the civil servants more retirement security."

"And I suppose a pretty penny for your coffers as well?"

"Very good. Yes." He almost winked at her, threw a wry grin. Steel realized he was enjoying the banter. "We don't run a charity, you know that, right?"

"Who was in your delegation?"

"I'm sure you have a list. Everyone had to be vetted by security. We spent a chilly three-quarters of an hour at the gate, in the shack, as we came in."

"Yes, we do have a list. I'm just trying to be certain that there's no one in the group that you think I may need to have a chat with."

"They were all my people. My top pensions specialists. Most from the Paris office. Some from Texas."

"All people you know well, I presume?"

"Yes. Surely. All people I have worked with in this side of the business for years. The best." He remembered something then—she saw a flash go by his eyes. He wanted to move on, figured it wasn't relevant. She wanted to deal with whatever had just crossed his mind.

"Each of them? You knew them all by name?"

Heaton stopped now and took a quick beat with his answer for the first time.

"No. Actually, not all of them. All but one. An American. He's new. I don't know him. Don't even know his name. He's from the Chicago office."

"Why was he involved? Why was he in the group?"

"It's a good question, that. He's a strong salesman, I believe. I think someone in the company is pushing him along. That's the sense I had. I think he's what we call a 'closer.' Very smooth. Lots of personality."

"Why would they need that when they have you, Sir David?"

Heaton liked her. He liked her cheek. He might have even liked the fact that she didn't seem to like him and didn't feel the need to hide the dislike.

"There's a good question, too. You've got yourself on a roll, Ms. Steel. Nevertheless, someone wanted him at the table, someone felt he'd be a strong asset, and in the end it was fine with me."

"Someone who? Can I get the name of the person who wanted him at the table?"

"I will get it for you. I don't have it on the tip of my tongue. It was someone in retirement services. You do realize I have three thousand people working for me, right, Inspector?"

Steel didn't volley back. She wanted to let him sit for a beat and wondered if this was anything, thought that maybe he was playing with her, having his idea of fun. Heaton just stared across at her, smiling, beaming, trying hopelessly to be charming, she assumed.

"And you don't have his name? The American? His address in the UK?"

"No. But my office does. You can feel free to get it on the way out. Even though I don't know his name, you can rest assured I didn't bring a terrorist into Number 10. It's not my style."

"I'm just doing my job, sir."

"Of course you are. From what I hear, you do it quite well. Make sure you let me know if I can help in any way. Okay?" He leered at her now, openly checking out her figure. "Feel free to call me anytime, Inspector Steel. I'm going to make it a point to leave my door always open to you."

She headed down to the private elevator.

There was something about people like Heaton that she couldn't stand. The odds were, she was sure, that he was clueless as to what had happened at Number 10, but a side of her wished he wasn't. She wished she could pin the whole thing on him. As ludicrous as it was, a smile came to her mouth just thinking about it as the elevator door closed.

THE PRESS WAS packed a good twenty people deep around the entrance of St. Thomas's Hospital when Georgia's Jaguar pulled up for her visit to Roland Lassiter. Poor Jack Early got out too fast, tripped on the curb, and fell straight onto the cement, picking himself up quickly as the cameras flashed and whirled. Georgia was sure this would be on the nightly news. It was typical Jack Early, though, and she didn't even mention it as he opened her door and got her through the noise and the nonsense into the hospital.

His Majesty, the king, was scheduled to visit, too. The palace had arranged for him to pay his best wishes and to make a public appearance with an early morning call in Lassiter's hospital room. It wouldn't do much good: they had the PM sedated and unconscious as they monitored his body and tried to ascertain which of the several courses of surgery were going to be most useful. It had been a full thirty-eight hours since the blast had opened him up, and the best the doctors could come up with was to keep his organs still for a few more hours and watch his vitals. No one was in too keen a rush to do extensive surgery. There wasn't a doctor on staff who could be sure that his broken body could handle any more trauma.

Georgia was there to await the king. She had managed earlier to get a minute with Lassiter as well, but there truly was no point. She sat by the side of his bed and spoke softly to her old friend.

"I'm so sorry, Roland, so sorry this happened to you. I beg you to please pull through, for your family, for me, for the country. Please, Roland, I suspect you can hear me. Please fight on."

There was no response, just more bleeping from the bank of machinery to which he was now coupled. She tried to get through to him anyway.

"You know, Roland, there's been a candlelight vigil for you in Whitehall for the last two nights. You're quite loved, it seems. The country is gutted—you should know that."

She was telling him the truth. It had been a shocking two days for the people of England. The news on television and radio spoke of little else. Even in America, the twenty-four-hour channels had churned it up as it became the biggest news event since 9/11. The Americans loved Roland—he had a higher approval rating than any president had had since the elder Bush threw Saddam Hussein out of Kuwait—and they wanted to know every detail as soon as it happened. There had even been a US network nighttime special report the previous evening that had preempted the finale of *Dancing with the Stars* and had broken all kinds of long-standing ratings records.

Meanwhile, at home, the borders, bridges, rail stations, and airports were all on a version of lockdown. Every line moved in the country like molasses as the authorities did their best to know who everyone was and where they were going. There was a manic frenzy at Downing Street, Whitehall, and New Scotland Yard to arrive at some sense of who had done this and what their next move would be.

Georgia leaned in closer to Lassiter's bed. She took his hand and held it in hers. "It's been quite a ride these last two years, hasn't it, my friend?"

Only Georgia, and most likely his wife, Kirsty, who was off getting the kids to school, trying to keep their lives on as normal a track as possible, really understood how rough a time it had been. She, Kirsty, and all the closest ministers and secretaries had done their best to shield the public and the press and other members of government from the truth of how much the helicopter accident had beaten him. Yes, he had walked away physically unscathed, but emotionally he had never fully recovered. He had refused to fly again: the G20 and any other summits he had some control over had all been on the continent where he could take the train, or else he found some clever way to cancel or to send Georgia. He had suffered from horrible nightmares and anxiety attacks, sure that something catastrophic was next on the horizon. He often broke into a sweat for no reason and was overly sentimental about everything. Worse, it had been like pulling teeth to get him to take a solid stance on any of the projects they had worked on for so long.

This was all kept under wraps and known to a very select few. For the most part he had held up fine, was as popular as ever, but, very much like Georgia, unknown even to her, the crash had also put Roland on a steady diet of the rock candy pain pills.

She pulled closer to the bed, softly stroked his full head of hair, gently adjusting the tubes coming out of his mouth.

"You're going to make it through, Roland. I have no doubt. I know that as surely as you knew we would take Elmet and Rothwell."

She leaned back and stared at her old running partner. He seemed so peaceful, so still. Even if he did pull through, this would only make him all the more fragile, all the more skittish. No matter how lucky he was, notwithstanding any medical miracle that he hopefully would have visited upon him, she couldn't help but wonder if Roland's time as PM had come to an end.

A CONFERENCE ROOM at the far side of the hospital had been fitted out as a room where Georgia could greet and speak with the king. The palace would want as much information on the crime as she had but, more important, it was set so the press could report that the government and the monarchy were in constant contact throughout the crisis. Georgia had met the king only a few times before at state dinners, during a visit that he and his wife had paid to Downing Street when Roland had first formed the government and, of course, at this very hospital, when he and his wife and brother visited them both after the helicopter accident. Roland met with the king at Buckingham Palace on a semiweekly basis, but even when he couldn't, due to travel or health problems, she had never been asked to substitute for him in those sit-downs.

The king's valet, Andrew McCullough, a rigid man in his late seventies with a Victorian-era beard and a boulder-shaped potbelly, waited with Georgia outside the conference room. When he was signaled, he nodded solemnly to Georgia that it was time and carefully opened the door, motioning her to follow into the room. The king stood in the room's center, ready to be received. Several aides perched firmly by the windows, waiting for their next orders. She bowed in a curtsy. He dropped his head for a half nod and held his hand out. Georgia wasn't quite sure what she was supposed to do next. *Do I bow again? Nod some more? Do I come to him? I completely forget the order of things I'm supposed to do. I can't believe this. I feel so damn feebleminded.* She moved forward and took his hand gently.

"Your Majesty." The king, tall and lean, with a smooth, pleasant face, seemed appreciative. None of his courtiers attacked her. She assumed she must have done it all correctly so far.

"Once again we meet on a somber morning, Ms. Turnbull."

"Yes, sir, we do. I am told, though, that he is holding steady. He is a fighter, as you know."

"I do. I know that, and I can only hope he summons all he has now." He was genuinely concerned for Roland. It was obvious, Georgia thought. The two men got along well, saw the world in many similar ways. Roland had forged as strong a friendship as one could form with the king of England.

"I'm told we have little firm in the way of answers here. Is this your assessment, Chancellor?"

"It is, sir. But, as you know well, we'll have all the pedals pushed to the floor. We'll have clarity soon, I can promise that."

"I'm sure everyone is fully invested. I have no doubt of that. This is a nightmare. Truly dark days."

"Yes, Your Majesty. They surely are."

"If he isn't to pull through? What is the plan then, Madam Chancellor?"

"I'm afraid there isn't one just yet. We are all hoping he will come through. In the meantime, the government is functioning. I'm at Number 10, in contact with all branches as well as the opposition." She made sure to look the king squarely in the eye on that, wanted to convey confidence to the monarch. He took the answer in with a gentle nod.

"Will you be able to form a government in the event of the worst?"

"We haven't gotten there yet, Your Highness. But, yes, I believe if it comes to the crown having to ask me that question, I will be able to answer to your satisfaction." He let the report roll around in his royal brain for a beat, his back still stiff and his feet firmly planted as he weighed out the severity of the moment.

"Very good. Please keep me informed, won't you?"

"I will, sir. Of course."

She half bowed again, wondering if that indeed was the proper way to say good-bye as she backed slowly to the door behind her, knowing well enough not to show the monarch her backside. She almost tripped over a chair and found the door. She nodded, bowed again, and quickly backed out of the room.

Adam lay on the bench in the musty jail cell for another hour or so. The old drag queen was gone. A Haitian man was brought in for a short time and then taken away, and he was by himself once again, alone with no idea what had happened. No real sense if he really had beaten the little blond call girl, as the man in the dress had said he did. He had never hit a woman in his life, had never even been accused of anything like that, yet he honestly didn't know what he had done or not done. The soreness in his battered hands wouldn't go away. He was sure someone must have put something in his drink. He was also reasonably certain that Heaton was to blame, or at least one of Heaton's bodyguards.

Still, he wasn't sure. That was the problem. His knuckles did feel like he had been beating something. He was scared—incredibly frightened. He had been terrorized a lot these last couple of years; he was actually getting used to it. Even after his criminal charges in Michigan were finally dropped, even when they moved on, when they lived in Illinois, he often had times when he wasn't sure what was real and what wasn't. He had heard people in their house in Wilmette twice, late at night, once someone rustling in their garage, another time in the den. He was convinced that someone was going through his computer files. Both times he called the police and grabbed a baseball bat, ready to use it. Each time he was told he had been dead wrong, that no one had been in the house.

The alarm was still on. It was just another in a long series of incidents that left Kate unsure of what to believe in as far as her husband's state of mind.

This was different. Some version of this had actually happened. He needed to stop his head from spinning and find out what and why.

NOT LONG AFTER he was finally awake, when it all truly started to sink in as to how much trouble he could conceivably be in, for some reason it was all suddenly over. Out of nowhere, a door opened. A uniformed police officer came down the hall, opened the cell, and motioned for Adam to follow him out. He walked him through the processing area, past the receiving desk, through the main lobby, down a stairwell, along a back hallway, and out to the street through a rear door. The officer then handed Adam his possessions in a plain envelope, minus his passport, turned, and went back inside, closing the door behind him.

Exactly like that, the officer left Adam alone, confused, and uncertain as to what to do next. The policeman hadn't said as much as one word to him. Now he just stood there on the corner of New Burlington Street and Savile Row, under a bright morning sun, once again not sure what the hell had hit him.

He walked a block or so and tried to start breathing again, wondering if it was a trap of some kind, if they were going to arrest him for trying to run. He decided it was best to move, that he should get the hell out of there. He hit Regent Street and sprinted for four or so blocks, until he couldn't move his legs any longer. He headed west and found a bench in the middle of Hanover Square behind a clump of trees and collapsed into it, struggling to regain wind, still having no sense of how he had gotten into or out of jail.

A minute or so later, Harris and Peet, Heaton's men, drove up in one of the company Mercedes. Harris, the stocky, muscular redhead, got out, opened the back door, and motioned from across the square for Adam to get in. Once again, there was a lot of summoning but no talking. Adam wasn't sure this was a good idea, but seeing as how he didn't have a better one, or any real idea where he was, he did as he was told, went over and got into the backseat.

They drove him through the Mayfair shopping district for a short hop over to Grosvenor Square. Still, not a word. As they pulled up at the hotel, Gordon was standing out front, waiting. Adam stepped out and on cue the bodyguards pulled away: once again, not a single syllable had been traded.

Bathed in remorse and confusion, Adam walked over and approached his father-in-law.

"Gordon, I don't know what you think happened, but I swear to you I did not do anything like what I'm being accused of doing. Also, I was not with any girl in any way that would make Kate—"

Gordon cut him off. He was good and upset, the old guy. He wasn't any more in the mood for small talk than the cop or the bodyguards were.

"Close it, boy. Close it now! I mean it. Stop talking. I know damn well what you did and didn't do. Anyone says you did anything close to what's been intimated answers to me. Understand?" Adam was surprised. He didn't expect Gordon to come on this strong, especially in his defense.

"The girl never existed, Adam. That's the way it is. She never existed, this bird, you got it? The charges are all dropped. Sir David's taken care of it. The police've asked that he keeps care of your passport until you're ready to leave the country, so he will, and that's that."

"I didn't do anything, Gordon. I wasn't with her, I know . . ." Once again Gordon shut him down.

"It's taken care of. Sir David's taken care of it. He's handled everything."

"I know, you said that, but what does it mean? What the hell does it mean?" He was on the verge of tears now, this big sturdy guy, the former football star and cop, the bottom about to drop out, seconds away from breaking down right here on the street.

"You know damn well what it means, Adam. Means he wanted to show you what kind of strings he has, imprison a man, just like that, get him out of prison once again as quick."

"But why? Why? I still, I just don't know why. Why am I here? What the hell is going on?" He looked at Gordon now; a bolt of heat shot through his chest. He made a fist with one of his hands, convinced he might take some teeth out of the gray-haired man's mouth. "What the fuck have you gotten me into?"

"Don't even start with me. Take that fist and put it up your bum if you need to put it someplace, but don't even think about a move like that. You hear me? This isn't my doing, and making me the problem won't help you one bit."

Adam took it all in. Gordon softened. Adam began to see that it might not be he who Gordon was upset with.

"What is going on? Please? Tell me. I'm so confused."

"I'm not entirely sure, son. He's brought you here to do a job, I know that."

"A 'job'? What the hell does that mean?"

"I truly don't know yet. I do know maybe it's not as simple as I was led to believe it was. I'm in the dark from this point on as well." He looked up at the hotel, toward Kate and the kids, somewhere up there in the fancy brick building.

"Now go on. Go up there and I'll back your telling Kate we all stayed out and had a late boys' night that turned into a messy scrap of a morning. Act like you've got a hangover."

"I do have a goddamn hangover!"

"Good for you. Go on. She knows nothing and she won't ever need to if you play this well."

"As long as I do whatever it is that you and Sir David have for me to do? Whatever it is I'm here for? I'm not stupid, Gordon. Something's going on, something not good."

Gordon stared at him long and hard.

"Yes. You're right. Maybe you should go to the police then."

Adam stared back, not liking the sarcasm. Gordon was done with this round. It was too much talk already.

"Go on. Go on up and be with your family. I have your back. I mean it. I'm gonna watch out for you here."

"I want to believe that. I do."

"Then go upstairs now."

The conversation was over: Adam was just as in the dark as when it began. He turned, went into the hotel, walked through the lobby, saw Trudy and the young French boy chatting up a storm on one of the couches, decided it was best to keep moving, and didn't bother to say hello. He had his wife to face, his thoughts to get straight. He needed to shut his eyes, clear his head. Heaton was up to something. He had been right all along—it was a setup, but nothing like what he thought he was being set up for. It had nothing to do with getting Kate to move home. Whatever "job" Gordon and Heaton had brought him to London to do wasn't going to be garden variety.

He got to the elevator bank and looked back out to the street, through the front door. Gordon was still there, standing firmly with his chest out. Adam couldn't help but notice that the old man looked good and worried.

AFTER ■ 4

It was half past four in the afternoon. They were coming on the forty-eight-hour mark since the bomb had exploded. Georgia had left the hospital and gone straight into a series of meetings, one at Treasury and another in the PM's small office at the House of Commons. Several of the leaders of her party wanted her and not Felix Holmby, the deputy prime minister, to do the Prime Minister's Questions in the House the next day. They didn't think Holmby was the right face, knew it may be the highest-rated turn at the dispatch box in years, and wanted to have a clear plan on who was going to be seen running the government through this phase. The consensus was Georgia. Eventually Holmby agreed.

Back at Number 10, she settled into her first meeting in the prime minister's office. Richard Sandville-Amply, the minister for Europe, had forced a meet to discuss, in light of the tragedy, the state of the upcoming referendum on Europe. The vote would be a serious reckoning on currency and trade and Britain's future in the European commonwealth. The decision point had been almost a decade in the making. A few years earlier there had been a referendum that almost sent Scotland out on its own. Since then that particular scenario was always in the air. Yet as realistic as this threat now seemed, it was nothing compared to the cloud that the referendum to leave Europe left hanging over daily life.

Georgia deftly put off an answer. If it were up to her, she'd see it through. She knew in her heart and in her polling briefs that it would pass, putting the final nail in the coffin of the decades-long "European experiment." Roland, however, much more pro-Europe than she had ever been, would have loved nothing more than an excuse to derail the vote.

After the tea with Sandville-Amply, Georgia led another emergency session in the Cabinet Room to hear from Darling and the others on what progress had been made in the investigation. Davina Steel, in her short-cut black leather jacket, dark blue skirt, and bright red silk shirt, led them through what they had, which was once again not much. They had canvassed many of the well-known informants with ties to ISIL and other radical jihadists groups, and were now even surer than yesterday that this was going to be something other than the usual bunch. Wiretapping of extremely high-level sources in all of the key terror cells had found them to be just as curious about the forces behind the blast as they were.

Just as in the meeting the day before, no one seemed too happy with Davina Steel's results. She faced another series of long faces; probing, almost accusatory questions. A bunch of scared, grimacing, whining faces, she thought. Wealthy, powerful people looking for someone to blame. It wasn't going to be her, she told herself. She was going to put this one to bed; she was going to win this one, make these overweight men with their throat-clearing harrumphing and their exasperated, over-the-top gasps truly sorry. It may take time, but she felt certain she'd have the last word.

Later, in a private meeting with the chancellor that Steel had requested, for the first time she spoke candidly about her misgivings. The two of them met in the prime minister's private den. It was Georgia's first meeting in the place Roland most liked to have important discussions. He was an expert in the one-on-one and had gotten his way more than often in this cozy anteroom turned work area. It was the "python's den" to his opponents. The nickname was bequeathed after Roland's famous, almost python-like ability to cajole, flatter, twist, turn, and, finally, charmingly bring an opponent around to his way of thinking.

Steel was nervous. They sat opposite each other on small fluffy couches across a finely polished dark wood coffee table. Everything about Georgia made Steel feel a little weak, not just because she was the most powerful woman in Britain, either. It was her confidence, her ability to look at people, and, as Steel saw it, almost see through them, into what they were feeling. She seemed older than her years to Steel, but also there was something about the chancellor that made her seem much younger, like a girl: an older sister whose parents had gone out and had never come home, leaving her in charge.

"There is one aspect to the events of two days ago that I wanted to discuss. I thought it would be best if I spoke to you alone. It's about David Heaton."

Georgia sat up. "What about Heaton? Surely you don't think he could be involved. I was in that meeting. I know Heaton well. I've known him for many years. I walked him to the door as they left; it was several hours before the explosion."

"Two hours. And I've seen the security tapes. I saw them leave. It's exactly as everyone is saying."

"You couldn't be insinuating that Heaton had anything to do with this? That's absurd."

"No. Of course not. But in his group, there was one person in it, someone relatively new to his firm. An American. Did you notice him? Have you had any dealings with him?"

"An American? No. It was mostly Heaton who spoke, Heaton and a fellow from Paris, Despone. He had prepared the brief from what I remembered. We were to give it a look through and have him back in. But I don't remember an American. What about him?"

"It's just that he was new. Very new. Doesn't seem to have much experience in the business at hand, nor have much of a reason to be at a top-level meeting. It doesn't seem right to me. I wanted to let you know I will be looking into it. I know Sir David Heaton is an important man. I also know that you and he have a history."

"Well, I don't see how this could add up to anything, but please do go ahead on any hunch that you have." She smiled at Steel as she quickly got to her feet. "And please, do not let the old dragons out there in the Cabinet Room get under your skin. I happen to think you and your group are doing a fine job in a trying time. Keep the back stiff, you hear?"

Georgia reached across the table and shook Steel's hand warmly.

Steel caught a strong whiff of her perfume, which she found surprisingly alluring.

"There's one more thing I need to tell you, Madam Chancellor, about the American, the one in Heaton's delegation. His name is Adam Tatum. He lives in Chicago, Illinois. He's originally from Michigan, just outside of Detroit. He's an ex-cop."

"Really?"

"Yes, ma'am. There's something else about him you should know."

"What is it?"

"He spent ninety days in jail in federal prison. Almost two years ago. The case was quite serious. It was very public. He admitted his guilt, but for some reason that we've yet to discern the charges were dropped and he was released."

"What was he arrested for, this Tatum?"

"Attempted murder."

"Who in god's name did he attempt to murder?"

"The governor of Michigan."

Kate wanted to make good on a return to the amorous moment from the night before. She had even looked past the fact that he had come in at eight in the morning smelling like someone had poured a gallon of whiskey on him and stuffed lit cigars in his pockets, or that he had smashed up his hands roughhousing with her father and some of his friends. She wanted him to have a good time, wanted him to enjoy London, to get on well with Heaton. It all played wonderfully into her game plan. She came out of the shower in his favorite orange pajamas, a pair that he always took great joy in peeling her out of.

It wasn't to be. He was fast asleep. She crawled into bed and went back to her book, a memoir from several years earlier by the comedienne Tina Fey. She, the sleeping kids in the next room, the snoring hubby, her orange "sexy PJs," and Tina Fey. All was fine. She was in London. That's what mattered. She was home.

The hotel phone did its thing once again. Like a clanging giant iron cat, the old mechanical ring commanded Adam out of a deep sleep. He sat up straight in bed as if he'd been hit with a hammer. It was another HGI rep on the line. Sir David wanted him to "pop round the house for a quick chat." It didn't seem to matter that it was eleven at night. Adam seemed to be okay with it. He actually welcomed more face time with

Sir David. Kate thought the hour was odd, but she happily helped him dress and gave him another sweet kiss at the door.

Gordon was there in the lobby, as usual. They almost had words as he walked him toward the Mercedes across the way, with Harris up front and Peet at the wheel.

"I'm gonna get to the bottom of all this shit right now, Gordon. This guy's going to come clean with what he's up to."

"I'm telling you to stay as calm as can be, son. Just listen. Do not bang pots. Do you hear me? It's not the way to play it."

"I'll do what I have to do. Fuck you, Gordon. I'm done playing with you."

The old man stopped him and pulled him back into the lip of the lobby, away from the eyes of the bodyguards.

"You watch how you talk to me! I am on your side, you hear me? I told you I have your back and I intend to keep my eyes on it. You need to be steady here. I know what you're up against. You don't have a clue."

"If you know what I'm up against, then you knew what you were getting me into, so quit playing dumb, Gordon. I'm getting tired of it."

He stared at him. Gordon wanted to smack him, it was obvious. Adam would have done more than smacked him back. That was also good and evident. Adam turned, left the lobby, crossed the small street toward the square, and got into the back of the Mercedes. The bodyguards didn't say a word as they pulled away. Adam hadn't expected them to.

HEATON'S HOME WAS on the Palace Gardens Mews, a mansion or two down from the sultan of Brunei's place and two doors up from the Lebanese embassy. It was five stories on two acres in the center of London, backing up to the Kensington Palace Gardens. It was a walled estate with more security than the embassies around it. As they drove through the gate, Adam saw several more men in nondescript suits similar to the ones Harris and Peet always had on. They all wore the same non-smile and were most likely armed. Adam wondered why a guy like Heaton needed all of that security, all this muscle.

Heaton met him at the front door, dressed impeccably once again, every hair in place. The mansion was landscaped to perfection, the front door an aged mahogany that must have been six inches thick.

"Tatum, good of you to come. Come on, I'll give you a quick tour and then fix you up with a very nasty drink."

Adam was in no mood: he couldn't make small talk if he tried, so he didn't.

"I don't need a tour, or a drink, Mr. Heaton. That's not what I'm here for. Let's get to it, okay?"

Heaton chuckled. "I've got your blood flowing, haven't I? I like that. Good for me. Come into the study. We'll show each other our goods and have a drink and the tour afterwards."

Heaton went inside as Adam followed across a highly polished marble foyer, past a massive stairwell that hugged the wall tight and coiled its way up toward a second-floor landing. They finally made it through the back hallway, into a wood-paneled study. The overly cushioned den was finely made up with expensive sofas and chairs, a Victorian-era pool table, and a ninety-inch flat-screen TV. There was a quietly subdued bar built in across the back wall.

Heaton immediately went to work making himself a drink. Adam just stared at him, waiting to unload. Heaton giggled and offered one up again. Adam declined with another version of his longest face. Heaton pointed to a set of chairs, took his drink, and followed Adam over.

"You're sore about the call girl? Is this it?"

"I'm sore about so many things, I'm not sure where to begin. Let me say up front, whatever it is you have me here to do, whatever 'job' you have for me, I'm not in. You understand? Not interested."

"Yes, you are. Trust me, you are, but go ahead."

"No, Mr. Heaton, Sir fucking Heaton, I'm not! Not in the slightest. You drugged me, had me thrown in jail, got me right out, all for what? To scare me? You didn't scare me. You just made me realize who you are."

"No, now, no, I have to stop you. Right there." Heaton leaned forward and grabbed a cigar from a box on the table between them. "The point wasn't for you to realize who I am. The point was for me to realize who you were. I liked that you didn't want to cheat on your wife. It was cute. It gave me a nice, warm, fuzzy feeling."

"Don't be an asshole. I mean it. I'm not here to play cute with you.

You may have all the money in the world, but it doesn't give you the right—"

Heaton cut him off. "Okay, come on. Yes, it was a little show of power. May have even been over the top, Tatum, but you're a cop, a son of a cop. I knew you wouldn't scare too easily. I was showing off, okay? I was setting the stage."

"Setting it for what? What is it that you want from me?"

Heaton cut his cigar, lit it, and looked Adam in the eye.

"I want you to leave something at Number 10 for me after our conference, something that I may not be willing to take the blame for having left behind myself. In short, I want you to be the fall guy if it goes bad. I want to be able to blame you, the nut job from America that even once went so far off the rails as attempted murder on the governor of Michigan."

Adam was surprised, blown away, even. He didn't expect Heaton to come out and be so honest about his intentions. Not that Adam hadn't, somewhere in the back of his mind, even mildly suspected such a scenario had brought him to London—he just didn't think Heaton would be this bold and up front about it.

"There's a brief—it's about five hundred pages long—in a thick, forty-pound binder like this one here." Heaton pointed to a wieldy, leather-bound folder on the table next to the box of cigars. He reached over and slid it toward Adam. Heaton motioned for him to pick it up. Adam did. He leafed through the pages of numbers and figures. He had seen a binder like this before, back in Barry Saffron's office in Chicago: it was a dossier spelling out the company's course of action to take over an expansive pension system. This was obviously one of the more detailed ones he'd seen.

"It's one of fifteen we've presented to the civil service. It's the only one that matters. It's the bible of the system we'd create. The new law would be written based exactly on what's in here. Precisely. They have one exactly like this already at Number 10. There's only one difference between the one in your hand and the one we've submitted to them, the one that has been okayed by the chancellor, the Treasury, and the minister of pensions for government workers. Turn to page 657."

Adam turned to page 657. It was just a lot of figures, a spreadsheet. He couldn't see anything worth looking at, only a sea of numbers.

"The one at Number 10 has a flaw."

"A flaw?"

"It's off. We messed up. It has what might be seen as a statistical error. If we say nothing, it's fine. That will be how the money flows for the length of the agreement. This is how the Treasury will write the law. Twenty-five years." He shrugged and sipped his drink.

"If we live with our error it will only cost us a billion and half dollars a year. No problem, right? Forty billion dollars over the course of the deal." He chuckled. Adam tried to see where the error was. Nothing jumped out at him.

"Trust me, Adam, several top people have been fired over this. I don't take it lightly. This is four and a half years in the making."

"Why can't you just tell them you made an error? Tell them you want to amend it?" Heaton chuckled even more at that remark.

"Obviously you've never dealt with Lassiter and Turnbull. They'll stick it right to me. That, plus the fact that it's done. The conference at '10' is a formality. Turnbull's signed off. It's a Lassiter deal, this one. If I have to go back in and make changes of any kind, that iron ass Georgia will send me straight back to the drawing boards and she'll enjoy doing it. It'll be another four and a half years if it's a month."

Adam followed it through in his mind, nodded when he had it. Heaton watched him closely.

"So, you want to sneak in a new 'bible'? Hope no one ever notices the difference? A new one with the right figure, so the law is written up in your favor? I make the switch, take the old one when I leave?"

Heaton nodded. "A new one with the new figure. The correct figure anyway. We're not doing anything wrong. We're fixing a mistake. No more." Adam just looked at him. It all seemed to make sense.

"And if for some reason the switch is uncovered? If it all goes bad? You blame the American. The 'nut job.' The mixed-up ex-cop who you hired as a favor for a childhood friend. The one that famously went bonkers in Michigan. He did it. The American. It was his error, and he made the switch at the meeting."

"You got it, Adam. Right on the money."

"Yeah. I got it. I'm the fall guy."

"You would be the fall guy. Yes." Adam couldn't believe what he was hearing. Heaton pressed on.

"Number one: it won't go badly. No one will ever notice the change, not even Georgia Turnbull. She has plenty more on her mind, I'm sure of that."

"If they do? If it's spotted?"

"They then have a case for fraud."

"Exactly."

"When we leave Number 10, you will get a fifteen-year contract starting at one million pounds a year. It will have no escape clause: if we fire you for any reason, you will be paid in full. Fifteen million pounds. If things were to go awry, which they won't, you will be long home in Chicago, and you would then of course be fired immediately, your contract settled. As per the contract, we will be responsible for all legal bills, and we will start a long, drawn-out legal battle with the British courts that would conceivably take them a good ten years to prosecute—a battle that I will have many tools at my hands to use to help force an ultimate settlement, of which I will bear the full costs."

"So in a worst-case scenario, I walk away with fifteen million pounds? You blame an errant employee for the whole thing while accepting all of the responsibility."

"And in a best case, you have a job for fifteen years and you work for us and learn the business. You grow with the firm as a key man that I personally look out for."

"Sounds great. I'm not interested." He got up and walked out. Heaton shook his head and giggled lightly as he quickly followed.

"You want the tour before you go? A drink? Cigar? Come on, you can say no. Don't be rude. Don't just run off." They arrived at the front door. Peet was waiting in the Mercedes. Adam stopped.

"Look, David, Sir David, Heaton, whatever . . ."

"Call me what you want. I'm not particular about that."

"Okay, how about 'shithead'? Does 'shithead' work?"

"It works if you say yes. Of course it does." Heaton was once again enjoying the back-and-forth, thriving on the heat coming off of Adam's forehead.

"I don't think you realize the toll it took on my life the last time I was talked into doing something else that absolutely 'couldn't possibly' go bad. I don't have it in me to do it again."

"The difference between that last escapade and this one is me. I don't think there was anyone in that prior debacle you took part in in Michigan with the resources that I have, was there?"

"No, there was no one in that group quite as charming as you are."

"Oh, look at me. Now I'm blushing."

"Heaton, I know that you're not a man who's going to take no easily. I know that's what the thing with the hooker was about. I get it. You have moves. I'm not your guy, though. If you want to find someone else, I'll never say a word to anyone. You can find another fall guy and give him my fifteen mil. If you fuck with me, though, you'll be fucking with my family, with my marriage. If you do that, we'll have a problem. I promise I won't let that happen to me again. Do you understand?" He leaned forward and got right into Sir David's space. Heaton just let loose the same cocky grin he was famous for flashing.

"I do. Of course. Your communication skills are excellent."

"Great. Have a good night."

Adam turned and walked out to the Mercedes. Heaton nodded to Peet to take him back to the Millennium. He watched them pull off the grounds of the mansion. Harris walked out onto the motor court porch.

"How did it go?"

"Went very well, actually."

"Did you give him the bullshit story? About the clerical error? About switching the binders?"

"I did. Figured it was best. He wasn't going to go for the truth. He's not quite ready yet for the truth."

"So he bought it? The 'numbers error' story?"

"Yes. He bought it. It played out perfectly."

"Is he in?"

Heaton turned to the burly redhead and smiled as he answered. "Yes. Of course he's in. He has no choice."

THE NEXT MORNING Adam and Kate and the kids went over to Shoreditch to have lunch with Beauregard and Tiffany and their two children. Gordon was to put the kids in a taxi and have them meet at the McCalisters' flat so that Adam and Kate could walk for a bit, cutting through

Soho before catching a separate cab over to Shoreditch. It seemed to Kate like a complete waste of time and money, but Adam needed the forty minutes of fresh air that hoofing through Soho toward Covent Garden would take; he also needed the time alone to tell Kate what had been happening and how he thought it was best for them all to leave England right away. He was actually hoping that there would be enough time. He knew it wasn't going to be an easy sell, especially when he factored in that he didn't dare tell her anything about the battered call girl, his arrest, or the sudden release from the police station.

Unfortunately for him, the discussion didn't go as smoothly as planned.

"What could you possibly be talking about? No! I don't want to go home. We've just gotten here, Adam. I thought you were doing well. You've obviously hit it off with Heaton and that lot; they wouldn't have kept you out all night if they didn't enjoy your company. He wouldn't keep calling you to these meetings. My father says he's very taken by you."

"Yes, but why? Have you asked yourself that, Kate? Why is he so taken with me? Why am I involved in this big meeting at 10 Downing Street? Aren't you curious? I have the least experience of anyone at the company. What's going on? What's he got planned for me? I'm curious what you think the answer to that is."

"What's going on is that my father has stuck out his neck and Heaton has agreed to bring you along on a key project, out of loyalty to my father; and you, out of some, I guess, either insecurity or resentment against Gordon, can only see it all as mysteriously contrived. It's very sad."

Adam could understand why Kate was seeing it the way she did. He was tempted to tell her about the whorehouse and the prison cell, but was leery to do so, as any mention of him in a prison cell would only bring on bad memories and a deeper level of argument. Kate was upset already; he didn't see an upside to pushing his luck.

"You didn't want to come here in the first place, and now you want to go home because you're a victim of some odd conspiracy that Sir David Heaton, one of the most powerful men in the whole world, wants to invite upon you. It's absurd."

They came through the top of Great Marlborough Street, cut into the small, cramped backstreets of the top of Soho, crossing down through

Soho Square. There was a lot of sun and a nice breeze in the air; hordes of the locals were out sunning themselves in the park, prepping themselves for serious burns on their pale faces that had all just weathered through a long, lightless winter. They were everywhere, the sun-starved, sandwich-chewing light worshippers, wherever they tried to step, requiring them to weave in and off of the path and forcing Kate to keep her voice down as she scolded Adam.

"I don't see why you can't enjoy this? A free trip? A chance to impress your boss, a legend, mind you, a national treasure, and a chance for me to be home, to relax, to show the kids London, to see my old friends? What about that doesn't fit your plan?"

They walked on a bit in silence. He didn't plan on saying what he said next. It just came out. Maybe he wanted Kate on the defensive for a change, or maybe he really wanted an answer.

"Is part of your plan here to look up Richard Lyle?"

She stopped cold, turned, and looked at him. "Why would you ask that?"

There was no holding back now. He had successfully changed the subject and the goal was to keep it off himself, at least for a little while.

"Because I got into your Facebook account and I saw that you e-mailed him. Told him how much you would love to see him while you were here."

She was surprised that he had that information, stunned, but only for a quick whiff. She was off her back feet almost instantly with a response she played perfectly, a volley that allowed her to hide behind the elephant that was always in the room.

"I thought you weren't allowed to be on the Internet, Adam. Wasn't that one of the key settlements to having your charges dropped? You were also not supposed to be drinking. From the way my father tells it, from the smell of our sheets this morning, there's been a lot of drinking."

"The drinking wasn't part of the settlement. Just staying off the Internet. I haven't been drinking only because it's something that had been making you uncomfortable."

"And now apparently you're not all that interested in my being comfortable?"

She was good. Damn good. One of the best. He always thought she should have been a lawyer. They walked on, crossing over Charing Cross.

The Richard Lyle thing had been left for dead back at Greek Street, not to be brought up again for a while. His whole life had been like this since his arrest in Michigan. He never had the upper hand. Any argument, any spat, anything Kate did wrong, it always somehow came back to the fact that Adam had lost his shit with a bunch of idiotic drunken union assholes and tried to frighten the governor by breaking into the mansion and trashing his office: the single dumbest thing he or, for that matter, any husband ever did in the history of marriage.

She could theoretically go fuck this guy Lyle, he thought; he had so thoroughly lost the right to complain when he joined an asinine union plot against the hated conservative governor. Every union member in the state was in arms: the protest in Lansing against the union wages bill was the largest attended in the state capital's history. Union men from all over Michigan and the Midwest drove to Lansing to rant and rave and flash signs and yell at the top of their lungs. The difference between him and all the other husbands there that day was that they got into their cars and drove home. They didn't stay in Lansing. They didn't drink and smoke and conspire lunacy. They didn't break into the governor's mansion in a misplaced attempt to mess with his head. To trash the neophyte governor's office and leave spray-painted epitaphs that spoke to the importance of having police well paid and available to protect the citizens. They didn't buy into an ill-informed guarantee that the governor was out of state and wouldn't be around when Adam broke the back door open with a crowbar. A "weapon" that turned the politically charged crime into an "attempted murder."

The husbands who went home that weekend still got to go toe-to-toe when their wives would e-mail and flirt with their ex-boyfriends.

The sad truth of that night in the governor's office is that the idea was never to hurt anyone. The governor wasn't even scheduled to be home. It was only meant to let him know how serious the workers were that he was messing around with, to let him know how vulnerable he was, how easily he could be gotten to. Only meant to make a point. Adam always thought that the only point that was made in that ridiculous drunken plot was how vulnerable his marriage was.

"Can I tell you what I think, Adam?" They had been walking silently together for a long block up Charing Cross.

"Yes, of course, go on."

"I think that you should be more than happy to do whatever it is that Sir David Heaton and his group ask of you. I think you should thank your stars for my father. I think you should just relax and enjoy yourself here in London and, for God's sake, let me and the kids have a little bit of a vacation without another round of your drama scurrying us up onto a plane and straight out of England."

She walked on ahead of him as he mumbled a pathetic version of the time-honored, "Yes, honey, whatever you say, dear." Once they made it through Earlham Street into the center of Fielding Court, he'd had his fill of "fresh air," so they caught a taxi over to Shoreditch.

THEY MET BACK up with their kids, plus Beauregard and Tiffany McCalister and their two children, Rolf, seventeen, and Serena, eleven, at the McCalisters' flat in a newish eleven-story tower of luxury flats off Charles Square. Beau and Tiff were a strikingly good-looking couple. Adam liked to say that they were both as tall as people were legally allowed to be. They were seriously tall. Their kids had some height as well. As a group they would have been damn close to being drafted by a world-class basketball team if they weren't so damn British.

Even Tiff, who was American by birth, was awfully British. This was probably what Kate loved so much about having them live in Michigan back when they did. Kate had always adored Tiffany and Beauregard. Back then, the kids were close as well. Rolf had even been one of the first of many to comically crush the young lovelorn Trudy's heart. Billy and Serena had been playmates as well, but the four years since they'd last seen each other had played so many tricks on all of the kids' appearances and adolescent attitudes that, at first blush, none of them really knew one another anymore. It was nothing but awkward the way the parents wanted them to instantly be best friends again.

After a quick drink and a tour of the flat, they strolled the two blocks down to Great Eastern Street to grab a bite at the Hoxton Grill. The kids walked ahead, struggling for things to talk about. Tiffany and Kate coupled up, chatting away as if they'd never not been in each other's life.

Adam and Beau followed up the rear with Beauregard catching Adam up on the changes that had occurred in his career.

"So, I returned here after the tax rebate for films in Michigan got tight and it turned out I couldn't get funding for movies here, either. I ran into a friend from school who sold me on a scheme to team up and buy the old Gloucester Studios, a small, run-down film complex from the forties in an industrial park just north of Kentish Town."

"Really? You own a studio now?"

"I do. My partner and I. Gloucester UK Studios. It's been refitted and is running chock-full."

"So, you're a big shot now?"

"I am. Massively important."

"Does that mean I have to be nice?" Adam and Beau were enjoying teasing one another, picking right up where they had left off, just as their wives were doing.

"It does. Indeed. Very nice."

"Yeah, that's not going to be easy."

"You need to come round and see the studio. You'll be impressed with the sets we've been building. We've just now built an amazing submarine set for Michael Bay, the American. The fellow who did the *Transformer* movies. We've also done a complete 10 Downing Street set for a sequel to a movie that the Working Title folks did. You wouldn't know it from the real thing. You should come round and see our carpentry shop. You may end up begging me to give you a job. Bring the whole family over here to London, live a proper life."

Adam stopped him, right as they came up to the restaurant. He lowered his voice as he spoke. "Listen Beau, speaking of Number 10. You know that's why I'm here, for a meeting there tomorrow?"

"Yes, you mentioned that. With David Heaton. You'll be in storied company there with that one and Lassiter."

"Well, the thing is, I'm not sure, but I think I'm going to get out of it. I think it could be trouble for me." Beauregard shrugged it off.

"I should think having anything to do with a ponce like Heaton is trouble, but that's just me."

"Really? I thought everybody loved him. He was like, a minister or a

European rep or something, right? Isn't he, like, a full-on power broker here?"

"To some, I guess. To me he's just part of the problem—his whole group. Nobody needs to get that rich, if you ask me. It can't help but go to the head. I don't blame you for not wanting to get into the thick of it with that one. But on the other hand, you're here, your wife is happy: go to the meeting at Number 10. What could it hurt?" He put his hand on his friend's shoulder and made a bad joke that he regretted as soon as he said it.

"But do me a favor, try not to go in the back door with a crowbar this time, won't you?"

"Very funny, dick!"

Adam knew making the joke was Beau's way of telling him that he loved him, that he didn't give a whiff about any stupid mistake Adam had made. In retrospect, it was way too close to the truth, but Adam didn't know that then, and didn't care. It was just good to be with a friend again. It had been way too long. They followed their families into the grill for lunch.

As they stepped inside, across Great Eastern Street, Harris and Peet, in one of the Heaton Global Mercedes, watched from afar. Their faces were stoic; even with each other they remained largely silent. They had spent the whole morning following Adam and Kate and the two kids all the way from Mayfair. To both Harris and Peet they seemed like nice people, the Tatums. Both had had thoughts to that effect. Each had separately assessed the American family positively.

That didn't mean that when the order came down, they wouldn't do their jobs, wouldn't follow through on killing the entire family. No, when the time came to act, they both planned to go through with it exactly as discussed.

AFTER ■ 5

Steel left Number 10 following another meeting in the prime minister's den with Georgia. She took the Underground up to Farringdon Street. The tube was jam-packed with commuters. It seemed as if every one of them was reading a newspaper article about the bombing. The *Sun*'s headline seemed to be addressing Steel personally.

3 DAYS LATER—WHO DID IT AND WHY?
INSIDERS: "SO15 STILL HAS NOTHING TO GO ON?"

She paid another call on the Heaton Global building. Things didn't move as fast for her this time; she showed her badge again, used all the right buzz words, but this round she was left waiting in the lobby for an interminably long spell, long enough to think about Georgia Turnbull: the clean slap her perfume delivered, the sense of pride she got from bringing her news, the thrilling feeling evoked by simply being in her presence. She'd never experienced anything like it before. She wondered what it was. She wanted to get her off her mind, but it wasn't easy. Even on the crowded Tube she could have sworn she smelled Georgia on her clothing. Three different times she thought she saw a woman who looked exactly like her.

As she waited, as she reflected on Georgia, she noticed a man watching her: a tall man, completely bald, with dark sunglasses on, trying not to look like he was watching her from the landing on the first-floor stairwell, observing her through the reflection on the mirrored wall across from him, eyes over a prop newspaper he was pretending to read. She was well aware of what he was doing. She'd noticed him the minute he sat down.

Finally, after a long wait, she was given an address for the Tatum family in London. They were staying at the Millennium on Grosvenor Square.

She left the HGI building to embark on another battle with the Underground: transfers at Moorgate and Bank, then a rush-hour slog along the Central line to Bond Street, all the time trying to fit together the floating pieces of what she knew about Adam Tatum and the 10 Downing Street bombing, while still trying to make sense of what she was feeling about Georgia Turnbull. She got off at Bond Street and hiked down through Mayfair, along the east side of Grosvenor Square, past the Canadian embassy, over to the Millennium.

Her badge and her papers earned her a much faster response than she had gotten at Heaton Global. The manager took the query very seriously. When he had gone through the records, it was revealed that the Tatum family had checked out three days ago, a little more than one hour after the bombing, eight days earlier than they had booked for, at six p.m., leaving both rooms empty for the night.

A further interview with Ronnie, the clerk on duty at the time the family checked out, painted for Steel a picture of a family in disarray: a fight in the open air of the lobby with a teenage daughter who didn't want to leave, some cursing, a father who was spooked and wanting to vacate the hotel right away, the wife demanding he calm down.

Ronnie, a nicely dressed black man in his late twenties with a thick South African accent, remembered them all too well.

"It was an outburst all right, then. I kept asking Mr. Tatum if it was something that the hotel had done wrong. I could not get an answer; in the end I could not even call a car for them. They left with their luggage right under their arms. A horrible hurry. I did not know what to make of the entire situation, ma'am. He just rushed them all off into Grosvenor Square. It was truly one of the very oddest things that I have witnessed."

Ronnie had now walked Steel out to the front door of the hotel. They stood on the curb, facing the redbrick-bordered square as the sun was setting for the day, the traffic whizzing by in front of them.

"I watched them until they got about to the middle of the square there, and then I had to get back to the desk."

"Did it seem to you like they were in some sort of trouble?"

"Yes, it did. Maybe they were in some kind of trouble. Why are you asking? Did something go wrong? Did something happen to them?"

"No, nothing that we know of yet. We'd just like to speak to them, ask them some questions."

Once the clerk went inside, Steel spent a few minutes walking into the square, trying to think where the family could have gone, what the options were in each direction. Why didn't they get a cab? Why did Tatum need to check out so quickly? She stood in the middle of the tony garden square, the FDR statue looking down on her, the Eisenhower statue at her back. During World War II the square was even known as the "Eisenhower Platz." It was truly the "American Square," a fitting place for a family from Chicago to vanish from in London.

She looked back and forth to all four different paths the family could have taken. At this point the puzzle was still a jumble. Nothing was coming together as quickly as Steel wanted: swirling objects; unanswered questions; Adam Tatum; an attempted murder charge in Michigan; a family on the run; David Heaton; high-end plastic explosives; an antique cupboard on the north wall of the White Room—fragments floating in her head, nothing making any sense.

Finally an image came to her: an Avis car rental place. Off Duke Street, behind the Brown Hart Gardens, she had caught a glimpse of the car rental location, the very corner of it, as she walked down from the Tube station toward the hotel thirty minutes earlier.

TATUM HAD INDEED rented a car, two hours and twenty-five minutes after the bomb went off. It was a good guess that had paid off. If they had wanted a cab, they would have gotten one at the curbside of the hotel; they didn't want a cabbie to be able to give information as to where they were dropped. The Tube would be covered on CCTV, every square inch of their journey start to finish, and he would know that. If they didn't want a cab or public transport, that left either their own car, which, being from Chicago, they didn't have, or a rental car that they could drive and then abandon somewhere in order to buy themselves some time.

The clerk on duty at the Avis center didn't really remember him. It was a Ford wagon, though. It was in the records. He had used his credit card for a return rental to this location. He was either coming back or planned on ditching the car. Steel was betting on the latter. Her blood was flowing. She wasn't sure what it was, but the puzzle had a few new pieces now.

As she walked back up toward Oxford Street, she thought about how she would couch it all to the chancellor, to Georgia.

THE NEXT MORNING, having breakfast at her parents' café in Bloomsbury, sitting at her perch in the window, making lists, fielding phone calls from the team of inspectors working under her, she noticed the bald man from Heaton Global across the street, down half a block, reading another paper, watching her, once again doing a rotten job of not looking like he was.

The Tatums hadn't come up on any hotel registers on the day after the bombing or since, in or outside the city. The rental car registered to them hadn't shown up yet, even though a bulletin was out for it. All roads would be watched. They hadn't flown out of the country, nor had they crossed through Folkestone, the Chunnel rail terminal to Europe, or taken any ferries over to Ireland or Europe. They were still in the UK, it seemed, but where? Who did they know? Where were they running to— or, more important, who were they running from?

Steel had briefed Darling, the home secretary, and a group from COBRA at Scotland Yard's Operation Center. She really wanted to wait and tell Georgia in the prime minister's private den about the family's dramatic flight from the hotel, but protocol and professionalism won out. Darling wanted to know everything that Steel knew in real time and not a second slower. Burnlee had already contacted the FBI in Washington for a brief on Tatum: what he had done in Michigan, why he had done it, and why the case was dropped. He expected to hear something back early that day.

Why was "Baldy" watching her? That was a nagging question. What was Heaton up to? He was too firmly planted in the center of power to be involved with something like this. Was Tatum just a whacked-out ex-cop? Was he off the rails? Why would he want to harm Lassiter anyway? None of it amounted to a smidgeon of sense, yet it was all, to her, incredibly fascinating. She looked over to her mother and father, serving up breakfast, rushing out the fried eggs and the sausages, day in, day out. She had escaped that treadmill, she thought, had found a life that suited her, that made her jump out of bed in the morning. She felt badly for them: they rarely ever left the block, left Bloomsbury.

She still lived with them, in the family flat just up and across the street, but that was more about responsibility than convenience. They needed her. She knew that. She would have to leave soon, but not quite yet. Her life had grown much larger, her swath of the city ever increasing. Now here she was, dead smack in the center of the biggest crime in London for possibly the last hundred years, working with the most exciting, historic woman to come along for decades. She wanted to pinch herself, it was all so intoxicating.

GEORGIA WAS BURROWED down deep into the couch in the prime minister's den. The night before had been another long one. Up until late working on plans to form a temporary government while Lassiter was on the mend, dealing with her Parliamentary secretary on another route to hold off on the newest European referendum, and getting forward movement with Treasury staffers on the budget proposal that would be coming due in a matter of days. On top of it, the bad weather in the north had brought in a horrible flood that indirectly killed seven people in a tourist coach accident. Georgia worked for hours with Alan Munroe, the director of communications and strategy, on a government statement in response to the tragedy.

Now, as noon approached, she was desperately in need of a few more pain pills, even if the pain was no longer restricted or necessarily pertaining to her leg. As always, she succumbed and dug further into what scarily was becoming close to the bottom of the little plastic bottle.

JACK EARLY POPPED in to tell her that Inspector Steel wanted to come by for a quick update. Georgia instantly perked up. She hoped that Early didn't see her rapid change in demeanor. Something about this young woman was incredibly stimulating to her. The other day when they were in that very room together, without realizing it, she had dropped the use of her cane. When she stood to say good-bye, she did so with a speed and an energy she hadn't had in the longest time. Something about Steel had an almost curative effect on her. She liked her energy, her youthful passion, yes, but it was more than that. When Steel was in a room with her, there was a zing to the air that Georgia wasn't accustomed to—a feeling she wasn't sure she was entirely comfortable having.

After confirming the meeting, she went over to 11 and up to her flat. She let her hair down, let it fly in a more casual youthful way, then changed out of her dress suit into a light-colored spring skirt and a loose-fitting sweater. In her entire life Georgia had never changed her wardrobe like this for a woman. She wasn't sure why she was starting now. She wasn't sure why she so quickly needed a couple more of the little pills.

Davina Steel, too, had dressed just a little more nicely for the meeting— just a tad more feminine. She put on a very small degree of makeup. She wasn't sure why she had done this, either. She simply knew that every meeting with the chancellor was more nerve-racking than the last instead of the opposite. She kept waiting to calm down in her presence, but it wasn't happening.

This time she had even worn a splash of perfume from a bottle of Yves Saint Laurent Parisienne that she had picked up when she went for a police conference on terrorism the summer before in Paris. She had yet to use it, and now here she was splashing it on, trying so hard to be subtle with it.

Georgia caught the scent the minute Steel walked into the den. It was the equivalent of a sweet mist of rose water.

"Ms. Steel, I must say I love the perfume you've on. It's lovely."

"Thank you. Got it in Paris. Last year. I like it, too."

Both not sure what next to say, they took a seat across from each other in unplanned unison. Georgia sat firm, her back straight, eager to get started with any update.

"So tell me your newest, Inspector. Where are we?"

"We're still working many angles, all the usual, but I have to tell you we are looking very closely now at the American, Adam Tatum. As it turns out, he and his wife and their two children were staying at the Millennium on Grosvenor Square."

"Yes, I know that hotel. They've a banquet room. The teachers union has their yearly membership election luncheon there."

"The point is, Madam Chancellor, the Tatums checked out in a hurry, unscheduled, almost four days ago—just a little over an hour after the bomb went off."

"Could they simply have had a problem with the hotel?"

"Maybe. They left in quite a huff, though. They rented a car and went off somewhere in an ungodly hurry. It's all very suspicious."

"Yes, it is. He's employed by Heaton, this one?"

"He is, but he's new and he has a troubled past, as we've discussed. The home secretary got on to the FBI, who did a very quick emergency search warrant and did a look-see at his home. They've come up with some very disturbing finds." Georgia's eyes went wide. Steel was enjoying having her paying such close attention.

"They've uncovered several boxes of literature and paperwork on Mr. Lassiter hidden in Tatum's garage."

"Paperwork and literature? On Roland?"

"Yes. He seemed to be obsessed with the PM. Apparently there were many articles about Mr. Lassiter's very public battles with the trade unions. Some of the writings that they've found on a cursory search of his home computer speak to something of a dark attraction to the prime minister and his union dealings over here. They've even found some comments he's made on chat rooms from that computer about bringing severe harm to the prime minister, as well as some very gruesome photo mock-ups of Mr. Lassiter, dead or being tortured."

"Oh my God. This is true?"

"I'm afraid it is."

"I don't know what to say. That's all quite upsetting. How well did you say Heaton knows this man?"

"We're not sure of what Heaton knows or doesn't know about Mr. Tatum at this point."

"Well, I would hope not too much. I can't believe that David would be involved in any way with something like this. It seems unfathomable. I mean, he does have a dark side, that's obvious, but not one that would play in this kind of water."

"Well, we're going to get into it. We'll have more facts on this American soon. I'll be sure to let you know as soon as the FBI sends the complete report of his case in Michigan. It should be late this afternoon."

"Oh really. That soon? Will you be stopping back?" She hoped she didn't overplay that last question. She felt like a lonely schoolgirl, needing a best friend's company.

"I shouldn't think to bother you. I could just call with any news."

"Either way. Whatever's best for you. Maybe I should give you my private mobile? In case anything new rears. I want to be ahead of the pack. Is that okay?"

"Yes, of course, ma'am." They exchanged mobile numbers. Georgia popped up again, her leg pain almost nonexistent now for some reason. They shook hands warmly, lingered there a beat longer than either one of them was comfortable with. Steel's face went flush red again; Georgia's breath went slightly labored. Each hoped the other had too much on her mind to notice any chemical change that had occurred.

GEORGIA HAD ANOTHER temper tantrum not long after Davina left. Something had gotten to her, right out there in the outer offices at Number 10, in front of a dozen staffers. It was almost a flashback of the meltdown she had let loose on Donald Stanhope, the Tory leader. Her cane had gone sailing once again, this time whacked down on a staffer's desk. Ostensibly the outburst was over a PR mess on the motion to shelve the coming referendum on Europe, but Georgia knew that wasn't it at all. The problem is, she didn't know what had gotten to her. Was it Roland's situation? The sorrow she felt for him, her horror and revulsion at this news of the American's home search? Was it a lack of sleep? Fear for the country?

Physical pain? Regret? Fatigue? Or even worse, was it just about Steel? Discomfort with the way the young woman made her feel?

She didn't know. She truly couldn't sort out her emotions; she didn't have the time or the tools. There wasn't even a moment to relax after making an embarrassed apology to everyone present as Early and his team rushed her along and into her Jaguar, over to the House of Commons for PMQs.

PMQS IS A long-standing Wednesday tradition in Parliament. The opposition leader, the MPs from the opposite party, and backbenchers from the ruling party all get to ask questions of the PM for half an hour. For years it was two separate fifteen-minute segments, but for some reason in Tony Blair's time it was turned into one long episode. Every Wednesday the prime minister shows up, makes a note of his appointments, and then begins to hear from the room. It is as unique and interesting as it is historical and heady. Sometimes it's a snooze fest, but sometimes it's a blood sport that refuses to let you turn away.

Lassiter was considered a genius at the dispatch box. Some would quietly say that was due more to the fact that he had the portly and dull Donald Stanhope to go up against; others contested that he never once answered a question with a straightforward answer. He was called "the Lord of Dodge." But in point of fact, his ease and elasticity there at the box, his way of mixing humor and honor, his smooth voice and his unique agility all made him an uncontested king of the realm. His was a tough act for Georgia to follow.

She had filled in for him only a few times: once when he was with the American president in Israel for the peace treaty signing and once when he was off for the G20 in Vancouver. Each time she got middling to good reviews, held her own, got some licks in, and elicited a few laughs. She wasn't in his league, though, and this Wednesday, with the PM fighting for his life and the country still numb and insatiably curious over news of the bombing, she had little room for error. The only thing she could hope, as she sat in the tightly packed, electrically charged House of Commons, was that the seriousness of the situation would force the opposition to come together and leave the knives and forks at home.

The Speaker of the House called on Stanhope, the opposition leader, to start it off. He tipped to Georgia who stood, as was custom, and gave remarks concerning her appointments.

"Thank you, Mr. Speaker. I have been at Number 10 this morning in meetings and conference, mostly on this most grave of matters, and will be for the rest of the day."

She sat back and let Stanhope lumber up to his side of the box.

"Thank you, Mr. Speaker. It is with great sadness that I stand today and I can only wish the best for a recovery to the highly esteemed and greatly respected Mr. Lassiter, while sending thoughts and prayers to his family. With that said, Mr. Speaker, would the most honorable Lady please explain to us why a full four days after this horrific event, the good people of Britain still have absolutely no idea who or what has caused this crime?"

This brought a rousing agreement from the opposition. *So much for leaving the knives and forks at home*, Georgia thought to herself as she bolted to the box and faced off to Stanhope.

"Mr. Speaker, many thanks to the right honorable gentleman for his kindly remarks on my good friend Roland Lassiter, and my warmest thoughts go out to all of you in this most calamitous time. We are all stunned, sir, we are all truly speechless, but what we are not lacking is resolve. We will find the perpetrators of this most hideous of attacks, and we will bring them to justice, and let not the good opposition leader or any member of this esteemed house think that we are not doing everything, using every facility, and employing our best minds to find the answers that we all desperately seek. To think that we would be doing any less is to truly underestimate this government, and I think that would be a mistake."

She got a strong response from the backbenchers and most of the opposition. The questions moved on, the majority of them concerning Lassiter's health and some on the European referendum, the latter of which in truth she dodged. There was a question on the government's response to the "flood and motorcoach tragedy," and one on who was running the country day-to-day, which she handled as adroitly and humbly as possible.

It happened while Stanhope was off on one of his long-winded tirades, toward the end of PMQs, in his last set of questions. Georgia fell asleep.

Fast asleep. As she sat there, in the PM's seat across the box from Stanhope, once again she dozed off, sitting straight up, and as before dreamt she was in her bed at 11. Holmby, the deputy PM, gently woke her as the entire room waited after the Speaker offered her a chance to rebuke, and it was painfully obvious she was fast asleep. Holmby gently jolted her again as her eyes finally popped open, at first not sure, as before, how she had gotten from her bed into the House of Commons. The room was suddenly awash with wild comic energy, all aimed at Georgia. Stanhope hopped back up to the box to throw in a zinger.

"Mr. Speaker, it's not a great time for any of us, and I believe that the chancellor deserves a good rest as much as the next one, but one would hope it doesn't have to be while I'm speaking."

This got a nice laugh from the House, mostly to ease the tension. Georgia perked up quickly and made her way to the box, locked and loaded, ready for bear.

"Mr. Speaker, I do apologize to my esteemed colleague; as he has said, the matters at hand are pressing and we've been round the clock these days at Number 10, as has all of government. With that said, I am most certain that I'm not the first woman who has fallen asleep mid-speech on Mr. Stanhope, and I surely won't be the last!"

She brought the house down with that one. It was a tremendous save of face, and a much-needed laugh in a troubled time. The Speaker of the House let the ruckus fly for a moment, then finally settled the room down for more of the business at hand.

LATER THAT NIGHT, up in her flat at Number 11, just as Georgia was about to finally get some sleep, her mobile rang. It was Steel. She saw the incoming name and found herself more than excited to take the call. Steel was calling from her family's two-bedroom flat in Bloomsbury, just down the road from her parents' restaurant.

"I hope I haven't disturbed you, ma'am. You had said you wanted to be in the front of the information line."

"Not at all, Ms. Steel. Please, call whenever you feel a need for me." *Did that sound wrong? A need? What could that possibly mean?* she nervously wondered.

"Do go ahead, Inspector."

"Thank you, ma'am. It's the rental car. The one the American rented in Mayfair. It's been found on a back road in Kent. In a thicket of woods, just below Tunbridge Wells."

"Kent? And the family? Have they been taken in?"

"No, ma'am, the car was deserted. The search for the wife and the kids in the area is active as we speak, but a dead body was found in the back of the car, under a tarp. A man. A wallet was found, with a Michigan driver's license, and they're running the DNA and fingerprint samples up the pole with the FBI. He'd taken quite a severe gunshot wound to the head."

"Is it the American? Is it this Tatum?"

"Yes, Madam Chancellor. At this point we're fairly certain that the dead man is in fact the American, Adam Tatum."

It was a quiet night. They had caught a taxi back from Shoreditch after lunch with the McCalisters and had a leisurely afternoon, then a light dinner from room service. Trudy went on a walk, and Kate and Billy were taking in a movie in the room. Adam watched her in the darkness, across the suite snuggled in with Billy, patiently viewing an animated film she had no interest in. He wanted to tell her he planned on informing the HGI representative assigned to him that he wouldn't be attending the conference at Number 10 in the morning. He knew that Kate would once again explain that it was a horrible mistake and wouldn't want him to cancel. He couldn't make her understand that he didn't trust Heaton, that something seemed off about the entire affair, so he finally gave up on any notion of even trying. He quietly left the room.

He needed some fresh air, needed to think.

The lobby was empty and calm. For the most part the guests were all checked in and up in the rooms for the night. The freshly mopped floors smelled like disinfectant and overly scented floral soap. There was a young man, Ronnie, a clerk at the front desk—a South African, nicely dressed in a suit and tie. Ronnie inquired if there was anything he could do to assist Adam. Adam explained that he was just going for some air, and he left the hotel, crossing into the tree-lined square.

He paced leisurely on the dirt walkway that wrapped around from leafy corner to corner. Halfway across he looked ahead and saw two young people passionately embraced, making out on a park bench. It was quite romantic, backlit in fact, and would have been like something on a postcard if only the young lady weren't his sixteen-year-old daughter.

"Trudy? . . . Trudy? Hello?"

He headed over to the bench. This was the last thing he wanted to deal with at that point. Trudy and the young French boy quickly uncoupled, as if they had each been told the other one had leprosy.

"Daddy. Hello. Hi . . . you know Étienne?"

"No, I don't think Étienne and I have had the pleasure."

He was an incredibly handsome young boy; he actually looked older than a teenager. He was nervous; his voice cracked as he stood and shook Adam's hand. He had a warm, thick accent and spoke a cute, almost comical version of broken English.

"It is a pleasure to meet you, sir. I believe that you and my mother are working in the same company, yes?"

"Yes, I believe we are." Adam towered over the young man and enjoyed the height advantage he had. He wanted the boy to be afraid of him. "Why don't you run back into the hotel, Étienne? Find your mother. I'd like to speak to my daughter alone."

"Yes, of course. I will do that. Again, it was a pleasure to meet you, Mr. Tatum." He was gone as fast as he could possibly move his body. Trudy wouldn't look her father in the eye. She was too upset. Adam sat down on the bench with her.

"That was rude, Daddy."

"Good. It's my job sometimes to be a little rude."

"Yeah, well, you acted like you enjoyed it."

"I didn't. Trust me. I get no joy out of seeing you behave like that. You're too young, Trudy. I don't see why you're in such a hurry to grow up."

"I don't know what you're talking about."

She was sullen, still not looking at her father. She had her mother's beauty, the same blue eyes and glowing skin. She had a way about her that made her sometimes appear older than a teenager, but she wasn't: she was a baby as far as he was concerned. A talented, bright girl, she had a wonderful singing voice that no one ever heard because she was too shy to sing in front of people. She had done well in school, well in her studies, at least until the last few years when she turned inward, wasn't as warm and open as she used to be, and she began to be focused on boys to the exclusion of anything else. He was crazy about his little girl.

They sat there in silence. He finally turned to her and spoke in a tone to let her know he needed her on his side of any argument he was in with her mother.

"Trudy, I want you to stick close to us while we're here in London. I'm not sure what's going on. I know your mother doesn't agree with me, but for a variety of reasons that I can't go into I don't feel safe here."

"What are you talking about, Daddy? Don't be silly. London's the safest city in the world."

"Is it?"

"Yes. We're safe. Grandpa's looking out for us anyway, him and the whole 'company' or whatever."

"I just need your help right now. I need you to stay close."

"I don't know what that means."

"Yes, you do, Trudy. You do. You are one incredibly bright young lady. You know what I mean."

"Mom says you want to leave. Quit your job. Get out of that thing tomorrow. The thing you came here for. She says you hate Poppa. Is that all true?"

"No. I don't hate Poppa. That's ridiculous."

"She thinks you're not all there sometimes. Because of what you did, what it did to us, she says you're paranoid or something." He moved a little closer, put his arm around her. She leaned back and slid into his side, resting her head easily on her father's shoulder.

"I'm not mad at you, Daddy. I never really was. I just never understood it. I was sad for you, but I was never mad."

"Thank you. That means a lot to me." They sat there quietly again, breathing in the gentle calm of the foggy night air.

"Why did you do it, Daddy? I know you didn't really want to hurt anyone. I know that, I do, but why did you get involved?"

In all the time, before, during, and since his troubles, he and Trudy had never had a private talk about them. He really didn't like to discuss them. He was tired of the whole subject, but she deserved an answer—he knew the weight she had had to bear for his transgressions.

"I had quit my job the year before, as you know. I had too much free time. I got involved with union politics, spent too much time at the protest rallies."

"I remember. Mom said it was a phase, that it would pass."

"When the governor wanted to pass a law that would basically weaken union power across the board, weaken the worker, the very group that made Michigan the great state it was, I was in shock. I really was."

"I know all this. What I mean is, why? I know all about it. I even know you only were trying to scare the governor, who was a new guy in politics and someone who you and the other union guys thought would buckle under if you scared him. I know all about that. I read it all online and Mom has told me all of that. What I don't get is really why you did it. It's so not you. Why would you do something so dangerous? So illegal? Did someone want to give you money or something?"

"No. It wasn't about money."

"Then what was it about?"

It was a good question. He had asked himself that one, too. He had answered it with so many lies. "Tales of stupidity," "alcoholic consumption," "false bravado," "following the crowd," but they were all lies. If he was going to tell anyone the truth, he was going to tell Trudy. Finally.

"I wanted to be special. I wanted to do something special."

"You are special, Daddy."

"Maybe I didn't feel special. I want to be more than just a dumb Ann Arbor detective, more than my father. I wanted to be part of history, someone who would and could live or die for the things that were important to him. I wanted to test myself, Trudy. Test my character." He stroked her hair softly as he spoke; she nestled further into his side.

"I fooled myself, sweetie. Convinced myself that what we were doing would change the history of the workers, like the original strikers back in the old days at the Ford Highland Park plant. I fooled myself . . . thought I had found a shortcut to greatness. Does that make any sense?"

"Kind of, but not really."

"All it got me was sent to the back of the line." She looked over at her father and gave him the little half smile that reminded him of a grin her mother would always deliver.

"I'm just glad you got out of jail. I hope you never do anything like that again. I was really scared for you. I never want to be scared like that."

"You don't have to worry. I promise." She leaned over and gave him a kiss on his cheek.

"Can you please not be so hard on Poppa? On London? On your boss? Okay, Daddy? Mom's happy here. Billy is having so much fun with Poppa. Mom really wants you to do well. She loves you. Go to that thing tomorrow. She doesn't want you to blow it all. Be nice to her. Okay?"

He sat there, ruminating on how much he loved being part of his family. That was something he once never thought he'd want to be: a family man. As a young guy he always figured there was no upside in having a family, in being nailed down, being a "dad." It sure hadn't done anything for his father.

He had been wrong, though. It was all he cared about. Three months in prison brought that home to him. Sitting in that cell, all night, all day, waiting for a trial, all he wanted was to be with them and to somehow make Kate and the kids happy again.

"I'll think about it. How's that?"

"I love you, Daddy."

"I love you too, button." They sat there in the square for a beat, listening to the wave of cars and buses in the distance, like the lull of a giant seashell, the gentle London night air blowing on their faces, the sweet jasmine scent wafting down from the trees lining the park. He so wanted it all to be over. Wanted his confidence back. Wanted to trust his intuition again, but he didn't. He hadn't in so long. Not since his arrest. Didn't even trust them now, with this whole obviously sorry deal with Heaton.

He finally got up and took her hand as she continued to lean into him while they walked back to the hotel.

"I think I'm in love with Étienne, Daddy. I think this is the one." He kissed the top of her head and answered her with great certainty.

"I can pretty much assure you it isn't."

"How can you say that? How could you possibly know?"

"I'm your father. It's my job to know."

AFTER ▪ 6

Steel was through with taking the Tube. The task at hand had evolved now to a new degree of difficulty. It was time to act, and act fast. She showed up at the HGI complex on Farringdon Street in a Metropolitan Police squad car with two others behind her. She strode into the lobby with three uniformed officers, mostly for show. She wanted to know what had happened with the surviving members of the Tatum family, what Heaton knew about Adam Tatum's past, who recruited Adam Tatum, and what Heaton and the good people at Heaton Global had to do with the bombing at Number 10, now a full five days earlier.

Once again she was given a lot of dead air. A noncommittal receptionist told her to have a seat while she got a representative to discuss the matters with her.

"Do I look like I'm in the mood to wait very long?"

"No, ma'am. I'll be sure to let them know that you're not. Please have a seat." She did wait. Almost five minutes. Too long for her. She wasn't anywhere close to the calm place she would need to be in to "have a seat." She was even dressed differently this time, in black jeans, high black leather boots, and a Met Police parka, plus a Glock 17 on her belt, mostly for show.

She had had enough waiting. She left the uniformed officers at the front, stomped down the back lobby to the private elevators, and went straight up to Heaton's suite. When she stepped off the elevator she was once again greeted by the young woman with the perfect hair and the pretty nose.

"Ms. Steel, hello."

"It's Inspector Steel. It's not often I require the title to be used. This just seems like the perfect time." The good-looking blonde hid a chuckle and a smile. There was something about Steel that she liked, something cute about her. She was a company woman, though, this blonde, so she played her part.

"Yes, of course. Inspector Steel. One of my associates is coming to see you right now."

"That's okay, I'm done waiting. I'm going in to see Sir David."

The pretty young woman tried to talk her out of it, but Steel pushed past her, barging into Heaton's private den. He was in the middle of a meeting with three Asian men. They looked like accountants to Steel. There were number-filled papers strewn over the couches and the table in between the couches. Heaton stood up, once again acting more than happy to see Steel, eager to banter, more than fine with how she had barged into the den. The shampoo lady tried to apologize.

"I'm so sorry, Sir David. I've called security—"

Heaton cut her off, as Steel knew he would. "It's fine, Rebecca."

He turned to the Asian men, spoke to them in Japanese. They bowed. Heaton bowed. They answered him in more Japanese. They picked up their papers, everyone bowed some more, and then they were gone.

Heaton waved a reluctant Rebecca out as well. It was now just he and Steel.

"Alone at last. Look at us. Should I order up some drinks?"

He had already gotten to Steel, two moves in. She didn't back down, though. She torqued her normally back-row Scottish accent up to the main stage, and gave it a bit of a Glasgow street lilt.

"Don't be smug. You know who I'm here representing and what I want to know. I'm not here to wait in your lobby or suffer your arrogant theatrics. Do you have a firm grip on that now? Do you, Sir David?"

He flashed his best "life's a big game grin" at her.

"I do. I get it. You're in a foul way. Don't want to banter. What can I help you with?"

"First off, I want to know how much you personally knew of Adam Tatum's past?"

"Very little. I'm learning more and more every day. In truth, the whole thing disgusts me. The fact that we—inadvertently—could have had something to do with all this. I had no idea of his prior criminal history until sometime yesterday. Neither myself nor anyone else at the company had any idea of what he did or, for that matter, what he was capable of doing."

"And you have no knowledge of who killed him? No knowledge where the rest of his family is or what happened to them?"

"Of course, I do not. I didn't even know he had been killed until just now."

"How is it that he came to be working here? Who here hired him?"

"I'm looking into that. As soon as I know, I'll get that name to you. As I've told you before, we have many thousands of employees." He sat back down for the first time since she'd come into the den and motioned for her to take the couch opposite, to get comfortable.

"I'm not staying long enough. Not this time."

"I am sorry to hear that he's dead. If he indeed was involved in the bombing, I'd have liked to see him stand trial."

"I'm sure you would have. In the meantime, I need to know who his connection was here at the company. We want to find his family before any harm comes to them, find out how much his wife knows about his involvement."

"Of course. I'll have that name to you by the time you reach the front lobby, Inspector." Steel turned to leave. He wanted to play some more. He was almost snickering. He called to her with a cackle as Rebecca and her head of great hair led her back to the elevator. "Burst in any-time, Davina. I'm going to make myself always available to you. How's that?"

She stopped dead in her tracks and turned back, her eyes glaring at him with an intensity he hadn't seen from her yet.

"I'm here under the direct authority of the head of the DPG and the home secretary himself. I'm investigating the attempted assassination of the prime minister. Our lead suspect was a member of your staff. There should be nothing about this that you find funny. That's the last time

I'm going to tell you this quite so nicely." Heaton kept his grin in check as much as he could and nodded sincerely.

"I'll take that as a fair warning."

As she left, she looked down the hall. She saw Harris and Peet on either side of her. She recognized Peet from his time following her. She wanted to laugh, to let him know how incompetent she found his work, but decided to let her unplanned outburst be her last words. She walked past Rebecca down to the private elevator and left.

At the front lobby desk she was given the name and phone number of a man named Gordon Thompson, an employee of HGI there in London. Thompson apparently had the day off, but Steel was told to call him at her earliest convenience regarding any information she needed on Mr. Tatum.

Barry Saffron was in Chicago in his office overlooking the river. It was five in the afternoon. Three plasma TV screens silently played ESPN, CNN, and CNBC. His cell phone rang. It was Tatum, calling from London. Saffron did the math: it must have been one in the morning there.

"What's up, Forrest Gump? You having any fun playing with the prime minister and that crowd yet?"

Adam was calling from a back hallway in the Millennium Hotel. He couldn't sleep, couldn't figure out who to talk to about the meeting at Number 10 in the morning. Saffron was the closest he could come to the name of someone he could trust.

"Barry, listen, I'm stuck here. I don't know what to do. I need some help. I'm out of my league."

"No shit, you're out of your league, you fucking yud-yud you. I could've told you that before you left Chicago." Adam could hear in his voice that Saffron was teasing, was in a good mood, that the sting of being passed over had passed over and now he was just having fun.

"Barry, I don't think this thing is on the up-and-up. I don't trust Heaton. I don't know how much you know about him, but I think he's dirty."

"Dirty in what way?" Saffron stood up, shut off CNBC. Adam had his attention now as he paced the office.

"That's the problem. I don't know what way yet. I just know something's up. You know about my troubles, right? We've never talked about them, Barry, but I assume you know."

"Everyone knows, Tatum. You're a legend. You're the nut job that went full idiot at the Michigan governor's mansion. What about it?"

"I think that's the only reason that I'm here. Why I was picked to go to Number 10."

"Well, there had to be a reason, didn't there? What the hell does being a moron and getting landed in a jail cell have to do with Heaton Global business at 10 Downing Street? Explain that one to me."

"I'm not sure I can. I just know that I'm here to be the fall guy in case something goes bad. He's admitted that to me, Heaton."

"The fall guy for what, Tatum? Start to make some sense here, please." He went over to his remote, turned off ESPN, walked to the door, closed himself off from the rest of the office, and waited for a reply.

"The story he gave me doesn't make any sense, Barry. Something about the dossier they accepted was wrong, a number was off. I was going to replace it so they wouldn't be out a billion something a year. 'No one would ever know.' I'd make out with a contract. Worse comes to worst, the lawyers would all settle it. It was a lot of mumbo jumbo. It was bullshit."

"Sounds like it to me. I mean I never even met the guy, so I can't give you much advice. I have heard from some London people that he's gone a little scary these last few years or so . . . but that's all second- and thirdhand."

"I think he's up to something. I think he's setting me up for something bad."

"Maybe you should call the police? Has that brilliant thought come to your mind yet?"

Adam explained to him in detail the events with the call girl and the police station. He laid out the whole trip up to then so that Saffron understood how going to the police in London was a waste of time. Heaton was too dialed in. Adam was too on the outside.

Saffron turned off CNN. All three screens were dark now. He went over to the window and looked out at the river ten floors below as he listened to Adam explain his situation over the phone. A pleasure boat had broken down or was out of gas on the waterway. The hapless driver and his wife were trying to get a rope to bystanders on the riverwalk to help him before the current took them for a nasty ride. A commercial boat was coming through the Dearborn Street Bridge. Saffron knew enough about boats to know that the big one wasn't going to be able to stop on a dime. There was a strong chance the maritime incident would end in tears. He was just as powerless to help Adam as he was to help them. The distance was similar. All he could do was peer through the glass and pray for the best.

"I don't understand any of it, Tatum. You may be dead wrong, for all I know. You're not all that bright to begin with so I don't put it out of the realm of possibility, but if you're at all right about any of this shit, if it's even close to what you're saying it is, if it were me, I'd turn in the opposite direction and I'd run like the hair on my balls was on fire."

AFTER ▪ 7

Bloomsbury goes dead quiet at night. The museums, shops, cafés, and luncheonettes all shutter early. The office buildings empty out by six, and other than the occasional hurried pedestrians coming to or going from one of the very few residences in flats above the shops, the sidewalks at night become lonely country back roads. The late-night wind whips louder than the distant traffic; the few streetlights left on twinkle softly.

The Steel family flat, just eight doors down and across the road from the café, on Theobald's Road, is one of very few residences on the block. It is a tiny two-bedroom pocket of London that no one even bothers to crane their necks up to see as they hustle on toward the city.

Davina's mother, Sheena, half German and half Scottish, and her father, Cawley Danaid Steel, were modest, quiet, and humble to a fault. They kept their heads low and lived their lives grateful for all that they had, all that they had built. The flat was bare-bones simple, but it was home. Warm with wear, the walls housed scripture framed for sharing, the carpets proudly boasting the scent of a thousand pots of homemade soup.

Steel sat at dinner with her mother and father. She was picking at a lamb stew, a plate full of marinated cabbage, and a piece of chocolate cake for dessert. Her parents both wanted to talk about the case she was working on. After all, it was the only thing anyone in the café was discussing. Steel did her best to change the subject. Her father seemed to get it before her mother, who kept on with the questions. Her dad finally, gently, took her mother's hand and ended it.

"She can't talk about it, lady. Don't you get it? It's not hers to discuss, so leave it be. Let her have a meal."

The truth is she could have spoken about it, could have carefully picked out bits to share, could have given them a pleasing earful. But she didn't want to. She didn't have it in her to engage them in small talk about a case this important.

Later in the evening, as her father watched the TV news on the bombing, while she and her mother cleaned up from the meal, she wanted to apologize for shutting them out. She wondered why she couldn't bother to be nicer to them, or at least think nicer thoughts toward them. But she couldn't, and that made her profoundly sad and even angry because she loved them both so very much.

DAVINA WOKE SUDDENLY from a deep sleep in her bedroom in the middle of the night. Her eyes popped open, having felt something pressed down on her face. She fell back blissfully asleep before she could figure out what it was that had been pushed down across her nose and around her mouth.

When her eyes opened the next time, what seemed like a few hours later, she realized that a man was sitting on the edge of her bed, staring at her. It was pitch-dark in the room; she couldn't make out anything about the man, his face, his height, or his weight. He was there on the bed beside her, that's all she knew. She felt his presence more than actually saw him, felt the way his weight dipped the mattress's edge as he perched there on the side of her bed. She realized that she couldn't move her arms or her legs at all. They were locked in place somehow.

It was when she decided to scream that she realized that there was a gag in her mouth. She couldn't make a sound and she couldn't move her limbs.

She began to struggle but the man leaned into her, put his finger to his lips, gently and sternly at the same time, motioning for her to be quiet.

He lit a match. The room awoke with a dancing orange flickering curtain of light, revealing that it was the redheaded stocky man who worked for Heaton, the one she saw in the hallway outside Heaton's private suite at the Heaton Global building that afternoon. The match gave off just enough flare to illuminate the outlines of another man behind him, sitting in the one chair in the tiny bedroom, up against the desk. It was the bald man. He was there, too. The flickering flame also told enough for Steel to see that her arms were firmly bound to her bedpost with heavy duct tape. She assumed that was the case with her legs as well.

She twisted against her restraints. She wasn't going to go without a fight. She squirmed and wriggled, cursing at them both even if she could only grunt or groan through the gag. The match went out. The blackness snapped back on. She continued to flail. The man on the bed left her to her battles, confident in the confining tape.

After a beat, there was a knock on her bedroom door.

"Davina? Darlin', are yous good?"

It was her father. She stopped twisting. The redhead lit another match, the flame and its shadows dancing around the walls, almost laughing at her. She had the clarity now to see the bald man with a shotgun walk slowly, carefully, toward the door. He held it right to the spot on the door opposite her father's head. The redhead slowly took the gag out of her mouth. No point in words. Steel knew exactly what she needed to say.

"Yeah, yeah, go on back to sleep. I'm good. I was dreaming. Go on."

The baldy kept the gun cocked at the door while all three of the occupants of the room waited for what seemed like forever for an answer.

"All right. Have a sweet rest of the night then."

They all waited and listened as the older man's footsteps creaked up the hallway, the second bedroom door shut, the far-off bed bristling under his body's weight as he burrowed back into his sheets.

As the redhead stuffed the gag back into her mouth, she tried to bite him. She even got a nick off, but it was no use. He shoved it in deep; she had to fight too hard to breathe through her nose to worry about nipping him.

The redhead lit another match. He smiled softly, almost warmly, and said nothing.

Before long she felt him finding and then lifting up her nightgown, slowly traveling down her stomach, his stout clammy hands, scratching their way into and under her panties as he looked straight into her terrified eyes. When his deadened fingers found what they were looking for, they plunged deep into her, two of them, as far up as he could go without dropping the match and starting a fire.

She wept, yet only because that's all she could do. She didn't dare put up a struggle or make so much as a sound. She knew on the next walk down the hall that her father would demand a talk, maybe some milk and another piece of cake. She knew it would be the last walk down the hall he'd ever take, so she didn't struggle. She let the man's grizzly fingers go wherever he needed them to go.

Once sure he'd made a point, he pulled his hand out, gently straightened back her panties, settled her nightgown down. The baldy came over. The redhead stood up, let the baldy sit down in his place. He stared at her, just gazed into her eyes for the longest time with a grin. She knew he had something on his mind, this one, something more than to make a point.

The flame went out on the redhead's third match.

The stocky little man walked back to the edge of the bed and handed the taller, balder one a large object. He nodded his head as if telling him to get on with it. As Steel's eyes finally adjusted to the light coming in from the street, she saw that the object he was handed was a gas mask connected to a metal canister. He leaned down and put it against her face. She understood now that this was what she had felt on her mouth and across her nose earlier. This is how they had bound her so unaware. The lights outside dimmed for some reason; the room went as dark as a cave. The two men had still not said a single word. They never did. It was just their way. Words to Harris and Peet were a waste. Actions were all that ever mattered.

WHEN SHE WOKE, it was morning. The predawn light came streaming in through her window off Theobald's Road. It was chicken-time early. She could hear her parents shuffling off and out the door on the way to the café, hear them discussing her night, a nightmare that she had had, her mother worrying about her as always. She looked down—her arms and legs were free. There wasn't a trace of the tape on any of the bedposts.

She was woozy, numb, and unsure of each movement she took. She needed to walk her body through each new function as if it were the first time. Sit up. Feet on the floor. Stand up. She wondered for a brief moment if maybe the entire thing had in fact been a nightmare, if it had even really happened?

Three burnt matches were left carefully on the desk across from the bed, a gentle reminder of an event purposely staged to not easily be forgotten.

GEORGIA MET WITH Major Darling and the home secretary at six a.m. the next morning. It had been five days now since the bomb went off in the cupboard at the back of the White Room. The chancellor's day was completely scheduled away, wall-to-wall meetings with urgent matters to tick off the list both at Treasury and in the prime minister's diary—important business that couldn't wait. On top of that, there had been a hostage situation in the middle of the night in Lebanon that had involved four British soldiers. Details were only dribbling in, but either way, it would be another crisis for her to deal with. The foreign secretary was due in half an hour with the latest report.

Georgia's pills were almost finished. She had been getting them from the back shelves of her father's pharmacy up in Finchley. It would soon be time for Early to drive her up at the crack of dawn one morning and for her to go into the shop through the back to replenish her supply. She hated doing it this way. Of course she had access to the staff physicians at Downing Street, but she wasn't the least bit interested in word getting out that she had gotten addicted to those lovely little pills of hers, not at the start of what would be a coming party struggle over leadership once it became obvious that Roland wasn't coming back to Number 10. No, she chose to get her medicine on her own, in the only way she knew how.

Meanwhile, Major Darling had news on Adam Tatum.

"The fingerprints and dental records the FBI have offered are distinctly not a match for the body found in the back of the Tatums' rented Ford. It appears the American may not be dead after all."

"Well, whose bleeding body is it, then?"

"We aren't sure yet, ma'am. This is all new and fluid. We'll know soon. The point is, he's out there, alive, which we feel is good news for us. I don't see any way Tatum acted alone. We need to know who he's involved with and why. Our best bet will be to find him safe, bring him in, and get him talking before the people who murdered whoever was under that tarp get to Tatum. The people that need to shut him down permanently."

Georgia agreed. She asked nonchalantly about Steel. She was told that the young inspector had taken a personal morning leave and that she'd be back this afternoon. Georgia expressed hope she'd be all right, quickly moving on to another subject, not wanting to give Darling or Burnlee any sense that Steel meant any more to the chancellor than any other civil servant or government helper who came in and went out of the offices all day at Downing Street.

The truth is that Georgia had spent a good part of the night lying awake in her bed, wondering, ruminating, pondering over Steel. She wanted to see her again, talk to her: discuss the case, her life, her hobbies, her family, and of course her perfume. She desperately wanted to chitchat with the youthful Steel about her perfume. She could see in Steel's eyes, when she had brought it up, a longing to have that kind of girl talk with Georgia, a similar urge.

When Burnlee and Darling came into the den that morning without Steel, all motion left the room, like a sailboat that drops one of its mainsails and comes to an instant drift. Georgia sadly reminded herself that she had used Davina as a reason to get up and out of bed that morning, had once again dressed and made up almost purposely to see her. She wanted to stop this, this constant contemplation of the young inspector. It made no sense. She blamed it on the pills. The pills were clouding her judgment. She was sure of it. They had taken her, changed her.

After the Burnlee/Darling meeting, Georgia had a quick meeting with the foreign secretary, Elena Dowl-Curtiss. The hostage standoff in Lebanon had been averted. A British soldier had been wounded, but all the others were safe and had been released. It was set to Alan Munroe to craft a statement, and Georgia had committed to put it before cameras in time for the evening telecasts. She thought it would be an advantage to have her going in front of the public on matters other than Roland's condition, to get them used to seeing and hearing from her.

GEORGIA WAS CHAUFFEURED, at the center of a motorcade, down across the bridge and over to the hospital to see Lassiter at her lunch hour. He had been awake for a full twenty-four hours, and Kirsty and his doctors thought it would be all right for her to pop in quickly and show support. There was still a large, unruly contingent of press from around the world camped out on the curb of the hospital. Security was naturally as tight as Georgia had seen it anywhere in London since maybe the king's coronation a few years earlier.

Roland was groggy, wildly medicated but coherent now, and more or less able to speak. The doctors wanted his visits limited to a very few and on a stopwatch always ticking, so he and Georgia had only a short time alone. He nodded when she came into the room and reached over for some water, his mouth too dry to speak. She saw him struggling with the cup and quickly leaned in to help. He was still shockingly handsome, even if he looked like he had aged twenty years in the last five days.

"You poor thing, you've been through hell, haven't you?"

The words came out slowly from both of them, his from the pure physical labor, hers weighed down with a lifetime of emotion.

"Now I know how you were feeling after the crash, Georgia."

"I know you suffered then, too. We were both in pain." She smiled at him. "I'm counting on you to pull through."

He smiled back, his eyes going distant. Already the short conversation had tired him out.

"It was an American? A nutter? That's what Kirsty's saying."

"We don't fully know yet, Roland. The details are coming out. He came in on Heaton's team. I don't think there's enough there yet to feel Heaton was anything other than a victim as well."

Roland took it all in. It was obvious that his thoughts were garbled, coming to him in static bursts. "He was there to sell his pensions package."

"Did he say anything to you, Roland, anything that would give one pause?"

Roland took what felt like a decade to answer. Then finally formed a thought. "He told me to look over the binder before you did, told me to be sure to read the summary at the back carefully, before you got to me. I told him I would. I was curious. That's why I went into the cupboard there. When it happened."

It was obviously too hard for him to replay the moment of the blast—too soon. His eyes watered up. Georgia's did as well. This was an answer that said so much. Heaton had sent him to the cupboard, had caused him to feel the full force of the bomb. It was an awful indictment. Or was it? Perhaps Heaton would say he was just selling his pensions package.

The doctors were back in the room, pushing Georgia politely now to move along. She gave Roland a sweet kiss and left, holding back her tears. He was too tired to even say good-bye and had drifted off by the time she left the room.

IN THE CAR on the way back over the bridge from the hospital, Georgia was told that Inspector Steel needed to see her. Apparently whatever personal matter she had in the morning was now straightened out and she had new information to share. Georgia okayed Early squeezing in a fast meeting. Once back at Downing Street, Georgia went up to her flat in 11 to straighten up, recomb her hair, and swallow one more quick little pill.

Steel was dressed casually: a tight cashmere wool sweater and a pair of designer jeans, her hair nicely blown out. She was wearing the perfume again, even more this afternoon than the day before. Her eyes were dark today, though, Georgia thought, as if she hadn't slept, or something had troubled her on a very personal level. It seemed as if recently she may also have been crying.

Early brought in a tray with some tea. He left them in privacy, closing the door to the den. As soon as they were alone, Georgia couldn't help but pry.

"Is everything okay, Inspector? You seem like you have the weight of the world on your shoulders this morning."

Steel wanted to open up with the chancellor, to tell her about the incident at her home the night before, but she felt it wasn't her place to burden her with her problems, even if Georgia was the one person she truly wanted to share it with, the only one whose shoulder she wanted to cry on.

"No, no, thank you for asking. I've just had a rough night."

Georgia knew that there was more to the story, but she didn't want to push. She walked over to the couch, not using her cane, sat down next to the inspector, and served her a cup of tea.

"Madam Chancellor, I know that Major Darling has briefed you on the status of the American: that it wasn't his body, that we're actively looking at the details to figure out whose body it was in the Tatums' rental car, and to find the present location of the Tatum family."

"The whole thing is becoming quite the mystery, isn't it? There's the assassination attempt, and now a murder."

Steel nodded as she sipped her tea. "It's Heaton. Heaton, ma'am. He and his people are behind this. Major Darling and the home secretary will be cross with me for going to you this strongly on this. It's not what they'll want me to say. They wanted to have more answers, but I don't need any more. I know without a doubt he's right at the center of this."

Steel waited for Georgia to answer. She didn't. She sat there on the couch, staring at Steel. She sensed somehow that this had become incredibly personal to the young officer, almost overnight. She moved closer, wanted to comfort her. She spoke quietly, confiding in Steel, thinking maybe that she would confide in her in return.

"I spoke with the prime minister this morning. He's conscious, just barely. He solved the riddle as to why he was in that cupboard when the bomb went off. David Heaton sent him in, looking for a dossier he was to read through ahead of me."

Steel took it all in and understood this to be Georgia agreeing with her on Heaton's complicity.

"It speaks darkly of Heaton. It scares me as well, Inspector. I'm sure he'll have a story on the backside of it. I'm sure he's prepared an iron-clad version of his innocence, but it troubles me. It makes me wonder who else is involved. He's a very, very well-connected man. This government is run sometimes by strings, strings pulled from the murky side of the shadows."

She and Steel sat there on the couch across from each other, trying hard not to telegraph or reveal the odd fascination or energy one was getting from the other. It was there, though, and it was then that a tear leaked, jumped, escaped, or was pushed out of the corner of Steel's eye. It sailed slowly down the side of her face.

The chancellor saw it at once. It took every ounce of will that she had not to catch it with her finger and softly wipe Steel's cheek dry. She reached over for a tissue instead and handed it to the young woman.

"Thank you. I'm sorry. I had a very hard night, ma'am." Again, she said nothing. She didn't want to unfold right there in the PM's den. She didn't think it right.

Georgia would have none of it. She took Steel's hand. It was warm, and soft as could be. Her thumb stroked the back of her palm, soothingly. "Tell me what's troubling you, Davina. Please?"

Steel closed her eyes and opened them again. She was ready to take the plunge and tell her story.

"Two of Heaton's men. They were in my bedroom last night. They came in the middle of the night."

Her words spilled out carefully. Georgia refused to let go of her hand. She wanted her to know it was all right to unburden herself.

"They gassed me. They had my arms and legs bound. One of them . . . fondled me, more as a warning than a thrill, I would suppose. But it was vulgar, and the thing is, I can still feel his fingers there." Georgia nodded. She understood.

Steel had more. "They threatened my father's life. The whole thing was a threat to me, to my parents, to our home." She stiffened now. Georgia's comfortable grip soothing her, she journeyed on from pain toward rage. Georgia could see her eyes go dark.

"I had seen them earlier. I had words with Heaton at his building. I told him I wanted answers as to what he knew of the American's past, of the incident here at Number 10. Of course, he claimed purity in the whole event, but he sensed I knew better. So he sent his in-house creeps to my home. To get inside of my head . . . inside of me."

Steel took a deeply bitter breath. She tried to soothe herself. Another tear fell. This time Georgia couldn't correct herself, didn't feel it necessary; she softly caressed the side of Steel's cheek with her hand and looked deeply into her big brown eyes. Steel's other hand clasped Georgia's hand wrapped around the one in her lap. She let both of her hands float and flutter around the softness of Georgia's satin skin.

"Have you made a report?"

"A rape report? Is that what you mean, ma'am? No. I can't give them that satisfaction. They'll duck it. I've seen what they can do. They can make it about me. They'll use it to muddy the waters on any case we now need to bring about them. I won't hand them that card."

"Have you discussed this with anyone else?" the chancellor asked warmly.

"Only Edwina Wells, my superior at SO15. She gets it. I can trust her." Georgia brushed away a piece of bangs that had fallen over Steel's eye. She tried to be as calming as possible. Steel wanted to impress Georgia with her resolve.

"I'll take care of it. In time." She started to tear up again. Georgia held her hands even tighter now.

"It's all right, love. We'll figure this out. We'll make sure a price is paid for this. I promise you, we will."

"We have to. We have to bring in the whole DGP. Get warrants. He needs to pay, Heaton. This is high treason. He has to swing for this. He needs to rot in a hole, this one."

"Yes. Yes, but we'll do it right. He's a very powerful man. He's a game player. We'll win with a calm head. We won't be ramrodding this. We'll take a breath and let the dust settle just a bit. There's a bigger story here. There has to be. He's too connected."

Steel nodded, looked down. Their two sets of hands were wrapped tightly now—four hands as one. Georgia was strong. Steel felt confident having a partner like this. What happened last night, what happened to the prime minister, to the country: a price must be paid. Someone had to pay.

She wanted to lean forward and kiss Georgia, kiss her deeply. She wanted their lips entwined like their hands now were. She couldn't even believe it had come to this—an undeniable attraction. How long could it be quelled? How could it not be anything other than a disaster? How could it not end in anything but shame and remorse?

They both heard Early's clumsy heels outside the den, stomping across the wooden floor into the office. Georgia could almost count the steps until he'd have his hands on the knob and then open the door to the den. They both wanted it to take so much longer than it would, neither wanting this moment to end. It did, though. Georgia politely pulled her hands free. She smiled and stroked Steel's hair.

"It's all going to be fine, sweet girl. I promise. You've done a wonderful job. I'm very proud of you." She stood up and broke free in one perfectly timed beat before Early opened the door.

I just don't see why you can't get your head past the fear and the spy talk and get into the excitement of the fact that you're going to 10 Downing Street, why you're not over the moon that you're going to meet the prime minister of England. Do you have any idea how many people would love to be in your shoes today, Adam?"

Tatum took a deep breath. She had given him a version of the same line about six times already that morning. He couldn't make her understand the trepidation he was feeling, couldn't quite clue her in to the danger he knew lay ahead. Her father wasn't helping. It was obvious that Gordon knew that he had Adam speeding along into nothing but trouble, was well aware something wasn't on the up-and-up, but he surely hadn't said anything to that effect to his daughter.

Kate helped him tie his tie and once again kissed him good-bye at the hotel room.

"You look perfect. Just put a smile on. You're going to remember this day for the rest of your life." He took the steps down to the lobby.

Gordon was waiting, as always.

"Looking every bit the part today, young man, I must say." He tried to make small talk. As usual, Adam wasn't interested.

"I don't know what this is about, Gordon, but I know if I were smart

I'd go right to the police here. Something's up. I know you know that. At the very best it's fraud."

"Well, then, I leave that to you. If you think going to the police is your answer, then you should go ahead and do that. If it were me, I'd get into the limo once it comes for you."

Adam wanted to slug him. He wanted to beat the old man's head into the wall. He bit his tongue and walked out of the lobby and to the curb. Gordon waited for the other HGI execs to come down from their rooms.

Outside, Adam took a deep breath of the midday air. He watched a flock of birds glide over onto the roof of the empty former US embassy. Crews were getting ready to rework and remodel the lonely old eyesore now that the inhabitants had all moved into the newly built embassy on the south side of the river. As he looked back, he saw his daughter and Étienne getting into a taxi. He was about to stop them, call to them, when Étienne's mother, Elise, came up behind him.

"They're going sightseeing. Your wife has okayed it."

Adam stepped off the curb. "Well, I haven't. Not today. Someone needs to go with them. Maybe tomorrow . . ."

"Adam, you need to listen to me. I don't want to do this any more than you do. These men, they are very serious. We need to take them seriously. Okay? I, too, am not sure. I just want to do this, then go home to Paris with my son. Okay?" She was scared. Spooked. Adam saw a resigned, jumpy, fatalistic fear in her eyes. He wondered if he was making it up? Was he overthinking everything?

He saw one of the HGI Mercedes behind the cab. He wasn't making that up. Heaton's two bodyguards, the redhead and the bald guy, were inside and preparing to follow the taxi. He called to the taxi but was too late. It headed off up Brook Street, and the Mercedes shadowed it. Elise, thin with a mild shake to her, in a Prada business suit, gave him a strained version of a smile.

"It's okay. They will be watched today. And I will be at the conference, watching you." She flashed her mobile phone at Adam. "Don't worry, if there is a problem, they will let me know right away, and of course I can let them know if there is a problem on our end."

The threat wasn't even close to veiled. She was reading lines off of a blatantly sadistic script.

"I'm sorry, Adam. I have no choice. I can't let them hurt my son."

Two HGI limos pulled up behind her and Heaton stepped out, straightening his suit. The French woman walked over, nervously kissed his cheek, and quickly climbed in. Heaton nodded to Adam and pointed to the backseat of the limo. Adam walked over and got right into Heaton's face.

"You think you can pull shit like this? Threaten my daughter? You're lucky I don't drop you to the ground right now."

Heaton didn't miss a beat. "Very heroic. I promise you, Adam, your daughter, your son, your wife, yourself: you are all fine. You're overreacting. I just need you to keep calm."

Heaton got into the car. The entire group waited as Adam decided what to do. It was obvious. The game had been played. Adam had been set up. He had no moves to make. He got into the limo. He was going to Number 10.

A SMALL GREEN building, a security shack similar in shape to an old cabman's shelter, sits just off Whitehall. It's the final hurdle to enter Downing Street. It took nearly forty-five minutes for the group of ten to go through the tiny shack. Even Sir David was checked and double-checked. As the Heaton Global execs were processed, their gear, books, handbags, and papers were put through a series of scanners and searches. Adam felt a measure of relief that nothing in the belongings set off any bells or whistles. It gave him a sense that whatever Heaton had planned wouldn't be so dire as to include any kind of weapon or banned device. He quickly thought about turning out of the shack and running, tearing away up Whitehall, maybe making a scene, screaming at the top of his lungs, stopping the whole conference from ever happening.

He thought about his daughter, about what kind of call the French woman would make, about what would happen to him in the bowels of any police station he was taken to. He thought about Kate, about how badly she wanted him to recover and rebuild his life.

As they came out of the shack, now inside the gates of Downing Street, the group headed up the road with the famous front door to Number 10 on their right and the Foreign Office on the left. Heaton made sure to catch up with Adam. He whispered into his ear as they walked.

"Our meeting will be upstairs in the White Room. As soon as you walk in, someone will hand you the new brief we want to leave with them. You'll sit as close to the front of the table as possible; when Louise Bloomfield, Lassiter's private secretary, retrieves the logged-in binder, you'll figure out a moment to slide the one you've been given across to Ms. Bloomfield and replace it. Elise will make it her responsibility to take the one of record with us as she leaves."

He didn't wait for Adam to respond. Once finished talking, he picked up his pace to make his way to the head of the pack as it reached the front door of Number 10. As soon as Heaton hit the stoop, the door almost magically opened from inside. Once through the front door, past the brass plaque reading FIRST LORD OF THE TREASURY, they were met in the front lobby by a contingent of civil servants. Leading the welcome party at the front of the line was Georgia Turnbull, the chancellor of the exchequer.

Heaton and the chancellor locked in a warm hug. Obviously they were old friends. David Heaton was comfortable with everyone there and with the home itself. Everyone else was in awe; to Heaton it was another day at the office.

Adam had seen the chancellor on television before and knew she was very important in the British government, but he didn't really know how or for what reason. He had no idea what a "chancellor of the exchequer" did. The truth was that he recognized her mostly for the cane she leaned on. He'd seen her using it before, maybe on the news at a visit to the White House or the UN. She was nice looking, he thought. There was something kind of sexy about her wild head of hair.

The chancellor and Heaton led the group up the stairway, past the photos of long-gone prime ministers, and into the White Room, a large, well-lit, ornately presented room that until the 1940s had been part of the prime minister's private family residence. Since Clement Attlee's time, during the postwar period, it had been used for staff meetings and later, starting in Harold Wilson's tenure, television interviews.

Adam was one of the last in of ten HGI members and another eight

Downing staffers. As soon as he entered the room, a man about his age in an ill-fitting suit thrust an identical version of the HGI dossier into Adam's arms. Once the man had surreptitiously given Adam the binder, he quickly disappeared from the room and into the hallway. The binder was heavy, much heavier than the one he had perused in Heaton's library.

Adam tried to make some sense of its weight as the group was seated on floral couches nestled around two large mahogany coffee tables. There was a smartly done antique wooden cupboard against the back wall underneath a painting by William Marlow, of St. Paul's Cathedral and Blackfriars Bridge. Another wall had an oversize portrait of Lady Thatcher staring down at the room, begging them to remember at all times that they were all inherently British.

A woman who Adam came to realize was Louise Bloomfield, Lassiter's private secretary, went into the wooden cupboard and pulled out a copy of the file in a binder exactly like the one Adam had been handed by the man at the door. This was the version that had been previously accepted by Treasury. Ms. Bloomfield sat on a couch across from Adam, setting the "logged-in" version on the table right in front of her, just opposite Adam.

The chancellor began the meeting, thanking Heaton and the group for coming. Heaton made a small speech about the work all the members of his group had done, thanking them and then throwing a nod to the present members of the Treasury for their contributions. He talked of the proud history of the civil service, of the importance in making sure the pensions of its esteemed employees were healthy, secure, and, equally as important, fruitful.

Henri Despone, a small, well-briefed Frenchman, stood and gave a quick rundown of the package, of what was in the report, and what the long- and short-term goals were on the Heaton Global side. Amos Harrison, the Texan who had gone with them to the high-end whorehouse, gave a report on the transition period between the civil service running the pensions and HGI assuming management. Adam looked over at the chancellor. She looked bored but not nearly as lost in the numbers and figures as he was; she seemed to be familiar with every aspect of the deal.

The prime minister came in. He made a strong, sturdy show of an entrance. Everyone stood as the chancellor introduced Roland Lassiter.

As they did, with all eyes on Lassiter, Elise, the French lady-scoundrel, quietly pulled the binder in front of Ms. Bloomfield toward her. Ms. Bloomfield was too busy listening to Lassiter greet the others to see what she had done. Elise now turned to Adam and motioned for him to switch the dossiers.

Adam knew it was a mistake. He knew he'd regret it. He paused and again considered getting up, walking out, excusing himself, and finding the head of security downstairs. He tried to make sense of it all. The French woman read the lines on his face; he read the dread in hers. She quietly flashed her mobile phone to him to let him know very clearly whom she intended to text if there was a problem.

As introductions to Mr. Lassiter and the others finished up, Adam carefully slid his weighty version of the binder across the coffee table in front of Ms. Bloomfield. She never noticed the change. The deed had been done. Once the room settled and everyone took their seats, the PM made a quick, funny, warmly taken speech praising his "very good friend" Sir David for all the hard work that he and the Heaton Global staff had done for the government.

Adam was taken by Lassiter's looks. He was a handsome man on television, but in person he was truly striking, with vibrant skin, an incredible head of radiant hair, and a large set of twinkling brown eyes. There was a sadness to him as well, one that could only be sensed up close. A weary kind of broken layer beneath the practiced politician's smile.

The PM finished with a nod to his chancellor for her work on the endeavor, and then he was on to his next appointment. He was a star, Lassiter. Playing a room like this was second nature to him. Other than Georgia, no one there realized the emotional pain he was in ever since the helicopter accident almost two years earlier. He was that good of a showman.

As the prime minister was about to leave, Heaton grabbed his friend and whispered something into his ear. Lassiter looked back, across the couches and coffee tables to the cupboard, and nodded. With one more slap on Heaton's back, he was off, and with that the meeting was over. Louise Bloomfield unknowingly took the binder that had been slipped to her over to the cupboard, piled several others on top of it, and then made a face and a remark regarding the weight of them all. No one responded—she didn't expect them to; she was more or less comment-ing to herself as the others said their good-byes and made small talk, sharing anecdotes about Lassiter and Number 10.

Sir David and Georgia Turnbull walked the HGI group downstairs and out the front door. Just like that, the field trip to 10 Downing Street ended. Adam had a sickening suspicion. That file was too heavy, way too weighty. He once again hoped he was overthinking, prayed that he was wildly off base, and that the file was just that, a file.

AFTER ▪ 8

At six thirty a.m., Cabinet Secretary Phyllis Dryden called all ministers to an emergency cabinet meeting. The heads of Scotland Yard, Special Branch, MI5, SO15, the foreign secretary, the director of COBRA, and even Stanhope, the leader of the opposition, had been summoned. The Cabinet Room was "standing room only." All hands were on deck. All staffers knew something was up—something big.

Georgia stood and addressed the room. Major Darling and Sir Melvin Burnlee flanked her. Steel was seated against the wall across from her with a direct view of Georgia.

"People, thank you for your prompt arrival. Six days ago this house was violated with a most hideous and disgusting crime. It has rocked this building, shaken our people, and saddened our souls. We have not stood idly by, as some have suggested; rather, with the good work of MI5, SO15, the DPG, Major Darling, and Inspector Davina Steel, today we have some answers. We have a suspect. He is an American. His name is Adam David Tatum. He is from Chicago. He has a history of subversive, aggressive behavior, and, it seems, a misguided inclination for violence as a tool for change."

There was a small murmur from the room as it was revealed that an American was the prime suspect. The "special relationship" with the United States had endured a few tough years starting all the way back during George W. Bush's disastrous foray into Iraq and on into the long, painful years of the battle with ISIL in the Middle East. Many in the British government had come to distrust the United States and Americans in general, and in fact the British public as well could be called "more than concerned" about the United States and its role in the world. The fact that they would now be turning west, looking at a US citizen as a possible perpetrator of this intimately horrible act, brought a new weight and a somber bass line to it all.

As the chancellor spoke, dossiers of Adam were passed around the shocked, silent, crowded room, one for each person. They contained his mug shot, a photo of the break-in in Michigan, and press clippings on the "Lansing plot." Georgia continued with her recap.

"His motive would seem to be that he is some sort of union activist, a man willing to do anything for his fellow workers. I will say there are many among the investigative team who aren't quite ready to believe that to be the case. They don't believe it possible or plausible that this was the work of one lone man. Some here feel he is part of a larger plot—a plot and a motive that we are still not sure of. Some fear very much that we may well be in treacherous waters today, that in fact this American's life could be in danger; the people who put him up to this would do well to kill him, to silence him. At one point we thought him dead already. This is not the case. He is very much alive. He is on the run."

Photos now passed around the room showing a gruesome shot of a dead body in the back of the Ford wagon that Adam had rented. As the photos circulated, Georgia and Steel made eye contact. Steel was so proud to be on her team and adored how strong and alive Georgia looked as she spoke to the assembled group.

"This man must be found. Every resource of our government must now be used to bring him in and to uncover where and to whom the trail behind him leads. His details and photos must be sent to the attention of every station house, border crossing, and police officer in and around every corner of Great Britain. The press should not have his name or any, I repeat, any knowledge at this point of his or this potential scheme's existence. We don't want them to know we are on the hunt just yet. We'll hope Mr. Tatum thinks himself free to roam and makes an unfounded move."

Her back was straight now, her chest out, and her voice clear. She was morphing, Steel thought, right before everyone's very eyes, into a true leader—a powerful figure, a Churchill even. Steel was crazy about her. It was clear in that moment, right then and there: she was head over heels nuts about Georgia Turnbull. How could she not be?

The room was thick with concentration, every eye riveted on the chancellor, her passion evident, the import, the severity, the calm resolve in her voice mesmerizing to the ministers and civil servants.

"This will be stopped. If it is in fact a plot, it absolutely threatens the very future and fabric of our nation. It could well bring along irreparable repercussions. It will not bear fruit. It will not pay dividends." She was speaking at the top of her voice now. "Our goal from this moment on is to shut down this island, to put eyes on every train, every plane, every boat, lobby, café, and shopping plaza. It is now, from this second on, job one of this government to use all of our powers and summon all of our convictions to locate this American."

With that, she sat down under the Walpole portrait, in the chair always left cocked to the table, and turned the room over to Major Darling who had more information on Tatum. As Darling spoke, Georgia looked over and saw young Steel looking at her. Her gaze brought Georgia comfort she badly needed—she had never once in her entire life been as frightened as she was at that moment.

PART TWO

ON THE RUN

ON THE HUNT

The limo dropped them all at the Connaught hotel. Sir David invited everyone in for a celebratory drink. Adam tried to beg off, to go back to the Millennium, but Heaton wouldn't hear of it.

"Don't be like that, Tatum. We've had a good day, a rousing success. You need to let a breath out and enjoy your win. Have a quick drink, man." Adam went in but stopped to call his hotel from the Connaught's lobby. Trudy answered. She was in the room with Billy. Kate was out somewhere, Trudy wasn't sure where. Adam took a deep breath. His daughter was safe. One major load had been lifted.

In the Connaught's smoky bar, the HGI group was in a good mood. Most of them wanted to talk about how exciting it was to be in Number 10, to meet Roland Lassiter and Georgia Turnbull. Heaton told a few funny stories about his first visit at Number 10 as a young man. They all drank expensive scotch and puffed happily on strong Cubans. None of it felt right to Adam. Not only did he sense that it would all end badly, but he also couldn't get over the fact that they had so blatantly threatened his daughter, forced him to do something against his will. Brought him to London to use him for some reason that he still didn't understand but was sure wasn't legal, ethical, or morally sound.

The French lady gave him a friendly, relieved half-smile across the table; he returned the darkest look he could possibly give. There was talk of "the deal," "implementation," "bellwether comparisons," and other "statistical anecdotes" concerning a package of this size, plus a lot of back patting on the historical nature of what they'd done, a "benchmark" set for years to come.

Adam finally excused himself. Heaton didn't want him to go, but he wouldn't stop him. Adam turned and left the bar before he lost his temper. He skulked toward the Millennium, his hands in his pockets and his eyes on the ground the whole way back to Grosvenor Square.

As he walked into the lobby, he noticed several people standing at the hotel's bar and café staring up at the television. They were all entranced by the screen. Others wandered over to listen. There was breaking news. The clerk, Ronnie, had left the front desk to see what everyone was looking at.

Adam crossed the lobby and craned his neck up to the television. His heart almost stopped beating when he saw stock footage of Downing Street on Sky News. A bomb had gone off at Number 10. That's all that was known. There were no other details yet, just word of an explosion— no idea where it came from or what part of the building it was in, and no news if anyone was hurt.

The newscaster and the people in the bar all wondered who could have done this. The first guess was ISIL. Someone else guessed the Syrians.

"Don't forget that last year we expelled their whole damn embassy. I bet good money it was the Syrians." One guest thought it was the Palestinians; another mused that it was Israel trying to blame the Palestinians. Everyone in the bar took a stab.

"It could be the Egyptians. That whole country's coming apart. I can see one of them doing something like that," said a well-dressed man at the end of the bar. An older lady, at a table near the back, thought it was the Irish. She almost got laughed out of the room over that one.

Adam knew better. He knew exactly what had happened. His hands could feel the weight of the report that Louise Bloomfield was fed to put back into that cupboard. He had the weight etched into his memory: the weight—in his hands, on his brain—of the bomb. He broke into an instant sweat. Every pore of his body leaked with a liquid dread. He left before anyone could see his soaking forehead and the near meltdown of his mind and body as he came to the realization that it wasn't ISIL, it wasn't the Syrians, it wasn't the Irish, the Egyptians, the Israelis, or the Palestinians. It was Adam Tatum. Adam Tatum had planted that bomb, and it wouldn't be long before the whole world knew it.

HE HAD TRIED to call Kate from his cell phone on his way down the hall to their suite. There was no answer; it went straight to voice mail. He didn't bother to leave a message, figured she'd see that he called. What kind of message could he leave, he wondered? *Hey babe, get home quickly. I just blew up 10 Downing Street. We need to talk.*

When he got into the room, Trudy was on the phone with the French kid and Billy was watching another cartoon. He distracted Trudy long enough to ask her where her mother was.

"I don't know, Daddy. She said she was going out to see an old friend, that she'd be back in time for dinner."

"Who was the friend?"

"She didn't say. She doesn't have to run that kind of thing by me. She's the mother, I'm the daughter, remember?" She shrugged. He ignored her, was used to her talking to him this way. It was another part of the price he had paid since his time in jail. In times of disagreement she spoke to him more like a sibling than a daughter.

"Why don't you just call her?"

"I tried. She's not picking up her cell."

"Try again." She went back to her phone call and starting giggling in a whisper, inwardly rolling her eyes at her father.

"You need to hang up the phone now, Trudy. Right now. I want you and your brother to pack your stuff. Right away." He stared at her. He gave her a beat to let what he said sink in. She looked at him, still listening to whatever Étienne was saying on the other end of her cell phone. She was still half chuckling at the French kid, half taking in what her father was going on about.

"I mean it, Trudy. Get off the phone now." She raised a finger in a way that told him it would just be another minute and he needed to be patient. He walked over, took the phone from her hand, hung it up, and set it on the table.

"What are you doing? I was in the middle of a conversation."

"Get packed. Right now. Help your brother. I mean it. We have to go."

She stood up. She realized for the first time how serious he was. She realized he was talking in the tone he usually talked in just minutes before he'd be yelling.

"Go where? What are you talking about? What about Mom?"

"We'll wait for her, obviously, but we need to be ready to go the minute she gets back." He went over to the television and shut it off.

Billy gave Adam a look like he'd just killed all of the characters in the movie, a movie that Adam knew he'd already seen at least five times.

"Daddy? Are you kidding me? Why did you do that? I'm in the middle of that."

"Not anymore. Pack your stuff. Right now."

"What? Why? I don't know how to pack. Mom packs me."

"You heard me. Both of you. I need you both to listen to me really carefully. We need to be packed and out of here in the next five minutes. We're moving to another hotel." Billy was still staring at the TV, wounded and hoping somehow it would magically come back on.

"But I like this hotel."

"Too bad. We're leaving. Pack up. Now. We'll meet your mother in the lobby when she gets back." Trudy held her ground and bore down with a strident glare to her father.

"Mom's not going to like this. You know that."

"She doesn't have a choice. Now for the last time, please go in there and pack your stuff. Both of you. Now!"

As they shuffled into their part of the suite, he tried Kate's cell phone. Once again, there was no answer.

RICHARD LYLE STILL smelled the same. Almost twenty years later, he had that clean, soapy, almost cologne aroma that he'd had the first night she met him, when she was sixteen years old—Trudy's age. Richard's place even smelled the same, a wild combination of sweat, chipped wood, burnt microwave popcorn, and hair care products. A tiny mews house a stone's throw from Paddington station, he'd lived there since finishing his A levels. He ran his music management company, his ticket-scalping operation, and his advertising consulting firm from the house, plus he did hair styling there. She used to tease him that he truly never had to leave home. That was when she used to do his food shopping and most of his cooking, so why would he bother?

Pictures on Facebook can be very deceiving. That's what she kept telling herself in the cab over from Mayfair. There's nothing to stop one from posting a fifteen-year-old photo and claim it's as current as the morning's paper. Richard wasn't that type, though. She knew that. She knew that his pictures were current. She knew that he wouldn't look all that different today than he had the last time she saw him in Michigan, seventeen years ago, the last trip he took over to try and convince her to come home.

She was ready for him to look the same. She just wasn't ready for him to smell so "Richard." She wasn't ready for his place to feel so familiar, as if time had stopped and waited for her.

"Well, aren't you a doll? Let me get a good look at you." He was dressed in a trendy jacket, a dark pair of jeans, and crocodile leather boots. He had dressed for her, exactly the way he knew she used to like him to dress. The fact that two decades had passed was another story, but "it's the thought that counts," she figured. She could have laid out the outfit for him herself, exactly as she had done so many times before in another life, in another world, another dimension—a dimension she had somehow suddenly stepped back into.

Richard Lyle truly had not aged. If he had, it had only helped. She hated men for that, for aging so well. His hair was shorter but still thick. His stomach may not have been as flat as it once was, but it was attractively maintained. There was no doubt he kept up his morning workouts, still followed his strict diet.

"You look lovely, Rich."

"And you, my doll. It's so nice to see you. I can't tell you."

"Well, I had a couple of hours to kill. Adam's at this business thing. I thought it'd be nice to say hello." She wasn't sure what to say, how much to say, what tone to say it in.

He made them tea.

The decoration and furnishings were as eclectic as Richard's résumé. There were Victorian-era antiques in one corner, video arcade games in another. The dining area/solarium was equipped with an impressive array of secondhand gym equipment. The breakfast nook had been turned into a one-chair hair salon. Three Himalayan cats perched lazily on a giant modern leather couch in the middle of the living room.

Richard and Kate went out back and sat on the terrace. He filled her in on all the things he'd been doing. He told her about the "pretty lady" who had just dumped him. He made her laugh with the stories of his travails with nutty women. She smoked a cigarette.

"Haven't had a cig in five years. Even when I did, it was a sneak, and I had to smoke it so fast it wasn't any fun." This one was fun. She smoked it to the nub—one of Richard's fancy French ones.

The tea was perfect as well. Richard made her laugh some more. They told and retold old stories, relived favorite memories.

"You know that I see Gordon every now and then, right? For breakfasts?"

She smiled, sighed. "He's lonely. He's so lonely."

Richard agreed. He refilled her tea, then lit another smoke and handed it over to her.

"That's why I like to have breakfast with him. That, plus he keeps me informed on 'all things Kate.' Allows me to keep up on current events. So I'm prepared to sneak back into your life when the proper time comes."

"Listen to you."

"Why start now? You never did listen to me." He winked. She grinned. They sat there in quiet, smoking and sipping. "You know, Kate. I know you've been through a rough patch. I know that your man's had a hard run."

"Well, yes, but it seems to be picking up for him. I hope. Gordon's gotten him a job, with David Heaton. He seems to be doing well there."

"I've heard. Like I say, I get filled in on all your comings and goings. Your dad, on the other hand, hates his job. He thinks Heaton treats him like a sack of trash."

"Does he really? He never says that to me, not a word on that. He tells me the opposite, in fact, how much he loves working for Heaton."

"Oh, great. Look at me now, back in the middle of a squabble with you two. The poor guy trusted me, opened up to me, and I blabbed to his daughter. Fat chance he's going to buy me any more breakfasts." She laughed.

"Well, don't worry, I'll probably keep your secret safe. Odds are that he'll speak to you again, one day." She thought about it some more, let what Richard said sink in past the playful banter.

"That's sad that he hates his job, though, that Heaton treats him poorly. It's horrible that he couldn't tell me that. We've drifted so far apart, Daddy and I. It makes me truly sorry."

They talked some more. She opened up to him a little, not a lot. She knew Richard too well. Knew if she revealed too much of her doubts and troubles with Adam, he'd use them. She was enjoying being with him, enjoying the attention he was giving her, but she didn't see herself here again, in this lost world, not permanently. Too much had happened. Too much time had passed. She was a woman, not a little girl. Richard needs a little girl. Kate was a mom, a mother of two, someone's wife. The visit was over. It was time to leave.

He walked her to the door. They took a long last look at each other. He still had a thing for her, it was obvious, and the truth is, she still had a thing for him—maybe not the same thing, but it was definitely a thing. He took her face in his hands, something he used to do in that other life, that other dimension. His giant hands wrapped her face, "like a cupcake," and in that one second she was one of his little girls again. He leaned in and kissed her. She knew he would. She didn't stop him. A little snog wouldn't hurt.

Her heart was beating. He was just as good a kisser as he always was, maybe better. He pulled her in and held her tight in a way that reminded her instantly of the intimacy they once had. He was the only person other than Adam with whom she had ever shared such tenderness. It whisked her back to scents and sounds, feelings and pleasures long ago locked away—replaced, but never exactly replicated. After a moment she finally pulled away and left. It wasn't easy.

ADAM AND THE kids and their bags tumbled out of the elevator and into the lobby. Billy was on his handheld game device, working a video game as they walked to the checkout desk, oblivious to where he was and where they were going. Trudy was the opposite. She was beside herself, trying to get her mother on the cell phone.

"You can't just do this, Daddy. You can't just make me leave. I haven't even said good-bye. We're supposed to be here eight more days. I had plans. You know that, right?"

Adam didn't even stop. He just soldiered on, over toward Ronnie, the clerk at the front counter.

"Things have changed, Trudy. I can't keep telling you that. We have no choice."

He looked into the bar on the way over. The crowd had grown. Sky News now had the God's-eye-view helicopter shot. Several soldiers and government workers were running in and out of the buildings that Adam had been inside of just over two hours ago. A Met cop could be seen running out of 11 and into 10 with a large fire extinguisher as a line of trucks and tanks pulled into the Downing Street concourse.

Adam walked over, dumped the keys to the room in the slot, and didn't even bother checking out. Trudy had the continuation of her melt-down. She started to cry, right in the middle of the lobby. Adam did his best to keep everything as quiet as possible. The last thing he wanted to do was cause a scene. He gently picked up Trudy's handbag, put his arm around her, and spoke softly.

"Trudy, I'm not happy about this, either. I am going to explain it all to you in just a bit, okay? I promise. I just need to get us all away from here. I get that you don't understand it, but I'm only looking out for all of us. All of you. Please trust me, for a little bit more. Okay?"

She didn't want to, but she reluctantly agreed. Ronnie the clerk came over on cue as Kate walked in the front door of the hotel, just back from Richard's. Right away she noticed all of their bags, hers included, laid out on the marble floor in the center of the Millennium's lobby.

"What's this? What's going on, Adam?" Billy popped up and wrapped himself around her legs before Adam had a chance to answer.

"Mommy, I want to stay here. I like this hotel. Poppa's gonna come over and we're going to feed the ducks again. Please tell Daddy we want to stay here." Ronnie the clerk was as concerned as Kate was.

"Excuse me, sir, is there a problem? Is something wrong with the hotel? With the service? Something that I can do to be of some help?" Kate watched Adam closely for an answer.

"No, no, thank you. It has nothing to do with the hotel. Our plans have just changed. We're going to go somewhere else. Thanks for your concern." Trudy broke into another round of tears. Kate looked at him, more confused than angry. Adam couldn't explain himself with the clerk hovering so close. He bent down and started grabbing luggage.

"Go where? What are you on about, Adam?"

"Let's go. Grab a bag. I'll explain later." He threw her a look, trying to tell her that she needed to back him and move along. Ronnie wasn't quite getting the hint that Adam needed some privacy.

"Can I arrange a car for you, sir, or a taxi?"

"No taxi, no car. We're good. Thank you." Adam headed out to the street. He looked in all directions and tried to make some sense of what his next move would be. Kate and the kids, and Ronnie, followed. Kate grabbed his arm, desperately needing to understand what was happening.

"Adam, you need to talk to me. Why are we leaving here? What has happened? Have you told my father? The people at your company?"

Adam came over, leaned in, and whispered to his wife, "I will explain it all to you when I can. For now, we have to go and you need to trust me. Our lives are in danger, Kate."

"What? . . . Have you been drinking?" Before he could answer, the clerk was in his space and in his face again.

"Are you sure, sir, that I cannot call you a taxicab? An airport shuttle? A sedan?" Little Ronnie didn't want to give up. He had been trained too well.

"No taxi. Thank you. It's all good. It has nothing to do with the hotel. I appreciate your concern. We just need to meet up with some friends that have invited us to come stay with them."

Kate's face scrunched up. "What friends? What are you talking about?"

He pulled her to the side again, talked low. "It's nothing. I'm just saying that so he doesn't think we're on the run or that we're in a panic."

"Gee, why would he think that, Adam?" she wondered with her most sarcastic drip. He wanted to get into it with her but decided against it.

He waved good-bye to the clerk and, with a mountain of unwieldy luggage balanced on his arms and his back, waited for traffic to clear, then crossed over into Grosvenor Square.

"Let's go, Kate, kids. We have to go right now. We're very late." Trudy and Billy begged with gusto for their mother to talk some sense into him, but Kate already had a solid feeling that that wasn't going to happen. She hiked up her share of the bags and went after Adam, ushering the kids to carefully follow her across the road.

Ronnie watched until they reached somewhere near halfway into the square and then finally let it go. He decided he had done his best, figured they were now going to be some other hotel clerk's problem.

Davina Steel, accompanied by Lieutenant David Bellings of Special Branch, Captain Andrew Tavish, and Edwina Wells, Darling's number two at SO15, descended on Heaton Global's building on Farringdon Street with eight uniformed officers and several different warrants for information pertaining to Adam Tatum. It was a purposely planned show of force. Steel had her Glock on display, next to a pair of handcuffs that were swinging on her belt. She hoped to run into the redhead and "baldy" and deal with the visit they paid to her parents' home. This time, much to Steel's regret, they weren't given any version of the runaround. Heaton was not on the premises and was said to be out of town, but his top people quickly convened with Steel and the investigators in the large wood-paneled conference room on the first floor.

There wasn't a lot of information to give, not if you listened to the sympathetic employees of the large multinational firm. According to the files, the Tatums came into town a few days before the bombing and stayed at the Millennium until they left abruptly after the explosion, which was now six days ago. They had disappeared since then, fallen off the map. No one seemed to have a straight answer as to where they were, where they could have gone, who picked Tatum to be part of the contingent, or why. Heaton Global claimed to be just as in the dark on Adam Tatum as SO15 was.

There was a man at the back of the room, an older fellow with close-cropped hair, a thick, sturdy trunk, and finely polished shoes. Steel watched him out of the corner of her eye. He was doing his best to stay out of the conversation. He always had one eye on the door to the conference room. Steel guessed by his overly firm posture that he was ex-cop, maybe ex-military. There was something weak about him, though, she thought, flimsy in his confidence in direct juxtaposition to his broad chest and thickened build. He had a frightened quality. He was too big to be mousy, but he looked shaken. She played a hunch. She turned and bellowed out across the room, her accent just a little more "street" than usual.

"Oy. Are you Gordon Thompson?" The man at the back wall froze and checked the door again, as if he might even run, then looked back. He wasn't sure how to answer. Finally he put words to lips.

"Yes. Yes. I'm Gordon Thompson, Inspector Steel. How can I help you?"

"Number one, you can start returning my calls. I've rung you three times this week. The receptionist gave me your number, said you made the hotel reservations for the Tatums, that you arranged to have them picked up at Heathrow when they'd landed."

"Yes. That's true. I did. I'm sorry to not have gotten back. I've been up north at one of Mr. Heaton's properties. The caretaker had to go abroad and it was left to me to take care of some logistics. Please forgive me."

She glared at him across the room for another moment, then started back in on her questioning. "So you made the reservations for them? At the Millennium?" He nodded. His face was white. Something was wrong with this man. It was obvious.

"I made them with the Chicago office. Actually, a woman called Ellen Doyle. In travel. It was she that cobbled together the arrangements. I just carried through."

"Who told you to do that? Who were you answering to at the time?"

"No one really. I was just doing what was in front of me. I took care of making sure the whole delegation got in and settled. That's what Sir David has me do. Whatever the job is at hand." He knew more, Steel could feel that.

"How did they seem to you, the Tatums?" Thompson thought about his answer. He wanted to get it right.

"They seemed like a nice family. Happy to be in London."

"How about him? Anything unusual with Mr. Tatum?"

"He may have been a bit nervous. This was a step up for him. I could see that."

"How well did Heaton know Mr. Tatum?"

"I couldn't say for sure, ma'am. I'm not in that kind of position to know how well Sir David would know anyone."

Steel knew this Thompson person was lying through his teeth. She could feel it. It only added to her growing anger toward the whole company, this whole place. She needed to figure out where he fit in. For now, though, she was done talking to him.

"Next time I call, you pick that damn phone up. You hear me? This is a very active criminal investigation into what may well be an act of treason. I don't have time to play phone tag or to play games with you. Okay, Mr. Thompson?"

"Yes, ma'am. I'll be sure to respond immediately."

Detectives Tavish and Wells shared a quiet chuckle. Edwina Wells was one of Steel's closest friends on the force, almost an older sister. For some reason she always perversely enjoyed seeing the pint-sized Steel make gruff old men quiver like frightened schoolboys.

WELLS AND TAVISH may have gotten a kick out of Steel's behavior in the conference room, but when the group left the building and walked toward the patrol cars double-parked on Farringdon Street, they witnessed a show of a completely different kind, a version of their young friend they had never seen.

Harris and Peet were on the far side of the concourse. Davina caught the redhead's eye, baldy's, too, both snickering at her, gloating over what they had gotten away with not only at Number 10 but also at her parents' flat. She lost it. She ducked behind a patrol car without being noticed, pulled out her Glock, and fired off into the sky.

The pack of cops, inspectors, and Heaton Global workers froze. No one knew where the gunshot came from. Steel jumped up from behind one of the Met cars, gun drawn, running full speed toward Harris and Peet.

"You two get down on your knees now!" She called out to the uniformed cops: "Over here. It was them, one of these two. They shot off a firearm." She screamed as she ran toward the two bewildered bodyguards. "On your knees, now!" She was over to Harris and Peet before they knew what to do or what had happened, the Glock up close in Harris's face. She slapped him.

"Get to the ground now. You, too, baldy, on your damn knees, now!"

The Met police officers were over there, too, guns drawn, circling Harris and Peet. Steel took control of the whole situation, barking out orders at the top of her voice.

"Cover these two. Cover him, the bald fuck. They both have firearms. One of them fired off." Harris was on his knees; she kicked him to his stomach and made him lie flat.

"Lie on the ground, now!" She cuffed his hands behind his back. The other officers and Bellings from Special Branch and Wells and Tavish from SO15 weren't sure what to do. All weapons were drawn, just in case. Steel was a blur. She made sure that Peet, too, was handcuffed on the ground, his hands behind his back. She quickly frisked them both, found their weapons, and held them both up to show the group.

"Right here, one of these was the one that was fired." She touched the barrel of Harris's. "This one here, still warm." Tavish and Wells knew full well that neither of them had shot off a weapon, knew Steel was up to something. They weren't sure where this was going. Everyone looked on in shock.

Steel bent down over Harris's body, took her Glock, rammed the barrel through the back of his legs, and shoved it into his crotch. She whispered into his ears.

"Ya listen to me, Red, you listen good. Ya ever come to my house, ya ever come near my parents again, I'll blow this battered little bunion of a cock right off. I'll burn your body alive in a field, a hundred miles from anywheres near where someone could hear ya scream. Do you understand?" Her accent was really thick now, as back-alley Scottish as it could go. "This is me being nice. This is my calm warning. Nod and tell me you understand." Harris nodded into the sidewalk. He understood.

She went over to Peet, rolled him onto his back, bent down, looked into his eyes, then reached up and kissed his bald head. She took her

Glock, shoved it down in his crotch now. Lieutenant Bellings moved to stop her; Edwina Wells, who knew what these two had done at Steel's parents' place, gently halted him to let her go.

Steel got real close to Peet's face, maniacally looked into his eyes with her gun up against his pants. She just stared at him, didn't need any words. She nodded to him and expected him to nod back that he'd got the message. He did. He nodded back. She pulled the Glock away from his pants and stood up. She looked around at the crowd of cops and detectives, all staring at her—the passersby, the HGI employees, the two men on the ground handcuffed, one on his stomach, one on his back. Her Glock was still drawn.

Everyone waited for her to calm down, to speak. She finally holstered her weapon. She turned to the Met cops and threw one of them her hand-cuff keys.

"I was wrong. It wasn't them that fired off. Might have even been a car that backfired. Let them go."

She walked over to the patrol vehicle she came in. As she opened the door to the backseat, she glanced back toward the building. Rebecca, Heaton's gal, standing on the top step before the entrance, watched her every move, hoping that Steel would meet her eyes. She did. Steel nodded softly as she closed the door and then calmly waited to be driven back to Scotland Yard.

Adam labored under the weight of the luggage all the way across Grosvenor Square to the northeast side, crossing over to Duke Street. On the corner, in front of the London Marriott, he looked back to see Kate and the kids having a rough time with the bags. He set down his load, ran back, grabbed as many bags as he could handle, and lugged them across the one-way lane, throwing them onto his pile.

Kate had had enough. She was more than a little close to melting down.

"Okay, Adam, you need to talk to me. What is going on?" The kids were far enough away, lagging back. Adam felt safe to share a little more information.

"We're in big trouble. Serious trouble. I was right. The Heaton thing was bad news. I've been forced to commit a crime, a big one. We have to move. Now. We don't have time to talk."

Kate's eyes flared. She wasn't one to follow along blindly, at least not this version of Kate.

"Make time, Adam. You've got the kids scared out of their minds, and I'm beside myself with fear that you're having some kind of psychotic breakdown, so make the goddamn time to explain to me what the hell is going on."

Adam looked over her shoulder as the kids crossed the traffic island onto Brook Street and caught up. He turned to his sixteen-year-old daughter.

"Trudy, I want you to stay right here, watch your little brother, and keep an eye on our luggage. For two minutes." Trudy, who had been in tears, segued into a junior version of her pretty mother's rage.

"Why, Daddy? Why? Why are you doing this? I have to go back. I have to be with Étienne, at least to say good-bye or something." Adam stood firm.

"Not now. Right now you have to watch your little brother. Do not go anywhere. Do not get on that phone. Keep alert. I need a moment alone with your mother. I mean it, Trudy, don't let me down."

"You're the one who's letting me down. You don't know what I feel for him, Daddy. It's never been like this." He softened, pulled her forward, and kissed her forehead.

"I need you to come through for me right now. Étienne has to wait. This is about your family."

He motioned for Kate to follow him into the front door of the Marriott. Kate reiterated to Trudy to keep sharp and to watch out for Billy. She promised her she would get to the bottom of this, then hurried to catch up to Adam who was already inside the Marriott.

In the lobby of the hotel, Adam found the house bar. Kate followed. It was about half as full as the Millennium's bar, but predictably the people there were riveted by the television. Adam motioned for Kate to look up as they watched the television together.

Rolling footage shot from a helicopter showed cops, workers, tanks, and trucks. The words under the screen flashed with breaking news of the bombing at Number 10 and the new information that the prime minister had been hit and had been rushed to hospital. There was no news yet if he had survived.

Kate looked over to Adam. She hadn't used her lungs in almost a minute. He stared at her. His eyes were red, his skin white; he was shaking. She asked him wordlessly if he did this. He answered with an affirmative nod. They were speaking in a way that a long-term marriage lets you speak in moments of crisis—almost telepathically. She felt as if she were going to pass out. She turned, looked for a place to sit. Adam quickly led her over to a lonely two-top against the front window. He could see the kids out on the curb. Trudy was still in meltdown mode; Billy was on top of the luggage, absentmindedly playing on his Playstation. Adam sat down across from his shattered wife.

"It's been a setup from the beginning. It's the reason I was given the job, a year and a half ago last November. It's been in the works that long—to set me up, to use the mistake I made in Lansing. We're in big trouble, Kate. We're in so much trouble."

She was shaking. The weight of the realization that things were going to go horribly bad from this moment on, very quickly, was already suffocating her. She whispered to him, barely able to form the words.

"You planted a bomb? Could that really be true? Please tell me you could be wrong."

"I'm not wrong. I wish I was. I was set up. I had help. There was someone inside, someone handed it to me, but the point of the whole thing was for me to be the one, the lunatic from Michigan, somehow over here with a hard-on for Roland Lassiter."

"That's insane."

"I know it is. That's the point. They'll say I'm insane. They'll say I've been setting it up for a long time. They've thought it through. I'm the perfect scapegoat. 'He's done it before; tried to kill a head of state, now he's done it again. This time he may have succeeded.'"

Kate said nothing for what seemed like the longest time. She turned, looked out the window, saw the kids on the curb, turned back, and stared at her husband.

"The police. We need to go to the police, Adam. Right now. Let's get up and call the police."

"We can't. Believe me, if we could I would have gone right away." He stared across the table and read the confusion on her face like a scary treasure map to the end of the world. He took a breath and forced out the story of the high-end whorehouse with Heaton, his arrest and subsequent release. He made her realize that it was offered up as a demonstration as to how futile going to the authorities would be. She hung there for a long, uncomfortable moment, stuck on the battered call girl.

"Did you do it? Beat that woman? The prostitute? Could that be possible?"

Again he needed a hit of oxygen to answer. He had thought it over so much in the last few days, played and replayed the night like a tape that he could rewind. He knew for a fact that the wounds and the pain in his hands that morning were real.

"No, of course not." They sat together for a moment as he thought about the girl again, finally turning to his wife, just a tad less certain.

"I was slipped some drug, that's all I know for sure. That and the fact that she and I were the only ones in the room. She was pushing me to a place I didn't want to go." Kate withdrew her hand, slumped back into her seat.

"We're in so much trouble, Kate. Everything, every moment has been a setup. Getting the job, taking this trip, it's all been a setup, a chain of events designed for me to end up taking a long, hard fall."

Kate allowed the darkness of the situation to sink in.

"What will happen?"

"We need to disappear. Quickly. The whole reason I'm a part of this is so that they can kill me. When I'm dead, it's over. 'He was crazy. He's dead.' End of story."

He gave her a moment. It was important that she clearly understood the stakes. He wasn't going to be able to do more of this stopping and talking thing. They had to move quickly, right away, and they weren't going to be able to speak in front of the kids. She realized that whoever would kill the prime minister wouldn't blink before killing a normal man, a man from Michigan.

"After I'm gone, the government and the press can speculate all they want. Anything else becomes folklore, another conspiracy theory to add to the others. And what's worse, Kate, is even if they kill me, I don't know who they'll stop with, who else they'll need to silence. I need to get you and the kids out of here. I'm going to take you to the airport. Right now. Put you on a plane. I can't leave. They have my passport, and by the time we get to the airport they'll be looking for me. Every minute counts. The bomb went off two hours ago. Watching the airport will be their first move. We have to beat them to it."

"Why do they have your passport?"

"It was taken the night I was arrested. They kept it. Heaton has it. I have to get you and the kids away. Out of England. Home. My uncles and my brothers can protect you once you're back in America. We have to go, Kate."

She started to cry. She couldn't hold it back any longer. She just started bawling. A couple at another table looked over.

"What will we tell the kids?"

"I haven't figured that out yet. Right now, there's a rental place a block from here. We're gonna get a car. I'll tell the kids we're going to take a drive. We'll figure out what to tell them on the way to the airport."

"We can't just leave England, not without you."

"You have to. I'll figure it out; I'll work out another way home. I promise." He reached across and took hold again of her hand in her lap. She was as cold as ice, numb with shock. A sudden realization caused another tear to suddenly leap from her eye, painting her big cheek with a deeper sadness.

"My father?"

"Yes. He's part of it."

Davina Steel sat on a small couch in a crowded vestibule outside the prime minister's office, the office that Georgia was temporarily working from. Georgia was inside with Jack Early, Major Darling, Burnlee, Edwina Wells, and several of the top COBRA people. They were discussing the investigation, but in actuality they were discussing Steel. Should she be taken off the case and put onto something else?

Steel's outburst outside of Heaton Global had caused a major rethink up and down the chain. Could something of this importance be spearheaded by someone as emotionally volatile and obviously immature as Steel? That was the question in play as Steel sat outside on the couch, punching away on her laptop, awaiting news if she'd be pried from the case, pulled away from her unique proximity to Georgia. Maybe that would be best, she thought. Being around her had become so fraught with emotion.

Inside, at Lassiter's desk, Georgia struggled to think clearly. She was exhausted. It was early. She hadn't slept once again the night before. Yesterday had been a long slog with the press demanding to know what Lassiter's future held. Would he be back? What would the party do in a reshuffle? Would it be Georgia? Munroe had wedged in a grueling series of one-on-ones with the top papers' editors, and most of them couldn't have been bothered to be civil.

The chancellor was scheduled to do a quick trip to Strasbourg to meet with top European ministers to discuss how to slow down the momentum regarding the upcoming referendum on Europe. The referendum would almost surely lead to Britain pulling from the union once and for all. Part of Georgia would have been overjoyed to let the referendum happen, just get on with it—to take it to the voters to decide. It was the only major issue she and Roland disagreed on. There was also a new inheritance tax cut bill looming that needed Treasury's guidance, another foray into a political minefield that would come back to haunt Georgia if she did in fact take over as prime minister. All in all, the entire load was more than she could have foreseen. It was a short walk from Number 11 to Number 10, but it felt more like crossing into an entirely different dimension.

On top of Georgia's exhaustion and her overbooked schedule was the utterly powerful pull of the pain pills. She was down to her last few. She had tried to wean herself but had only become more irritable, less able to sleep. In her vulnerable state, she was nagged by thoughts of this young inspector. Maybe it would be better, she wondered, if she let these people talk Major Darling into benching Steel. Maybe it was too much for Georgia to process. There was nothing all that comfortable about the feelings she had for Steel. It had been years since she felt this way about a woman, not since university; Steel's obvious reciprocal passion only made the situation more difficult to bear.

Representatives from COBRA and DPG, along with the director of Special Branch, all implored Georgia and Burnlee to remove Steel at once.

"She's crossed every line there is to cross."

"Bringing Heaton into it is absurd—acting that way to a former minister."

"Threatening those two men with a gun? Whether or not she should be brought up on charges is what we should be discussing here, not keeping her on."

"This American, Tatum, is who we should be focused on finding, not harassing Heaton and his people. Heaton is just as concerned about this as we are. His barrister is Lord Winkle, and he's preparing to make a formal complaint. This young girl is trouble. She needs to be taken off."

In spite of these arguments, both Edwina Wells and Darling still thought that Steel was the right staffer. They agreed that she had gone too far but felt certain they could rein her in. They promised to give her plenty of support and to have backup ready in case her anger were to improperly express itself again.

As the debate raged, Georgia's mind was drifting. She badly needed another dose. Her eyelids felt as if they were made of iron. The last thing she wanted was to fall asleep in the middle of another meeting, not after the drubbing she'd taken in the press over falling asleep in the middle of PMQs. The photo of her fast asleep at Parliament was on the cover of every single one of the dailies that morning, and not just the Murdoch-owned ones.

In the middle of the discussion Steel interrupted by bolting into the office, pushing away the red-faced staffer imploring her to let him announce her. She had her laptop in her hand and her eyes were wide open with exuberance. She had placed another piece of the puzzle.

"Gordon Thompson is Tatum's father-in-law. Tatum's married to his daughter."

Darling, Georgia, and the others quickly tried to process the news. It went against anything they had known at this point about Thompson, an innocuous figure at best.

"He has a daughter, Kate Thompson. She left the country to go to school in Michigan. Met Tatum in Ann Arbor where he was a local cop."

Burnlee wasn't quite making sense of it. Something was bothering him.

"Why wouldn't he tell us this? It seems like an easy enough thing to eventually find out. I mean, it's a strong case to be made for Heaton to be involved—the fact that one of his people, an old friend, is related to the bomber. It's sloppy. Almost too sloppy."

Steel agreed. She'd thought that through, though.

"Maybe Thompson is another player who's only in the game to be taken out. Maybe the point will be for the trail to go cold after he and Tatum accidentally turn up dead one day. He seemed shaken to the nub when we were talking to him. He's likely made out the same story line. He's more than a bit spooked, that much was obvious. It's odd I know, but in truth nothing really makes much sense and we still haven't the faintest clue who the dead man in the back of the Tatums' rented car is."

They were good questions, all of them, yet the newest puzzle piece did nothing but dislodge others. They answered no questions, only raised more; pointed further toward Heaton, but also made Steel wonder why a man at his level, with his clout, would put himself so close to the blade on something like this. It didn't seem to hold any water.

It was obvious to Steel that Georgia felt the same way. The connection to Heaton made it all the more confusing. The way some of the others were quick to not let any blame land on Heaton, the fervor that was building to have Steel stand down—it gave the air an uncertainty that she didn't need, not with all of the other inconsistency floating around her life at the moment.

"No. Steel will stay on. All information from here on in will come through me, through this office."

Burnlee stood. He objected to this course. "Georgia, it cannot be done that way."

"It can and it will. I want Inspector Steel to keep me as close to all this as possible. I want her to have as much access to me as possible."

Jack Early's head bobbed in recognition of his marching orders. With various shades of reluctance, Burnlee, Darling, and the rest of the group more or less acquiesced. Georgia and Steel shared a quiet nod with each other across the crowded office, neither of them certain if closer access to the other was the healthiest of personal choices.

The rental of the car from the Avis at Brown Hart Gardens was uneventful. Adam calmly chartered a Ford station wagon while Kate and the kids waited outside. Trudy begged her mother to explain what was going on. Even little Billy was concerned enough to pull his face out of his portable electronic toy.

"What about Poppa? When are we going to see Poppa?" the little boy implored Kate with his big, innocent brown eyes. "What if he thinks we're still at the hotel and he comes there to see me? We were going to feed the ducks in the park. Won't he be sad? Poppa and I are special friends. That's what we said."

"No, sweetie. Poppa will be fine." Even talking about her father brought about a stabbing emotional pain. She didn't want him in her head. She was too mad, too sore, too angry. Her father had conspired against her, put her whole family in danger. It was a blend of burn that she couldn't deal with, a hurt she felt for her young son who thought he had finally connected with his long-lost mythical "Poppa." He had no sense of what a colossal shit the old man really was.

Kate spoke to them both in clustered wisps of careful words, doing everything she could not to burst into tears.

"Your father's had a very rough day with his business, kids. He badly needs our support. We're going to take a ride and help him calm down.

I want you both to do whatever you can to just let Daddy relax. Please? Right now is not a good time to argue with him about anything."

Both of the children reluctantly agreed to be on their best behavior, both taking Kate at her word that very soon she would give them an explanation for everything that was happening.

IT WAS QUIET in the car as it snaked down below Hyde Park and out onto Cromwell Road, following the A4 until it became the M4. Adam stared ahead, resolutely moving forward, driving without saying a word, only occasionally speaking to honk or swear at a cabbie or a truck driver who had cut him off. Trudy repeatedly asked her parents where they were going. Neither of them would answer. Every now and then Kate would start to weep and then catch herself. Billy kept asking what was wrong, only to be told again and again with a softly whispered tone and a motherly pat that all was fine. The little boy was on the verge of tears himself now; at one point in the backseat he mouthed the word "divorce" to Trudy, who nodded affirmatively. That could be the only answer.

Sometime later, as the Ford wagon wound its way along the bottom lip of Gunnersbury Park, a little more than halfway to Heathrow, Kate's cell phone rang. It was Gordon. She picked it up, part instinctively, part purposely, wanting to lash out. Once she did answer, however, in that very second, she realized how few words there were to say, not only how little she could discuss in front of the children but also how utterly and completely he had devastated her. She spoke quietly, in measured tones.

"What is it that you could possibly want?"

"I need to speak with you, love."

"I have nothing to say to you. You disgust me." Adam looked over and caught her eye. He took her arm and motioned for her to cover the microphone. She did.

"Do not tell him where we are going. Do not say a word. He's going to ask. Tell him nothing." She nodded, silently agreeing. She listened as her father prattled on about his innocence.

"I had no idea what was happening. Please know that, Kate. I thought this was a simple white-collar crime that would have no bearing on anything other than Adam making a lot of money for taking a stupid risk.

I was told they would cover all the downside. I was told nothing of a bombing until it was too late—nothing whatsoever. I promise that to be the truth."

Kate wasn't letting him off the hook, not even a little. She kept her voice down to a whisper, yet her words were couched in a sharp, decisive cadence. She wanted him to know there was nothing he could say to convince her of anything other than that they would never speak again.

"I don't believe you. How's that? And if I did, I'd be agreeing to the fact that I now understand that you're stupid and foolish beyond belief—a malleable old buffoon who has put everything I love and care about into serious jeopardy."

"Listen to me, Kate. It's much more complicated than you know, than I could ever have known. This is deep water here. We need to keep close now. I need to help you. Your man, even you and the children, could be in a serious predicament."

"You think? Really, Daddy?" she snapped at him. She had not the slightest hesitation in cutting him off at the knees at every turn the conversation would take. If the kids weren't in the car, the sword would really have been unsheathed. She was boiling over: she so wanted to let him have it for years and years of being a petulant, cowering, simpering, and whimpering fool. She desperately wanted to take out her rage and anger over this whole horrible debacle on him, but she held back with the kids behind her. Instead she sat low in her seat and covered her mouth as she whispered another dark blast of invective.

"Who do you think put us in this predicament? Who can be blamed for all of this? What were you thinking? What could possibly be in your mind? How much were you paid for this? Does he own you that much, this man, so much so that you'd do something this cold and callous to your own family?"

There was silence on the other end. She could hear Gordon struggling. She could hear his mind trying to form the right combination of words to make her understand whatever flimsy version of an excuse it was that he wanted to convey. Finally he just leaked out a short, lifeless query.

"Where are you right now? Where are you going?"

"That's none of your business."

She looked over at Adam. His eyes burning into the windshield, trained on the open road—on an unknown, perilous future. She turned to her kids in the backseat. Billy was watching her, Trudy, now oblivious, was tooling on her iPhone, playing a game or something, she figured. She returned her gaze up front, whispering quietly to Gordon.

"I don't want to ever speak to you again, as long as you live. Don't ever call me."

She hung up the phone, staring ahead to that same rocky version of a murky road that Adam was heading into.

A moment later Adam's cell phone buzzed. It was Gordon. He showed the phone to Kate. She hit ignore. Another minute later the old man started texting him.

"I must speak to you, Adam. Urgent."

"Call me right away."

"Urgent."

"All of your lives are at risk. Call me straightaway. I know you are
        upset but so am I. We must speak."

Adam looked at the phone and decided that it could only be used to track him. He would have to get all of the phones away from the rest of his family. They would be closing in on them fast.

He would be the one who the police would turn to once the shock of the bombing settled down: "the American," "the Michigan radical, attempted murderer." He thought now about the noises he heard in his garage and in his living room that winter. He realized he wasn't out of his mind. They were in his house, planting evidence: maybe an Internet trail of him buying the materials, a convenient e-mail speaking of his plans to kill their prime minister. Who knows what they planted? It all made so much sense now: how he got his job, the reason he was picked to come to London, why Heaton had such an interest in him. The clues would fall like dominoes once they started looking into him. It wouldn't take long for their version of the FBI to come after him. Heaton and his people would probably very quickly make sure the authorities were aware of the "nut job" they may have accidentally let into Number 10. They would think they were geniuses, the British police or Scotland Yard or

Sherlock fucking Holmes, whoever it was that they sent to find him, not realizing that they were being spoon-fed fake clues. All this would take time. He just wasn't sure how much time. He hoped at least enough time to get Kate and the kids on a plane and out of the country.

He rolled down his window and quietly put his hand out into the open air, in a very leisurely way, so that the kids couldn't see what he was doing. He dropped his cell phone onto the highway and watched in his side-view mirror as it hit the pavement and bounced onto the shoulder as they headed on toward Heathrow.

What Adam and Kate didn't know, couldn't know, was that Trudy and Étienne had been texting each other since Brompton Road.

"I miss you, Trudy."

"Me, too. My parents are both going crazy. It's insanity right now."

"Why? What is happening?"

"I don't know. My parents are both freaking out. I think they're
    getting a divorce. It's gnarly."

"Where are you going?"

"I'm not sure. Everyone's freaking. My parents are both so dramatic."

"Where are you now?"

"In a car. We rented a car. We're driving somewhere."

"Where are you going? I need to see you. You aren't leaving, are you?
    Leaving England? I can't let you go. I'm in love with you, Trudy,
    you know that, right?"

"I feel the same way. You are everything to me. I want to spend my
    whole life with you. I know you may think that is childish or stupid,
    but it's true. I want to be with you. For the rest of my life."

"I feel the same way. I don't think it is childish at all. Where are you?
    I want to come see you. I want to hold you in my arms. I want to
    hold you tight and kiss you and not let you go forever. For my life
    as well, Trudy. I want to come see you. Right away."

"Not poss. I am in a car on some highway. No idea where we are
    going."

"Can't you ask your dad where you are going?"

"I just tried. He isn't answering. They're both in the weirdest moods.
    Such losers sometimes."

"I know. My mother, too. She is in a bad mood over something. I love
   you."

"I love you, too, Étienne."

"Ask again where you are going."

As they pulled onto the Tunnel Road turnoff, as the signs started
guiding traffic to Heathrow, Trudy realized they were leaving the country and started to cry.

"Oh shit. We're going to the airport. The airport. Damn it!"

"Daddy, what are you doing? We're leaving? We can't be leaving? I
can't go. You can't do this to me. You don't understand. This is my soul
mate. You don't know what you're doing to me." She started to get desperate, leaned up, almost climbed over the front seat, begging.

"Look, look, Daddy, Mommy, I know you two are splitting up or
whatever, something's going down with you two, but don't take it out
on Étienne and me. Please. We're in love. We are. We both are so in love.
Mommy? Mommy, please, just let me stay. I'll stay with Poppa. Just for
a week or so. Please? Please, Mommy? Please!" Billy jumped up now and
joined in on the panicked pleading.

"The airport? We can't leave. What about Poppa? I want to stay here.
I want to live with Poppa."

Adam ignored them. Kate couldn't look back, couldn't face them as
they pulled into Heathrow, prepaid on the longest parking ticket possible
for short-term parking, and found a spot. Adam looked at his watch. It
was almost eight p.m. There was an American Airlines flight at nine
thirty. He had a short window to walk around freely. Right now, he figured, was all about mass confusion and hysteria at 10 Downing Street.
They wouldn't be looking for him quite yet, but they would clamp down
on people leaving the country soon, especially unplanned exits. He was
hoping he had a few hours before they got to that place.

He ignored his children's whining and rustled up a luggage cart and
rushed the family through to the ticket counter of the crowded departure terminal. He quickly checked a newsstand. The papers still had
nothing. He tried to spot a television set but there were none in the

departing terminal that he saw. He thought the police presence was heavy, but it didn't seem any more than it was when they had landed.

"Are you at the aeroport?"

"Yes. I don't know what to do. What should I do?"

"Can you please talk to your father into letting you stay?"

"I tried. It's no use."

"I love you, Trudy."

"I love you, too. What should I do?"

"Do you see signs for the Heathrow Express? They should be all over
   the place?"

Trudy quickly scanned the walls around her. She saw the signs on the walls advertising the Heathrow Express train to London.

"Yes. I see them. I see arrows."

"If you follow the arrows, it is a direct train back to London. It only
   takes fifteen minutes. I could meet you."

Kate and Adam didn't look at each other as they waited in line to purchase tickets. Gordon kept calling Kate. Adam could hear her phone buzzing. He figured it best not to make a scene right now and bust the chip. He thought he still had time. He took Kate's hand. She wrapped into his shoulder.

"It's going to be okay. Okay?"

She turned and looked at him. Her eyes were as dark as he'd ever seen them—blue eyes that had closed down, gone black with fear.

"No. No. It's not okay. I'm so scared, Adam. I'm shaking."

"I know, sweetie. I'm scared, too."

He bought his wife and crying children three tickets. He was worried as the attendant at the ticket desk punched the family name into the computers. If they were on a list already, if there was a filter of any kind, looking for anyone leaving the country, he'd know it in seconds. But the ticketing went smoothly. The attendant could see that the family was grieving for some reason. She figured this was an emergency flight home. That someone had passed. She was overly gentle and sympathetic and gave them passes to wait in the First Class lounge and use the VIP customs line. Adam played along and thanked her with a bowed head, trying to put on the soft whimper of a man who was wrapping his head around a new loss. It was an easy part to play.

As they headed to the customs line, right as Adam began to feel hopeful about his family getting out safely, about having made the window, he looked back and couldn't believe what he was seeing. Trudy was texting. He lost it. He stormed over and grabbed the phone right out of her hand.

"What are you doing, Daddy?"

"What are *you* doing? What the hell is going on here?" He quickly read through the texts and went white with rage.

"How could you do this, Trudy? How could you do this? You told them right where we are. Do you realize that?" It threw the teenager. She wasn't used to this. He was talking to her as if she were a criminal.

"What are you talking about?" She was at a loss. Her father's anger made no sense. He had never spoken to her like that. Adam didn't care. He was blind with rage. He opened her phone case, took out the chip from the top, dropped it to the ground, and broke it into pieces with his heel. Several other travelers stopped and noticed the commotion.

"What is your problem, Daddy?"

"My problem is you. You've betrayed us. Don't you see that?"

He regretted saying that as soon as the words left his mouth. Events had caught up with him. He had lost his balance. Trudy was a victim of his knees going out from under him. He wanted to pull her in, hug her, but he couldn't. He was enraged. Kate came over, rolling the luggage cart with Billy on the top, stepped into the wicked silence, father and daughter glaring at each other. She saw the broken cell chip on the floor. Trudy's face flushed with anguish.

"What's going on?" Trudy didn't bother to reply. She looked at her mother, then back to her father.

"I hate you both. You both make me sick."

She turned and ran. She ran as fast as she could through the terminal, away from them, into the crowd. She bolted, fled, escaped, darted away with all the speed and emotion of a scared young girl in love. Adam gave Kate the tickets.

"Wait here. Right here. I'm going after her."

He chased her through the terminal, down a long winding hallway that kept sloping down, lower and lower with each turn, the walls adorned with large arrows and signs pointing to the Heathrow Express, bragging about the ease of the fifteen-minute trip right into the center of London. Trudy was running as fast as Adam had ever seen her move. The terminal was crowded and Trudy, being smaller and thinner, was having an easier time slipping through the people and the carts and the kiosks. With every turn of the hallway she pulled farther and farther away from him.

When she finally reached the ticketing area, after running almost a quarter of a mile through sloping hallways, she stopped to figure out the boarding process. Adam came around the corner faster than she thought he would and lunged for her as she was looking up at the departure board. The run had taken its toll on him. He was winded and as he went for her she quickly stepped aside. He went crashing past her, falling forward and sliding along on the newly polished floor. She watched him crumple and fall and was torn about what to do. She wanted to make sure he was okay but knew that if she stopped, he'd grab her, make her come back, fly home, leave England, leave Étienne.

She seized her moment. She turned and fled down the steps to the train stalls. She took them two, three, and four at a time. Halfway down she looked up, saw her father, once again on her tail. He was coming fast, his eyes on fire. She hit the bottom and ran toward the one of two tracks that flashed a message that it was now leaving for London.

She ran as fast as she could, blasted into the track tunnel, and then onto the closest car, right as the door clamped shut. She made it with less than a second to spare. She looked out and saw her father coming into the tunnel as the train slowly began to pull out. He caught sight of her watching him through the door window and she quickly ducked. An older woman with a frilly coat and a throwback of a hat, seated in the last seat of the next car, stared at Trudy as she sat there on the ground of the middle car's entranceway, hiding from her father as he banged on the window, desperately yelling for someone to stop the train. Trudy saw the older lady look up to an emergency button that would immediately grind the train to a halt. She saw the woman consider it and heard her father outside, still yelling, still banging.

The older woman didn't reach for the button. The train didn't stop. It lurched out of the station, slowly picked up speed, and headed off toward London.

Adam was at the end of the tunnel ramp, watching it disappear. He was begging his battered body for the faintest version of an easy breath, soaking wet with sweat, trembling with white, airless anger.

He had lost her. Lost his window.

BACK IN THE departure terminal, he found Kate and Billy right where he had left them. Kate had seen him coming from the far end of the hall, saw that Trudy wasn't with him, and read the look on his face from four long ticket counters away.

"She went back to London. To find that French kid."

Kate held Billy close. She wasn't sure how to react.

"Maybe this is good. Maybe it gets her out of trouble. Maybe she needs to be away from us until—"

He cut her off. "It's not good. He's a phony. I don't even think that he's that French bitch's son. She's with them. Who knows what they have on her."

"What are you talking about, Adam?"

"They used Trudy to force me to go along with them today. They threatened me with her life."

"Who threatened you with her life?"

"Étienne's mother. She's part of all this. She's with Heaton in some way." Kate eked out another groan. This all just kept getting worse and worse.

"Trudy's in trouble, Kate. I need to go back into London and find her. Fast. You need to go through security and get into the boarding area. Get on the plane as soon as you can."

"What if you're not back before the plane leaves? That's an hour from now?"

"You take off. I'll put her on the next plane as soon as I find her. You need to get out of this country right now, Kate. Get Billy away."

Kate just stared at him. It was all happening too fast. This new reality didn't make any sense to her—the need to escape Britain, her own home-land.

"I won't leave Trudy. I won't leave you."

"You don't have a choice! You need to do exactly what I tell you to do right now. Please. Tell me that you understand this." He glared at her. She didn't know how to answer. She was too off balance to go head to head.

"Yes. Yes. I understand."

It didn't matter. As the words came out of her mouth, Adam saw Harris and Peet coming down the far steps. He saw them before they saw him. He grabbed Kate, Billy, and the bags and pulled them behind a currency exchange kiosk. He watched the two old thugs coming through the terminal. They went over to the ticket desk he had just come from. The bald guy asked for someone. The attendant who had helped them was called over. The window of opportunity had closed. They were on to them. It was as bad as he imagined it would be.

He turned to Kate as he grabbed the smallest bags and threw them over his shoulder.

"Grab your handbag. We're leaving."

"What? What about the cart? All the luggage."

"It stays. Let's go." Billy grabbed his suitcase.

"No. My toys. My books. No, Daddy, we have to take them. Please. Please."

"Fine." He grabbed Billy's suitcase. Billy stopped him again.

"Where are we going now, Daddy? I'm scared. You're scaring me. Where is Trudy?"

"You said you didn't want to leave, right? Well, now we're not leaving. Let's go, Kate. Now." She grumbled as she picked up her carry-on bags. Adam picked up Billy along with his suitcase, guiding them carefully back toward the elevator leading out to the parking deck.

"What are we doing, Daddy? Are we getting on the plane? You and Mommy are both acting funny. I'm getting really scared."

"It's fine, Billy. Mommy changed her mind. We're not going to leave after all."

"Can we go back to that one hotel? The one with all the movies? The one near the park?"

"We'll find a better one."

He shuffled them carefully behind a newsstand as he waited for the elevator to land. When it did, as he pushed them on, as the doors closed, he and Peet made eye contact. They were spotted.

THE ELEVATOR DOORS opened on the parking level and Adam, Kate, and Billy bolted out and across the long covered bridge to short-term parking. Halfway across, Adam craned his head back and could see Harris and Peet on the outside stairs running up to meet the bridge. He still had a good three hundred yards on them, but they weren't carrying an eight-year-old boy and an assortment of luggage.

They hit the parking garage, turned left, and ducked behind a row of cars. Harris and Peet entered the parking deck and turned right. The Tatums caught a lucky break. Their car was in the west stalls. They snaked their way quietly through the parked cars, finally reuniting with the Ford. Adam opened the car, winced as its alarm chirped, got Kate and Billy in, and left the west deck as quickly and quietly as possible.

THEY HEADED BACK onto the M4 toward London. After a quarter of a mile, Adam checked his watch. It was useless. He couldn't beat the express train. He pulled off the highway onto a small road, stopped the car, and got out. He needed air to think. There wasn't even time to mull it over or contemplate a way out. He walked over to the car and motioned for Kate to roll the window down. She was crying again. Billy was dutifully trying to calm her down.

"Give me your phone. I have to call your father. He has to go to Paddington and meet that train." She stepped out of the car and closed the door so that Billy wouldn't hear her.

"We can't call my father. I don't trust him. I never want to speak to him again."

"I'm not sure we have a choice. That train will be in Paddington in eight minutes. If we lose her, I don't know what the next move is. I'd call Beauregard, but it'd take too long to get him over there. Your father may have resources: some friends, ex-cops, someone. It's his granddaughter, for Christ's sake."

She just stared at him, her phone in her hands, not sure if she wanted to give it to him. She thought about something for a long beat, another option. She wondered if it was the right move and realized she didn't have a choice. She started dialing.

"Who are you calling?"

"Richard Lyle. He lives a block from Paddington station. I was there this afternoon."

Adam couldn't believe what he was hearing. It was like a punch to a gut that had already spent the day taking incoming shots.

"Great, so while I was knee deep in this shit that you coaxed me into, you were sneaking around with your old boyfriend? At his apartment?"

"No, I was innocently seeing an old friend." She turned to him with icy eyes. "I was having a tea. You were blowing up Number 10. Please don't even think to lecture me about how I spent my afternoon."

Luckily for her, Richard picked up his phone before they could take the useless banter any further. She deftly told Richard their predicament without going into too much detail. She told him he needed to go over to Paddington immediately and intercept Trudy. She told him it was an emergency, to not let anyone else talk to her or persuade him to do anything but put her right back on the very next express train. He was more than happy to help. He could hear the stress in her voice. He didn't need to know too much, only that he now had the chance to play the hero for Kate. He had the chance to see her again. He was in.

"Thank you so much, Richard. You're a doll. But please, go this instant. Yes? Thank you." Adam motioned for her to cover the phone.

"Should we text him a photo of her?" She took it as a good idea. She ran it by Richard and waited for a reply. She was nodding.

"Okay, sweetie, then just go. Go fast and call me once you have her. Thank you so, so, much." She hung up and turned back to Adam.

"He says not to bother, says he knows what she looks like from her photos on Facebook." Adam just threw his hands up. He walked away mumbling something about Facebook being the worst thing ever invented.

Georgia had a whale of a nightmare. Roland had died, succumbed to the wounds of the bomb blast. The entire city was in mourning. There was no one in the streets. The television stations had all signed off. The king gave a statement and then Buckingham Palace went dark in quiet remembrance. Numbers 10 and 11 were empty. Everyone had gone home to their families. Georgia was alone.

She walked out onto Whitehall, naked—not a stitch of clothing. It didn't matter, though; no one was around. Maybe there was the occasional odd, old woman, crying on a bench. An empty bus rolled by, but the driver didn't look at her. She walked toward Parliament, her wild hair the only thing covering any part of her body. When she turned the corner into Parliament Square, she saw it was filled with people—filled with everyone she had ever known: her parents, her childhood friends, cousins, even David Templeton, her first boyfriend. They were all in the candlelit early morning square, mourning over photos, posters, and drawings of Roland Lassiter.

She quickly stepped back into a nook in the base of a building—they hadn't seen her yet. She was suddenly embarrassed to be so blatantly naked. A car pulled up across the way, an old Bentley in beautiful shape. The passenger door opened, and it was Roland driving. He looked perfect.

He had a Cheshire cat's grin on his face. He waved her over. She quickly crossed the street and jumped into the Bentley and drove off.

They tooled through the empty streets, laughing and telling old stories, the windows down, the warm air blowing in as he took the Mall past the Palace and Constitution Hill up toward Hyde Park Corner. She wasn't the least bit bothered to be undressed in front of him; it was just happiness and laughter, juvenile notions, and odd remembrances. Music was playing from ages ago: Wham!, Mick Hucknall, Annie Lennox. He soared into Hyde Park, which was as free of people as if it were still the king's private hunting ground. He took the car up onto the walkway to the Serpentine. He asked her if she remembered that they came there early on the morning when they won the first general, when they stayed up all night talking about truly being able to change the world.

She remembered, she told him she did, and now she was dressed, dressed from that night, and then she was dressed in the suit she wore the morning they crashed into the sea together, and it was ripped and covered in her blood, and now he wasn't laughing—he was angry and intent on driving the Bentley into the Serpentine. He picked up speed. She begged him to stop. He wasn't having it. They drove into the empty pond and the car sank, sank as if it were a cold blue ocean they were sinking into, not a slimy pond, and then she was unclothed again and he was laughing once more, wildly alive and happy as they both drowned together.

She woke up uneventfully—not a jolt up, not even immediately. She just woke up, covered in a light night sweat. The dream could have been hours earlier, but she remembered it perfectly. She still smelled the stewy leather of the Bentley. She sat up. She needed more pills.

The bottle was empty.

JACK EARLY LIVED south of the Thames just below Croydon with his wife of twenty years, his two young daughters, and his fifteen-year-old son. It was a small three-bedroom home. He'd been Georgia's private secretary for almost eight years. He knew her as well as anyone, which meant that he didn't know her well. It was a nice-paying job—nothing extravagant, but the benefits were solid and he mostly enjoyed being part of "Team Turnbull."

It wasn't his first job at Number 10. He had been a "garden girl" for ten months before she took him on. The "garden girls" were the steno pool that typed up the speeches and documents that went out of 10 and 11 in a steady stream. Their warren of offices overlooked the back garden. The sobriquet dated as far back as Churchill's day and stuck through the years, regardless of gender. Jack almost lost his job there once. He stood up to Gordon Brown, who had pushed aside a young typist in a fit of rage and took over the job at hand himself. It was the manner in which the PM spoke to the young woman that got under Early's skin, and he had said so. Gordon Brown looked up at him as he typed, considering going off on the lanky young civil servant, the way a bear may consider eating a broken deer he'd found by the side of the river, but he grunted and thought better of it and went back to the computer terminal he had commandeered. Early's job was saved, only to be lost a year later in a cutback.

He returned again in another year, tucked deep behind the coattails of the new chancellor of the exchequer, the very protective Georgia Turnbull. He took the job seriously, even if he did make a bit of a clown of himself from time to time, falling, tripping, and constantly saying the wrong thing. The fact was that she needed him. She needed someone watching over her at all times, someone to have her back. He was that someone and was proud of it, even if he had to do things he wasn't sure were right. His job was to keep Georgia running. Georgia in turn would keep the trains, the clocks, and the banks flush and on time. He had to wrangle just her, and for his money he had the better end of the stick.

He sped into London from Croydon at four a.m. on a chilly Wednesday morning. He usually took the bus when he came in later, but this run was an hour or so earlier than normal. The streets were barren, he'd made almost every light, and so the ten-mile trip in to Number 11 that could sometimes take ninety minutes took only fifteen. He pulled around the back of the Horse Guards to the little-known rear entrance of Downing Street, used his key card at the rear security shack, drove his Ford Focus up to the lip of the garden, and stepped out into the cold morning air. It smelled of dry sand and horse manure. There was the usual fog in the air, so it remained rather dark despite the hour. He was going to light a smoke as he waited for Georgia, who, according to their time-tested drill, would wait for the most recent pass of the night guard on the back lawn, then sneak quietly out the rear door onto the Horse Guards Plaza. She had called him eighteen minutes ago. He had woken from a deep sleep, stumbled out of bed, and gotten here, but he was sure, knowing her as well as he did, that he had a good-size wait on his hands, so he prepared a hand-rolled cigarette.

The smoke never happened. She stepped from the shadow of an old elm tree. She had been waiting for him—maybe a first. She wore an oversize scarf that covered her hair, a large pair of sunglasses, a heavy brown wool overcoat, and an odd pair of boots that she hadn't bothered to buckle up. She looked homeless, or at least hospital bound—nothing like the powerhouse she was. She had her walking cane with her again, something she hadn't used much these last few days, he realized.

"Put the cigarette out. We don't have the time. I want to beat the traffic."

He nodded. "Yes, ma'am."

She made a face and got into the passenger seat. She didn't wait for him to come around and open the door. She was in a hurry.

They raced through the deserted streets, north now, up the hill past Holloway, past the gray streets of East Finchley and into Finchley proper. Thanks to the early hour, the trip took only twenty minutes from Whitehall. The only other vehicles on the road were by and large delivery trucks and vans. The traffic lights once again seemed to be on their side and they made good time, which made Early happy. He never felt right about taking Georgia on these little excursions, skirting security and protocol. He knew that he could lose his job for it. He also knew he could lose it for saying no, so he took the option that left Georgia as happy as it was possible to have her.

They pulled onto High Street, rolled past the Turnbull Pharmacy— her father's place—drove up to the end of the block, and circled back around through the alley. Early pulled as close to the back door as he could get and kept the car running while she got out and fumbled for her key. Neither said a word to the other. They had already made this trip several times in the last year or so. Lately they were spaced closer

and closer together. He wondered, as he watched her sneak in the back
door of the shuttered chemist, if he should speak to her, sit her down,
talk about seeking help of some kind. The idea seemed like a disaster as
soon as he had it. He promised himself to not consider it again.

GEORGIA HAD WORKED in her father's store as a teen. She worked in the
musty shop alongside him all through school. He'd opened it when they
first moved down from Glasgow in the late seventies, when she was just
a year old. She knew the alarm code, knew which tiles creaked and which
didn't. She didn't need to turn on a light; she made her way behind the
counter and into the shelves of medicines and medical equipment. The
work light on her father's spot at the counter was always left on: part
superstition, part security. It was the eternal beam, a small tubular
beacon of shielded light cutting through the blackness that led her way
back to the shelf she needed, to the little bottle of help that she pulled
down off the top rack and placed in her pocket.

In this moment on each previous trip, she always considered taking
a second bottle in order to make it easier on Early, so that they didn't have
to sneak back as often. She never did, though. One, because her mind
always fooled her, told her she didn't need them because she was about
to quit and was ready to kick this dreadful need. Two, and more important, was the inventory process she knew the shop had, the rigorous pill
count that one of the young employees would do once a fortnight.

One bottle gone would constitute a refill order. Two would demand
that a pill audit list be cross-checked with past sales and then against
current sales slips, which was the one thing she never wanted to trigger:
the cross-check. She feared her father more than she feared the press,
the party, the Tories, or the voters. "Dad" was the one thing she never
wanted to go up against, never wanted to sully, embarrass, anger, or
provoke. She loved her father profoundly, loved how proud she had
made him all these years. She lived for his encouragement and support. These trips were launched against every fiber of her being; the very
thought of letting him down in any way was horrid to her, so she never
took more than one bottle.

This morning, though, she thought about a second bottle. The events at hand had weakened her. The odd thoughts swarming her mind, awake or asleep. Steel. Her lips. Her eyes. The way she looked, talked, laughed, and listened. The tough, cute, stern little inspector. Steel and Roland. Life and death. The Party. Power. Roland. The responsibility she would now have. The opposition. Europe. Taxes. Donald Stanhope. David Heaton. The *Mirror*. The *Telegraph*. The *Sun*. So many things were on her mind at all times these days. It never stopped, never slowed down. Even asleep she was tortured.

This morning was a morning for a second bottle. This was a different time. It had to be worth the risk. She stepped back to the shelf, reached up, grabbed another bottle, put it with the first one in her jacket pocket, and briskly left the shop.

The Great Western Railway Paddington Band was performing on the main concourse of the cavernous Victorian-era rail station. The band of older men and women, brass and woodwind players, performed on most Friday nights, and when they did, they trumpeted their special version of old-time joy throughout the congested rail terminal. The station was packed with travelers. The express from Heathrow was just settling into one of the glorious train sheds first built in the 1860s. Trudy Tatum was the first passenger off.

She scanned the crowd for Étienne. She couldn't text him because her father had destroyed her phone. There would be hell to pay for running away like she did, she knew that. She couldn't think of that right now. She needed to find her Étienne. She needed to hear him say what he had last texted her, that he wanted to spend the rest of his life with her. She had to see him say it, watch his lips move as he did. She needed to touch his face, stroke his hair, and hold him close as she responded in kind. She would figure a way to make it up to her mother and father later. Right now, Étienne was all that mattered.

Trudy searched every face, looked up and down, walked in and around the various benches, through the reuniting families, past bored travelers with their e-readers, others with noses buried in newspapers or chatting away on mobile phones. Each face that wasn't Étienne's was harder and harder to endure. She thought for sure that he would be there, waiting for her the minute she got off, as eager to make the connection as she was.

She moved slowly, sadly, toward the end of the train, closer to the concourse and the crowd of people listening to the big band, when she saw Elise, Étienne's mother. Her heart almost burst. Why was she there? Had something happened to her sweetheart? Had her parents contacted her? Was she just going to be put back on the train and sent back to the airport, home to Chicago, never to see him again? She walked over to the woman, who was on her mobile, excitedly telling someone she had found Trudy. She hung up and addressed her in a similar comic version of the broken English that her son spoke.

"Trudy, thank God you are here. I was very upset to have not found you. Come quickly. We must leave."

She didn't wait for a response; she took Trudy by the arm and headed out toward the front of the station. Trudy stopped. The woman turned to her, annoyed as Trudy peppered her with questions.

"Where's Étienne? Why isn't he here? Why are you here? Where is he?" She was crushed that her love didn't show, that he had sent his mother.

"He is at the hotel. He is very excited to see you, but we must go now, Trudy. Right now." Once again she took the teen's arm and led her down to the concourse. Trudy stopped again, her eyes liquid with the pain of a dream that had been doused by cold reality.

"He couldn't come himself? Why didn't he come?"

Why are you here? is what she wanted to say. *After all I went through to be here, he sent his mother?*

The woman was through playing. She turned with a harsh glint to her eyes.

"We go now. It is enough talking. We go now. You must listen to me. We are all in trouble if you don't." She was harried, this woman, spooked. Her words had a strain to them. She was flailing around at the end of her wits. She snatched Trudy up and pulled her along.

Very suddenly someone grabbed Trudy from behind—a tall man with a dark head of hair and a friendly face. He clutched her firmly, stopping both the French woman and Trudy in their tracks.

"Hello, Trudy. I'm a friend of your mum's. You'll be going with me, Princess."

He had a thick British accent and a deep, comforting voice. She had no idea who he was, but he sure seemed to know her.

"I've just spoken to Mum. She wants me to ring her straight up, so you two can speak."

The French woman pulled Trudy away, her voice cracking in desperation, "No, you come with me, Trudy. Right now." She pulled her by her collar, ramming them through the crowd of people, but the British man, the one claiming to be a friend of her mom's, wasn't giving in.

"No, sorry, love, but this girl's going with me tonight. Back to her mum and dad."

He brushed Elise off Trudy, pulled Trudy close, and stood in between the young girl and the French woman. Once again the crowd of departing and arriving passengers washed over and around them, cascaded past, oblivious to the struggle taking place over Trudy. Elise came at her again; the tall British man pushed the tiny French woman away with a long, strong arm just about as thick as her whole body. Elise fell backward and tumbled against a pillar. The man took it as a chance to move on, and he did. He put his arm around a very confused Trudy.

"I recognize you from Facebook, in case you're wondering how I knew it was you. Your mum and I are Facebook friends. Of course we go back a hell of a lot further than Facebook, that's for damn sure." They had just about made their way out to the front of the station, past the brass band, when Trudy was aware that Elise was back. She didn't see the knife, not at first.

"This girl goes with me!" She got up close to Richard and flung herself at him. He made a face, a grimace. She pulled back. Now Trudy saw the knife, covered in blood. She saw the side of the big man's shirt pool with dark liquid. She saw him hobble back on the balls of his feet, unsure what had hit him. A few people started to recognize the drama unfolding. Someone yelled, but they were so close to the brass band, now playing a tune from *Mary Poppins*, that not many people heard the scream.

Trudy was grabbed again. She was dizzy with fright. She wanted to throw up. Elise used the confusion to whisk her away. She held the small girl tightly now, the knife hidden in her pocket, purposefully hurting

Trudy's arm, twisting it. She had been sternly told not to make a scene and now she had done even worse. She had stabbed a man. It wouldn't be long before the flames of panic would ignite the station. She needed to flee, needed desperately to get Trudy out of there.

As they got free of the crowd, Trudy had had enough. She pushed Elise off her with a violent lunge. She had seen the bloody knife even if everyone else somehow hadn't. She screamed at the top of her lungs and shoved Elise again. The French woman went flying into the back of one of the brass players seated in the folding chairs. Several of the band members stopped playing, Elise got up quickly, ran toward Trudy, and grabbed her by the hair, her eyes crazy now. The knife was out of her pocket again, suddenly making her way toward Trudy, attempting to jab it into her side.

Out of nowhere Elise was torn off her and thrown a good five feet into the middle of the band members. The show was now over. People were pushing and yelling, screaming and running away in the early stages of terror. It was the man, the tall man who claimed to be a friend of her mother's. He grabbed Elise and threw her forward with an angry intensity, slamming her headfirst into a pillar. She hit the post with a velocity that stopped her cold. She fell backward and dropped to the ground like a bag of rocks.

The British man turned, saw Trudy, ran over, picked her up in his arms, and tore through the crowded station as if he were a stallion breaking free from a barn. Trudy didn't know why Elise had flipped out like she had, but for some reason she felt safe with this man; she somehow knew he wasn't going to harm her. His shirt was covered in blood but he kept going, smiling at Trudy, telling her to be calm, that everything was going to be okay. He was even trying to make her laugh.

"I was actually enjoying those old folks in the band, too. Shame they had to cut it short."

The entire station was ablaze now with hysteria. Trudy looked back over the man's shoulder and saw that Elise was up again, with the knife, slashing at several people who were trying to help her out. Two policemen had run over and were carefully trying to calm the madwoman down. The man whose arms she was in used the excitement to run through the crowd and outside toward Paddington station's taxi entrance. Once

outside, he set her down and quickly moved them along, never looking back, never missing a stride, until the two men in suits stopped
them both cold.

They were younger, thick like him, in nondescript business suits. One
of them, a man with a thin mustache, punched the man claiming to be her
mum's friend in the face, and when he did, her stallion's knees gave out
and he fell to the ground. The other one of them, a smaller man, grabbed
Trudy and tried to whisk her into a waiting car. The stallion quickly got
to his feet. The mustached man pulled a gun. Trudy screamed but she
needn't have worried. Somehow the stallion wrestled the gun away
and just as swiftly turned it around and began to beat the mustached
man on the head with the gun's butt until the man finally collapsed to
the ground in pain. Before he could land, the stallion had come over to
the littler man and pulled him off Trudy with twice the force he had
used on Étienne's mother. The little man put a gun to Trudy's head and
threatened to fire it, but even that didn't stop her stallion. He grabbed
Trudy away and wrestled with the little man, slamming his head into
the side of the car over and over, until the small man finally passed out.

A crowd had developed. The stallion was winded. He tried his best
to steady himself. He saw Trudy and saw the mustached man getting
back up to his feet. The stallion came over in a flash and kicked him hard
in the head before he could rise: the man dropped flat to the cement.

The mysterious man—the stallion, her mother's friend—turned once
again to Trudy. He nodded, was strained from a lack of oxygen, but somehow managed to pick her up over his shoulder and run. They crossed
quickly to another street, hit the main road, and then darted off into an
alleyway of small mews homes just a block or so up.

He pulled a key from his pocket, opened the door to one of the small
homes on the back street, made sure no one had followed them, and then,
once convinced they hadn't, quickly took Trudy inside and closed the
door.

IT WAS THE oddest place she had ever seen—video games in the dining
room, a workout set in the living room, several cats perched on a modern sofa in the middle of the hallway. She actually liked the way the place

smelled. It had an acidic fog of a scent, like hair products, which made sense seeing that there was a hair salon chair in the kitchen. The strange man was over at the sink, catching his breath and checking the wound on his stomach. She slowly came over. He glanced back and winked at her as he looked over the gash on his midsection.

"It's gonna be fine." After another beat, once he had gotten his breathing right and made sure the wound wasn't going to kill him, he stuck out his free, freshly washed hand for a shake. He gave Trudy a big friendly, toothy, almost goofy smile.

"It's my great pleasure to meet you, Miss Trudy. My name is Richard Lyle."

ADAM AND KATE were glued to the radio as they drove, heading back toward London, waiting to hear from Richard. They were listening to BBC reports of the bombing, desperate for some knowledge of what they had been thrown into. Billy sat quietly in the back, scared, oblivious, and unsure of what was happening, he retreated into the only place that was safe for him to go, deep into one of the many worlds of his Playstation.

The news was still sketchy. A bomb had gone off and the prime minister was in the hospital, gravely injured. The chancellor, Georgia Turnbull, was set to speak to the press soon. That's all anyone knew at this point. It wasn't much. *That would change quickly*, Adam thought. *They would be looking for an American. There would be talk of a madman, an unstable ex-cop, and then the press would have his name, Adam Tatum. It would happen soon.*

They drove in a dreary silence that was instantly interrupted when a Mercedes in the next lane over violently rammed into the driver's side of their car. Their rental slammed two lanes across the highway, toward oncoming traffic. It was Heaton's men. They had tracked them from the airport.

The bald guy was driving. He rammed them again. Billy cried out from the backseat, suddenly out of his video game bubble. The Mercedes battered them again, flying ferociously into their side, pushing Adam farther into the opposite lane. With cars and trucks barreling straight on at seventy miles an hour, Adam threw the wheel left and hit the gas, scurried across the oncoming wall of wheeled missiles and the brutal symphony of horns and squealing brakes, careening toward the opposite side of the road.

They reached the dirt shoulder by inches. It was useless to stop. The momentum carried them off the road, airborne now, flying into a field, touching down violently, instantly shooting forward. They torpedoed wildly across a young crop, tearing through the poor farmer's neat rows at eighty miles an hour, never on all four wheels more than two seconds at a time.

"Adam, you need to slow down," Kate begged, her hand dug deep into the armrest. He ignored her, kept pressing on. He knew only one thing and that was that he had to get as far away from those two psychopaths as possible.

"Daddy, please, slow down. Please, please, slow down." His little boy was crying. There was nothing he could do. He didn't even want to take the energy to answer. He had both of his hands and all of his concentration on the wheel as the car whipped and jumped, rumbled and roared at a dizzying speed. They finally came up to a small fence alongside of a road and he plowed through, smashing the fence, never lifting up so much as a fraction on the gas pedal.

He climbed through a ditch and hit the back road, traveled south, turned right after a quick quarter mile and sped forward for a good ten minutes until he came to the top of a hill. The road behind him was empty. He turned into the parking lot of what appeared to be a shuttered shipping warehouse, drove behind the building, and snuck into the back lot so that he could watch the road they had just come from, down to the misty valley.

Finally, feeling relatively safe, he turned the engine off, gave the car a break and leaned back and tried to breathe again. They sat in a languid, loaded silence. Adam had no idea what to say. At least now Kate would understand the danger he had been going on about. She couldn't form a thought either. She was too terrified. Billy as well. He sat there in the back, wondering if this was real, waiting for his parents to speak or to wake him from his dream.

Kate's cell phone roused them from their collective daze.

"It's Richard." She answered it.

"You have her? Oh, thank God, Richard. Thank you so, so much." She looked over at Adam, who let out a visible sigh of relief. She listened to what else Richard was saying, her perfect face contorting in disbelief.

"Dear Lord, no! She attacked you with a knife? Elise? Oh my God, what is happening? What is going on?" She turned to Adam. The tears were back.

"Tell him we need to meet up, get Trudy. We can't go back to the airport. We have to figure something else out. Ask him if he has any idea where we can meet, safely. Tell him we'll explain everything when we see him." Kate nodded, went back to Richard, and repeated what Adam had said verbatim. She listened as Richard shot back with an idea.

"Your father's place? The mill house in Kent? Your aunt owns that, doesn't she? Yes. Yes. I do. I do remember how to get there, I think." She turned to Adam.

"He has a place—technically it's his aunt's now, but he's fixing it up—a mill house in the middle of nowhere, in Tunbridge Wells, near Kent."

"Does your father know where it is?" She thought about it. She wasn't sure. She asked Richard. She listened while he answered, finally turning back to Adam.

"Says it's a shithole, he only goes there to get drunk and watch football, but no one knows it exists. Just he and his auntie, who's in a home in Dulwich." Adam nodded, and Kate went back to the phone call.

"Richard, thank you so much. You're a doll. I mean it. Thank you so much. You're a lifesaver." She hung up the phone and mumbled out loud, more to herself than to him.

"Thank God. At least there's someone we can count on."

Adam wanted to take issue with that sentiment for a variety of reasons, volley back with a good strong response, but for several reasons even better he decided to let it lay.

At home in her parents' flat in Bloomsbury, Steel was on the phone with the prosecutor of Adam Tatum's attempted murder case. It was ten o'clock at night in London. One full week after the bombing at Number 10 there was a suspect, that was clear, but the motive was missing. Nothing seemed to make sense to her: Tatum's involvement, Heaton's involvement. Neither seemed to be sitting up straight yet. She wanted to download as much information from the US prosecutor as possible, learn as much about Tatum as she could.

While she spoke, her mother brought in a pot of tea and sat across the coffee table from her in her bathrobe, listening to the whole conversation. She watched closely as Steel took notes, probed, asked more questions, and rummaged through a small mountain of papers and many more files on her laptop. It seemed all very exciting to Sheena Steel, so utterly different from her dreary life in the sandwich café.

When Steel finally hung up, her mother sat there, beaming.

"What's gotten you?" Steel asked her mother playfully.

"You're sharp as a tack, girl, that's a given. You could be a Georgia Turnbull yourself now, couldn't you?"

"That's the last thing I'd want then, isn't it?"

"What? Come on, I thought you'd thought the world of Georgia Turnbull?"

"I do, but I'd never want to be in politics."

"Maybe something in business then, with that head on you? Maybe you'll be a lady of finance somewhere." She sipped her tea and looked at her daughter, as smitten as she could be.

"I like what I'm doing. It's just fine."

"I know that, baby. It's just, how long can you do this kind of a thing without it, you know, getting to you? All the killings and the bombings that you're needing to be sorting through. It's bound to take a toll. I worry about you."

"Well, don't waste the worry. I love what I do. It's a puzzle. I'm putting the puzzles together. I enjoy it, Mum. You know I do."

Sheena smiled and nodded. "Tell me about this one then, this puzzle?"

Steel looked at her sweet mum's face. She had held her away long enough. She wanted to let her in a bit, maybe show off a little. She leaned closer.

"I've just found another clue, another piece. Not sure yet where it fits. Number one, he didn't want to kill the governor in Michigan. He never even planned on it. They didn't know the governor was in the mansion when they broke in. He's not a killer."

"Go on then." Sheena's eyes were wide with curiosity.

"The whole thing was an amateur's prank. He isn't even close to a terrorist, this one. It was cheap theatrics. It was a misguided stunt gone bad."

"Then why come all the way here and place a bomb in Number 10? He obviously planned on the PM to be home, that's for sure, and he was." Sheena was getting into it now, loving the fact that Davina was including her.

"Here's the thing, Mum. All four of their plane tickets were purchased together. From here in London."

"So maybe someone framed him up? I like that. It's juicy. Someone else placed the bomb and this fellow takes the fall. I saw this in a Dirk Bogarde film once."

"Sometimes a puzzle piece fits; sometimes you jam it in and you lose view of the bigger picture. Maybe he did try to do this. Maybe he's just rotten to the core, or loony bin–bound. One doesn't know until you know. It doesn't feel like it to me, though. Why would he bring his family to London if he was coming here to murder the PM? It hints to me of another piece of the puzzle."

Sheena sat up. Shook her head as she thought it all through. Steel looked over to her mother who suddenly had a big silly smile on her face.

"What's on your mind now, you daft goofy thing?"

"I'm just proud. That's all, Davina, my love. As proud as any mum could ever possibly be."

The old mill house just off the Derry Road in Tunbridge Wells was easy to find. Kate spent many weekends there with Richard's family in her late teens. It was beaten down by the years—the gardens and the lawn had long been unattended—but the old brick home with the walled courtyard seemed strong and sturdy and still had the same lulling calm. It was obvious that Richard, or someone, had been working on the place; it seemed frozen in the early stages of a renovation.

Adam, Kate, and Billy waited a few hours for Richard and Trudy to arrive. When they finally did, Kate leapt from the car to head for Trudy; at the same time, Trudy jumped out of Richard's car and ran to her mother. Kate pulled her in tight and cried. Adam came over, softly stroking Trudy's back.

"I'm so, so sorry . . . Mommy, Daddy, I'm so sorry." She pulled Adam in and hugged him firmly.

"I can't believe how stupid I've been. I feel like such an idiot."

"It's okay, Trudy. You're here with us. That's all that matters."

"They used me. Used Étienne. It was all fake. It was never real. It was all a game to them, wasn't it, Daddy?"

"No, it wasn't a game. This is very serious. I'm sorry that you've been put in the middle of it. Both of you." He turned to Billy now, who was tightly holding his sister's hand, listening closely, a dark look of dread on his young face.

"We're in a tough spot, kids. Some people have gotten me into trouble. It's going to be okay, though. We will get through this. I just need to know that I can count on both of you to do what I say, to trust me. We need to work together. Is that clear now?" Trudy nodded. She had little doubt. Billy had more questions.

"What about Poppa? Is he going to be safe? Are we going to see him again?" Adam looked to Kate, wondering if she wanted to take a swing at an answer. She didn't. Adam turned back to his son.

"I don't know, Billy. I don't know yet when we'll see Poppa again. I'm sorry."

"Because you hate him, right? Just like Mommy has always thought, right?" Kate came over to Billy.

"No, Billy, this isn't about your daddy. This is about men that Poppa works with. It has nothing to do with your father's feeling toward Poppa. Do you understand?" She tried to comfort her son, but he pulled away.

"Yes. I understand because you're all lying." Trudy piped up to help her brother understand what he was hearing.

"They're not lying, Billy. I thought so, too, but they're not. The men at Poppa's company have done something really, really bad and they want everyone to think Daddy did it. Mommy and Daddy are not lying."

"Daddy is. Daddy's lying. He's a criminal. That's why the people want to put him back in jail. He wants to blame Poppa, but he's the criminal."

Billy had had enough. He turned away, ran to the back of the mill house, and started to cry. Trudy went after him, reassuring her parents.

"I'll talk to him. Don't worry. He'll be fine."

Adam and Kate watched them go. The children's absence left an uncomfortable void. Kate crossed the courtyard and gave Richard Lyle a warm hug.

"Thank you so much, Richard, thank you so, so much." She held him close as Adam came over to thank him as well, noticing the bloodstain on his shirt. She saw the halfhearted attempt at bandages on his side through the rips in his flannel top.

"She got me a good one. Not too deep. It's gonna be okay. From what

I can tell, she's your daughter's boyfriend's mother. She didn't seem happy that I was there to look out for her. Gave me a nice little sticking."

He turned to Adam and stuck out his hand. "Richard Lyle, Adam. It's a pleasure to meet you."

Adam reached over and shook Richard's hand. "I can't thank you enough."

"Think nothing of it, then. Seems to me like you've gotten yourselves in with a bad crowd."

Kate looked at Adam, not sure how much to say. Adam took the ball. "Richard, we're in trouble. The whole family. We're in a world of shit."

"Seems like it. What'd you do, rob a bank?"

Kate hit him playfully. "Stop it. It's no time to joke. We're in trouble, Richard. Big trouble."

Adam noted how closely and comfortably Kate stood alongside Richard. He decided this wasn't the time to be jealous or small. This man had just saved his daughter's life.

"It's true. We're in a lot of danger. I was about to get them out of the country, all three of them, but then Trudy ran off to see her boyfriend."

"But the mum had different plans? Sounds like she's part of the reason you're in danger."

Adam nodded in agreement. "She's involved. Yes. The boy's nothing more than a tool to manipulate Trudy. They've used her. They've played with Trudy from the beginning, using her to manipulate me, to get me to commit a crime."

Richard nodded affirmatively, even though he had no idea what they were talking about.

"Maybe you should both come inside. I'll open a bottle. Seems like it might help."

INSIDE THE HOUSE, with the kids still outside by the mill, Adam explained what had transpired. For some reason, none of it seemed to faze Richard. Maybe the years spent bopping along through life in London, getting by nicely but never growing so tall that he had to fit in with the crowd that ran the world, left him with an innocence, a desire to believe people when they told a story. He believed Adam's accounting. Never for a moment questioned its veracity.

"Truth is, I'd just heard of it on the radio on the way down. Poor Lassiter. I didn't want to dwell too long on it, what with the girl in the car. I did wonder, seeing as you had said Adam was at Number 10 today, if he had gotten mixed up in it, but I was thinking in terms of getting hurt or getting delayed. Wow. You really are in a bit of a wringer."

Adam wanted desperately not to like Richard. He wanted to confront him about e-mailing his wife, about having her over at his apartment, but he knew not only that it was absurd to think she didn't have the right to do what she pleased, but also that he didn't have much of a leg to stand on at the moment. He had no claim to righteousness. Richard had given them shelter in a dark hour without which Adam would have no idea where to turn. He knew that animosity toward his wife's old boyfriend would get him nowhere fast.

They drank some wine and talked about the security of the house. Kate went outside to check on the kids. Billy was already on to the next agenda, which was that he wanted to play on the mill wheel in the pump house by the small river out back. Normally Kate would say no—worry about the pitfalls, the danger—but today it seemed safe compared to the rest of the world. She wanted time alone with Trudy so she caved, begged him to be careful, and watched as he ran off to play, to be eight years old again, to shed the burdens of the last few hours.

Adam hid the rental car in a field down the road behind a thick row of brush. He couldn't take the chance that anyone already had the license plate. As he got back to the house, he saw Richard through the front window. He was on his cell phone. By the time he got back inside, Richard was finishing up a conversation with someone, not the least bit worried about Adam seeing him. He said good-bye and hung up the phone.

"Who was that?"

"Just a friend." In truth it was Gordon. He was sick with worry. He had called earlier. Richard was only letting him know they were all safe now at the house, that he'd call later, once they'd calmed down. He was just trying to be a good friend and, truthfully, a good potential son-in-law if things stacked up nicely for him one day.

"Listen, Richard, I have to ask you not to call anyone. Not to tell anyone where we are. In fact, I need your cell phone."

"You do? What for?"

"I need to hold on to it, to make sure you don't call out, or worse, that someone uses it to track you here. I promise you that's a reality. Please give it to me." He bore down on Richard with his eyes, refusing to avert his stare, his hand out. Richard gave in with a shrug, handed him the phone, and watched in shock, keeping his temper in check as Adam took out the chip in the back.

"I'm sorry, Richard. I have to protect my family. I can't afford to make a mistake right now."

Richard nodded. It was obvious that he and Adam weren't going to be best pals, which probably made sense seeing as how Richard had long-term plans to win Kate back. His mind was quietly racing. Maybe this Adam was in fact a nutter. Maybe he was guilty, was involved in this blowup thing at Number 10. Even if he wasn't, it seemed like a good chance he was going to take the fall, and a better one that he'd spend a long block of time alone in a jail cell. Richard's plan was shaping up: Be nice. Help out. Let events unfold. Sit by Kate's side as a family friend through the ordeal, and when she's alone and the tear ducts are empty, after the trial and hoopla, she'd come back to her Richard. That was the plan. Just be the good man.

"Another glass of wine, Adam?"

"I don't think so. Thank you, though." He looked back at Richard again.

"Do you have a weapon? We may get visitors. Not soon, but if we stay here, I'm gonna need something."

Richard went to a closet, opened it, and pulled out a shotgun and a box of shells and showed them both to Adam.

"My father's. He was a hunter. I've never shot it once. I don't believe in guns." Adam didn't respond. There wasn't time to have a gun control debate.

"He has a pistol up there, too, on the shelf somewhere. Again, I've never had much use for it all." Richard put the gun and the shotgun shells away just as Kate came back from the yard. Adam went to his wife.

"How's Billy?"

"Better for now. He's playing on the mill, distracted."

"He doesn't want to believe your father's in with them, does he? Doesn't believe he had a hand in it all?"

"He's eight. He's finally connected with an old man he's been longing to know, someone he thought he'd lost forever. Now he's losing him again. He doesn't believe in anything other than that. For what it's worth, Adam, he doesn't think you're a criminal. He believes you. He's just terrified to be going through it all . . . again." He understood clearly that she was talking about herself as well. She now turned her gaze back to Richard Lyle and his tattered shirt and bloody side.

"Do you need me to look at that wound?"

"I'm not sure. I think I need some help with it. Maybe some supplies. There's a pharmacy in the city center. In Tunbridge Wells. I could go and get some stuff. It seems like we may be here for—"

Adam cut him off, "I'll go. I'll go now, before it gets too dark."

What he wanted to say was before it gets too hot, but he didn't want to alarm Richard and Kate. He figured he had another small window. It had been four or five hours since the bomb went off. It wouldn't be long before his face would be plastered all over the media. Could be hours. Could be a day or so. Not a lot more. He wanted to take advantage of this last chance to go out. Get some time alone, time to process all that had happened.

He took Richard's antique Volvo into the village for supplies, just in case they were already on the lookout for his rental car. There was no telling how quickly Heaton would throw him under the bus. His sense was that "Sir Dickhead" would let it play out awhile. Let the detectives on the case come to it naturally. Then play shocked and dismayed.

THE VILLAGE, ABOUT twenty minutes south of the mill house, was a typical English country borough, on the big side of a small town. The high street had a row of fashionable shops and the congestion had a minor-league scent of London traffic to it. It was bigger than Adam had expected. There was more foot traffic than he had hoped. He put on a painter's cap that he found in the Volvo and went into the pharmacy.

After getting everything on Kate's list from the pharmacy, he walked the streets looking for a grocery. He gave a quick scan to the late afternoon *Evening Standard*, which had news of the bombing but, thankfully, no mention of any suspects.

He passed an old pub, looked in through the leaded windows and saw a small crowd glued to the television in much the same way that the two groups had hovered around it back at the hotel lobby bars in London. He went inside, happily noticed that no one paid him any attention, pulled his cap down, and sat in a booth at the back to watch the news on the flat-screen TV mounted on the front wall.

Georgia Turnbull, the woman from the conference who had sat across the table from him, had just come out of an SUV on Whitehall outside of the main gate to the Downing Street complex and walked straight into a churning sea of pandemonium and confusion. She began speaking at a podium surrounded by a horde of insatiable microphones and flashing cameras. As she spoke, the network showed pictures in a separate box of Roland Lassiter and her over the course of their lives as politicians.

To Adam, she seemed in shock—displaced, disoriented, much different than the powerfully assured figure she had cut earlier that afternoon. She spoke slowly, her voice somewhat deeper, as if she were trying to exude control and calm. Yet Adam, not knowing her in the slightest, didn't see that at all. To him she appeared on the verge of tears as she tried to speak sweetly of the wounded prime minister.

The locals in the pub hung on every word. For the hearty group, some of them already several pints in, it was the first statement from the government since the bombing and, needless to say, attention was paid. The crowd continued to grow. Word on the street had obviously spread. The people in the pub looked as stunned as the chancellor. Roland Lassiter was undoubtedly a beloved politician, but this was beyond even that. Britain had been attacked at the masthead. This was a personal blow.

Adam couldn't help but wonder how this crowd would react if they knew the bomber himself was seated just behind them in the booth by the back wall. He envisioned the patriotically fueled beating he would take. The final line of Ms. Turnbull's speech did little to calm his fear of the coming reprisals. She looked straight into the camera, and, for the first time now, looked dead certain of her words.

"In short time, as the dust settles, we will piece together the events of

this dark day, and then, with the warm light of a clear morning, we will come for you, we will find you, and I promise, on behalf of our United Kingdom, there will be hell to pay."

Some people in the pub were even crying. Even the ones who weren't had mist in their eyes. Some cheered; others bandied about conspiracy theories. Everyone seemed to be a pundit—a pub full of half-drunken experts on international terrorism, pontificating on how the government should right this wrong, who was to blame, and how much firepower to use. Adam picked up his shopping bags and headed off to find the grocery store.

TRUDY AND BILLY were both asleep in an upstairs bedroom. Neither had had a full night's rest since they had left Chicago. Kate checked on them. Even though it was early, they both were out. She sat on the edge of the bed and lightly stroked Trudy's hair. Kate understood the agony of a young heart. She wanted to somehow take Trudy's pain away, but all she had to trade it with was more misery.

She left the bedroom and made her way down the hall past the master. She looked in and saw Richard in the shower, naked. He didn't see her watching as he stepped out and wrapped a towel around his waist. As she turned away she saw the size of the knife wound on his stomach and saw him grimace as he stepped to the tile floor. She went to him. He allowed her to inspect the wound.

"I'm gonna be fine. Don't you worry."

The towel conveniently dropped to the floor. He stood there proudly, as he always did, loving to show off the bells and whistles of his manhood. Oddly, she wasn't the least bit embarrassed, though she shut the bathroom door in case one of the kids woke up.

She took a hand towel, dried the wound, and looked closely again. He would be okay. It needed dressing, though. Without thinking about it, she began softly drying his chest while looking worryingly at his injury. She looked farther down and saw Richard's erection.

He gazed into her eyes now and grinned a devilish half smile that only a former lover could deliver. She thought for a second how nice it would be to hide in something so carnal, so base, so "wrong." She wanted to reach down and take him in her hand, stroke him, and have him take her, whisk her away to a place free from fear, even if it were only for a few moments. She considered whether to use the escape route, whether to lash out at Adam in this way, whether to fall into a moment and let Richard have her right there in the bathroom, or not. She saw his reflection in the bathroom mirror, a want and a need smoldering so strong she even thought for a second it was he that was steaming up the glass.

She dropped slowly toward her knees, looked up past his penis to his eyes, which were as wide and ready as she had ever seen them, even when he was twenty years younger and the game between them was still new. Their views locked on each other. He looked down longingly, she up fondly, both wondering if this moment here, these naked seconds, would open a door to a past that both of them privately owned together.

She broke from his gaze, picked up the towel, stood up, wrapped it carefully around his waist, then left the bathroom in search of supplies for his wound.

AT HEATON'S MANSION, on Palace Gardens Mews off Kensington Gardens, it was a somber, foggy night. The security detail, tense with news of the explosion, was on high alert, along with all of London.

Heaton and Gordon were in the kitchen. Sir David was making himself a sandwich. He had let the cooks and the kitchen staff go home early and was having a good time making himself a bit of a feast in the giant server's kitchen. He was more than a tad tipsy, having had one too many at the Connaught after the conference. Now, with the house almost empty, he would have a nice meal, smoke another cigar, and watch the news coming from Downing Street. It was a perfect plan until Gordon barged in and demanded a face-to-face.

"It was supposed to be a 'nothing bomb'! Isn't that what you said? A 'dud'? To scare the PM? To send him over the edge? That's what you told me! That's a far cry from the truth, David." Gordon was hot, as worked up as David had seen him since they were kids.

"You need to calm down, Thompson. You're getting yourself lathered over nothing." He cut his sandwich, set one half on a plate, and slid it over the polished, stainless-steel countertop. Gordon looked at it and pushed it away. Heaton saw the burn, the black of Gordon's glare, knew this wasn't another time he could just push his old sheepdog of a friend down the road and have him fetch a stick. He wasn't going to be petted and rolled over.

"Yes. Okay, Gordon, yes, it was supposed to be a dud bomb. Just scare the piss out of Lassiter. Jangle his already beaten nerves. It was supposed to be a nothing incident—"

Gordon cut him off, his voice raised, his own nerves now good and "jangled." "I don't care what it was supposed to be! I care what it was! This boy could be looking at murder now. We all could be looking at murder, David."

"If I didn't know you so well, I'd take that as a threat."

"It's not a threat. It's a reality. This is a mess."

"I'm well aware. Trust me. There's an aspect of this that has gotten out of hand. You are spot on. But you have no idea how big this is, how far back it reaches, how much of it is out of my purview."

"That doesn't concern me. What concerns me is that you've brought my family into this."

"No. You brought your family into it, not me. I didn't even know they were coming over with Tatum until you'd gone ahead and made it happen. You went around my back on your own and had your daughter and the kids come along as well. I never would have okayed that, Gordon, let's remember that. It was a serious mistake."

"I did that because I trusted you, that what you told me was the truth: that we were going to use him to fix a 'bookkeeping snafu,' that at the very worst he'd do a couple of years, and they'd make out 'like royalty.' You know damn well I would have had no part of something on this level."

"But you knew about the bomb before today, Gordon, didn't you?"

"Yes, I did. But by then it was too late, and what you told me, even last night, was that no one would be hurt and that he would be protected. If Lassiter dies, if this thing truly does erupt, you won't be able to protect him."

Heaton took a sip of a drink he had poured. "Your daughter and your grandchildren will be safe and well taken care of. I've given you my word."

"And what about Adam? What's the plan there?" Gordon didn't need an answer. He knew full well what the plan was. He knew there was no way that anyone involved in all of this could afford to let Adam live through this whole damn cock-up.

"Honestly, I don't yet know what the plan is. I'm not moving the pieces around the board at this point."

"Bullshit, David. Just come out and say it, damn it. Look me in the eye. They're going to kill him. That's the plan, isn't it? He takes the fall, and Lassiter dies or resigns?"

Heaton just stared back at him. He gave him the body language that read he was tired of pretending they were equals. Gordon pressed on.

"This is about Europe, isn't it? The referendum. Just come out with it."

"Yes, Gordon. It's about Europe. Europe and so much more." He finished his half of the sandwich and began cleaning up after himself. "It's about saving this country, okay? This isn't a bunch of kill-happy thrill seekers enjoying the job at hand. This is all in service of an important turn. You can trust that."

"I don't trust anything. This is about my family."

"I have promised that they will be fine. Your family will not be hurt. You need to find them, like we planned."

"So Adam can be sacrificed?"

"When things settle down, sooner rather than later, your daughter and the kids will be flown quietly out of the UK. She has a policy from the company that covers him when he's traveling abroad in case of an accident. We'll honor it to the letter, and she'll be well looked after."

"And he'll be dead?"

Heaton chuckled, rolled his cigar in his hand and smelled it.

"Are you wearing a wire, Gordon?"

"Of course not."

"Then why do you need everything spelled out for you?"

"We're talking about my son-in-law."

"Whom you can't stand. Who embarrassed the hell out of his wife. Remember? You were all for this when he was just going to do a small turn in prison, weren't you? When he'd have been destroyed and she'd be back here in London? Now that it's worse than that, you've found your line in the sand. Is that what you're telling me? Because I'm sorry, the game has changed. The stakes have been raised and you are seated at the table, Gordon, whether you like it or not. You don't get to pull back. You don't get to just cash in and walk away, not now. Neither of us does." He finished putting everything back in place and gave Gordon a moment to resign himself to the circumstances.

"You were on the phone with the former boyfriend two hours ago. Your mobile to his mobile. He's with them. He has your granddaughter. Where are they?"

Gordon was stunned. The tentacles these people had were as long-reaching and quick to react as he feared. The resources Heaton was dealing with were infinite.

"We're all-in here, Gordon. Deep. Do not even think about going wobbly. It's nowhere near close to smart." Gordon finally nodded. He knew Heaton was right. He had no choice.

"Royal Tunbridge Wells. His family has got a mill house on the Pill-gar Riverway, about ten miles east."

"Where is it?"

"Somewhere on the Derry Road . . . Kate and the kids. They need to be golden."

"Yes. Good. Golden. That's a boy. You have my word. Stay firm, Gordon. It's all going to work out."

As Georgia billowed through the back halls of Number 11 into Number 10 with a dust cloud of assistants and secretaries, on her way from an education meeting into the Cabinet Room to be brought once again up to running speed on the investigation, she saw an elderly man sitting in the waiting area. The image froze her to the spot. It was her father.

Harry Turnbull was seventy-eight, as nice, sweet, and calm of an old gentleman as could be. Georgia and her father mutually adored each other. The walls of his chemist shop were papered with stories and magazine photos in a shrine to her career. Her mother had died when she was only six, her father having never remarried. He busied his life raising his three children, Georgia and her two brothers, running his shop in Finchley, playing with his grandchildren, watching sports with his pals, going to church every Sunday, and religiously smoking one cheap cigar every single day. He wasn't one to ever bother his busy daughter. He never needed a favor, never wanted in or around any of the canyons of power and glory that his daughter regularly played in. He had never once in all her career ever dropped by unannounced.

The fact that he was there at Number 10, obviously waiting for her, could only be more bad news. She could see Jack Early and his team of blondes hovering over him, getting him a coffee, obviously trying to let him know how busy the acting PM was. She went straight over to her

father. They'd only talked once in the last few days: the night of the bombing she had called to let him and the family know she was okay. Her
father spoke only of his pain for Roland and his family. He wanted to
know if he could help in any way. That was Harry, to a tee.

"Daddy, how are you?"

"I'm well, love. I need to see you."

Early interjected. He wanted the chancellor to know Mr. Harry had
been well taken care of but told of the full schedule. Georgia thanked
him and put the parade to the Cabinet Room on pause. She excused herself and escorted her father into Lassiter's office. She closed the door.

"This is where you're working out of now?"

"Yes, Daddy, for the time being."

"It's nice. I've only been in here once, for Roland's birthday a few years
back, to have cake."

"I remember. It was a beautiful morning. He was thrilled you were
here."

"Is he going to make it?"

"I hope so, Daddy. I so hope so."

They stood for a moment. Harry looked around, not thrilled about
getting to the heart of the matter that brought him over.

"You don't look well, Georgie. You look like it's taking a toll."

"I'll be fine. I'm not going to lie to you, though. It's been a horrid
week."

"I know. I follow the news. Normally I don't, but this week I think
it's all I can do."

"Daddy, is there anything wrong? Anything I can help you with?"

"Some pills have gone missing, Georgie. At the shop."

"Pills?"

Her heart sank like a lead balloon. She felt like a nine-year-old girl.
A cloud of shame mushroomed around her body.

"Missing? As in stolen, Daddy? Is someone stealing from you? If that's
true, it's horrible, and we can have a police detective . . ."

"I've put in cameras last month. The new manager, Byron, had the
idea. I okayed it." Her chest froze up now, worse than her feet had done
before. She felt as if a giant rock were sitting on it, even though she was
standing straight up.

"You've cameras? Inside the store?"

"And the back. The shelves. Twenty-four hours. It's you, Georgie; I knew it was you without the cameras. I'm very, very worried for you. These are incredibly strong pills."

She didn't know what to say. She just wanted to cry but wouldn't allow herself to. The thought of letting him down, of her father seeing her in this light, was pure horror. She was caught. Revealed. Stripped bare.

Harry came closer, his eyes stern, concerned, sadly resigned to the truth. There was a new Georgia. Events, time, age, life, and too much responsibility had taken his baby away. This wounded woman with the wild hair had replaced her. She was a drug addict. He took her hands in his; they were as big and warm and friendly as they had always ever been.

"I know the pain you're in, love, but these are very strong pills you've got yourself on. They were fine for the two weeks when your body was broken and you needed calm to start the heal, but being on them now regularly, you'll not be yourself. You'll make very bad choices. You'll lose yourself, Georgie. I can make you that promise. You need to get some help, right away." He gently brushed her busy bangs away from her face as tears cascaded down her cheeks. "I've told no one. I've no one to tell."

"I love you, Daddy. I am so, so sorry." She could barely look at her father, she was so embarrassed.

"Don't be sorry. Get help. Right away. That's what I've come for today—to look you in the eye, to tell you to reach out to someone. Right away."

TWENTY MINUTES LATER Georgia was in the meeting in the Cabinet Room that had been postponed for her sit-down with her father. She had washed up and had done her best to recompose. Darling, the COBRA reps, the home secretary, several cabinet members, and, of course, Steel and her minions were there to convey the latest on the hunt for Adam Tatum. There were developments, an embarrassing group of revelations.

Steel was the bearer of bad news. Georgia was just glad to see her face. She would have loved to be able to talk to her alone, tell her all about the private hell she was in, tell her how she'd let down her father, how she'd been caught red-handed stealing pills from his shop. She wondered if Steel would sympathize or if, instead, she would be forced by her convictions to turn the matter over to the DPG.

Georgia's mind went a thousand places in a fraction of a second. Telling Steel. Cleaning up. Getting free from those things for good. Admitting it all to the press. An inquiry. A scandal. A resignation. She had truly left the room, as badly as when she had fallen asleep and woken up again sure that she had just been in her bedroom upstairs. It was that dramatic of an exit. Steel's lips were moving but she wasn't hearing her. She nodded desperately, wanting everyone so badly to believe that she was in sync with them.

Steel sensed it. Instinctively saw the hidden cloud over Georgia's head. She felt the confusion, wanted to somehow lend a hand, to hold Georgia's arm all the way from across the room. She stopped, took a sip of water, was quiet for the longest time, pretended to be confused in her presentation. Darling finally broke the silence.

"Inspector Steel, can you please go on?"

"Yes, of course. I was just—I lost my train of thought. I don't know why . . . if it's all right with the chancellor, may I just quickly start over? From the top of the report? I'm so sorry. I'm having a long morning. Please forgive me, everyone."

Georgia agreed, the men in the room grumbled softly, and Steel started from the top. Georgia knew clearly what she had done. She listened now to every word.

They were important beats, too, words that Georgia needed to hear. They had uncovered something from the day of the blast, something that had somehow fallen through the cracks for a solid week now. Tatum's wife and his two children had gone to Heathrow just three hours after the bomb went off and suddenly booked flights to Chicago. Not Tatum himself, but his family. Even odder was the fact that they never made the flight.

"We figure that they were on the run, that someone had caught up with them at the airport."

Darling wanted to know why this was coming to light a week later. Why wasn't this known in real time? The home secretary had the head of COBRA's liaison officer, Reginald Atwell, explain it off.

"We weren't aware of the ticket purchases until Tatum's image was distributed to the airport security staff. They never passed through customs or security, so a bell wouldn't have gone off along that line. Once his photo was circulated within the system, within hours he was recognized as being there at the airport last Friday, and in fact he is on the CCTV files, for some reason chasing his daughter through the terminal."

Darling tried to cover tracks by reminding the chancellor how busy a Friday it had been, how thinly spread assets were making sure more bombs weren't going off, that major installations were secured. Steel had even more news. A fight on Paddington's concourse that Friday, an incident that was put down to a wild woman fueled by drug use on the atrium landing, was now seen to be somehow connected.

"How could it be connected?" Georgia was focused now, keyed in, thanks to Steel. Focused but confused.

"Tatum's daughter. The same girl that he chased through the airports. She's on the CCTV files. Talking to the French woman who had the drug meltdown. It matches with the files from Heathrow twenty minutes earlier. We know she was on the Express, ran from her father, came to Paddington, and then was caught in the middle of a strange scene once she disembarked. Then she disappeared. We've pieced it together in a sense that we feel someone was fast on the family's tail."

"What has happened with the French woman, the drug addict?" Georgia winced as she said the words.

"She was taken to Transport Security for questioning and a checkup."

"Then?"

"She was let go. We don't yet know why. Let go, with no record of a name or an address. It's being looked into, Madam Chancellor, but she's disappeared. I'm sorry, but that's all I have on that for right now."

There was more, though. Steel opened another file.

"We have phone records now from a rented mobile Mrs. Tatum obtained from Heaton Global. The records were given to us by them."

"Do they tell us anything?"

"While in London, she was speaking quite a bit to a former boyfriend, a man named Richard Lyle, a local. Grew up and lives in London. A music promoter of some kind. That's all that we have on him yet, but more is coming."

"Do we think this Richard Lyle is somehow involved?"

"We don't know yet. This is all developing quickly. We do know that Mr. Lyle also made a call from his mobile to Tatum's father-in-law, Gordon Thompson, later that Friday evening from an area in Kent. Since then, he hasn't used the phone again. In fact it's gone offline."

"Kent? Isn't that where the rental car was found? With the dead body?" Georgia was wide alert now, sitting straight up. A picture was emerging. She couldn't help but think it was about bloody time.

"Yes. Just outside of Kent. We're not sure yet what the connection is. Why Kent and, for that matter, where? His name hasn't yet come up on any property searches or hotel ledgers in that area. Once we get deeper into the who and what of Richard Lyle, we believe we'll have an answer. We're on that now and expect something very soon. I would say by early this evening we'll know exactly where they've holed up down there in Kent."

It was late at night at the mill house. Everyone but Kate was comfortably asleep. Kate was wide awake. The silence scared her. Everything had gotten too quiet, the night air too flat. The wind on the back fields coming up the tiny river normally whipped past the old wooden mill house, giving it a familiar creak, but this night, for some reason, the wind had nothing to offer her as she lay next to her sleeping fugitive husband.

They had been there for four full days now. The first night, and even the nights after, she hadn't slept; no one really had. Richard and the kids, maybe, but not her, nor Adam. They had tried to talk about what had happened, but there was nothing worth saying. It was too much of a nightmare to make it real with too many words.

It was eleven a.m. that first morning there at the mill house when Sky News reported that the prime minister had survived the attack. He was in a hospital just on the other side of the Thames from Number 10, and Adam and Richard watched the news together as both the young king and Georgia Turnbull, the chancellor of the exchequer, visited the hospital. Kate and Adam each let loose a silent sigh. At least what they would be discussing, when they could finally speak about their situation, wouldn't be a murder. There was something to be grateful for in that.

The first two afternoons and evenings were uneventful. Kate took the kids on several hikes through the long golden fields on the other side of the tiny tributary. Most of the days Adam watched the news, all day, his head lost in his hands. Richard did light work out on the mill, work meant to kill the hours, to keep him out of the house so he wouldn't have to spend too much time talking to Adam. They had a few dinners together, Trudy and Billy watched movies on the television, and Adam took a series of long walks alone.

There was a numbness to the air—a quiet, gentle, floating sadness. The kids weren't sure what to say or how much to press. Maybe if they all said nothing, it would be as if nothing had happened. It seemed to be the most comfortable position for everyone trapped at the old mill house to take. So on that last night, the house sat still and quiet until finally, sometime around three a.m., the wind changed. There were visitors.

A car had pulled up a short way down the darkened road. Two men had crept up to the house in the pitch-black country air and scooted over the courtyard wall. Richard heard them first—sensed them. He got up and quickly dressed. Adam woke just seconds later. He turned to Kate, surprised to see her awake. They said nothing. Both listened quietly as Richard clomped down the steep wooden stairway, putting on his boots as he went. They heard him open the front door, heard him talking to two men out in the courtyard.

Adam went downstairs barefoot, still in pajamas, over to the front hall closet, and took out Richard's father's shotgun and the box of shells. He grabbed another pair of Richard's work boots and slipped his bare feet into them. He pulled out an old brown workman's jacket and shoved the box of shells into the pocket. Kate was at the top of the steps. She looked down to him.

"Stay in here. Please? Don't go out there. Stay with us." He looked up to his wife, her hands tightly throttling the banister railing. He didn't respond. He wasn't sure what his answer was, so he didn't give her one. He went over to the window, looked carefully through the sheer curtains, stood at the edge, and watched Richard out in the courtyard. He was talking politely to someone outside of Adam's field of vision. He didn't seem to be too concerned. He was giving out directions—guidance back to Royal Tunbridge Wells.

Adam watched. Kate wanted to know what was happening. He signaled for her to be quiet. He looked back: two men came into view, pretending to listen to Richard's navigation tips to the village. It was Harris and Peet. In what seemed like a jump cut, everything about the air outside changed. The redhead, now very close to Richard in the center of the courtyard, stopped pretending to listen and took out a handgun with a silencer on it and fired twice into the center of Richard's head, killing him instantly. His legs buckled under him like a cheap parlor trick. He collapsed in a broken heap on the cobbled brick surface.

Adam turned around, whispered loudly to Kate, "Go upstairs. Get into bed with the kids. Lock the door!"

"What's happened? What was that? Was it a gun? It was quiet. Was it a gun?"

"Now. Go. Do it."

"Where are you going? You can't go out there."

"If I don't go out there, they're coming in here. It's one or the other. Move it!"

She turned and ran to where the kids were sleeping. Adam raced through the kitchen, took a back door to the side yard, and crept as silently as possible through the dewy shrubbery to the front of the house. He saw Harris and Peet going through Richard's pants. They found his wallet. Harris showed it to Peet. They were in the right place. Harris dropped Richard's wallet as they both stepped over his blood-soaked body, each with a pistol loaded and ready, closing in on the front door.

Adam marched toward them. He fired the shotgun just as they sensed him coming. Peet went down. Adam stood his ground and fired again. Harris fired back at Adam and missed by inches. He grabbed Peet and ran in retreat as Adam reloaded, guiding his partner back toward the street. The two of them barreled over the moss-covered wall. Peet had been hit in the shoulder. He was oozing blood like an old-time schoolhouse drinking fountain. Harris helped him under the cover and confusion of darkness, pulled his shirt off, ripped it in half, and tied off his shoulder to close the wound. Peet was hurting bad, but at least he was alive.

Adam fired again, wanting to change that equation. He scurried around the wall, ran through the gate, pumped in another load, and waited at the ready for a stage direction to bubble up from the quiet. He finally saw the shadows of the two men running. He followed after them firing again and again.

He waited now for a reaction. The night went silent once more, just as quick as it had flared into terror; the world was now mute, muffled, and dark. Every moment was its own eternity. Harris and Peet were out there somewhere. He wasn't going anywhere. He wanted to fight in the open air, away from his family. He reloaded and tried to discern shapes or movement in the pitch-black country stillness. Tried his best to calm his labored breathing.

A car door opened a short click up the road. An interior light went on then went off. He sprinted toward it, not wanting to take the chance that they were after more weapons, or calling for help. He raced as fast as he could in Richard's untied boots, reached them as the car started. It was another one of Heaton's endless supply of black Mercedes.

He fired into the car. He shattered the back windshield and shot out the back latch of the trunk, which popped itself wide open. He busted a taillight. He fired his last blast just above the roof of the car, aimed high on purpose; he didn't want to thwart their escape—that wasn't the goal. The aim was to send them packing. There was no upside to having them stick around to stand their ground. He knew well the dark mettle of these men. He'd watched them murder Richard Lyle in cold blood. The best thing for everyone was for them to hustle away into the night and lick their wounds. He knew they'd be back once they could regroup, that was a given; the point was to get them to scuttle off for now.

The car squealed onto the road, kicked up dirt and gravel, and raced away. Adam quickly reloaded and flared off another shot in case they had the idea of turning back and barreling into him. He watched as they picked up speed; he focused on the red and broken white of their tail-lights for a quarter mile. They'd return—no question. With any luck Adam and his family would be long gone.

HE RACED BACK to the house. Richard's body lay stone cold in a pup-pet's clump, his eyes staring up toward the moon as Adam passed him, gazing eerily toward forever. He went into the house. Rummaged through the front hall closet in a blaze of desperation. Found Richard's father's pistol. Made sure it was loaded. Bolted up the steps.

He quietly announced himself, carefully opened the door to the room. The kids were up, concerned, wanted to know what the shots were.

"Firecrackers. Some older kids were out playing pranks. It's fine, kids. Go back to sleep." They didn't believe him—they both protested—but he didn't have time to respond. He signaled Kate out to the hall. She was scared out of her wits. The firecracker story wasn't going to fly with her, either. She hugged him tight and whispered, so as not to startle the kids any more than they'd been startled.

"Oh my Lord, Adam, what's happened. Are you okay?"

"I'm okay. Yes."

"Where's Richard? Is he okay?" He wiped her wet cheeks. He took a beat to find the courage to answer with the truth.

"No. No, he's not okay. He's dead. I'm sorry."

"He's dead? How could that be? What are you saying?"

"Two men came. I shot one of them. They ran. Drove away. They're gone."

"They've killed Richard? No, no . . . who were they?"

"Heaton. They're with Heaton. They work for him." She pulled back. That made no sense to her, no more sense than Richard being dead and gone could possibly make.

"Kate, we have to leave. I want to hide the rental car. We'll take Richard's aunt's car, the one in the garage, but we have to be quick." He pulled the pistol out of his jacket pocket and handed it to her. She took the weapon in a daze, not sure what it was until she felt its weight.

"You stay in the room. If anyone comes in that door but me, you point this straight at him and fire. Keep firing."

"Wait . . . what? Don't leave."

"I'll be back. Five minutes. No more. Be ready. We'll take the kids and go."

He sprinted through the dark up the road again, then crossed the field to the west and through to the back trail where he had abandoned the rental car in the scrub. He drove it back to the mill house and pulled into the motor court, right up to Richard's body. He lifted the corpse and put it in the back of the Ford wagon. He found a tarp in the garage and covered the corpse. He picked up Richard's wallet from the ground and exchanged it with his own. He wasn't going to get very far being Adam

Tatum in the days ahead. He thought he'd at least let Richard sub for him when the car was found and maybe throw whoever came looking off the trail for a beat. Lord knows, given the condition of Richard's face, no one was going to be recognizing him for a long time.

It was cold, calculated thinking, but he had no choice. Every move from here on in would be forged by a burning desire to keep himself and his family alive. He drove the rental car back into the brush and hustled up the road to the house. He pulled the old Volvo from the garage, went into the kitchen, got as many of the supplies as he could carry, and threw them into the back of the car.

Kate brought the kids down; they were groggy and scared. Both of them wanted to know where they were going.

"We're taking a ride. I'll tell you where when we get in the car." Trudy stopped him and spoke to him with a maturity he hadn't heard before.

"Daddy, are you going to be okay?"

"I am, yes. Thank you."

"I love you and know that you're innocent. Billy does, too. He's just sad, that's all. But I really know it. I know you'd never do something like that. You know I do, right?"

"I do, sweetheart. Thank you for saying that. It means a lot to me."

They led the kids out to the Volvo. Adam had parked right over the large and gory pool of blood so Kate wouldn't see it. She whispered to him and wanted to know where Richard's body was. He shook his head; he didn't want to discuss it.

They pulled out of the cobbled drive, went in the direction opposite the one in which Harris and Peet had fled.

After a few minutes and a long round of groggy questions, Billy finally fell back asleep. Adam picked up speed. They sailed up and down lonely wooded roads for forty frigid minutes. It was quiet enough now for Kate to think about the reality of Richard Lyle being dead, of all the memories, all the joy, all the pain, all the idiosyncrasies that made up the man she'd known. He was gone now and why? Because he had helped her.

She wished for a quick second she had let him take her in the bathroom the night before. She made another wish—that those images wouldn't be the ones that she came back to for the rest of her life: the foggy way his eyes met hers in the damp bathroom mirror; the hungry, longing look on his face. She let it go unformed; she didn't have the energy to allow it to percolate. The idea of Richard dead was a darker, more encompassing pain than any specific notion would hold. He was over. There was no room for "if I had" and "I wish I hadn't." Richard Lyle's larger-than-life story was finished now, closed out, because of her.

"Where will we go, Adam?"

I don't know. I don't know, he thought to himself. *It's a goddamn island.*

He didn't answer, just kept driving.

They drove a bit longer, until he finally pulled over to the side of the road and stopped. He took a deep, troubled breath and turned to face his frightened wife. He wanted to soothe her, but no words sprang to mind. He had no idea what to do or where to go next, no sense of whom to turn to, only whom to turn from, which was everyone. Her lips quivered in a way that told him that she needed to hear a reassuring word, so he did something that he had resolutely promised never to do again: he lied to his wife.

"Give me a beat, Kate. I know exactly what we need to do."

Steel and a contingent of officers took the mill house early in the morning. It was eight days now since the bombing and she was more than bothered. Her face bore a full-time fretful glaze. She had let whoever was behind him, whoever was chasing him, put too much time in between herself and Adam Tatum.

Adam and his family were an essential piece of the puzzle. They would know the who and the why, the truth of how he came to be involved in a bombing of Number 10. She had seen the evidence taken from his home computer firsthand now: the website comments he had made, the sick photos in his hard drive of Roland Lassiter. She didn't believe they were real. Everyone else did—all the forensic gods and goddesses at Scotland Yard and on the home secretary's team. They swore to a person that it was all verifiably Tatum. Steel didn't buy it.

As the uniformed officers tackled the historic-looking stone walls of the driveway's courtyard, she leaned against the squad car that had brought her. She knew there would be no one inside, knew the house would be empty. There would be no one present to flash the warrant to. The Tatums, if they were alive, would be long gone, she was sure of it.

The blood work had come back on the body from the ditched rental car. It had been found, sadly, two days earlier, not an eighth of a mile from here. It belonged to Richard Desmond Lyle, Tatum's wife's boyfriend from years back. Two .30-caliber bullets straight into his forehead had felled Mr. Lyle. It had taken time to run his blood, which had no matches, until the connection was made from his calling the cell phones of Kate Tatum and Gordon Thompson, and his place near Paddington was gone through and DNA samples had been collected. Memorabilia had been found linking Lyle to Tatum's wife. Richard Lyle had lived a clean life as far as the law was concerned.

His wasn't an easy trail to walk back. The mill house wasn't even in his name; it was in the name of an aunt, a Penelope Ann Jordan.

Forensics estimated that Mr. Lyle had been dead almost four days. The way that the body was hidden, away from the house, told Steel that Tatum hadn't done the killing. If Tatum had killed Richard Lyle, he would have hid the body on the property and laid low. There would be no point in moving on. This remote country shack would have been a perfect place to sit tight. Someone else did this, someone who was also on Tatum's trail, someone who had gotten there before Steel had.

She was guessing that the Tatums left right after Lyle was killed, which meant that she was at least four days behind. Why else would Tatum have placed his own wallet on the dead man if he wasn't trying to purchase time? Scheming to confuse the next group to come along? The former police detective knew better than to stay around after Mr. Lyle's killing.

A large, faded bloodstain was found seeped into the center of the brick courtyard. It was sampled, logged, and sent to the Yard. Steel was certain it was from Richard Lyle. He had been killed there in the court-yard. Shotgun shells were found in the motor court and in the ditch heading out to the road. Tatum had stood his ground somehow, run whoever killed Lyle off, then hid Lyle's body in the rental car and taken another car, leaving immediately with his family.

Steel phoned Edwina Wells and had her put someone on finding out what kind of car Richard Lyle drove. Again, nothing came up. She then had them find out what kind of car the aunt drove. Finally, within twenty minutes, there was a vehicle worth tracking: a 1969 Volvo, registered to Lyle's aunt. Tire tracks coming into and out of the garage seemed to suggest that the Volvo had been there recently. DPG shot a loud flare through the system. Somewhere in Britain, someone would have seen that old Volvo.

Steel slowly walked the road and found another spent shell in the grizzled brush off to the side. As she called the others, she saw something else—a steady dripping trail of blood that had seeped deep into the road and soil, coming off the vine-covered stone gate by the side of the road. She overturned four more spent shells, all leading to scattered bits of broken taillights on and off the asphalt. She found a battered piece of metal that she deduced was once the keyhole to the lock on the trunk of a car. She paced the road, saw it all in her mind, second by second, like a flipbook at a gum shop. Tatum had hit one of them. He had hit the car twice, a third time, maybe. One of them would have a bullet wound. That would help. So would piecing together the taillight and lock for a make and a model. Tire marks squealing out in a long line of desperation raced away from the area around the broken taillights like a junkyard dog whose foot had been stepped on, then kicked with a steel boot in the head. The tire tracks told Steel that the car more or less tried to leap away.

Tatum. He had sent them running for their lives. Of course the family had to leave. He was sure they'd be back.

Steel knew who the men that killed Richard Lyle were. She saw them there in the courtyard, as if she were watching overhead as they snuffed out Lyle's life four mornings earlier. They were Heaton's men, the men who were in her bedroom. She knew firsthand that they could sneak up in the cloak of night and make the pitch-black even darker still. She would play it out in her mind with a near-perfect clarity, the stumpy redhead and the lanky baldy, driving away up the road, sweaty wide eyes, shotgun sober, silently praying that they made it out of Tatum's range before the backside of one of their heads exploded.

She smiled to herself. It would all lead back to Heaton. She was sure of it now. It was time to sit Georgia and the others down—time to draft warrants.

LESS THAN THREE hours later Steel was presenting her identification at the stuffy little security box at Downing Street. She met in the Cabinet Room with Darling, Munroe, Burnlee, Edwina Wells, and several Scotland Yard detectives and the foreign secretary. They were waiting for the chancellor. She had been upstairs in the private residence after a long morning of meetings.

Up in her bedroom, Georgia changed once again for Steel. She redid her hair. What was it that made her do this? Every time she thought of Steel, she harshly judged her own clothing choices. She reminded herself how she dressed like an old woman already. She thought back to how easily Steel seemed to present herself, how her skirts just seemed to hang off her little body in a perfect drop. She had put on a light blue pantsuit, frustratingly combed her hair out for a third time, and was putting a little red on her cheeks when Early knocked and told her they were ready for her in the Cabinet Room.

The now daily meeting went as well as could be expected. They were starting to have a "gang that couldn't shoot straight" feeling as a group; Georgia could feel their confidence on the wane, especially Steel, who oddly seemed to have the most to lose, the most on the line. The ever-rigid Darling was calmer; he had a comfortable manner, as if it was only a matter of time before they found the Tatums and what was at the bottom of the box. Munroe was on edge, though, particularly at the suggestion that now was the time to release Tatum's image and name to the press.

"Until we know more about this man, about what his motives are, about who is behind him, I don't want to run off and blame an American because that's all every front page will say. *'It's a Goddamn American!'* Believe me, we will hear from the White House on that, straight off," Darling scoffed openly.

"And what if we do? It clearly is an American. That doesn't mean America. It means one American." Burnlee wasn't on the same page. He stood up and faced the room.

"It won't end well if we look like we're rushing into calling this out on an American. I don't need to remind everyone in this room how dicey our relationships are with the US these days. We don't need to give the British people another reason to hate America unless we absolutely have to."

Georgia weighed in now. "Should we at least let the White House know? Give them a window on this?"

"I don't think we can afford the time," Steel said, agreeing with

Darling. Tatum needed to be found. They weren't the only ones looking
for him. Tea was served. Georgia pondered. She read through the reports,
the file on the mill house, and the events in Kent. She sipped her tea as
she read, and fiddled with her hair.

Davina sensed her apprehension. Going public would make it all very
international. Adam Tatum from someplace as all-American as Michigan would change the fabric of the story in a profound way. The volume
level would make everything harder to hear through, even if, yes, it would
make it harder for Tatum to hide. Georgia had to think like a politician,
like a head of state. Steel had a thought toward a compromise.

"Maybe we can buy you some time. Release the nonrelated story of
the discovery of Lyle's death, his car, and the incident in Kent. Use the
press from that to see if we can get the public to help us find the Volvo. It
would give you the time to deal with the White House and the American
embassy." Georgia looked across the table. She wanted, once again, to
wink, thank her, but knew to Darling and Burnlee and the others that it
would look as if Steel had crossed a line and had dabbled in politics, in
direct violation of her role as an investigator on a case of dire importance.
She shot a darkened look across the table, as if the idea were distasteful
at first, as if she, too, thought her tail had been stepped on.

Major Darling, however, liked the idea.

"I say yes. We need to go public, and we will soon. We can't hold this
back much longer. I can promise you that in a blink the press will get on
to Tatum and it'll make our one big problem several much bigger problems. Let's give Burnlee the day to deal with the White House, and let's
get the public tracking that Volvo for us."

It was time to speak of the elephant in the room. What was Heaton's
involvement? How could it be possible? Steel tried to explain it as fact.
She was sure that Heaton's men had murdered Richard Lyle. Other than
the fact that the broken taillights and trunk lock were sure to be from a
new model Mercedes, she had no evidence, but her gift, if she had one,
was a God-given, highly developed sense of intuition.

Lyle had died in the center of the courtyard. The blood work on the
broken bricks confirmed it: two bullets to his forehead from close range.
He hadn't been running, hadn't been hiding. He was killed by either

someone he knew or someone he didn't consider to be a threat. She was sure it was Heaton's two men.

Heaton was at the back of the theater of this entire shit show, watching with a proud smirk as all of the actors ran his lines. This wasn't detective work; this was just plain sense. The chancellor and the others had to see that. She wanted a warrant. She wanted to have him brought into the Yard for a proper sit-down. The home secretary led the side of the group that urged restraint.

"David's a very connected man, and very public. To go after him now, without a shred of evidence that he's involved in any way other than one that's as distasteful to him as can be, is foolish. It would only get the pans pounding out there in exactly the way we don't want them to. It will turn this all into a lurid twenty-four-hour soap opera and will not bring us one beat closer to capturing our bomber. Yes, Tatum did work for him: it doesn't make David guilty. We've all known him for too many years to believe he would ever be involved with something like this."

Georgia suggested a second compromise.

"I want to call him in. Right here. In the den. Sit with him as a fellow member of government. As a man of Britain. Ask him his assessment of the situation. Go from there. Major Darling, Sir Melvin, you'll both join with us. We three will take a measure of David's view on this. I can't think of another way. I agree with the home secretary. We can't go riding off toward him. He's done too much for this country, as has his family. He deserves the benefit of the doubt, and we will give it to him."

Steel piped in with a request.

"I would like to sit in as well, please, Madam Chancellor. I need to hear his take, if it's at all possible."

Burnlee answered for the room. "At this point, that would be a breach of Sir David's confidence. This will be a talk and nothing more, not an inquiry." Everyone in the room knew what the HS was really saying. It wouldn't be the time for cheap theatrics, and that's what they would presumably get with Steel in the room. *A loose firecracker.* She'd labeled herself early on. The sit-down was above her pay grade. There was nothing she could do but nod in unpleasant acceptance. Georgia tried to soften the response.

"I will personally fill you in on every detail, Inspector Steel. You have my word. I understand your need to have this file, and I'll be sure you get it."

"Thank you, ma'am. I appreciate that." Georgia gave a friendly smile. She didn't care what Burnlee and the others thought about how much attention she did and didn't pay to Steel. She wanted Steel to know that the pushback was from the others and had nothing to do with her.

GORDON THOMPSON READ the news of Richard Lyle's death in a copy of the *Daily Mail* someone had left behind at the Potted Cobbler, an old Tudor pub he regularly stopped at in Tewkesbury on his way to and from Heaton's stables where he'd been up feeding the dogs. The news of Richard's death, the police manhunt for his aunt's Volvo: it was too much for Gordon. He was well aware who had done this and knew what it meant.

It had been years since Gordon had cried—maybe as far back as when Helen, his vivacious wife, Kate's mother, had passed. Maybe it was when he realized once and for all that Kate was staying in America, that he was indeed a man alone. It had been that long. Yet now, here, he felt like bawling.

He blamed himself. He had done this; he had killed Richard Lyle. He had adored him, for years. Richard had become his link to Kate, who was his link to Helen, who was his last bond to his mother, his final connection to his father, now both gone so long that Gordon some days couldn't even remember what they sounded like or even looked like.

Richard had been one of the last people left alive whom Gordon cared about. He felt a woozy kind of weak as he left the Cobbler heading south. He tried to drive but couldn't. This was his fault. There was no one else to blame. He had been played by the same slick version of Satan that had been playing him since he was a child: David Heaton.

He stopped by the side of the narrow East Road, heading down just before it merged back with the Trinston Road leading to M45. He drove the car up onto a small grass embankment, toward a rolling, fenced-off blanket of green, got out, and walked in the crisp fresh air that was laced tightly with the acrid smell of fresh cow dung. He stumbled into the field through an ancient easement gate, trying like hell to keep breathing steadily.

Heaton had murdered Richard. He wasn't going to stop. Adam. Kate. The kids. Himself. They all would have to go the way of Richard. There was no one to turn to, either. The police? Gordon knew too well the folly of that.

The press? That would be his only option. It would take a beat, though. In the meantime, he'd have to find Kate and Adam before Heaton did. There was no way he would let Heaton harm his Kate. Trudy. Billy, that fantastic little grandson. No, he'd spend the rest of his life in jail first; he decided that then and there in that hay-strewn field in Tewkesbury.

He and Heaton were done. Forever. "Sir David" was now officially down one porch jockey. Gordon drove back to London, carefully putting together a plan.

They had headed east from Tunbridge Wells and spent the next few days and nights in a small cabin at the far side of a traveler's lodge just west of an area called Lamberhurst. Adam had used Richard Lyle's identification to rent one of the units at the back of the property. They left the cabin rarely, only for the kids to play in a run-down common playground, or for Kate and Trudy to drive to a Tesco for supplies. Adam watched the news whenever the kids were outside, trying to keep as close to real time as he could.

There was chatter on all of the cable outlets, all around the world. The press were hanging on even tighter than Adam. Thankfully, there was still no mention of him, the conference, HGI, Heaton, or, worse, "the Michigan radical that tried to kill the governor." The talk was all politics, terrorism, the health of Lassiter, and who would run the Labour Party in the days ahead.

Inside the press glare, even as the dark drama washed over the airwaves, there were moments of levity that were, of course, lost on Adam. He watched wearily as the world news played and replayed footage of Georgia Turnbull falling asleep in the House of Commons at PMQs as the press heartily enjoyed her quick riposte to the portly opposition leader.

It was the evening of their fourth night at the cabin when it became time to leave. The *Daily Mail* had the story of Richard's murder. The killers were said to have escaped in Richard Lyle's aunt's 1969 Volvo, of which the paper ran a photo. It wouldn't be long before someone recognized the antique Volvo in front of the cabin. Adam figured that the powers that be were by now on the trail. For some reason the media had been left to twist in the wind as he was quietly hunted. He knew it wouldn't be long, and even if the government didn't make a formal statement, the media horde would put it together soon enough. The connection to the Heaton Global conference and "the nutter from Michigan" would be a new pail of chum for the sharks any hour now. In the meantime, he was checked into the lodge as Richard Lyle, a man who had been recently shot through the head, and was driving an old car being sought by the authorities and the press. They had to leave. Now.

They had nowhere else to go so they headed back, west and north, toward London. The best plan he could muster was to see Beau and Tiffany in Shoreditch.

ADAM MADE KATE promise not to say a word to Tiffany. The kids wouldn't because they were embarrassed, he knew that—embarrassed and in shock at the thought that their father may once again be involved in an intense criminal scandal. No, the kids weren't going to be a problem. It was Kate. She would crack soon. It was only a matter of time before she lost her composure, said something to someone she shouldn't say. He could feel her, a dam ready to burst.

As they neared London, Adam had a troubling thought: Gordon. He broke an icy spell of silence that had persisted since Lamberhurst.

"Does your father know where Beau and Tiffany live? Does he know anything about them?"

"No. Why would he?"

"I don't know. Have you ever mentioned them to him? I need to know if he knows anything about Beauregard, about us having friends in Shoreditch. I don't want to be surprised again by Heaton's thugs." What he really wanted to say was that he didn't want to get Beauregard and his family killed.

"No, my father doesn't know about them. I've never breathed a word to him about them."

"How do you know? How can you be so sure?" She took a moment, then finally spoke, as if telling a truth on herself she hadn't intended on sharing.

"Because I didn't tell him on purpose, from the beginning, when we made friends in Michigan."

He turned to his wife. She sat in severe rigidity. Her skin was tight, her jawline hard. She was bracing herself, preparing to put the ice wall back up, yet still trying to stay in the moment with him, trying to be there for all of them as they drove into a chapter of their lives that had nothing good to offer.

"I didn't want him to be jealous that I had made friends with people from home. I know that sounds stupid, but you need to remember how wounded he was that I wasn't coming back to Britain, that I was firm set on living in America forever."

"He could have easily hopped on a plane, you know. All those years, it wasn't all on us. Other people do it all the time, visit family far away." Kate nodded. It wasn't a debate she wished to pursue. Whatever had gone wrong between her father and her had happened too long ago, and too far away. Gordon's actions in the present were enough to upset her for a lifetime; she couldn't be bothered with what did or didn't happen almost twenty years ago.

ADAM AND KATE and the kids dropped in unannounced at the McCalisters' flat at around eleven p.m. Beau and Tiffany were, to say the least, shocked. In the age of smartphones, people don't just surprise one another, and certainly not whole families. Adam quietly pulled Beau aside and explained that there was trouble, that they needed a place to stay until he could sort things out. Beau didn't blink; Tiffany wasn't the least bit fazed, either. She just turned and headed toward a closet full of spare sheets and blankets.

Within minutes the Tatums had taken over the guest room. The kids would sleep on the floor in sleeping bags; Adam and Kate would have the lumpy oversized spare bed. Beau and Tiff quietly checked in with each other when they were first briefly alone. It was fine. They both assumed that Adam had lost his job. Somewhere in the back of his mind, Beau wondered if the bombing had something to do with their stricken visitors. Perhaps, he thought, the unexpected event had crimped Heaton Global's business model, which would then have adversely affected Adam. In no way could Beauregard imagine the real reason the Tatum family was on their own, lost, slightly disheveled, knocking on the door of his seventh-floor flat in the middle of the night.

Adam suggested that he and Beau take a ride around the city. He needed some time to unload and strategize. He spoke in short, clipped, grim clouds of speech, his voice for some reason slower and an octave lower than Beau remembered it being. Of course he said yes. It was obvious that Adam was in the middle of something profound. Who could say no to a friend in a moment like this?

When they got to the curb, Adam walked over to the old brown beat-up Volvo.

"Where the hell did you get this one, Adam? It's got to be thirty years since it's had a car wash."

"It belonged to Kate's old boyfriend. We had to borrow it. Can you follow me for a while in your car? I need to get rid of this and then I can't walk back or take a bus or the Tube. Too many cameras."

"Too many cameras? . . . I don't get it. What are you afraid of?"

"I'm afraid of everything."

"What's going on, Adam?"

"I'm gonna tell you. I just need to get rid of this car first. Can you follow me?" Beau thought quickly and nodded yes. He wasn't sure how many more yeses he could offer, but he got his car from the building garage and followed Adam in the old Volvo out into the London night.

They drove through Shoreditch and snaked their way down toward the river on Brick Lane into Osborn Street, taking every turn as if Adam knew precisely where they were going, but he didn't have a clue. He just drove, wanting to put as much distance between Beau's house and the car when he dumped it, but without going too far away, not wanting to be spotted or stopped on a long ride back. Beau played along, following in his car. He wanted to ring Adam on his mobile but knew Adam had "lost" his phone, so he put up with the wild, curious drive for as long as it would last.

When they hit Wapping Gardens, a block or two north of the river,

Adam ducked into the parking lot of a block of council flats and found
an empty spot. He waited for Beau to pull in, got out, and jumped into
the passenger side of Beau's car. There was nothing to take: what luggage
and supplies they had, along with Richard's father's shotgun and pistol,
were all hidden in the guest room back at the McCalisters' flat. Adam
even left the key in the ignition.

"Go. Quick. Take off." Beau looked at him and wasn't sure for a second that this wasn't a put-on. Adam locked weary eyes with Beau and
told him with a look that there was no punch line coming.

"Drive, Beau. Please, let's go." Beau pulled out. Adam burrowed low
into the depths of the bucket seat. The streetlights came and went; the
car interior flickered between piercing brightness and calming dark,
surfing from one pool of light to the next as they drove away from the
Thames.

"What is it, Adam? Tell me what's going on." They barreled ahead,
taking one short turn after another, slithering through the empty city
streets. Sometime later, about halfway to Shoreditch, Adam told Beau
the whole sordid tale, beat for beat, the unvarnished truth. He had nothing to hide; there was no reason to leave anything out, so he didn't.

The BBC ran an hour-long special on the life of Georgia Turnbull, a what-if on the woman who very well may become the next prime minister. A week and a day had passed since the explosion and the press had no choice but to focus on a presumptive successor. Georgia was clearly the most attractive. The inevitable comparisons were slapped into place to underline her Thatcheresque humble origins, right down to the shopkeeper father and the stern, steady rise to power. Much was made about the way she would rule, with whom she would govern, and even who would rue the day she came to power. It was sensational, tawdry, speculative, and completely compelling.

Steel watched from her family's flat in Bloomsbury with her parents. She tried her best to be blasé. She wanted so badly to tell her mother how well she thought she knew "Georgia"; how strong she felt the bond between them had grown; and, yes, how madly in love she thought she had fallen. She said nothing. She watched coolly, playing the part of a detached co-worker who had no real opinion one way or the other on the famous woman being profiled.

It was later, alone in her bed, in the dark, while she thought of gently kissing the chancellor's naked body, her head arched back deep into her pillow, when she finally let her face show how truly enthralled she was with all things Georgia Turnbull.

———

THE NEXT MORNING Davina woke early and drove down to the Kensington Palace Gardens to wait for Heaton. She stood stoically beside a patrol car, her hat off, her short fine hair blowing in the wind, as Heaton's driver pulled out on the way to Number 10. If she wasn't going to be included in the discussion among Heaton, Turnbull, Darling, and the home secretary, she wanted some shelf space inside his mind. She wanted him to know that she would be there when it came time to arrest him, when it came time to put him into the pit at the end of this ordeal, when she finally placed the last piece of the puzzle and saw the unmistakable figure of a man who had betrayed his country.

She followed closely in traffic as Harris steered the way through Knightsbridge, down the back of Belgravia, behind Buckingham Palace to the Birdcage Walk, and finally onto Whitehall. Any chance she could, she'd have her patrolman driver pull up next to them, and she'd sweetly half smile at Heaton and nod as he proudly nodded back. He was so clever, so calm, so confident that this would end well for him. She needed him to know that it wouldn't. True, it didn't seem to faze him, his grin as cocksure as ever, but she knew it made a dent. He would fold, Heaton. He would crumple one day soon. She was convinced of it.

She chuckled to herself at the last traffic light when she saw Peet in the passenger seat up front and realized his shoulder was bound tight in a sling. He had taken a bullet, she had no doubt. Tatum had scored a hit. She couldn't help but feel a devious sense of joy. When Harris turned the freshly washed Mercedes onto Whitehall and then quickly onto Downing Street, Steel and her patrolman slogged on up along the bottom of the busy boulevard. She had done what she needed to do. The rest was in the capable hands of her lovely partner Ms. Georgia Turnbull.

"I'M TELLING YOU, Georgia, we are all sick about this. Everyone at Heaton Global, from myself on down. It's a heartbreaker is what it is." Heaton's cologne was stronger than Georgia had ever noticed it to be before. She had known him for years, even went out on a few unmemorable dates in the late nineties, and had always been aware of his propensity to wear too much cologne, but this was a lot, even for Heaton. She couldn't help but wonder if it were because he was nervous, if the thought of this "sit-down" had gotten under his skin.

"We hired this man as a courtesy to my oldest friend in the world, Gordon Thompson, after his son-in-law had had some legal trouble in Michigan, and I had little idea, by the way, what that entailed. He subsequently went to work for our Chicago office. At best reports he did well there, and somehow or another Thompson got him along on this delegation we took here. Again, I didn't know the man, had never set eyes on him until a few days before the final conference." Heaton felt the weight of uncertainty in the room, the pressure to force some version of the truth about Tatum, about Heaton's connection to him.

"Georgia, ask yourself, how well do you remember the man in that meeting?"

"Not at all. I don't recall him saying a word."

"That's because he didn't. Nor to me, before or after. To this day here, I still have no idea how he got anything in or was able to leave anything behind."

Darling had the answer at the ready. "It was inside a large notebook that was left behind and placed in the cupboard—the dossier that you had instructed Lassiter to look over personally."

"Before I could get to it," Georgia added. All eyes were watching Heaton as closely as humanly possible, hoping for a telltale sign of inconsistency, a hint of deviousness or deception. Heaton remained calm, steadfast in his own victimization in the matter.

"You must believe that we were all floored when this came out, of his past, of his complicity in this, of these threats he had made toward Roland on the Internet. It just defies logic how this could be the truth. No one who worked with him at the company has anything at all to report in terms of untoward behavior, deviancy, or the slightest hint of aggression. Nothing. By all reports that we have put together, he was a very, very personable man. Quite charming in fact. Yes, he had been in some trouble in Michigan, but somehow or other, which we can only blame on his father-in-law, he had been able to hide the full nature of his legal transgression from the Chicago human resources people when Thompson first got him his interview."

"So you're saying that Gordon Thompson was able to get him in under the wire in terms of a background check?"

"Yes. Sadly, that is what I am saying. HGI is a very large company. Too large, maybe, it now seems." Georgia listened as Heaton spoke, leaned back on the couch, and tried her best to take it all in.

"So you're thinking that the father-in-law conspired? Is involved in the bombing? In whatever is behind this?"

"And where is this Thompson now?" Darling wanted to know.

"He's been up at my farm. Outside Worcestershire. He's supposed to be back in London today. We'll be doing an inquiry ourselves after we've made him available to your people to question. That takes place at one p.m. at Scotland Yard." Georgia looked over to Darling for confirmation. Darling agreed, the meeting was set, but he seemed troubled. None of this seemed to sit well with the grizzled Darling.

"And tell us again, David. Why had you asked Mr. Lassiter to look into the brief? What was it that you wanted him to see before Georgia got to it?"

"That was merely business, Major Darling. We had spent three years on a deal to more or less privatize a financial service system that has done nothing but given its members short shrift in terms of retirement packages. I just wanted Roland's help in putting the whole thing to bed. You see that, don't you?"

Darling answered halfheartedly. "No, actually, I don't entirely. What is it that you wanted Roland's help with?" Heaton took the query in, actually chuckled slightly.

"Well, I hate to say it like this, but I needed him to help me sell Georgia. She's a tough one to get over and was the final hurdle. No one could work the good chancellor over quite like Roland. I begged him to put his back into it, so to speak."

Darling followed the answer with another nod, yet still, for some reason, didn't quite see it as true.

Something seemed off to Burnlee as well. His face gave it away. The home secretary, twenty years older than Heaton, Turnbull, and Darling, had known Heaton's father and his uncle, both members of Parliament in their day. In fact, the uncle, Edmund Heaton, had once held Burnlee's title. He was a wary watcher, Burnlee, and didn't say much in moments like these. He let others do the talking so that he could hear between the banter. His way had always been to listen to the larger tone of the room and not the short bursts of words that were thrown fast and loose around this storied building. His stony silence hinted at his suspicions. Heaton was lying. Burnlee had no doubt.

"Maybe it's an American thing. Has anyone put any thought to that?" Heaton quietly asked. Georgia and the others were stunned.

"An American thing? What could that possibly mean?"

"He's an ex-cop, maybe he's CIA. I don't know. I am aware that the Americans would love us off our balance right now. I know they aren't anywhere close to fans of Roland's. I know they'd love a freer hand in the Middle East and I know they'd love the referendum to work out and for us to leave the EU. Let that money and those contracts flow west to New York and Los Angeles. It's wild speculation but what isn't about all of this, really? What if the CIA got to Gordon Thompson, paid him to set up his son-in-law, then planned to nicely do away with them both?"

"That's rich pudding. As far out as it gets," Burnlee protested.

"I agree, but it's all rich pudding at this point. Isn't it? None of this makes any sense."

The room went quiet. There were no more questions. Heaton didn't have any other theories. Georgia politely ended the talk.

After Heaton left the PM's office, an accounting was taken, and Georgia and Darling agreed with the home secretary. Heaton hadn't uttered a single truthful sentence. They sat in silence, wondering who would say it first: Heaton, and whoever his conspirators might be, had sought to destroy the government from the inside. This was officially a national disaster. It was no longer speculation. If Heaton was involved, then he had key insiders helping him. The brazenness of the attempt was breathtaking. Darling and Burnlee were both sure of it.

Georgia's worst nightmares had sprung fully formed into an awful reality.

IN THE BLACKEST hour of the morning, Georgia was awake, lying in bed, wondering where this would end, where tomorrow would take them. She truly had if not the weight of the world, then the weight of Great Britain on her shoulders.

Her thoughts wandered and settled on Steel. She wondered if the young detective realized what murky waters she had waded into. She wanted to chat quietly with her about how scary the world had suddenly become, to speak of the events on the scale of their national gravity, but more important, she wanted to speak in shades of the personal and intimate, in terms of being a frightened girl, wide-eyed inside a woman's body. Steel would understand that, she thought. She would understand and maybe softly brush Georgia's face with the back of her tiny hand. Maybe kiss the tip of her nose and slowly run her fingers through Georgia's thick hair. They would lock eyes and discuss the gravity of being caught up by history. She sat up, pulled her knees close, and thought of calling Steel, and then, when the impulse grew and took hold she went over and grabbed her phone and brought it back to the warm bed with her, burrowed back in, and phoned Steel.

"Hello?" Steel heard her mobile buzz on the nightstand next to the bed. She woke from a deep sleep. She had been dreaming of skiing in America with her parents, who were both somehow younger and incredibly adroit at downhill. She woke so quickly that she remembered the incongruent fantasy and was still living it for a beat as she reached for the phone.

"Hello." It was Georgia, according to the caller ID. But her voice seemed different. She spoke quietly, more slowly than usual. "I'm so sorry to wake you, Inspector Steel."

"No, no. Don't be sorry at all. Is everything all right?"

"As all right as it can be, what with the world as it is."

"Yes, I can only imagine what you have on your plate. I shudder to think of it in terms of a workday."

Georgia took a moment to answer. She sipped cold water from a cut crystal glass at her bedside. "It's beyond madness, Inspector. I can't begin to tell you. It feels like a mountain has slid right over on top of me." Steel nodded silently. *What must that be like? To be suddenly thrust into this position, where everything comes down to you? Every decision that's made is yours to make, yours to muck up?*

"You must feel so alone right now." A tear rolled down Georgia's cheek as a response. Steel didn't need to see the tear to understand the silence floating along the line. The pain she heard in Georgia's voice.

"Is there anything I could do for you? To make it easier? Anything at all, Madam Chancellor?"

"You could call me Georgia. I do appreciate hearing you use my name."

"You do? Truly?" That seemed unreal—Georgia Turnbull getting joy from Davina Steel of Bloomsbury addressing her one-to-one, yet she sensed maybe it was the truth.

There was yet another waft of silence between them. Steel's heart was beating wildly as the chancellor spoke to her. "I do enjoy talking with you, Davina. It seems like I have no one to talk with these days. Oh god, how pitiful must that sound?"

"No, no, I feel the same way. I enjoy talking with you, too, Georgia." Somehow saying her name made Steel slightly giggle. Georgia responded with a laugh of her own and it went on that way, the two of them serving back and forth simple rounds of small talk and chitchat. Life. Childhood. Stress. Weight gain. Weight loss. Hair care. Fashion. Dogs. Cats. Tennis. Uncles, aunts, Britain, and even Adam Tatum. They were all touched on for over an hour until suddenly there was silence. Steel waited for her partner's next volley and it didn't come.

"Have you fallen asleep on me? Georgia? Georgia?" After a moment she was back. Her voice was even groggier now.

"Yes, I think I may have. I'm sorry. I don't mean to be rude."

"It's not rude at all. I'm going to let you go. I'm sure you have a full day ahead of you."

"I wish you were . . ." Another silence.

"Wish I was what? Georgia?" She had stopped herself. Steel sensed it. She knew she had stopped because the words that would have come out would have been hard to take back. They would have been too emotional, too laced with longing. They were both better off saying good night, so they did.

"Good night, Georgia."

"Good night, Davina. Thank you for a wonderful talk."

Kate went shopping with Tiffany the next day, who jokingly said she wanted to "show off" the giant Whole Foods on Kensington High Street. It took everything Kate could do to keep from breaking down in tears, but she had promised Adam to keep it together while he figured out their next move. Tiffany made small talk as they squeezed and weighed vegetables and fruit. Kate pondered sadly to herself at how mundane life can be, how rote the day-to-day steps can become, and in the same moment she found herself envious of Tiffany and the uneventful future she would most likely have. She saw her own family's future as cold and unforgiving. She tried to envision a time when she'd casually weigh and bag the evening's vegetables again, but she knew life wouldn't be anywhere close to carefree in the near future, if ever.

As they waited to check out, Tiffany talked about Beau and his ailing father, about living in London, about being an American in Britain, about raising the kids so far from her parents in Indiana. Kate nodded, did her best to carry a small part of the conversation, but all she could think about were the last seven days: Adam forcing them to run, the realization that her father had knowingly set up her family and her for a horrible fall, about Richard, his face in the steamed-up bathroom mirror, his murder, the blood on the courtyard that Adam was sure she didn't see, the fact that she and her family had caused the end of his beautifully awkward one-off of a life, the constant gloom on Adam's face, the way he watched the news with certain knowledge that a wave would wash him away at any time—toss them all away.

KATE FINALLY COULDN'T take it anymore. Interrupting another one of Tiffany's anecdotes about her kids, she started to cry, a deep, guttural moan that took her breath away as the car rolled along on the pock-marked roads back toward Shoreditch.

Tiffany jerked the family's BMW wagon over to the side of the street. She had felt the sullen, sour air floating around Kate and the family since the moment they had arrived, but this level of anguish was well beyond her expectations. Tiffany had no idea what to say. She figured it best just to let her cry it out.

"It's okay, it's okay, Kate, just let it out. Let it out, babe." That was really the best that she could do. Kate squeaked out a silent thank-you and did in fact "let it out." She cried for another few minutes until there were no more tears. As Tiffany warmly took her hand, Kate did the one thing she promised her husband she wouldn't do. She told Tiffany everything.

LATER THAT NIGHT, after a silent dinner where none of the adults spoke, while the kids hypnotically watched a Pixar film they had each seen a dozen times before, Beau spoke candidly with Adam on a leisurely walk in the early evening among the cold, tan brick buildings of Great Eastern Street.

"I'm afraid you're going to have to leave, Adam. Tiffany's upset and she has every right to be. No matter how innocent you are, you're going to be the prime suspect any moment now and you know as well as I do that hiding you here will be a crime. There'll be a steep price for us to pay, even if you somehow wriggle out of this godforsaken nightmare."

Adam understood. He'd seen it coming the minute Tiffany walked through the door from her excursion with Kate that afternoon. It made sense, too. They couldn't afford to drag the McCalisters into their mess. It had already cost Richard Lyle his life.

An old woman was digging through a garbage can outside a block of

office suites, hunting for recyclables. Two young boys on bikes were spinning circles in the middle of the turnoff to Garden Walk. No one seemed
happy. Not the boys on the bikes, not the pedestrians on the street, not
the people on the buses that floated by. It was if the whole city had been
robbed of joy along with Adam and his family. He had taken the ultimate darkness to Richard Lyle, dimmed the lights of the McCalisters'
life, and now it seemed as if he were soaking the entire city, blocks at a
time, with despair. He was cursed. He felt that then, in that moment,
with his friend who desperately needed to distance himself from Adam
and his doomed family.

"Just give me the night to figure out what to do, Beau. We'll leave
tomorrow. I think that I have a plan. Just give me the night to come to
terms with it."

Beau answered sincerely. "I'm sorry, Adam. I truly am. If there was
anything I could think of to do for you, I would do it."

Adam nodded as they kept walking. He searched as intently as he could
through the windows of pubs and restaurants to find one person laughing,
even smiling. No one was. The curse of Adam Tatum loomed like a thick
cloud over Shoreditch. It would stay there for as long as he remained.

WITH THE FIRST light of day, Beau's family BMW wagon pulled up to
the main pavilion of the sparkling new American embassy in the Nine
Elms area of London. The embassy, recently opened, looked like an
installation dropped to Earth from another planet. It was a large gleaming
cube sitting proudly, defiantly secure, looking out onto the river, daring
anyone to breach its perimeter. Adam and his family got out of the car
with the few handbags they had left. Richard's father's guns had been
thrown away in a trash can on the ride down.

Adam thanked Beau again. Kate gave him a warm hug. There was
no need for small talk. Beau got back into his car and drove off with his
normal stoic grace. Adam solemnly led his wife and the kids across the
street, up to the pavilion, eager to throw himself at the mercy of his government; to have his family taken from the country, and for him to be
put into a jail cell for God knows how long. This was his best-case scenario: an unknown time in a series of prisons, maybe even for the rest

of his life. It was the most he could hope for unless the curtain opened to expose Heaton and what he'd done.

As they crossed the street, Trudy heard someone call out her name.

"Trudy. Trudy . . . My love. Please . . ." She turned around to see Étienne standing beside a Heaton-issued Mercedes. She stopped in her tracks, the very sight of him stirring her, causing her to flutter. Despite knowing all that she did, she crossed the street toward him. There was so much she wanted to ask him, so much she wanted to say. Her heart had taken control of her feet.

Adam and Kate both turned back a beat later, already well on the way to the front gate of the embassy. Adam instinctively knew someone had lagged behind. When they saw Trudy, crossing over to Étienne at the Mercedes, with Harris and Peet, Heaton's gunmen, now stepping out of the car, all he could do was scream at the top of his lungs.

"Trudy. Trudy, no! Stop!" She turned back in the middle of the street; her father's voice had broken the trance. She saw the fear in his pleading eyes as he and Kate, with Billy in tow, raced back to the street for her. The lovelorn teen knew in an instant, when she saw Harris and Peet shuffling menacingly toward her, that she had made a grave error. She was about to run for her parents and try her best to get away when another Mercedes barreled up the road and stopped in between her and the Heaton men. It was her grandfather, Gordon.

He slammed the brakes in the middle of the road, his window rolled down, and called to his granddaughter.

"Get in love, quickly." He reached back and opened the rear door. Harris and Peet, whose shoulder was still in a sling, were on their way over, her parents coming up from the other side. She jumped into the car. Gordon stepped out; in a blur he threw his arm over the roof of the car and fired a pistol toward Harris and Peet. They both ducked for cover, buying Adam, Kate, and Billy time to get over to the car. Gordon turned to them, his face as sour and hardened as either of them had ever seen him.

"Get in the car. Now!"

Adam tried to reason with him. "We're going to the embassy, Gordon, and I'm turning myself in." Gordon turned back and fired off another two rounds in an effort to keep Harris and Peet on the back of their ankles.

"It's a mistake. You're playing with people that can melt minds inside of that place. Top-drawer people. You're in real rough waters, son. This isn't the plan. I have one. I promise. Get in." He turned to Kate. She was staring at him in a disgusted way that made his heart drop to his groin, little Billy burrowed into her side, scared out of his young mind, looking up in confusion at his now gun-crazed granddad.

"Trust me, Kate, you need to get into the car. Right now. On your mother's soul, I've nothing but your best here. Get in!" She turned to Adam right as Harris found a parked car to hide behind and shot off his revolver, smashing out Gordon's side window. A siren went off at the embassy. Red lights flashed on the gates. It would be mere seconds before the street would rain with embassy soldiers pouring out of the intergalactic cube at the top of the plaza.

Adam nudged Kate and a crying Billy into the back of the car with Trudy. He jumped in behind them as Gordon tore away up the street under a storm of gunfire coming from both Harris and Peet. The Mercedes raced through the back streets, snaking its way up to Battersea Park Road. Gordon pulled out a manila folder and threw it back to Adam, who was huddled up into a ball doing his best to calm his terrified family down.

"It's passports. The best fakes money can buy. I have a friend. He's putting a boat together on the west coast to get across the St. George Channel to Bray. From Bray, you'll cross over to Galway. We'll get you on a cruise ship to New York." Adam opened the envelope. He found the passports with all of their photos and an impressive amount of cash: the Davis family from Greenwich.

Gordon punched the car now and made a final speedy tear on the pavement until he came up to the intersection at Queenstown Road. Then he made a sharp, squealing turn. Kate spoke for the first time.

"How did you know that we would go to the embassy?" She was probing. Still not ready to trust him.

"I didn't. Harris did. Heaton did. I've just been following them. I knew job one for them was to find you. They've been here on and off waiting for you for two days. Figured I'd be here when they finally caught up with you." He turned down a small street, went slowly under an old brick railway underpass, and parked the car.

"First thing we need to do is get you as far away from London as we can." He jumped out of the Mercedes and motioned for the family to follow him across to a late-seventies Volkswagen van, also parked in the shadowy tunnel of the overpass. It was loaded down with fishing rods and family bikes, folded easy chairs strapped to the roof, fishing licenses, and ripped remnants of semi-funny bumper stickers plastered all over the front. Adam instructed the group to do as Gordon said. They piled into the dusty old hippie wagon. Gordon put on a large, oddly shaped fishing hat. Adam sat in the front seat as his father-in-law handed him another version of the same silly cap.

He turned back to his granddaughter.

"There's a bag of sandwiches in that cooler there, luv. Some drinks, too, and a couple of travel games I picked up for you kids." He caught Kate's eyes in the rearview mirror and winked at her as he turned the van back, slowly ambling onto Battersea Park Road in the very same direction that they had come from.

The other lane was filled with police and embassy vehicles barreling by them, lights and sirens, shouting and dancing. Two embassy helicopters were escorting the squad cars with a wild windy whip from a hundred yards above the earth as Gordon slowly wheeled the van away, right under their noses.

Kate wasn't sure yet what to make of it all, what colors she wanted to show to this new rendition of her father, but inside, in her heart, she was smiling for the first time in over a week.

In yet another meeting in the Cabinet Room the next morning, Munroe and Burnlee wanted Georgia to agree to allow Munroe to release Adam Tatum's name and likeness to the ravenous press corps. It was high time to tell the whole story and hopefully tighten the net around Tatum and his family. The minister of communications was convinced a loud bang to the announcement would make it not only almost impossible for Tatum to move around, but even more difficult for anyone to quietly dispose of him. Burnlee agreed.

Steel sat in the row against the back wall of the Cabinet Room behind her boss, Major General Sir Donald Darling, who was noncommittal, almost quietly mumbling to himself. He seemed to be taking the hardest brunt of the nine days since the bombing, and the fact that Tatum was still out there, he and whomever he was working with, thwarting the ex-soldier, the decorated Gulf War vet. They were razzing their noses at Darling with each day he was left twiddling his thumbs. He sat in the chair fuming, his close-cropped hair almost melting into his forehead. No one could feel the major general's helplessness like Steel could.

Steel was, of course, also strongly attuned to Georgia's tension. She looked across the table and thought the chancellor appeared at times to be underwater with the weight of it all, almost drowning. She sounded different than she did with her on the phone last night. Last night before she passed out, she had a vibrancy to her voice. The conversation gave her an energy and a vitality that her tone didn't seem to regularly have these days, or even this morning. Last night at the height of their talk Georgia seemed to have a strength that was bigger than all of the problems at Number 10.

"Have we covered ourselves with the Americans? With the White House?" Georgia asked. Burnlee nodded. He was a pro. Always several steps ahead. "I had a long talk last night with Elliott Anderson, the president's new chief of staff. He called me early this morning. We're on the same page. They just want to be kept up to speed."

"Do I need to call the president?"

"No. She's well aware of where we are at." Georgia took it all in. If she was going to be the prime minister, she was going to need to start out on the right side with America's historic female president. She didn't want to kick off a new relationship on a sour note, yet at the same time, she needed to find this Tatum. It had already gone on way too long.

"Good. Let's go then. Inform the public on everything there is to know about Adam Tatum. I want his picture on every TV show, website, magazine cover, storefront, and smartphone in Britain. Enough is enough. Let's put the people to it. Let's find this man."

As the conference room dispersed, Georgia couldn't help herself any longer. Knew full well she was in full view of Burnlee, Darling, Early, and other staffers, yet she was well beyond being in control of herself in matters pertaining to Steel.

"Inspector Steel? Might I just have a quick word with you? In my office?" Darling looked over with a question mark embossed on his face. Georgia answered before he could move his lips. Before either he or Burnlee could form a pair of complaints.

"I'd just like a moment alone with the inspector. Nothing pressing. Just a girl thing." She smiled and casually walked out of the conference room.

Steel looked over to Darling and the others with a shrug, trying as hard as she could to look as if she had no idea what this could possibly be about.

———

ONCE IN THE PM's office, as Davina followed her in, as she closed the door behind Steel and her palms broke into a sweat, she turned back to Steel, hoping she could remain calm.

"I just wanted you to know, Davina, that I so, so truly enjoyed our phone visit last night."

"As did I, Madam Chancellor. The time just flew by, didn't it?"

"Georgia. Please." She playfully scolded her. "When we're alone, 'Georgia.' Okay, Davina? I told you, I really do love to hear you say my name."

"Of course. Georgia."

"Thank you. These are loaded times, aren't they?" Georgia stepped closer to her. "Loaded days. Everything is so full of peril. Laced with purpose. Sometimes, just to talk, just to not say anything important for once, it's invigorating." She hadn't planned to, but she was stroking Steel's hair now, gently pulling a strand down the soft side of her face. Steel responded with a noticeable deep breath. She gently touched Georgia's arm, and before either of them could check the moment for sanity, Georgia leaned in and kissed her.

She sweetly brushed their lips together, then thankfully, Georgia pulled away. They just looked at each other, for what seemed like the longest time. The moment was broken by a small knock at the door and the head of one of Early's perky blondes who had come in with a sheath of papers.

"Excuse me, ma'am. I have the notes from Treasury's meeting this morning."

Georgia barely turned to her, hardly took her gaze off Steel.

"Yes, thank you. Just place it on the desk." The staffer did as she was told and quickly made an exit.

It was just Steel and Georgia again, the only difference being the half-opened door. It was enough, thought Georgia. She had said what she had wanted to say, had done what she wanted to do. She and Steel nodded to each other. They took each other's hands, squeezed them both together. Steel turned and left as Georgia leaned against her desk, trying to figure a way to get her head wrapped around the job at hand.

———

NOT MORE THAN an hour later, in Heaton's den atop the Farringdon Street HGI complex, Sir David sat quietly with Harris, Peet, and two others. Rebecca, his office aide, brought in a tray of drinks on a Lucite cart, along with a plate of scones. Heaton had been in Strasbourg in the evening and his new home in Switzerland after that, and then quickly back to London. The long day and night of constant movement had taken its toll. The whole week was bringing him down, deflating his normally swelled-out chest. He hadn't slept in four nights. His frustration had boiled over. Harris and Peet knew it. The two, never ones to waste words either, had none to offer. They had both thought the job at hand would have been much easier than it had turned out to be. They knew Heaton well enough to know that bad had turned worse. They were rarely, if ever, brought into the den like this.

"Gordon Thompson has gone underground. He was supposed to have come down from the farm; I had him up there with the dogs as the care-takers are in Zurich opening my house for the season. He was to be here yesterday, to make a statement to the police. It was set up through Darling and the DPG. He was a no-show. It means he's left the squad. I'm sure of it." The men in the room nodded. They understood the severity of what Heaton was saying.

"I've known this man for too many years. I underestimated him. I thought he'd stay good through to the end, but in fact there isn't the stomach there." He got up and paced the small den, almost talking to himself, trying to figure out how he had got himself into the present fix.

"I should have done this quicker. Bolder. I should have known he'd jam the works. This needed to be all put to bed on the very night that it started. My mistake was wanting him spared. Now he'll do what he can to thwart all this and I'll pay for it from the others. I'll bear the brunt if it can't be fixed."

He looked over the four men in the room: Peet and Harris, his two top men; and two younger men, Dorman and Childs, both tall, lithe, and coldhearted. This would be the foursome that decided his future. If they couldn't fix this now, not later, not in days or weeks but now, it would be over for Heaton. He would be a ruined man. Everything he had and more would be taken, he'd be labeled a traitor, and most likely he would spend the rest of his life in a prison cell. Four men stood between him and a personal apocalypse.

Why? Because he loved his country. That's why he'd pay. Because men forty some odd years ago had started to slowly give it away, parcel it off, soul first, body second—men his father saw as traitors, men so addicted to empire that they'd trade away country, trade it for money, for power, for Europe, for crumbs. This was what Heaton and the others wanted. They wanted England back. Were they criminals? Traitors? So be it. Lassiter clearly felt the strong winds that demanded a referendum and yet couldn't be bothered to muster up the passion to let the people vote. He had to be removed. There was no way around it.

Heaton knew what Gordon Thompson would be planning right now, working on getting his family, his son-in-law included, out of country. Heaton had resources all tethered together, all in sync, but the clock had run out. He had just gotten a quiet call letting him know that moments earlier, Munroe and Burnlee had talked Georgia Turnbull into releasing Tatum's name to the press and to the world. The odds of Heaton's men finding the Tatums before the authorities did had grown very long indeed, but he could not give up now. These four men had to understand that they were his last chance.

He took a small manila envelope off the coffee table and pulled out a photograph, a frame from a security camera.

"This is from the caretaker's lodge in Worcestershire last night." He passed it around the den. It showed Gordon, Adam, Kate, and the two kids, getting out of a run-down camper's van.

"He went straight back up. He knew no one would be there. It's just them and the dogs. They won't stay long. He'll move west, I'm sure of it, try to get them over to Ireland, and from there to New York. You have one chance. Tonight. There's no other way. It ends quietly in Worcestershire, for all of them."

The men nodded minimally, as a group, not one of them proud of what they were all agreeing to do, no one wishing to oversell his confidence. They all understood though: they had no room for error. Heaton nodded back. The room cleared quickly. He sat into a padded leather club chair and took a deep, wistful breath. He told himself this could all still be righted. He took another full-bodied breath with shuttered eyes and palms held out flat. *Stay confident.* Then another. In. Out. *Stay clear.* A final deep inhalation, then a vigorous exhale . . . *Stay strong.*

THE BONGO BAR is an odd little joint in Shepherd's Bush, just off Shepherd's Bush Green. It's a trendy little watering hole for young professionals and working singles. What it lacks in volume, it makes up for in a darkened moody ambience, tailor-made to melt away the stress of a long day spent in the throes of industry. Rebecca Donton sat at the bar, her wonderful hair catching the low-wattage bulbs overhead in such a way as to give her a halo effect. Like so much of her life, Rebecca and her long waves of blond beauty looked, as she leaned against the bar sipping a martini, as if she were posing for a magazine ad.

She had come to London from South Africa. Her friends, family, and many strangers had routinely told her how much she resembled a young Charlize Theron. Growing up in the suburb of Lakeside, she was often approached with offers to model or even to take acting lessons. Some were legitimate, some were merely come-ons from local men, and some were from workers at the stable where her mother and father were also employed. She had no interest in modeling or acting. She would leave that to the performers and the poseurs of the world.

She dreamt only of business. She wanted to work in the world of fashion maybe, or sport, or even media, but all from the side of business. It was as far away as she could get, she thought, from the life of her parents who were both third-generation horse groomers. It was a chain she was determined to break.

She earned a degree from a small university in Johannesburg, and with money borrowed from her aunt she traveled to London. After a long year working in a Pret A Manger, she managed to get an interview for an executive assistant position at HGI. It wasn't until her fourth interview that she realized she was being sussed out to be the new first assistant for Sir David Heaton, the world-renowned CEO of Heaton Global.

Once hired her life became, to her, a true fairy tale. If it hadn't turned out to be exactly "high finance" in the sense of what she'd learned at university, the cool factor of having a fold-down seat on the bus alongside Sir David Heaton's larger-than-life reality more than made up for it.

There were private planes, dinner parties, and exquisite celebrity luncheons. Yes, she was the "help," and more than often out in the hallway waiting for Sir Paul McCartney or Sir Bob Geldof to leave Sir David's office, but she was there inside the whirl, living a movie montage of an existence.

Heaton was a taskmaster. She was on call at all hours and was expected to have no life. He rarely showed any interest in who she was or what her opinions were on anything. He paid her more than amply, was always respectful, and although he constantly had a starlet or a model floating in his jet wash, she was never called to take a place under his arm or in his bed. In the early days he had been nothing but professional with her, even on long trips in exciting situations where she would have maybe welcomed a call up to his suite for a champagne ride in his Jacuzzi. It never happened and was never even joked about.

Later, when she had come out to him, in a time when she was in a relationship with a woman she had met at Wimbledon, he was nothing but respectful and supportive. It was a dream job. It had been the best four years of her life. It broke her heart that it would now be over, but she absolutely had no choice.

Inspector Steel arrived at exactly half past eight, as she had said she would over the phone. She ordered a drink for both of them as they took a private booth in the back of the restaurant. They had a run of idle conversation. Steel wasn't exactly unaware of Rebecca's beauty. Under the warm light of an overhanging lamp in the center of the rounded booth, she looked even more radiant than she did in the HGI executive suite. Steel, not usually one to spend too much time or concern on her own looks, had no idea how alluring she herself looked to the young South African. They doubled down on the chitchat, life in London, the differences between London and Johannesburg, and Rebecca's flat nearby in Shepherd's Bush. Steel comically described her life living with her parents and her desperate need to get her own place.

More drinks were ordered. Rebecca considered accidentally dropping the "her" in a story of the relationship with the tennis fan that had just ended, a shot into the air that she was a lesbian, that she was single, but she knew there was serious talk to have, talk that would quash any leanings toward romance, notwithstanding the fact that Rebecca didn't really size Steel up as a woman who would find other women attractive.

It didn't matter. Steel sensed that Rebecca was a gal's gal, not that Steel was herself as a rule. Georgia Turnbull was the third woman she'd had strong feelings for, and the first two were both just more or less fun weekend playdates. Both of them maddeningly adorable, she had immensely enjoyed their quick company, but before Georgia she'd never felt anywhere near close to what she was feeling now.

She could easily see this Rebecca as a plaything, someone who would be fun to giggle and cuddle and tease with if it weren't for Georgia. Georgia had her heart now. She wasn't interested in anyone else, no matter how perfect her hair and teeth were.

"Why don't you tell me why you called, Rebecca? You said it was important."

"It's more than important. I actually feel cheap making small talk. I'm just nervous."

"What is it that you're nervous about?" Rebecca finished her martini and looked around. A young man sat at the bar, in a suit, by himself. She was sure she was overreacting but felt he was watching her; a common occurrence, yes, but tonight she felt a different kind of naked than she normally did when strange men were observing her.

"Could we leave? Go for a walk?" Steel sensed her fear, wanted her comfortable.

"Yes. Let's get out of here."

They walked through Shepherd's Bush. It had rained while they were in the bar but had conveniently let up. The streets glistened sweetly, the moon dancing happily in the reflection of every surface that would have it. The small trees on the roads dripped with tiny drops of a mildly pleasing spray.

"He's involved. I'm sure you must know that." Steel stopped in her tracks. Her heart pounded as the South African beauty slowly began to weep.

"I've known something was up for a bit now. He's been so sullen. There has been so much whispering. So many quiet meetings. Not business meetings. Meetings with men that he uses for his . . . security. Shady characters. You know?" Steel nodded. She knew quite a bit about Heaton's shady characters.

"He's been different. For the last three months or so. On edge. All the time. I travel with him less. Never really know his schedule anymore. Then, a week ago, after the bombing at Number 10, about the time you started coming around, he withdrew completely. I knew. I knew. I could tell." She looked deep into Steel's eyes.

"Today, he was in the den. With all of his security. I brought in a snack. He'd been traveling. He needed to eat. I set the tray down, on the coffee table. The edge of it, I didn't know it, but it had rested on the phone. On the button for the intercom. When I got to my desk, I heard them all, clearly. Was going to get up to let him know, to move the tray, when they started talking about doing this. I couldn't stop listening. I couldn't pretend anymore. I couldn't be around this anymore."

"What is it, love? Tell me. You can. I promise." Rebecca nodded, wanting Steel to know that she trusted her.

"I can't hold this back anymore. I need to tell someone. I don't think they're safe. Any of them. Not even Mr. Thompson."

"You're talking about the Tatums?"

"Yes. Yes . . . I think they're going to kill them. They know where they are."

"Where are they?"

"Up in Worcestershire. At Sir David's farmhouse in Tewkesbury. Dorrington. They're not safe." Steel nodded, her eyes trained on Rebecca's.

"I hope I'm wrong. I could be wrong."

"No, no. You're spot-on. They're not at all safe."

"Can you help? Help them?"

"Yes. I think I can. In fact I'm going to give it everything I have." Rebecca broke out in a sliver of a smile at Steel's confident response. Her eyes brightened as much as they could under the circumstances.

Within another fifteen minutes Steel was in a patrol car with Captains Andrew Tavish and Edwina Wells, heading to the London heliport, bound for Tewkesbury.

Gordon pulled into the winding driveway onto the two-hundred-fifty-year-old estate and rolled past the main house, down a long tractor road, to the caretaker's lodge at the north side of the property. As the shaggy fishing van snaked back toward the cabin, a chain-link fenced pen came into view. It was alive with the rabid energy of eleven catch dogs. Large, angry Cane Corsos, snapping at them as they drove by. Adam thought the beasts looked hungry. Gordon knew full well that they were. In his race to retrieve Kate and the kids, he had forgotten to feed them. He made a mental note, once the family settled into the back lodge, to quell the pack with food.

The caretaker's lodge was sparse, cool, and calm. The steady bark of the hounds was the only sound from outside. The place seemed to be shut down for the season. Gordon explained that the caretakers were in Switzerland opening Heaton's summer home. He had been the only one up here for the last month or so, only to feed the dogs and walk the property, scouting for any problems to report to the maintenance crews down in London. He had come to like the lonely, quiet work. In the last six months, as Heaton and his world grew increasingly crazed, Gordon preferred the solitude nestled inside the three hundred acres, with the stars in the sky at night and the birds in the trees come morning—just the dogs and him.

He had stocked the kitchen in advance of bringing Kate and the grandkids up. He showed them around the sparsely furnished maintenance lodge. He gave Kate and Adam the nicest bedroom suite and told them to get some rest while he organized his plans to get them over to Ireland and then back home. He had Adam stow the fishing van in a garage by the dog pound while he backed out a new Mercedes station wagon that they would load in the morning and take to the west coast. He was trying desperately, with actions rather than words, to show Adam that he had been played as badly, if not worse, than Adam himself had been.

Something about the way that Adam went along with the preparations told Gordon that his son-in-law seemed to understand, if not condone, the actions Gordon had been forced to take. The ice was still there between them, but perhaps it had begun to thaw. He hoped he'd soon feel the same energy from his grandson and, even more important, his daughter.

Later that night, with Kate and the kids in bed, while he and Gordon nursed some of Heaton's scotch, Adam saw the latest chum that Downing Street had thrown to the world's media. They had released his name and face. He was on every channel. CNN was interviewing everyone he ever knew about the "attempted murder" at the governor's office in Michigan: all of his old friends, and they even got to Jenny Plena, his high school girlfriend, who told through tears about Adam bringing flowers to her mother on her deathbed.

Every channel would be running the story for hours, fueled by photos, testimony, theories, and profiles. By morning there wouldn't be a soul on Earth who wouldn't know his name.

This latest news had taken Adam lower than Gordon had ever seen him. As he pried himself up off the couch, Gordon took the remote and shut the television off. He put his arm on Adam's shoulder.

"It's gonna be okay, boy. We have a plan, we stick with it." Adam nodded. It made sense but he couldn't picture the end, couldn't imagine a time when he walked away from all of this, from his mistake in Michigan, from the fugitive version of himself that he saw on the news. However efficient a plan they made, it all seemed pointless, like a fire drill in a town about to be nuked.

———————

EARLY THE NEXT morning, Gordon, standing in the kitchen, could hear Kate's feet moving on the thin wooden floor above him. He made a fresh pot of coffee and put out a pitcher of orange juice. He sat at the table and waited for her to come down. When she did, as she poured herself a cup of coffee, he opened his heart and hoped for the best.

"Kate, please know I would never have knowingly put you or Adam or my grandchildren in any harm. I'd rather die a thousand deaths than to have that on my head. I was duped. I am an old fool. All I wanted was for you to smile once in my direction, to be happy and know that maybe I was part of the cause. I thought I was doing a good thing getting Adam in with Heaton. I swear to you, darling, on the grave of your beautiful mother, I swear it's the truth." Kate turned to look at her father seated at the table. He seemed smaller now than he ever had. His eyes red with anguish. His hands bent inward from stress.

She walked over to the table and kissed his wrinkled forehead sweetly. She could almost feel her kiss melt his aching limbs. She sat down with her coffee next to him and took his hand. He leaned down and kissed hers. A tear sat solemnly on his bottom eyelid.

"All I've done for years is miss you, girl. Miss you, miss your mum."

"I know, Daddy. I know."

"When this is all over, when I get you and the family out, when I clean up my side of the street, I want to come over. To Chicago. I don't need to live underfoot. I have money. I'll get a place. I'll start a new life. I've been a fool. I should have done it years ago, but I thought I couldn't leave England. Thought I'd be leaving your mother, my mum, my dad. I could feel them here still, but I can't now, you see? I don't feel them anymore."

She hugged him. He wept outright. They held each other with bittersweet joy. There was nothing to be happy about in either of their lives, but this moment here had waited patiently to arrive, so they each danced in it warmly, hungry for any bit of light they could find.

Steel and Captains Andrew Tavish and Edwina Wells arrived at the south side of the Dorrington property just before noon. Wells had asked the local authorities to stand down for the first blush and let them determine if the Tatums were there or not. The last thing they wanted was for Tatum to flee before they could get to him or, worse, have gunfire to conclude the chase with the Tatums' death, playing right into Heaton's hands. Radios keyed, guns at the ready, they proceeded on foot onto the estate, using the thick line of woods for cover as they scrambled from tree to tree toward the main house.

Steel wondered if Georgia was aware of the present operation. She fought the urge to break from the pack in order to call her, tell her everything. She wanted to impress her, energize her, titillate her with news of the final siege, but she knew a break in ranks would only put Georgia in an awkward position. She understood it would be the wrong thing to do and quickly tried to find another reason to call and to hear her voice—some pertinent excuse to engage in a quick conversation. She wondered, as they passed through the woods, what Georgia was up to right at that moment. What could the minute by minute in her daily life possibly be, a life with so much responsibility, with so much at stake? She tried to think about what she was wearing, what kind of mood she would be in. With each step through the musty forest, she thought deeper about where the road ahead led for herself and that beautiful chancellor.

AS GEORGIA'S WEEKLY meeting at Treasury ended, Jack Early took her quietly aside in the hallway and told her of a phone call that had come in. It made her heart beat quickly, like a drum. She hustled the whispering Early over to Number 10 and into her new perch in Lassiter's office, where she quietly closed the door.

"Tell me everything, Early. When did the call come in?"

"Just now, ma'am. He said he needs to speak with you. Says it's urgent." Her face flushed. She knew now that every personal or private call she had with Heaton without consent of Darling or the home secretary was a mistake. She knew Heaton well. He would be calling to draw her in, to position her as cover.

"If you do make the call, ma'am, I'd suggest that you record it." Early seemed to come alive with the tension. Georgia was of an opposite state.

"I don't know if I can do that, Jack. Surreptitiously recording a call from Heaton—I don't know if I have it in me. Where will it lead?" She turned to him, sincerely searching for an answer. Early stood mindlessly, scratching at his forehead as he ruminated on a proper reply.

"No, I suppose not. I suppose if we do record it, it's there to hang in the wind, isn't it?"

"I should call him back, though. Return the call quickly. If I don't, he knows full up that Darling and Steel are spikes into him. Do we want him to have that information?" Early agreed. It needed to remain business as usual. She collapsed into Lassiter's chair as Early dialed.

"I REALLY JUST wanted to see how you're holding up, Georgia. None of this could be easy on you. In your position."

"No, no, thank you for calling, then. It's all a nightmare, isn't it? I wake up every morning and still can't believe it's the truth."

"Do you think he'll make it? In your heart of hearts? Do you, Georgie?" He teased her with a schoolboy's nickname, reminding her in one snap how deeply the ties between them were laid: all the wins they'd had, the losses, the two silly stabs at sorry sex, the arguments over well-prepared meals. There had been years and miles of motion and emotion between them, and now this, too, all recalled with the simple use of a friendly moniker.

"I don't know. I really don't know if he'll survive. I'm not a doctor, am I?" And with that, she took all hope for a warm call off the table. "What can I do for you, David?" Heaton chuckled. He knew her well enough to discern her hidden meaning.

"You can take it all slow. That's what you can do, love. Take it all slow. There's much at stake. Right? Let's let cooler heads prevail. That's all I'm asking. Don't charge anyone up, not until you have a strong handle on how much there is to lose. For everyone." It wasn't even a veiled threat. It was an order he was giving her now. She wanted to lash out but knew there was no upside. *Let him talk*, she thought. *Let him keep talking*, she decided as she swallowed air, let him be David-charming, David in control. Sly David. Chess player David.

"Someone will hang for this, there's no doubt, Georgia. The dust will settle. You needn't worry. Just know this, if it's me, if I'm to hang, there will be a smile in my heart. I'll know I was looking out for England, for my country. Do you see? I'll know I did what was right. Will you be able to say the same?" She let it all rumble on the line, the threat, the intonation, the cocky cackle. She didn't have it in her to respond to the level of gamesmanship that Heaton wanted to play at.

"I have to go, David. I think it's best for you not to call again." She hung up and stared across the desk at Early, who did everything he could not to meet her eye.

STEEL, TAVISH, AND Wells walked behind the pen and small feed house that comprised the dog compound. The animals thrashed violently at the fence as they passed. Steel felt her knees wobble.

"I hate dogs. Always have," she confessed to Wells, a known dog lover.

"How could you hate dogs, Davina? What's there to hate? Look at them, poor things, they're just hungry." Tavish wasn't as sympathetic.

"Those are vicious dogs. Cane Corsos. And they do look hungry. And angry. They're actually very rare in Britain. They have the most bite force of any breed. Jaws like sharks." He looked gravely at Steel before a sly grin pulled at the corner of his mouth.

"Seriously, Davina, if any dogs were to give you the willies, these are the ones to get them from. They are trouble. Just look at them." He tossed a stone at the fence. The dogs charged and gnashed, hatefully barking at them all. Tavish, in his early thirties, a tall, lean ginger with a handsome baby face, had a good flirty laugh at Davina's expense.

They tucked behind a nearby tree when they heard a car roll from behind the main house. A new Mercedes parked on the other side of a grassy hill and its occupants disembarked. Harris and Peet, the latter still with his arm slung and shoulder bandaged. Two younger men accompanied them. Steel hadn't seen them before. They seemed to have the same affectless disposition common to all of Heaton's paid guns. Under cover of the cacophony of canine howls, the four men headed past the manor home into another clump of trees, sneaking to the lower area of the estate. It was obvious they weren't making a social call.

The three investigators decided to split up, hoping to flank and contain Heaton's team. Steel tried to ignore the baying dogs and stay focused. She flipped off her gun's safety and chambered a round. She sensed in her bones that things were about to go from bad to rotten.

Gordon heard an electronic beeping from a closet in the front hall of the maintenance lodge. He rose and walked toward the utility nook. Adam and Kate both figured that the washer or dryer had finished its cycle, but when Gordon stepped out of the closet, there was a noticeable lack of blood in his face.

"Are you okay, Gordon?"

"I'm fine. All is well. I need to run up to the main house. It's an electrical thing." Adam was more than curious about this concern.

"Should I come with?"

"No, no, you stay here. Once lunch is finished, get everyone in the car and we'll head out. Yes?"

"That's fine."

Gordon waved to the others and then took a maintenance golf cart up the tractor road toward the big house. Adam didn't believe his story for a second. He saw what he thought was a handgun-size bulge under Gordon's shirt when he emerged from the utility closet. The kids and Kate were busily not talking to each other, gazing mutely into their respective iPads. Adam tried to open the closet door but it was locked. He rifled through some nearby drawers and found the key.

Inside the closet there was a bank of monitors running the feeds from security cameras positioned around the property. It appeared to be an intensely sophisticated system, obviously more attentively manned when Heaton was on the property, and now reliant upon motion sensors. It beeped again as Adam saw an image of Gordon driving up the tractor trail.

Another monitor above showed Adam what had sent Gordon off: the Mercedes. At the main house. Heaton's men. They were here. On the opposite wall was a finely engineered rack of rifles and handguns, a precise spot for each and every weapon. One was distinctly missing.

ADAM SPRINTED NORTH through the woods, a Barrett REC7 automatic rifle in one hand, a .44 Magnum in the other, dodging through the dense field of trees and growth, making his way up to the main house, hoping to cover Gordon. Adam had started to contemplate forgiving Gordon for his cluelessness. But now, running and gunning, trying hard to maintain a steady breathing pattern, he was as mad at the old fool as he'd ever been.

Adam had come from the closet into the kitchen and demanded that Kate and the kids finish packing the Mercedes that Gordon had for them, and then get into it and wait and be ready to leave in a hurry. Of course, Kate wanted explanations, but there was time only to yell and insist in a tone that purposely scared her and the kids into immediately doing exactly what he wanted, so he had done just that as he bolted from the lodge.

The trees thinned out at the top of a gully. He heard yelling on the other side of a clearing. He saw Gordon, standing beside the golf cart, in a heated conversation with Harris, the man who had killed Richard Lyle. Another two men listened on, Peet and a younger colleague.

Adam got low and crept closer, advancing from one tree to the next. As his breathing steadied, he could hear what was being said. There were angry shouts now just ten yards away. Gordon was enraged. All four of them had guns drawn, each of them warily trying to figure how not to get killed once the firing started.

"You're a fool, Harris. You, too, Peet. How long do you play his stooges? Don't you see where this has all gone? You'll kill Adam, and then what? Kill me? Then what does he do?" He pointed to the young stooge.

"He has Dorman here kill you, and where does it end? He's got himself in a corner. He'll take you out, too. You need to understand that. Understand it clearly, man!" Harris moved closer to him and chuckled. "No, Thompson. You have it wrong. Very wrong. Heaton is in control here. You jumped ship too early." Gordon didn't back down, raised his gun.

"I have it spot-on. Heaton will be arrested. In any scenario. Where does that leave you, and how does killing us help?"

"But he's not going to be arrested. You're wrong as usual, Thompson. He's got an inside player on this one. All the way at the top. No one's going to be arresting Heaton. He's going to be calling the shots." Adam leaned into the clearing. He wasn't sure what he was hearing. Harris spelled it out for the two of them.

"Georgia Turnbull, you dumbass! She's gonna be prime minister, and soon. He's not as dumb as you think he is. Now you either drop that gun or shoot me now. And when you do, Peet shoots you. This is too much talking for me."

Gordon turned to the bald and slow-eyed Peet: a handgun in his good hand was pointed straight at his head. Then he turned back to Harris, his stubby Beretta angled at his brow. The younger man, so confident they had the jump on Gordon, didn't even bother to lift his pistol from his side. He just shot a cocky grin at Gordon to let him know it was there.

Adam put Harris's red head in the center of his scope. He would take him out, then the younger guy. The element of surprise would allow him to get both. He hoped Gordon would be quick enough to shoot Peet. As his finger curled around the trigger, a voice rang out.

"Freeze! Right where you are! Metropolitan Police! Drop your weapons!" Adam looked up and saw a police officer, Andrew Tavish, gun drawn, badge out, on the crest of the hill. A shot rang out. Before Tavish could finish his orders he was dead, a fatal head wound. Tavish was blown off the ridge where he had been standing. The shot had come from Adam's tree line. He spied a fourth Heaton man, another young guy, west of his position, prepared to fire a long-range rifle a second time.

Adam turned back to the clearing in perfect time to see Harris deliver to Gordon the same cold-blooded good-bye that had felled Richard Lyle. Right to the center of his forehead from three feet away. Gordon flew back onto the lawn, landing flat on his back, gone before his body touched the grass.

Adam reacted in a spark of rage, firing twice at the hidden sniper. He heard an instant groan. He'd hit him. He wasn't sure if he had killed him or not, but he'd been hit. He brought his aim back toward Harris and fired. The bullet missed its target but caught Dorman in the chest. A wet pop sounded out as his sternum cracked. He spun to the ground next to Gordon's body. Harris and Peet hesitated long enough to grant Adam another shot. He hit Peet squarely in his good shoulder. Tatum slung the rifle over his back while rising to his feet. He pulled out the Magnum and marched dead ahead to Harris, blasting bullets through the crackling air as Peet painfully loped away to the safety of the woods.

Adam came within twenty feet of Harris, ten feet from Gordon's lifeless body. He was good and ready to avenge his father-in-law. He had the jump on Harris and he knew it. He stopped firing and moved slowly toward him. He wanted to be right up close when he fired on him, exactly as Harris had just done to Gordon, as he did to Richard Lyle.

Harris stood his ground and didn't say a word. He smiled in a demented way that told Adam there wasn't a chance in hell that he would drop his weapon. Adam was once again about to fire when someone shouted out.

"Metropolitan Police! Drop all of your weapons! Now!" It was a young woman, small, maybe midtwenties, with a badge around her neck on a chain and a handgun that seemed to Adam to be as big as her whole arm.

"Drop both of those weapons now, damn it! I mean it! Drop them!" Adam wondered who the hell this little thing with the big Scottish voice was but also realized in the same instant that the Heaton man knew exactly who he was dealing with and obviously had no use for her.

Harris turned and started firing away at the young woman, and in his ruthless abandon he got under her skin. She ran for cover but fell onto the grass at the crest of the hill. He reset his aim and was about to fire off another shot, but he was too late. Adam had put a hole the size of a large fist into the center of the back of his grimy red head. Harris buckled to his knees and fell face-first into the grass, loudly coughing up blood. Just seconds later he was good and finally dead.

Steel peeked over the ridge and knew exactly who had saved her life. It was the American, Adam Tatum. Adam had no inkling as to who the young Scottish woman was. He just knew well enough to take the few seconds of confusion he had purchased to run quickly away into the relative safety of Dorrington's woods.

Steel heard shots fired from the west. She heard Edwina Wells scream out. She was racing through the forest after the American, chasing him around and through each and every clump of trees and stretch of bog, staying right on his tail, in and out of the lush woods, chasing him hard, up and down the rolling moss and vine-laden ground. She wanted to turn back and help Edwina but didn't want to lose Tatum. She chased him with every ounce of energy she had. He kept looking back, thought for sure she would give up. He was wrong.

Edwina called out again. Steel stopped now, had no choice. She had to go back. Edwina Wells was her mentor, the biggest supporter she had had in SO15. She couldn't leave her alone out there. Tatum would have to wait. She watched him sprint into the far side of the forest. She turned back to the sound of Edwina's shouts and caught sight of a real-life nightmare bounding toward her, down the winding tractor road.

Eleven rabid dogs, running at her, full pace. Peet, out of breath, in the distance, was bloodied and mangled but happily watching from a rise in the road. His wicked grin told the tale. He had let them free to feast on the first thing they could find.

Steel turned in a panic, ran back into the woods, and tore through the scrub and the bramble over a pile of dead trees, down into a soggy brush-covered valley, the dogs tight on her trail. Her lungs were spent, her legs were aching, and there was sharp pain in her feet, but the fear of death powered her forward as she ran back up another wooded hill with the pack of miserably tempered hounds now snapping their jaws at her heels.

At the top of the hill she fell. The dogs attacked, eleven at once in a frenzy. She curled into a ball. She covered her face as they bit and clawed and jumped up on top of her. This was the end, she thought. Such a horrible way to die: torn to ragged bits by animals. She flashed quickly on her mother, on her father, on Georgia. The dogs barked and bit and tore into her clothing. She felt blood on her back. Her skin had been ripped. Her right leg. A bite there had broken skin. It didn't stop. A pummeling of teeth. Gnashing teeth. Stinging. Biting. Pulling. The constant roar of barking, the disgusting rain of angry canine saliva washing over her, slapping her, washing onto her arms and her face. She was crying now, wishing it would end, wishing they could somehow get to her heart and just tear it out and be done with it.

A gun fired. Several shots. In a flash the dogs were off her. Gone. Just like that, it was over. She looked up. Tatum, from the bottom of the hill, had shot over the pack and was waving them down to him, goading them, yelling at the top of his lungs.

"Come on! Go on, you ugly fucking mutts! Get the fuck off her!" He had saved her life a second time. The dogs did exactly as he ordered. They angrily chased toward him. Their downhill run surprised him—they moved faster than he thought they would. He turned and ran but they were on him now, and as he sped through the thicket of vines and stumps he tripped as well. His rifle flew to the ground as his body landed flat on a bed of mud.

The dogs pounced. They tore into the American, who didn't have the time to curl into a ball. Steel watched from the ground in horror as they chewed into him, as they'd done to her, only worse. She tried to stand but her legs were too beaten, too soaked in blood and wrenched with pain to respond to mental commands. She wanted to pass out but knew if she did, if she ever woke, she'd find the dogs gone and the American's chewed dead carcass.

Somehow she got to the bottom of the hill, to his rifle. She picked it up and fired into the pack of insanely feeding dogs, praying she didn't hit Tatum. She killed two dogs. They dropped like sacks of flour. Then she wounded a third. The rest of the pack finally got the headline and were gone in a lick, racing away through the silent trees.

Tatum stirred. He looked over and saw Steel. He was bitten badly, but he could move. He stood. She was about to pass out. He knew it. He wanted to thank her, but the badge on the chain around her neck flashed the reality to him that he had to go. Had to get back to his wife and his children.

Steel wanted to command him to halt as he scuttled off, but she didn't have the energy or the vocal strength to speak. She collapsed onto a moss-covered stump. She tried to right her broken breathing as she watched the American limp his bitten body up the hill, disappearing off into the forest.

THE AIR WENT suddenly quiet. The branches on the trees gently sashayed with the wind in what seemed like a natural reset. The dogs ran in their miserable parade somewhere off into the distance, their surly din growing quieter and quieter until they would have been a dark memory were it not for the blood and the shredded clothing, the burning ripped skin on her arms, legs, and back.

She sat still for several brittle minutes. Her breathing settled. Her body was beaten, but the wounds weren't fatal. The bleeding wasn't constant. She'd survive, she thought. There wasn't time to think about much more. She saw through the trees onto the tractor road as Peet pulled up in the Mercedes and a younger man, the sniper from the woods, limped into the vehicle, his clothing painted in blood. She stayed hidden in the brush and watched as they drove away, a broken duo.

A few minutes later Edwina Wells called out again from somewhere in the shrouded distance.

STEEL SPENT HALF an hour roaming through the darkening woods searching for Wells. She kept her weapon at the ready for whoever returned, be it human, dog, or anything else. She came upon Wells at the crest of yet another damp hill, seated, spent, leaning quietly against a tree.

Wells smiled when she saw Davina. The veteran detective waved peacefully as Steel trudged her way up the incline. When she got to the top Steel could see that Wells had been shot. Her chest was liquid black, her shirt soaked with blood. She smiled wearily once more at the young prodigy, and as her body bled out she nodded softly, then closed her eyes and died.

Adam thanked God when he got back to the lodge that Kate and the kids were in the car, apprehensively packed and waiting, ready to go. He was a mess. He knew it. He had horrible news to impart, but it all had to wait. They had to leave immediately. There was once again no time to explain anything to anyone.

Kate was speechless. He looked like he'd been fed through a shredder. His hands and his face were covered in blood. He was limping, soaked in sweat and mud, thoroughly out of breath. Little Billy saw him and instantly started crying. His daughter felt his pain all over her own body. It was the worst sight any of them had ever seen. It had taken all of the dark, scary, miserably horrible moments of the last days and made them all seem like picnic memories. He stumbled to the car, fell into the backseat, and screamed at Kate to start driving—immediately.

"Where's my father? What's happened?"

"He's fine," he lied. He had to. There wasn't time to let her grieve; it wasn't fair to tell the truth.

"Where's Poppa?" The kids were in a raw form of shock, also afraid to speak, afraid to ask anything they instinctively knew they didn't want the answer to.

"He's back there. Just drive. He's gonna meet up with us later. It's fine. I was attacked by the dogs."

Kate looked into the rearview mirror as she pulled past the main house onto the long drive out to the road. She saw only her young son, leaning over the far backseat to look down sadly on his blood-soaked father, who struggled for air, struggled to form words.

"Keep driving, Kate, whatever you do, whatever happens. Don't stop. You hear me? Don't stop." He knew the badges on the chains around the necks would be there in large numbers any minute. He knew they had to be long gone from Heaton's farm, was sure there weren't even seconds to spare. He tried not to picture his father-in-law's broken dead body in a tuft of dirty grass, but it's all he kept seeing as he shut his eyes—that and the dogs.

At the main drive he had Kate take a left onto the road leading to the highway. He could hear sirens in the distance, coming on like locusts.

"Left? I thought we were going—"

"Change of plans. Head left to London. Get on the highway."

She did what she was told, pulled onto the road, merged over to the highway heading south.

"You don't stop, Kate. No matter what. You get to London."

"What about my father? Tell me what's happened."

"It's fine. Keep driving." He was fighting to stay conscious. "Go to London. I need to get to London."

"What are we going to do in London, baby? What's happened? Talk to me, please, I beg you."

"I have to see Georgia Turnbull."

"Georgia Turnbull? . . . The chancellor? What could you possibly have to see her about? Adam? Talk to me. Please? I am so frightened. Look at the kids. We're all petrified, darling. Talk to me. Please, I'm begging you."

Adam gathered enough breath to answer.

"Go faster. Don't stop until we get to London."

"Why Georgia Turnbull, Adam?"

"I need to see her."

"See her for what? How do you expect to see her?"

"Just drive." Each word was labored; they were fewer and farther between. Each breath was harder to manufacture, harder for the children to hear, and harder for a terrified and unnerved Kate to comprehend.

"What are you going to do when you see her, Adam? What are you going to do when you see her?" He didn't answer for the longest time. No one said another word as the finely tuned engine of the German marvel purred perfectly along the road at eighty miles an hour. Billy's teeth clattered as he shivered in fear, Trudy's soul quietly ached as she finally knew what real pain of the heart felt like, and Kate could only silently whimper. Whimper and drive.

Out of nowhere, Adam spoke. With one last burst of semi-cohesion, he made an odd, incongruous, final statement.

"I need to see the chancellor of the exchequer."

PART THREE

TURNBULL

—

TATUM

—

STEEL

Georgia had another dream about Roland. They were in the helicopter the morning of the crash. The sun was much brighter than it had actually been that day. The light was blinding, and they were laughing and drinking champagne. Roland was performing for her, doing naughty impressions of the other MPs at the conference in Brighton. There was a buoyancy to the mood as the aircraft flew mere feet above the ground, right over cars and pedestrians' heads. They both thought it was so clever and cute for the pilot to show off like that. Roland reached out the side door and swiped off a man's hat as they both laughed, uncontrollably.

The helicopter landed safely at Shoreham Airport this time. The entire crash was reworked, rewritten, and replayed into just another day at the office. They disembarked, giggly and drunk, and out of nowhere Roland kissed her. She was stunned. Her face grew bright red and her heart pounded as he told her that he had always loved her. She cried as he held her close and kissed her some more. He ordered the helicopter back into the air. They hopped in and floated low over the beach at Brighton, laughing together at the world passing peacefully beneath them.

She woke to feel a cloud of sadness hovering over her like a heavy quilt. The dream, no doubt triggered by the day's scheduled visit to Roland, was unsettling.

———

IT WAS THE fourth time she had visited in the nine days since the bombing. It was clear for the first time that his body would, in fact, eventually heal.

"There's so much out there to bring you down, isn't there, Georgia? Once you get up on top of that heap? Once you're the one that needs toppling?" She nodded. Simple speech was still an uphill climb. His one free arm moved ahead of his mouth as if it were trying to help it along.

"Kirsty thinks it's an inside job. I tell her that's science fiction. I still think it's Islamic radicals. That lot. My brother thinks it's the Americans. The CIA. How absurd is that?"

"It's a theory being floated all over the panel shows and Internet, from what I've been told," Georgia explained. She wanted to tell him she was pretty sure the talk had all been launched by Heaton, but she didn't want to upset him.

Roland reached over, needed water. She helped pour it. He smiled in a tiny way, not sure how grateful he wanted to be for needing help to have a simple glass of water.

"I'm done either way. I can't do it. This is just the end. The crash was the beginning of it, but this is the end. I'll be up on two feet soon. I feel it. They can't keep me down. But I can't play on the stage anymore. I need to let the parade pass."

She squeezed his hand, kissed his cheek again, and then the drugs walked him into the back rooms of his mind, left his broken bandaged body to lie there, not awake, not asleep. Georgia sat next to him as long as she could, then quietly left.

BACK AT NUMBER 10, she met with several Labour MPs who had been sent over to discuss the transition—almost as if they had placed a wire in Roland's hospital room. The timing was uncanny but, in truth, everyone in Whitehall had been discussing nothing but the timing of when to make it official. Georgia needed to convince the party leaders that it was time for her to stand forward and lead a call to form a government. She would then see the palace and have the king ask her to do the same. None of the ministers meeting in Roland's office thought she would have much competition. Maybe Andrew Rogan or that television whore Deandra Potter, the MP from Hendon who had seemed to Georgia to live in a television studio this last week and a half. *Not the Deputy PM, Felix Holmby*, thought Georgia. He had no standing in the party and was severely personality challenged.

She had been the face of the government during this tragedy and had been a popular figure in the party for almost fifteen years. Polls showed her to be the most familiar player in the party next to Roland. She responded positively to the delegation that had been sent over to address the matter and agreed to make a statement in advance of a party conference the following week. As they left, she wondered what they would think if they knew that she had been behind the plot to place the bomb in the first place. Would they still think she was the "most likely, best face to put forward"?

ANOTHER CALL FROM Heaton had come in while she was dealing with the party reps. Early scheduled Heaton to meet her. It was time to have a face-to-face. They convened an hour later in the White Room, the very place where the bomb had gone off. Heaton brought an aide with him, a young man with a device that swept the room for surveillance equipment as they waited for Georgia, who arrived mid-sweep. She chuckled at the audacity. Heaton shrugged.

"There are no chances worth taking at this point, are there?" Once the young man with the electronics had finished up, Heaton nodded for him to move on. Some tea was brought in. They were alone.

"There's been a shooting. Up at Dorrington. Two officers of DPG have been casualties. You should know about this. You will in a short time anyway, I'm sure." Georgia lost her breath for a second. *Was it Steel?*

"Two police captains, a woman named Edwina Wells and a man named Tavish. It's all very sad. Also an old mate of mine, Gordon Thompson." Georgia caught her wind again. She knew she wouldn't have been able to control herself if he had said "Davina Steel."

"Gordon Thompson? Isn't he the father-in-law of the American?"

"Yes, exactly. It's a mess. It will be cleaned up, though. It will all have actually occurred on land just to the east of my property. It'll plummet down as 'drugs related,' an arrest gone bad. It's being handled as we speak. No need to make this more of a mess than it is. It shouldn't intertwine with the Roland thing. We're keen to keep them unrelated." He poured himself some tea. She marveled at how at home David was in matters of intrigue, as if this were his natural state: planning, scheming, hiding, scrambling.

"We need to talk now, you and I, Georgia. We are both in this together and in fact need each other more than ever before. I want to be sure our middle legs are tied tightly and we're running in proper sync. It's imperative. We have to be in lockstep. You and I. Understood?"

"I understand that you're saying that I need to listen to whatever you have planned. I'm getting that loud and clear."

"Why are you being like this? What will being combative award you? Nothing really. Not at this point." He sat down in the couch across from where she was standing, stirred his tea, and waited for her to sit. She did.

"David, that bomb was never supposed to go off. It was supposed to be a 'dud,' just enough to unnerve Roland, nothing more. To play on his already shattered state. Wasn't that your original pitch on this whole idea?" Heaton started to answer. She didn't give him the chance.

"You have lied to me, deceived me, and committed a horrible crime. You put someone I dearly love on the brink of death and through an awful amount of pain. I can never forgive you. I can never trust you. You realize this?" Heaton nodded and agreed with everything she had said.

"Very good. As usual, you've laid out your point of view clearly—always one of your strong points." She shook her head; his confidence was insufferable.

"I'm sorry, Georgia. In the end, it was felt that a 'dud' wouldn't have been enough to frighten Roland to retire. I know you thought it would suffice, thought he was on edge, looking for a reason to pack it in, but you were alone in that assessment. I do agree that the amount of explosive was overdone. I truly had no interest in inflicting that kind of damage on Roland, the whole thing just got out of hand, but with that said, we are here, he is alive and will recover, and now you have a job to do as far as the path we've all chosen."

She stood and paced the room. She hadn't been using her cane these last few days, a by-product, she thought, of so many things: the adrenaline, the pills, Steel. Steel—God, how hard it was sometimes to think of Steel. How badly she wanted to walk out of this room away from this billionaire buffoon and find herself a quiet nook to call Steel and hear her soft flutter of a voice.

"I want us to have a clear plan now, Georgia. You're going to get what you want. You're going to be the PM. The party will kneel at your feet, but you'll need to make good on the referendum. It won't be able to wait. We don't want Strasbourg to go into conference and make amendments that would give the Libs a good reason to balk or, worse, sue for more leverage. We want this done now—in weeks, not months. I need your commitment."

She looked up at the portrait of Margaret Thatcher, then over to one of David Lloyd George as a wave of shame bolted through her body. How had it come to this? How had this slick-suited, silver-tongued reprobate gotten one over on her? Surely she was brighter than this. *It was the pills*, she thought. He never would have played her this way had she not been under their command.

"You will lead forward as planned. There is no choice."

"Don't talk to me that way, David. I am not going to become your servant. It won't happen, do you hear me? If you think you'll run Downing Street with me as a puppet, it will not happen!" She was shouting now. "You tell whoever it is alongside you, these faceless men, that I will not be your marionette! I will resign office first. Step down. Leave you with nothing. I promise you this!" Heaton gave her a beat to calm. He knew she would. She always did.

He got up, came over, and put his arm on her shoulder. She wanted to shake it off, pull away from his touch, but didn't.

"It won't come to that, Georgie, I promise. You aren't to be anyone's water carrier. It's just about the referendum. That's all anyone's going to get churned up about. Rest assured." She turned and looked him in the eye.

"I'm very scared, David, truly frightened, for all of us."

"Good. You should be. There's plenty to be frightened about." He leaned farther in, kissed her cheek, and made his exit.

TATUM ▪ 1

The Tatums paid cash for a week in advance on two rooms in a broken-down hotel in Earls Court. Kate had gone in alone and rented the rooms from an old Chinese woman who had no interest in who or what would be in them, only focusing on the cash. A television on the wall blasted a Ping-Pong tournament with Chinese lettering scrolling along on the bottom of the screen. The newspapers on the desk behind her were all copies of the *People's Daily*, in Chinese as well. It seemed to Kate that this may well be the one place in Britain that didn't have images of her husband strewn from wall to wall.

They had driven into London, arrived as the sun set, and then dropped off Adam in an alley not far from the hotel. Billy stayed with Adam as Kate and Trudy dumped the car at Canary Wharf, then took a taxi back to Earls Court. Adam was still pale and needed medical attention, but, thankfully, his bleeding had stopped. Kate had improvised a bandage out of Trudy's scarf, binding the wound on his thigh, which seemed to be the worst of his injuries. Kate ran into a Boots pharmacy along the way and bought bandages and supplies. It was everything she could do to keep moving, stay with the job at hand, not think too much about anything—about her father, about Richard, about a bomb in the prime minister's office, or about her husband being the most wanted man in Britain, maybe even the world.

Once it was dark and they were certain of a path free of CCTV cameras that would record Adam on the way from the alley to the hotel, she and the kids helped him across and inside, past the old woman who was on the phone arguing with someone in Chinese, then into the elevator up to their floor.

A musty yellow film covered almost everything in the two adjoining rooms. The water in the bathroom sink even had a yellowish tint. The mattresses were hard as boards and the blankets old and tattered at the ends. The rooms smelled dank and wet, like the floor of a bus station phone booth. The window shades were also aged and frayed. Nothing in either room was less than forty years old: appliances, furniture, bedding, or literature.

Adam passed out on the bed as soon as they were inside. Kate and Trudy washed his wounds while he slept. Kate did her best to close up anything she could and to disinfect what she couldn't. Billy sat on a creaky chair and cried in the way one whimpered after having cried so much that nothing was left but gentle shivering. In the middle of the night, as Kate slept with the kids in the other room, Adam woke and turned on the television, the volume low. He watched the news. The Adam Tatum show. There was wall-to-wall chatter and clatter on what seemed like every channel about "the American." Several panels of pundits used the occasion to reiterate long-standing claims about America's dark part in everything currently going wrong with the world. This "Adam Tatum" had opened up the conversation once again about what could and couldn't be done to stop America and its reckless behavior in all facets of modern life.

Later the BBC ran a program about Georgia Turnbull and the government, hypothesizing on who would align with whom once Lassiter was officially out—a quarter hour of talking heads finally not talking about Adam. It was almost refreshing.

On the subject of Georgia Turnbull, the experts were in agreement, and all surmised that she would be the next prime minister. Adam stewed while watching, wrapped in musty blankets in a room that felt like one stop before the curb. He sulked and steamed, mumbled and muttered to himself as he tried to fix his mind on an idea, a plan, a way to stop her, bring her down, clear his name.

Then he saw Jack Early. It was during a piece on the life of Georgia Turnbull. Early was briefly mentioned—her private secretary. There was footage of Georgia now, Early always at her side. One of the panelists, a British comedian, was even showing slow-motion footage of Early from a few years earlier standing behind Georgia while she made a speech, picking at his nose. Another splotch of video showed the man falling as he got out of her car as she arrived at the hospital to visit Roland the day after the blast. The panel made a quick barrage of jokes, then moved on to her various cabinet members, trying to determine who would back her bid and who would turn and run.

Adam wasn't interested in moving on, though. He was fixed on Jack Early. He knew him. They had met. This was the man who had handed him the heavy replacement dossier that day at Number 10. It had been eleven days, eleven long days, but the memory was clear. This Early character, this skinny clown of a man—he was in on it. He had given Adam the bomb. He forced himself to sit up straight. This Jack Early—he was the key.

LATER, KATE HELPED him shower. Talk was clipped, conversation sparse. He used his weakness as a wall, a reason not to say too much. He handed her one of several lists he had made while lying in bed.

"We need these items." He tossed over an envelope that Gordon had given him. It was filled with cash, passports, and driver's licenses.

"I need these supplies." Her eyes trained on his every move now, her voice broken and stilted.

"What about my father? When are you going to—" He cut her off, sadly snipping the words as they left her mouth.

"He's gone. I'm sorry, Kate. Heaton's men. They killed him. I'm so sorry." She took it in, said nothing. She just nodded and stared at him. She fought the tears and wiped away each new barrage before they could flow into a steady stream. He sensed it wouldn't be long and the dam would explode. She'd crumple in pain, double over in agony. He didn't have the time to wait.

"You and the kids are leaving. Once you get me those supplies, you're going to make some changes in your appearances and use those passports and fly out of the country. My brothers will take care of you in Ann Arbor until I can get home." She buckled into a ball and collapsed. He rubbed her back and held her as she sobbed. But she moved away from him, making it clear that she didn't want him touching her. He backed off and let the sorrow take hold of her.

After a beat she looked up from her tears and faced Adam, her eyes swollen and puffy.

"He was going to come to Chicago with us. Near us. He wanted a new life."

"I'm sorry, Kate. I'm so, so sorry."

Fifteen minutes later she took Trudy and left to go find the items on the list. They caught a taxi over to Oxford Street. Kate wanted to talk, wanted to tell Trudy what was happening, but she couldn't find the words to tell her that her grandfather was dead or that they were going home, so she said nothing.

She didn't want to fight; she knew that neither Trudy nor Billy would want to leave Adam. Kate did, though. She was good and ready to go home, ready to be done with it all, to be done with Adam.

The New Testament Church of God in the Wood Green area of North London hosted the funerals of both Andrew Tavish and Edwina Wells, Andrew's in the late morning and Edwina's just an hour or so after. They were work friends, not a lot more, but their brutal murders in the woods of Dorrington had brought them closer together in death than either of them ever imagined they'd be.

Steel watched from the middle of the church as Edwina's sister gave a passionate and humorous, tear-splashed speech about her older sister and best friend. Steel's gut ached with bitter pain, not the sting from the bite wounds but the angry pang of knowing that these deaths were to be forever shrouded in lies. The morning papers had all told the same story, the one reported by the Met and the local authorities in Tewkesbury.

The two investigators were killed by drug runners, possibly Turkish. It was an arrest gone bad, a tragedy in the line of duty that had taken place in the woods a mile south of the closest home. There was no mention of Dorrington.

There was no reference to Gordon Thompson or of Harris or Dorman. All three of them had been airbrushed away in the cold morning Tewkesbury air. Steel pounded the desktops of Darling and the others, but this was to be the official story. It was from higher up than Major Darling could reach. With his mind, as well as Steel's, still bent on seeing Heaton swing for this whole sad wrinkle of sanity, Darling wanted Heaton and whoever it was Heaton was trotting and plotting with to think that they had indeed dotted all of their *i*'s and crossed all of their *t*'s.

Steel needed to believe in someone, and she did in fact trust in Darling, so in the end she went along with the cocked-up story. She sat there now in the bosom of an aching extended family as they wailed and moaned, sneezed and sniffled over the tragic loss of sweet, sweet Edwina Wells. Steel didn't have a tear to shed; her mind was too busy with dark thoughts of revenge and retribution.

SHE TOOK THE Piccadilly line, reasonably quiet on a Sunday afternoon, from Wood Green down to Russell Square, which was walking distance to her parents' flat in Bloomsbury. Several of the passengers were reading the morning papers with cover stories on Georgia and what was universally now seen as her inevitable rise to the prime minister's office. Lassiter had all but made official his inability or desire to return to office when he healed from the bombing, which had occurred two weeks earlier. The world was ready to move on, Steel thought. The Downing Street bombing was just another media story now—an unsolved riddle, a nagging ache that the public inherently knew would be solved eventually—but the anger and the fear had somewhat subsided, and what had been just a few days earlier on a high flame on a front burner was now replaced with the taunting question of what normal would be like, what face tomorrow would flash. According to all of the papers staring across at her, it was the face of Georgia Turnbull.

She wanted to call Georgia so badly. She wanted so deeply to soothe Georgia's nerves and, even more, wanted to tenderly kiss away her doubts.

Then, as Russell Square became the next stop, another thought flashed across the young inspector's mind, a thought that had been there before, one that she hadn't wanted to pick up and place, a puzzle piece that she wasn't ready to find a hole to snap into. What if Georgia was involved? Someone was, someone very high up. To have made the connections, managed the coercions that were enlisted in dressing over and stitching up the murders of Wells and Tavish, someone had to have powerful strings available for Heaton to pull. Who stood the most to garner from all this? Who could have had the inside track it would have taken to place a bomb to set off a conspiracy from this high up? Who had profited the most from Roland Lassiter's fall? The answer was clear: the woman on the cover of the Sunday magazine, the heir apparent.

Steel slowly picked the puzzle piece up in her mind. She tried not to remember how sweet and cool Georgia's breath felt wrapped inside of a soft quick kiss as she twirled the notion around in her mind. When the Tube came to a stop at Russell Square, she sat there numb as passengers hobbled off and new ones shuffled in. The only two things that didn't move were the photo of Georgia Turnbull and Steel herself.

She stayed frozen into place as the train left the station, replacing it with a sea of blackness and rail clatter. The final piece fit perfectly on all sides. All the little puzzle-type knobs and bobbles slipped into the adjoining space with ease. It was a flawless landing, a perfect placement. How could she not have seen this before? She'd been blinded by infatuation. That was the only excuse. All of her powers, all of her talent, all of her instincts had been easily felled by a simple schoolgirl's crush.

Heaton had had inside help at Number 10 and, like everything else Sir David had in his life, it was the best there was to have. His partner in all of this would be the new prime minister. You couldn't do any better than that. Numb and slapped senseless with an obvious truth, breathlessly taken with a sharp reality, Steel didn't move as much as a muscle until the Tube finally pulled into Holborn, where she disembarked and headed home in her very own self-contained fog.

TURNBULL ■ 2

Her Jaguar and a follow car pulled into the side gate of Buckingham Palace. Upstairs, outside on the landing to the regal drawing room, Andrew McCullough, the king's valet, held ground at the large wooden door while Georgia waited patiently to be given the sign that the king would be ready to see her, ready to ask her the question the press and the pundits were all asking: would she be able to form a government?

Once inside, she nodded to the king, did a slight bow at the door, and was summoned into the seemingly never-ending room with the ornately coved ceilings and the silk-lined walls. She made her away across. They were alone in the room. He held out his hand. She took it, suddenly not sure if she should bow again. *Do I bow only at the door, or here across from him? Do I kiss his hand? I know it's all different when it's a private meeting at the palace, but I forget exactly what I should do. Damn this all. Why don't I have this all down?*

For some reason she couldn't settle on what to do, so she bowed slightly again. Awkwardly, she thought. The king seemed fine with the response and invited her to have a seat on the couch across from him.

"How are you holding up, Miss Turnbull? These can't be easy times."

"No, Your Majesty, they are not."

"I have sent a note to the prime minister. My heartfelt thoughts on news he would be leaving public life. It's a loss."

"Yes it is, sir. A horrible loss."

"I guess it's all to you then, now. Can you form a government?" He was wasting no time. There was no small talk to be had. That was it, the big question. She had always imagined there was more to say in private meetings with the monarch, little wisps of truth to be shared, wisdom passed on, but it wasn't to be. He wanted an answer to the query the constitution forced him to put forward, and nothing more.

"I believe that, yes, I can, sir, form a government. That will be my task."

"Yesterday's dispatch box had a summary to me of your objectives. I've looked them over and feel that all of them are sound. They not only carry on Roland's work well but will give the people a good sense of continuity. I do have concerns on the referendum, Miss Turnbull. I can see that it's going to be a high priority of your government. Is that true?"

"Yes, I believe it is. I should think it's an idea whose time has come."

"I guess you could label me sitting on top of the fence on this one. All I have really is a strong desire that it's a majority vote. There will be unending repercussions, I'm sure."

"Yes, Your Majesty. It's a course change fraught with peril. But one we believe needs to be taken."

"It would cause massive change. You'll need it to be a resounding decision of the electorate to leave the union. I would hate to have it feel as if it had the fabric of a backroom deal by big business or any other collective or pressure group. It has to clearly be the people speaking. I'm sure of that much."

"Yes, of course, Your Majesty. I'm in lockstep with you on that."

He looked across at her now for what seemed to be the longest time.

He can see through me, Georgia thought to herself. *He's staring right into my soul. Knows all. No. That couldn't be. He's just a man. He's the king but, in the end, just a man. Dear God, why is this all so unnerving?*

After a pause, the king broke the silence.

"You'll have the weight of the world on your shoulders, won't you?" he asked with complete empathy, a knowing kind of compassion.

"I'm sure it comes with the title, sir, but, yes. I can feel it already, to be honest."

"You'll take it in drips and drops. It will become part of you, the weight. You'll learn to live with it." He took another quiet breath. "I'll be saying my prayers for you."

"Thank you, Your Highness."

"Thank you, Miss Turnbull. A pleasure to see you again." He stood. She quickly followed. They faced each other. The meeting was over. She started to panic. *Do I walk backward now all the way to the door? It's an incredible length. Not sure that I'll be able to do that without tripping or doing something silly. Damn, why can't I figure this out?*

The king smiled, almost as if he were in fact reading her mind. He nodded his head, turned, and walked toward the rear hallway leading to his residence. Georgia waited for what seemed like a season for him to cross and leave the endless room, then turned and scurried out as quickly as possible.

"I'VE JUST ACCEPTED an invitation from His Majesty the king to form a government." Georgia was speaking to the British public through the press, outside Number 10. It was early morning and a pleasant sun favored her face as she read a short statement on the priorities of her new government, number one of course being to bring to justice the persons responsible for the bombing that had taken place there. To the great dismay of the assembled journalists, she finished her statement, took no questions, and briskly strode back through the black door behind her, away from their glare.

Several days had passed since Georgia had taken a pill. She felt better, yet in moments alone, when darker thoughts consumed her, she'd find herself fending off an impulse to run to her flat and reunite with her helpers. She had so far resisted and had been free of the little beasts for almost seventy-two hours. With all that there was to be done, she needed to have as clear a head as possible. She was aware that unless she pushed through the storm of the inevitable withdrawal, the clarity she was longing for would never reappear.

She had a light breakfast with Holmby, the deputy PM, Arnold Haddon, the minister for the cabinet office, and the very pregnant Lucy Barnathanson, the cabinet secretary, in the den adjacent to her office— Roland's office. There was little doubt that she would have the numbers in Parliament. She would bring a vote in and have the backing of her party. She would indeed form a government. Georgia Turnbull was going to be the prime minister. It was done, set down in stone. All that was left to do was lead—lead and breathe.

She had hoped to avoid making any cabinet changes at such an early point, but the cabinet secretary sensed that many felt that a reshuffle was due—in particular, Burnlee had made clear his desire to leave the home secretary post and take up Treasury as the new chancellor of the exchequer. There was also talk of unrest at Justice, Health, Work and Pensions, and Energy and Climate. Georgia begged Lucy and Haddon to postpone all that they could, at least for the time being.

The requests would likely be granted. There would be much goodwill toward Georgia now, not only in her own party but with the Tories and the Lib Dems, and even UKIP as well. This was still crisis time they were in: the new PM needed backing and would get it. Everyone was on the same page. Hopefully.

IT WAS BEFORE the cabinet meeting, while Burnlee was bending her ear on how he needed to help her by taking over at Treasury, that Jack Early let Georgia know how desperately Inspector Steel was trying to get ahold of her. She had insisted the matter was urgent. Georgia took a breath. Simply the thought of Steel was enough for her to lose her calm. How had it happened? After a lifetime of not letting anyone into her center, this young woman had climbed the gate and gotten in. Even a simple flash of a thought of her made Georgia's head go a little light with too much oxygen.

She wouldn't see her today, though. She didn't have the strength, not without the help she couldn't let herself reach for. She had the cabinet meeting, the address at Parliament, and sit-downs with the BBC, ITV, and then Sky News, plus a dinner planned with her father. Steel would make her heart race at too fast a clip today; she couldn't take the chance. Early pressed again, not aware of how loaded his inquiry was.

"Should I schedule her to come by once you've returned from Parliament? She says it's most important. I assume she has news on the investigation. We need to stay at the front of her trail, ahead of the pack. Didn't you say that, ma'am?"

"Yes, I know. But I can't. Not today. I just can't. Do you hear me? Have her see Darling. Let her convey whatever she has to him. Tell her I'm fine with it."

"Yes, of course, ma'am. I'll tell her."

Georgia made her way over the finely woven rug runners down to her initial cabinet meeting as prime minister to be, something she had waited for her entire adult life, yet David Heaton, her own gnawing ambition, those "damn pills," and, yes, even Davina Steel had all conspired to take any sense of joy from the moment or the victory. Everything she had ever wanted had come true, yet here she was, deeply demoralized and dispirited. The historic hallways of 10 Downing Street all seemed to be bouncing around a cackling form of laughter, one wall to another. The joke was entirely on her.

TATUM ▪ 2

Adam, Kate, and both of the kids dyed their hair. Kate cut Trudy's short—short and dark, a look she kind of liked. It was the only time the teenager had smiled in days. Billy went blond, basically white. He looked almost albino, like a spy in a James Bond movie, and elicited just as rare a laugh from them all. Adam shaved his head and began growth on a goatee. For a moment it was as if they were prepping for a costume party, putting on disguises to go out into the world and have some fun. Then for each of them, a wave of truth would waft over the hotel room and they'd remember what it was that they were dressing up for.

The dye and the haircutting accessories had been on Adam's list. Clothes, souvenirs, and maps were accoutrements to make them look like three tourists heading home to New York. Kate had gone online and bought three plane tickets. She had checked every item off the list. She had been a good wife, agreeing to help her husband with everything he asked of her, and yet she constantly consulted her watch, she could barely endure the minutes and hours before their departure time. Before she could fly away from him.

Adam watched the clock for a different reason. He needed to steady himself to say good-bye. He knew this send-off would be different, knew that it was more than probable that he would never see any of them again—at least not as a free citizen. He was in tune enough with Kate, even in light of all that had gone on between them, that he felt what she was feeling—that she was spent. The last three years had taken everything out of her as far as he was concerned, as far as "they" were concerned. He knew it was over and his heart was broken. He didn't have the words or the will to try to change her mind. All he wanted now was to get the kids and her to safety.

Sometimes at night, as he lay alone in the mildewing hotel room with her in the room next door, bunched in with the kids, he'd think of the early days when he won her heart in Ann Arbor. He remembered how full she made each moment, with her beaming smile and syrupy laugh. He'd flashback on how much he used to love to make love to her, how happy he was to come home to his lady in Royal Oak after a night on patrol in Ann Arbor. It was all a distant world away now. The memories were ashes, remnants of a house fire, flames he himself had started and events had taken and stoked to a blaze. He had lost Kate and Billy and Trudy, lost them in the fire.

BEFORE THEY LEFT, before he put them in a taxi to Heathrow, he wanted to speak with them all. Especially the kids. He wanted to try to explain to them what had happened. He wanted them to have some sense of who he was in the light of who he'd become. He sat the kids down in the rickety desk chairs in the room he slept in.

"I want you both to know that I love you. I love you so, so much."

"Why can't you just come with us, Daddy?" Little Billy wanted to comprehend it all but he didn't. "Why can't we all just go home together? Why is it so important to for you to see Georgie Turnstile?" Trudy rolled her eyes, but knew enough not to make a sarcastic remark. "Let's go see Poppa and make him come with us to Chicago, please?"

Kate felt a strong pang of guilt at her inability to tell her boy what had happened to his grandfather. She turned away and steadied her jaw as Adam responded.

"I have to make things right, Billy. I can't run away. You three are all that I care about. I have to set things straight, Billy. If I don't, we'll all be hiding, running forever." Kate knew he was about to choke up a good ten words before he did. She knew Adam rarely let his emotions get to him or overcome him, but she saw it coming on like a lonely car's head-lights floating forward on a darkened road.

"I have to clear my name—our name. Okay, Billy?" His son nodded. He wrapped himself around Adam's shoulder and announced that he was never letting go. Adam started sobbing but bucked up, stayed the course with his explanation.

"Some people have made everyone think that I did something that I didn't do. They've used the fact that I had made a mistake once before, so it was easy for them to make people believe that I had done it again, but I didn't. Powerful people. Do you see? They've done some very, very bad things and they have to answer for them. I have to make sure they do. All of them. Then I can come home, home to you."

Out of nowhere his eyes erupted with a rain of pain. A steady wash of fear and anger buckled him farther to the floor at his son's feet. Kate's eyes caught the same storm. She couldn't help herself. In that moment, she knew she wasn't free. She wanted to be harder, tougher than she was, but it wasn't so. She was still his wife. It wasn't going to be as easy as she thought. She hadn't in fact emotionally emancipated herself from him.

She wandered alone into the other room and collapsed onto the bro-ken, doughy mattress. There was no one else left in her life but Adam, everyone else was gone now, and though she hated him for that, against everything she was feeling, everything that made sense to her about her life, she couldn't abandon him—not now, not here. It was over—she was more and more sure of it every day—but she also knew it wasn't how she would be able to let it end. She didn't have it in her to leave Adam alone in London.

She picked herself up and went back into the other room. She spoke low, with a steady surety.

"We're staying."

"Excuse me?"

"You heard me, Adam. We're staying. Here. We'll wait. We'll all leave together."

"No, no, Kate. No. You can't." The kids were relieved. Billy held on to his father even tighter, locked his arms around his legs with all his might.

"Please, Kate, don't do this." Billy reached up and put his hand on his father's mouth, his eyes flushed red with an overdose of youthful anguish.

"Yes, Daddy, yes! We are staying. I'm staying with you." Trudy fell to her knees, grabbed Adam by the waist, and locked her arms around him in another bout of tears. Adam looked over the crumpled kids to his weary wife.

"I can't let you stay, Kate."

"You don't have a choice." It was obvious she was set on her newest course.

They would stick firm, live there in the hotel room, and help him. She and his two children would support him in any way that they could. If she didn't, if he met any form of danger—was arrested or, worse, killed— her children would never forgive her and she herself would live with nothing but unbearable guilt. Her only path was laid out clearly. She had no other road to take. She would dig in and fight, and in the fight maybe, just maybe, she would find some way back to Adam.

STEEL ■ 2

Steel kept herself busy in the time since Edwina's funeral, kept to herself and nursed her wounds. She still hadn't said anything to Major Darling about her sense of Georgia. She couldn't even think about it, let alone talk about it. She would lie awake at night and pray that she was wrong. She would go over it all again and again, looking for the ludicrous in all of her assumptions. She didn't find them, though. She still saw the puzzle piece as a perfect fit, and it only made her shattered heart bleed with a need for retribution.

SHE WENT UP and into the woods at Dorrington again. She took photos and ran as many forensic exercises as she could, but the forest had been swabbed clean. The scenes of Edwina's and Andrew's murders had both been meticulously lifted and relocated to a property two miles south, restaged as a drug arrest gone bad. It had been the work of experts, experts, Steel assumed, that she had been working alongside for the last six years. These were people she knew and trusted, who were now putting their talents to work for the sake of conspiracy and corruption.

She walked the now peaceful woods and pondered how common all that must be. She was new, as green as the saplings vying for light beneath the great oaks. Did the world really work this way, the way cynics and conspiracy theorists always claimed it did? Was subterfuge the order of the day, even at the highest levels? Maybe she wasn't as adept at discerning the big picture as she was at the little ones. Maybe she had an eye for the pebbles and the sand, yet the faraway horizon never came into focus.

The wind whipped around as she went back to her patrol car. Her intuition was failing her. She couldn't remember when she had ever doubted herself as deeply as she did now. What else had she been this wrong about? How could she have found herself to be in love with someone so duplicitous?

HER PARENTS BOTH knew something was seriously wrong. Her mother had been in a panicked state since Davina came home a week earlier with her arms and body bandaged and stitched. Davina slept later and talked even less than she normally did. Her shoulders seemed to droop with each and every step. Sheena stayed quiet when she could. She pried carefully when she couldn't. Davina of course denied that anything was wrong, but it was no use: Sheena felt the pain she was carrying.

Steel's heart was broken in the common way that a young woman's heart breaks and bleeds, but this was different. This was something from the movies and from spy novels, something greatly uncommon. Every time she turned on the television the news was in some way or other lashed directly to her own personal plight, her own private pain. It was all "Georgia" all the time, and when it wasn't "Georgia" it was "Adam Tatum."

Had she been used? Was it all to keep her close, to know what she knew, what Darling knew? How much had she said? How much had she spilled out into that late-night intimate call? She wanted to retrace every bit of the conversation, but it hurt too much to go back over it or any of the other interactions they had had.

She called Georgia a third time. She didn't want to make the call. She wanted to be standing on much firmer ground than this, but she dialed, held her breath, and waited as her mobile rang with a nauseating buzz. Georgia answered. Her voice, soft and throaty, comforted Steel, comforted and frightened her.

"I want to see you. I've been trying to call. I've left messages."

"I know, love. I want to see you, too. It's been such a thunderstorm these last few days. You must know that."

"You're the prime minister now. That feels so strange. It all feels so different." There was silence. Georgia waited for a powerful current of emotion to settle back down. Steel could almost feel it through the phone.

"I want to see you, Georgia, so badly. I have so much to tell you. There's so much that we need to talk about. I just need . . . you." Once again a word had jumped from her mouth like a fish from a bucket back into the ocean, never to be seen again. She wished she hadn't said it that way, casting herself as so weak.

"I need to see you as well, Davina. I do. It's just that we're in high drama here right now, do you see? Every hour is key, every minute spoken for."

"What about now? Can I see you now? Can I come to see you, please?" She was one beat short of begging, but she didn't care. She had a need and a purpose and was desperate to fulfill them both. Georgia knew it wouldn't work to bring Steel to Downing Street—into the hot light cascading over her every move. She promised her a quick answer, hung up, called Early, woke him in the middle of the night, and against every bit of her better judgment had him come round and drive her to Bloomsbury.

THEY WALKED SILENTLY through the foggy streets. Early walking just behind them, while Stacey Rimple, the MI5 guard whom Early had insisted on bringing along, stayed back in his car outside Steel's parents' flat. Georgia hadn't wanted Rimple along, but Early had prevailed upon her that her world had now changed and that caution was needed, even in moments like this, when it was being thrown to the wind. Georgia had her scarf over her head, once again covering her face. She wore her old ratty wool jacket, which made her look a true chemist's daughter out for a windy night stroll with a young female friend.

They tucked into Bloomsbury Square. A tiny, authentically square patch of unhealthy green nestled alongside a tall office block and a row of old homes. It was dark and forgotten. The trees were not large or full enough to hide drug use or illicit sexual encounters, and there was no real place for shelter or sleep, so it sat quietly at night, waiting for the morning and the pedestrian traffic or the first rumble of the parking lot buried below it. Early hung back and gave Georgia the privacy he knew she would never have again. Georgia and Davina instinctively found a nest of small trees to shade themselves from the moonlight.

They kissed, softly and carefully, neither sure who had initiated the embrace. Steel went weak in the knees. She didn't want it to end, wanted to pull her even closer, but instead pulled herself back and looked at Georgia. It was a razor's edge, what she was feeling. It was lust, love, bile, and hate, all in a perfectly wrapped bow. She did what she could to mask the dread. She wasn't here to confront her. She wasn't after drama. She was hunting truth. She knew she needed to keep the flame on the front burner. She stroked her cheek, teased her.

"Madam Prime Minister. What must that be like? You must be so thrilled." Georgia chuckled in reply.

"I don't know what I am. I really don't. I'm a bit adrift, if you must know. I'm taking it all on a minute-by-minute basis. So much of it doesn't seem real. Does that make any sense?" Steel nodded, yes, and spoke in a gentle whisper.

"I've been wanting to talk to you about so much—about us, but also the investigation."

"Have you uncovered anything new? Is there a break?" She led Steel over to a bench. They sat down holding hands.

"No. It's more of what I thought, though. Even clearer now that someone very high up is involved. The murders in Tewkesbury last week of the DPG agents—" Georgia cut her off with a concern that Steel knew was inauthentic.

"The drug bust?" Steel struggled again to stay in the light, to give her the benefit of the doubt.

"Yes. But it wasn't a drug bust. It was murder. Heaton's men were responsible, and it took place on the grounds of his Dorrington property."

"That's absurd. It seems to be a cut-and-dried case of a drugs bust. I read the report."

"I was there, Georgia. I saw it all with my own eyes. I watched Edwina die." The blood drained from Georgia's face. "Heaton is a monster. He's behind all of this. He's murdered that Gordon Thompson, the American's father-in-law. He tried to murder Roland Lassiter. It's him. I'm sure of that now." Steel's eyes went cold. Georgia saw the change and held her hand firm.

She wanted to tell Steel everything, let the truth escape from her soul, fly out and up, right there over Bloomsbury Square, but she knew that she couldn't. She'd be revealing herself not to a beautiful young thing who had somehow stolen her heart, but to an investigator dead set on the truth. She wanted to tell sweet Steel how badly she had been duped, how sick she was with it all. She wanted to confess and collapse right into her arms, to hear young Davina tell her how right it all was eventually going to be, how much she was going to do to protect her. Each breath she took as they silently held each other's hands brought her closer to releasing her burden—to confession.

Steel somehow sensed it, somehow gleaned through the old wool coat and the now pushed-back scarf Georgia's desire to open up to her. She tried to prod the conversation along to her benefit.

"Do you have any idea who in the government he could have aligned with him, any sense of it?" She looked deep into Georgia's eyes, begging her to volley back with the truth. Georgia sat there for a loaded moment, waiting for a response to percolate, praying for the right combination of words to come together. What should she protect? Her life? Her job? Her freedom, or her heart? She finally spoke, stroking Steel's hands as she did.

"No. No. I have no idea who he's colluded with. I couldn't even begin to think who would stoop to that. I wish I had an answer, love. I do."

They spoke just a while longer. Georgia laid out promises about uncovering it all—about them finding a time to be alone together, in some safer version of privacy, nothing, though, that had a sincerity to it. It was time to move on—they both knew that. They kissed gently once more, held each other in small fits of warmth, and then Georgia left. Early walked her back to Rimple's car.

Steel watched as the government vehicle lumbered off. She had had this one chance to get Georgia to confess. It hadn't happened. It was over between them. She was sure of that.

She knew Georgia had cleverly held her tongue. She was sure, as well, that she'd never get as close to her again. It was all now past tense between herself and the new PM. Steel stood alone in the frigid night air on the vacant, sterile, concrete street. She opened her coat and ripped out the useless recording device she had taped to her chest.

Heaton wanted Georgia to call for an emergency session at the party conference scheduled that weekend. He wanted her to propose and implement an up-and-down referendum on leaving the European Union. They were in Georgia's office at Number 10, once again locking horns. She was in as foul a mood as he could ever remember. She had grown to despise Heaton now. "Hate" was too weak a word. She could feel a flame in the back of her throat every time his name or even the thought of him arose. His cologne made her retch; his careless, classless cackle was like nails on a chalkboard; and his incessant demands had been taken to a new level in that they were now voiced openly as orders.

It had been a full week since she had addressed Parliament and accepted her party's call to form a government. It had been one long, never-ending series of meetings, dinner parties, and conferences. It felt like it had been a year or more, not anywhere close to a mere seven days. She was tired but she was stronger. She had been off the drugs for almost two weeks and was already standing firmer, sleeping better, and even eating full meals again. She wanted to stand up to Heaton but wasn't yet sure of just how to do it. She needed to keep him as close as she could until she could strategically end their affiliation.

"The time is right, Georgia. Now. Not later. The public is ready. They've experienced drastic change and it hasn't been the end of the world. You've overseen a smooth transition, Roland is going to survive, and so is all of this." He waved his arms around the finely crafted room with the ornate souvenirs.

"We are ready to move on and ready to reclaim what's been lost. I'll tell you there's a majority of the Tories ready and waiting to anoint you with the mandate to do this, you've got all of the UKIP vote, and Andrew Bate-Hydely at party policy tells me that he thinks a good third to almost half of our party is ready to take the plunge. Even some of the damn libs are on board. The stars may never line up like this again."

"I'm not sure. I don't think it's time. Not yet. I'm not saying to wait much longer, but Roland was very vocal and public on his not wanting a referendum, on choosing a series of protections and amendments. His white paper stands as record. The ink isn't dry. I'll be seen as a provocateur taking advantage of his misfortune."

"You'll be seen as a heroine, the woman that brought England to its senses! Every poll we have done tells us it's more than feasible."

She turned away. "I won't do it. Not now. We've already done enough damage. I need to let the dust settle and run the government. We have other fish to fry here, David. It isn't all about your grand scheme. I have an agenda to discern from this convention and I need to put together a team to put it in place. We have holy hell still brewing in the Middle East, a crime rate on the ladder up, and unemployment ticking high again for the first time in three years. Give the people a chance to catch their breath. Give me a damn chance to catch my breath. I'll not be pushed this quick."

There was a slight knock on the door. It opened quietly and Sir Melvin Burnlee entered. He reminded her of a tall gray distinguished spruce. Dapper, dignified, and perfectly elegant, Burnlee was a last link to another kind of Englishman. He had been in government or service his entire life; so had his brothers, his father, and his father's brothers. There were very few families in Britain that had roots and rivers that ran as deep and as true as Burnlee's did.

Georgia was shocked to see the home secretary there. He wasn't one to come by unannounced. It wasn't his way. He was a "by the books," old-fashioned sort who would have meetings on preset attendance; even phone calls were scheduled and calendared.

"Are you with him on this then, Sir Melvin?"

"I am. Have been all along. Yes." The wind left the room for Georgia. Heaton had often waved the idea of the "others" in the scheme, how deep the mine had been dug, the pedigree of his pals, but for some reason she never suspected the prim and proper Burnlee to be one to ride along with the strong scent of new-moneyed cologne that Sir David embodied, but apparently he did. He stood right next to Heaton, now firm and proud.

"It's time to get on with it, Georgia. We've come a long way. There's no turning back."

This was a body blow. If Burnlee had come along, then there were surely others. The party was aboard as well. This had all been planned, consecrated, and anointed by a cabal with incredibly rooted ties. On one level she felt safer, not as alone, more sure-footed in terms of being able to ride along and complete any cover-up. On another, much broader and more profound plane, she felt thoroughly saddened for her country, for what they had done, for the trust they had squandered, obliterated. Yes, they had their patriotic reasons—they yearned for a true referendum above the reach of politics, to "let the people speak"—but they had done it in a way that was beyond sinister. It was malevolent and ultimately nothing shy of unfiltered evil. They must have all, on some level, known that and decided not to let it stop them.

Burnlee nodded to her. She had no response. He left the office. Heaton looked back once more to Georgia. He seemed to want to say more, maybe even to comfort her. He knew her well enough to know that now wasn't the time. He kept his head low and made his exit.

She let Jack Early know that she needed a break. She went wordlessly up to her flat at 11, closed the door, and tried to stop herself from spinning. She went to the bottom of her drawer and pulled out a small Dopp kit. She fished out the bottle, backed over to the bed, tried to breathe as she sat down, and popped open the bottle. She didn't even fight herself, knew that it was useless. She swallowed two of her little "candy" pills.

TATUM ▪ 3

Adam left the family at "the fleabag," as they now called it, and walked several blocks to a local printing shop that still sold Internet access. It was a blessedly foreign-owned shop whose owners weren't tuned in to the daily blast of British politics, or the "Hunt for Adam Tatum" show that locals were still reading about regularly. He had shaved his head and grown a solid goatee, lost at least ten pounds from stress, and truly did look like another person. He felt like another person as well. The man on the television, the face flashing from newsstands, wasn't him anymore. That was a different man, from another time and a far-off place. That man had a sense of who he was, what he wanted, a head full of dreams and goals for himself and his family. This man—this bald, goateed, skinny man with the limp from the dog-ravaged leg bites and the haunted memories of his father-in-law's brutal death—had no dreams, no plans, and no schemes. Nothing concerned him now that didn't deal directly with survival.

He googled "Jack Early." One result was an entry on a wordy blog about the activities of Britain's civil service workers. The post described a 2007 banquet in a town called Skegness. The roll call of those attending listed a Jack and Darleen Early. This was his man: a civil servant with a one-off work address—10 Downing Street.

He searched for "Jack and Darleen Early." The names came up on several property tax roll calls in someplace called Croydon. They owned a home. He looked up the address and scrolled through estate listings on the property. Jack Early and his wife, Darleen Early, were listed as owners. He read through a mortgage history of the home listed on Dulcette Way in Croydon. The owner, this "Early," had stated he was under the employment of the national civil service. He laughed to himself that it was so easy.

A Somali woman at the next computer over smiled his way. She was happy to see any form of joy. Her big, toothy beam warmed him for a brief second.

"Got him," he exclaimed, not even sure why he was communicating with a stranger. "I got my man." The woman smiled brightly once again, a vacant flash of her teeth. She didn't speak a word of English.

He took a bus down to Croydon the next morning. He found the home on Dulcette Way and was there by 5:30 a.m., perched on a bus bench across and over from the suspected Early house. He had a full view of the door. He waited. No one came out for two hours. Then a young man, maybe fifteen, gangly and thin who looked like a younger version of Jack Early, left the house, unchained a bicycle from the front garden, and pedaled off. A half hour later the door opened again. A woman, a thick one with a curly shock of gray hair, shepherding two younger girls, maybe ten and twelve, walked out and away up the street.

He waited another two hours. Still no Early. The sun came out loud and proud, and then it rained. The thick woman lumbered back home and banged the front door closed. People came and went. He let each and every bus pass, seated diligently until it became obvious: Early wasn't there.

He took the bus back to London. He decided he had been too late. *Early leaves early.* He picked up a magazine left behind on the bus and read a story about himself, about his life, his bomb-making techniques. He read about a murder he committed in Kent: Richard Lyle, his wife's ex-boyfriend. Apparently Adam was a deranged bomber and also a jealous, scorned lover/murderer, on the run and extremely dangerous. It was all laughable fiction but read well. When he'd had enough, he turned to a story on some famous pop star's favorite soups. It seemed to have more truth to it, so he read it through as the bus made its way back over the Thames.

The next night he caught the final bus south. One a.m. He needed to be there well before first light, before the first bus left London. He got to Croydon at two a.m., had a coffee from a place called the Two Brothers Café, which was open late, and walked the chalky streets until four thirty a.m., taking his place on the bus bench across from Early's house to once again wait patiently.

He still hadn't told Kate and the kids his plan. They were also waiting patiently: still numb, not a lot of talking, watching old movies, playing games on an iPad, eating takeout, quietly huddled in the musty room next door, the kids' room, the one that Kate was now living in. He was alone, limping around on his side of the family hovel, quietly muttering to himself.

He would tell them soon. He would carefully tell them all that the plan was to kidnap one of Early's children, to make Early help them. He would force Early to tell the truth, tell the media. The scheme wasn't fully formed enough to inform his family yet. Kate and the kids were all he had and he would need their help, particularly Trudy's.

At 4:50 a.m., Early came out his front door and walked across the street, straight toward Adam with purpose. He had been spotted. It was over before it began. He wondered if he should run but decided not to. He decided he wouldn't get too far with his legs bandaged up the way they were. He would let Early confront him, then he'd bellow back, accuse him of attempted murder, treason. He would let him know that others knew. He sat firm and let his heart pound as the lanky little man crossed over to him in the cold, dark morning air.

Early sat down on the bench next to him. There was a pause. He looked over, half smiled, pulled out a newspaper, and began to do the crossword puzzle. Adam took his first breath since Early had come out his front door. He was just waiting for the bus and hadn't suspected Adam in the slightest.

The London-bound bus came. Early climbed on and so did Adam. He took a seat at the rear and watched the back of Early's head in the middle of the mostly empty bus as it rumbled north through Brixton. Early finally got off just below the river. Adam disembarked and followed as he went into the Underground at Vauxhall and caught the train for Westminster. On the Tube, much more occupied than the half-empty

Croydon bus, Early stood holding a strap, staring out the useless windows into the fleeting black of the tunnel as the train barreled its way toward the seat of power.

Early's gaze was vacant, Adam thought. There was nothing seriously worrying him. He wasn't in any danger; his family was safe and warm. With a good job with the most powerful woman in the country, he had nothing to be troubled about. So big deal, he had helped place a bomb that almost killed the prime minister, had committed an act of sabotage that could have him imprisoned for life. His silly, smoky face revealed no burden of the weight of seditious activity. His kids were off to school and, according to the Google search, his mortgage would be fully paid in six years. Life was running along nicely for this "Jack Early." He was most certainly not on the run; he had no reason to shave his head.

Adam let him go at Westminster. He didn't need to follow on through to the final leg of his commute. That wasn't the point. He stayed on as the Tube rocketed off. He had seen what he needed to see.

Steel visited Edwina Wells's grave in Hoddesdon. There was a light rain that fit the occasion. She was buried next to her father, a former officer of Scotland Yard, and her sister who had died of leukemia at age nine in the 1960s. The family graves were on a slight hill behind a large stone church.

She missed her already. She thought about her so much more now than she did when she was alive, but that's how it was, she figured; you only realize what you have when you've lost it. Edwina had been a good friend. It had been Edwina who was on duty when sixteen-year-old Steel landed at Scotland Yard with a wild tale of taxicabs being used to disrupt the Queen's Jubilee. It was Wells who first sensed there was something to her story. Something to Steel. It was Wells who had convinced her parents to let the young Davina take the courses she took and then to serve her country.

"You've made me good and proud, Davina Steel." She heard that, over and over. She missed her friend, and she burned bright now, smoldering with anger. She had been duped. She had been lied to. She had been treated with disdain, by a traitor. Georgia was somewhere laughing at her, she thought, laughing at her and reveling in the power she had stolen, laughing at the people that she was supposed to be looking over. Steel would bring her down, make her pay. She would make Edwina Wells proud.

––––––––––

SHE WENT TO see Darling at SO15. She realized there was a possibility that the major general was involved with the bombing as well. There were considerable resources spent in the reframing of the Dorrington murders. It would take someone high up in that world to push those kinds of buttons. It didn't make sense to her, though—not Darling. He wasn't a clubby political type. He was a soldier, a man of virtue. He was too rigid to chase that breed of fox. She didn't see Turnbull or any of the others even having the audacity to confront someone like Darling with such a scheme.

She felt strongly that she knew people, could sense the superficially unseen. Events had proven that right. Her reputation spoke of it regularly. Yet she missed on Georgia, missed that one completely, hadn't she? Could she be this wrong about Darling? She thought not.

"THE PM'S INVOLVED. From the beginning. She's aligned with Heaton. I'm sorry, sir, but it's true." Darling sat wordless, a good three minutes— an eternity when you're sitting across from someone whom you've just dropped the world on. Darling kept staring at her, chewing his lip underneath his bushy mustache. His spartan office walls were closing in on her. She was about to beg him for an answer when he finally spoke.

"It's preposterous, but it makes some sense." Again more silence; then, "I mean the whole thing makes no sense, yet oddly, this does make some sense. If it's true, if you're correct, then it's a horror. A tragedy for England." He got up, paced. "If you're wrong though, Steel, if you're off on this, it's going to be the end of you, you realize that? It'll gut you. From here on in. You'll be done. Can you see that?"

"I'm not wrong. She's involved. There are others as well. I was there. I saw what happened at Dorrington. I still have the bite marks." Darling looked back to her now. She knew what he was thinking: Dorrington. A conspiracy. It all could be true. High-level connections? It would make strong sense with Heaton involved, but this was the prime minister she was implicating.

"I could set a trap for her, sir, make her reveal herself to you. Would that help?" He went back to his desk, sat across from her, played with his facial hair for another interminable amount of time, and then finally looked over the desk intently.

"What kind of a trap do you have in mind, Steel?"

TATUM ▪ 4

Ryan Early never liked the Croydon Youth Center at the West Croydon YMCA. It had a feeling of being like a kid's version of an old folks' home. The furniture smelled like his grandmother's place in Liverpool and the chubby counselors who made the rules and kept the kids in line all had a dull, vacant drone to every proclamation they made.

He was there because his mates were there, almost every day after school—playing football, watching movies, drinking Cokes, and stealing smokes. Ryan, fifteen, was a good kid. He was thin and sort of gawky. Like his father, he had a birdlike face. He also had a serious acne problem, one that came with the package of being fifteen and a lover of fried foods, candy, and sugary soft drinks. He liked girls in a way that he was too young and too closed down to realize wasn't anywhere near as unhealthy as he thought it was.

That was the other thing about hanging around the YMCA youth center with all of his friends after school that interested him: the girls. The girls were there every day, not that they were much to look at, this pack, not that they spent any time looking back at him, but they were there, and happy, skipping, singing, and laughing, and he could look at them and dream. Girls like Chandra Johannsen, who was a neighbor and had incredibly giant breasts, or Mindy McTavis, whose dad worked for the government like Ryan's dad did. They were the two top-tiered girls at the center, and neither ever bothered to say as much as a word to Ryan. They definitely didn't seem to be inclined to do any of the "things" that he had his mind set on doing with them. He couldn't even get them to acknowledge his existence.

The new girl had been coming around for about three days. She was, all of a sudden, out of nowhere, always there. She was beautiful. She was American. She was new in the area, from what word of her leaked down to Ryan and the oily boys in the cheap seats. No one was really sure where she came from.

The girls all took to her. She seemed always to have gossip or something to dispense and was constantly the center of attention in the middle of a pack of them, making the group laugh and squeal as one. Chandra Johannsen seemed to get a big kick out of everything she said. She had dark brown, bushy short hair that Ryan was sure must have smelled like a meadow, dark brown hair that Ryan would have no way of knowing was freshly dyed. She was a little older, maybe sixteen, with blue eyes and Hollywood teeth.

Maybe she was a movie star researching a part, studying how to play a girl from Croydon. That's the notion that Ricky Finnegan was floating. They all wanted some good reason for her just being there, having landed among them. It wasn't real unless there was a reason. She was too good to be true.

On the third day she said hello to Ryan at the water fountain. She was sweet, and luckily his breath was able to keep pace with his words and he didn't embarrass himself too much. She looked into his eyes when she spoke to him. She had to have been an alien. *She's here studying life on earth. That's all there is to it.*

On the fourth day, as he was heading from the school over to the center, he saw her out and about on George Street coming out of an Orange mobile phone store. She was by herself, fiddling with a new phone. She even had the box and the bag still clumsily in hand. He watched for a bit and saw that she was frustrated. As she stopped and read the instructions, she turned and saw Ryan coming up the street. She showed a flash of embarrassment for having the problems she was having. The awkward teen wasn't sure what to say or even how to say it. He just knew his heart was racing and he needed to move his lips, so he squeaked out a quick monosyllabic burp.

"Hey." She smiled, appearing happy to see him.

"Hi. You're from the center, right? I'm Trudy. Hello."

"Ryan." She reached out her hand. He shook it. Her skin was as friendly as she was—soft and warm to the touch. He was right, he thought. Her hair did smell like a meadow.

"Do you go to school here?"

"No. I'm from Illinois. My dad is here on business. I'm with him."

"I didn't think you were from around here."

"I wish I was. I kind of like it here."

"You do?"

"Yeah. I like the center. It's fun. Plus it's the only place my dad lets me go in the afternoons when he's off working." He wanted to say something clever but knew it was a bad idea, so he just nodded and stared at her.

"Do you know anything about phones? I've just got this new one and I'm trying to hook it up so I can text my dad, let him know I got it, let him know I'm okay. That I haven't been taken or run away." She made a comical face to empathize how lame she thought her father was. Ryan looked down at the phone as if he'd hit a jackpot. It was the same phone he had, the one he knew everything about. He wasn't an expert at much but, boy, did he know the ins and outs of his phone.

"I know that one. It's the same as mine, isn't it?" He pulled out his phone and showed it to her so she knew he wasn't lying.

"Oh, that's great. Can you help me set this up? Is there any way?" It was everything he could do to contain himself.

"Where can we go?" she wondered as she turned to the coffeehouse across the street. "Can we go over there, grab a table? Have a coffee? I'm buying."

She's stunning. That's all he could think about as they walked up to the corner and crossed at the crosswalk. Over and over to himself. *She's stunning, she smells amazing, her teeth are perfect, and she keeps touching my arm. Don't mess this up. Don't say too much. Don't let her smell your breath.*

———

LATER, AS SHE and her father drove back in the rented car her mother had gotten using her fake passport, Trudy was quiet. Adam sensed she wasn't too happy to be involved with what they were doing.

"He seems like a nice boy."

"He is." She looked out the window of the compact car as they ambled north, up by Streatham Common, toward the city. She once again started thinking about the last few weeks. All she was doing was what Étienne had done to her. He and his crazy weirdo French mother had been using Trudy, and she was just doing the same to this little goofy kid with the acne and the big nose. She wondered if maybe Étienne felt the same way about her. Did he just pretend to find everything she said funny? Find her "adorable"? Was it all an act? Had she really been used that badly? She finally turned back to her father.

"Promise me again that we aren't going to hurt him."

"Of course not, Trudy. We'll make his father worry, but we won't hurt him at all. I promise."

"Okay. I mean it, though. I get why we have to do this, but I don't think it's fair if we just become like them." He looked over at her and managed to smile.

"What?"

"You're growing up. I like it."

THAT NIGHT, AS Ryan was about to go to bed, his phone buzzed. It was Trudy—the angel. He had used his phone to make a test text that afternoon when he set her phone up, so she had his number. This wasn't a test, though. She was actually texting him now. He looked at the phone as if it were radioactive, worried that if he touched it she'd know, and he'd have touched it wrong.

"Thanks again for setting my phone up, Ryan. You're the best. See you tomorrow."

Should he respond? Should he just keep cool? Be digitally aloof? No way. She texted him and he wanted her to know that he was there for her. Maybe she was just lonely enough that she'd want him to be her boyfriend while she was in Croydon.

"It's cool. I can help more. Do other things."

Jesus. That sounds weird. Creepy.

"To your phone. Not to you."

Even stupider, he thought. *I can't believe I sent that.* He mulled over what to text next, how to dig himself out of the hole he thought he was in. He almost went into a panic when his phone buzzed again.

"You're funny. That made me laugh."

It was followed with an emoticon of a face giving a big red kiss. Then it buzzed again.

"See you tomorrow at the center."

He didn't sleep a wink that night.

ADAM AND KATE got into a spat over what he had brought Trudy into. They talked quietly on Adam's side of the connected duo of fuggy hotel rooms. He did his best to make his wife understand that they had no other choice. Things were speeding now to an inexorable conclusion. It was "us or them." Jack Early needed to be coerced into helping him expose Georgia Turnbull and the others in order to clear Adam's name.

"I'm just worried she'll live with this forever, live with all of this forever."

"I'm sure she will, Kate. There's no doubt of that. This is a nightmare, for all of us. It's pretty obvious, though, that if these people have their way, if they catch us, they'll do to us exactly what they did to Richard and to your father." She turned her head into the ratty bedcover on the lumpy bed and covered her face so he wouldn't see the tears.

"I'm sorry, Kate, I don't mean to scare you, but I don't think we have a choice."

ADAM, BILLY, AND Trudy drove down to Croydon the next morning. Adam didn't bother to wake Kate to say good-bye. She was sleeping these days fifteen or sixteen hours at a time, cloaked in depression and fear-fueled self-pity. Adam couldn't fix that. He made a decision to steer straight ahead. Let her be. She was safe asleep in that rat hole of a hotel room.

He would do what he had to do. He didn't need her approval anymore. He was waiting for her to admit that she was wrong, waiting for her to apologize for not believing him when he told her that he was in trouble, that he was worried about the whole trip, that he didn't want to go to Downing Street. For not trusting him when he told her the whole thing smelled bad and that her father was involved, but it wasn't Kate's way. She didn't accept blame. She was a permanent victim. It was always she who had been wronged, and nothing about the state of their sorry lives right now got in the way of that familiar pattern. *Let her fucking sleep*, he thought. *I have shit to do.*

TRUDY SPENT THE afternoon at the youth center. While she was there, doing her best to subtly further the friendship with Ryan, Adam spent the afternoon with Billy, waiting, killing time, having pizza, and playing arcade games. He tried to talk to his son, wanted to see where he was on all that was happening, but Billy wasn't taking the bait. He didn't want to talk. All of his answers were quick and clipped, brittle bricks in the sturdy barrier of noncommunication that he had erected around himself. Adam decided not to push. He could only imagine what must be going on in that poor little eight-year-old's mind. He couldn't help but think little Billy was actually holding up damn well.

He was proud of both of his kids. They may not have been wanting to say much, but the overriding emotion they were conveying, both of them, after the fear, was a protective desire to stand alongside their father, to do what they could to support him, to let him know they were there for him.

It was inside a yogurt shop in Croydon, while they were waiting for Trudy, sitting in plastic seats by the window, looking out onto the High Street, each slurping down a tub of frozen yogurt, that Billy finally started talking.

"Poppa's dead. Right, Dad? He's dead? Someone killed him up at that place in the woods, when you got bitten by dogs? Right?" Adam took a minute to answer. The subject up until then had been sidestepped. Kate had made the decision for them. She didn't want Billy to know. She felt he had enough on his plate to deal with. They had told him they were going to see him again once they were home. In fact, they had lied to him. He was now instantly done with that. He turned to his son.

"Yes, your Poppa is dead. That's true."

"I'm never going to see him again?"

"You aren't. I'm sorry."

"I didn't really know him that well."

"No, but he was crazy about you, Billy."

"The people who killed him, are they the ones that are trying to make people think you're bad?"

"Yes, the same people."

"I wish that I could kill them myself, all of them. Shoot them."

"I understand that."

"I mean, how would they feel if someone had killed their Poppa? How would they feel, Dad?"

"I'm sure they wouldn't like that." Billy let it all roll around in his head some more. He sat in saddened silence while he looked distantly out to the street. After a few more minutes, Adam got rid of their trash. They left the shop without talking, walking down to the car. He opened the rear passenger door for his son, made sure his seat belt was fastened, closed him in, and walked around to the driver's seat. As he sat in the car and fished for his keys, he looked into the rearview mirror to see and hear Billy bawling his eyes out. He waited quietly, with nothing to add. He decided it best to let his young son have a good cry.

———

THEY PICKED TRUDY up around the corner just before dinnertime and drove back to London in the middle of rush-hour traffic. He had her text the Early kid once again as they crossed the Thames.

"Good seeing you today. My phone works great. You're a star!"

He had her throw in another gooey emoticon for good measure.

RYAN ENDURED DINNER with his mom and two sisters in their tiny, newly redone West Croydon kitchen that night. He wanted to talk to someone about the girl, Trudy, the divine one. Her mom would just tell him not to waste his time. His sisters would giggle—they giggled at everything, especially things that Ryan felt strongly about—so he said nothing.

His father worked late, as usual. He had an important job. He was an important man, and now that his boss was the prime minister, he was even more vital. He didn't have the time to come home to have dinner with them, let alone the bandwidth to talk to Ryan about some girl whom he helped set up a stupid phone for. He decided he wouldn't mention Trudy to anyone. She would be his secret. He would eat dinner and go to his room in solitude and stare at his phone with a devotional hope that she would make it vibrate, praying that she would text some version of light into his lonely, drab, acne-scarred life.

In the morning he was up at the crack of dawn. He had fallen asleep with the phone in his hand. She hadn't texted him at all that night. His father had just gotten in from a trip out to Chequers with Miss Turnbull and her entourage, which was most likely what had woken him. It was going to be a long day, waiting and wishing. His father having stumbled off to bed and his mother already headfirst into the laundry, he was given a handful of chores to do, a list of things to run out for, which he gladly took on as a diversion. Each and every moment and movement was wrapped and filtered by a guttural longing for his phone to buzz. It finally did.

He was on the High Street, just leaving a Toni and Guy hair salon where he'd picked up a set of brushes for his sisters. His list was completed and he was going to meet some friends at the pizza place just on the other side of the overpass.

"Do you want to come to our place and watch a movie on my iPad? My dad and my brother are going to Brighton for the day. I'm sooooo bored."

The world changed for the boy. The color of life lit up with a vivid brilliance he'd never seen it have. The wind had a beautiful brace to it. The cars seemed to motor along in a synchronized melody. He was taller, it seemed—taller, firmer. He didn't feel the bumps and grinds on his face for the first time in a long while. This was how life was supposed to feel. His eyes teared up and his hands shook as he answered the text.

"Sure. I'd love to come over. What's the address?"

ADAM HAD A long day ahead of him. It was a key day. Things had to work out or he would have no future. If today fizzled, all the days after would be more of this: more running, more hiding; more mildewed hotel rooms; more fear; more fright. And that was a best-case scenario. Today had to be successful.

He went and saw Beauregard McCalister at the Gloucester Studios. He waited for him to arrive, flagged his car at the gate, and hopped in alongside him. When Beau first saw Adam, he was relieved that he was alive, then was quickly perturbed that he had come back.

"I need help, Beau."

"I told you I can't be involved. You're as hot as can be. Even with that shaved head and the goatee, you're still gonna get picked out, and if it's with me, I'm gonna pay for it."

"I don't have a choice. I need help. Do you understand? I need help. Tonight. I need one of your stages."

"What are you talking about?"

"You can have it all cleared out. Shut it down, send the guard home, but I need it. Tonight." Beau looked over. He wasn't one to turn away a friend, not one in this much need, but this was insanity, a borderline lunatic rant.

"I need that set of the prime minister's office you have. I need it set up and lit on one of the stages. Build it, leave it lit. Walk away. That's all I want."

"The prime minister's office? What in hell do you need that set for?"

"You said it was authentic. Detailed?"

"It is. It's a beauty. You'd never know it from the real thing."

"Good. Leave it up and lit. I need it tonight. I'll never bother you again." He and Beau locked eyes. Adam begged himself not to tear up. Beau saw it. It wasn't an act. He was at the end of his rope.

"I'm innocent, Beau. I'm an innocent man. More important, my wife and my kids are innocent. I'm the only one looking out for them. I have no choice here. I'm in serious danger. We all are. They killed Gordon, Kate's father. Murdered him in cold blood. I watched it happen. I can't get it out of my head. This is a nightmare. I'm living in a nightmare. I have to end it." They both sat there in silence while Beau took it all in.

"I'll be back tonight. I need that set built and lit, Beau. I have to have it."

He stepped out of the car and took the narrow walkway out to the street, turned up his collar, and hustled off. Beau clocked him in the rearview mirror. Once he was sure he was gone, he reached for his mobile and dialed. He took a deep breath, wasn't the least bit happy about what he was going to do.

"Henry, it's Beau. I need that prime minister's office set built on stage three. Now. Need it lit and set up for tonight. It's for a friend. It's a private deal. They've got their own crew, their own security. Just set it up and give the late shift the night off. With pay . . . It's for a friend, that's all I can tell you, Henry." There was a pause as the man on the other side questioned the order. Beau chuckled. "No, it's not the Rolling Stones again. It's not a music video. I'd tell you this time, I made you that promise. It's someone big, but not them."

IT WAS A chilly night in Croydon. It was just past eight p.m. on Saturday evening. The light from the nearly full moon filtered through the spotty fog, giving the street outside of the Early home a sleepy haze, as if it were much later. It had rained earlier; the streets were wet and shined vibrantly, the whole block for some reason smelled brand new tonight. Jack stood on the stoop overlooking his diminutive garden, having a smoke after a meal. It had been a nice day for Jack: no work. It was the first time in a long time. There was nothing scheduled, and "she" hadn't called him in on one of her ludicrous quests. She left him alone for the first full day in maybe forever. These last few months had been holy hell. He was glad things were finally calming down.

He slept late. What a blessing. Until ten. He took his girls out for breakfast. He helped his wife by cleaning out the back shed and caught up on some reading. He wanted to spend some time with his son, but he had been out all day. He apparently had run errands for his mother in the morning, brought back the goods, and took off like a bat fleeing hell. He probably spent the day with his mates. Early had a memory of his own boyhood. He was glad that his son had missed out on all the pain he had had to go through. His kids would have a better life. That was nice.

So was his smoke. The misty air made it all better. The whole world was a gentle place tonight. It was the first time in weeks that he didn't feel dark and dirty with a nagging secret.

After a few minutes, as his smoke warmed and then threatened to burn his fingers, he looked across the way. A man who had stood up from the bus bench—he'd seen him before—was walking over to him from across the street. Was he coming here? Who was this fellow? Something about him seemed familiar. He came closer, the bald man with the goatee. He was limping and had something in his hand, maybe a tablet of some kind. Was he coming here? Sure enough, he was. He came right to the front of the house and let himself into the little gate. He walked straight up.

"Hello, Jack. My name is Adam Tatum. It's nice to see you. Again."

Early froze. His arms and legs seized up; his blood stopped flowing. It was him. The American. In the flesh. What was he doing here? *The entire world is looking for this one, and here he is, off my stoop.* He couldn't form words.

They just stared at each other for a beat. The American opened his iPad, pulled up a photo, and handed it over to Jack, who cautiously took it.

Jack's face broke into an instant sweat. It was his son, little Ryan. It was a photo of him playing with a young lady, the American's daughter. The two them were on the ground, playing a card game of some kind, forced to look up and smile. The girl was holding today's edition of the *Sun*. It was clearly his Ryan. Tatum had planned for Jack to be speechless. He was prepared to do most of the talking, so he did.

"I have your boy, Jack. He's happy, but I promise, he's not safe. You're going to do what I say. Beat for beat. You're not going to call anyone, tell anyone, or do anything stupid because I promise you, Jack, I'm not someone who would take pity and let the kid go. I don't have an emotional streak that bends that way. I'm basically a caged rat, Jack. You and your friends have seen to it that I have nothing to lose. If you trip me up, I'm going to kill this boy. Rest assured. I'll put a knife through his heart. I'll jam it straight in and I'll twist it slow. I'll stare right into his eyes as he dies. I'll be the last face he sees. Do you understand?"

Early said nothing. He couldn't move, form words, or process it all.

"Nod, Jack. Nod and tell me that you understand." Early finally nodded. His entire body was now wet with sweat. *How is he here, this man? How did he find me? Why me? I had the least to do with it all.* He finally saw a way to words and spoke for the first time.

"I thought it was a fake bomb. It was only supposed to scare him. It was going to be a dud."

"It wasn't a dud, though, was it, Jack? It wasn't fake bullets that killed four people either. My father-in-law, Richard Lyle, two cops. This is murder. Treason. You people have crossed a very dark line." He handed Jack a mobile phone, a cheap pay-as-you-go.

"It would be a shame if your son had to settle up for all this with his life. Take this phone. I'll call you in an hour. Don't say a word to anyone. You and I are spending the night together. As far as your wife and girls are concerned, you got called in to work. Got it? Nod again." Early bobbed his head on demand, like a trained parlor act. Adam grunted back, turned, and limped away, down the road, the opposite way from the bus bench.

Early was suddenly whimpering. Adam could hear him from three doors away as he walked back to the rental car. That was good, he thought—he had taken something that Early couldn't bear to lose. He normally would have felt bad about all of this, about taking an innocent boy and scaring his poor father to death, about showing his own family this type of behavior. They had changed all that, these people. They had made Adam a different blend of a man, the kind that didn't feel bad anymore about any of it.

STEEL ▪ 4

Steel had requested a private meeting with Georgia. She had been denied and was told it would be better with the PM's schedule if she waited until the next SO15 meeting on the investigation that had been scheduled for Saturday morning. It was now Saturday evening. The meeting had been pushed back all day and now had been rescheduled for nine. She had tried to call Georgia several times. There was never any answer, and now this morning, when she tried again, a message thundered on that the number had been discontinued.

She had tried to drop in on her, which apparently was laughable. She was denied access at the security gate. She wanted to tell the security officer who she was—not who she was professionally, but about the private place she held in the PM's heart. About the gentle kisses they had shared, the way they'd been affecting each other's breathing patterns.

She wisely decided against it and left.

On Saturday night, when they did have the meeting, as she was led down to the Cabinet Room with Darling and the others, she took a minute to dodge left and sneak a craned head into Georgia's office where she was sitting alone at her desk, reading.

"Can I grab a quick word?" Georgia looked up and saw Steel. She had forgotten how beautiful she was.

"Yes, of course, Davina. Come in. Come in." Steel entered. Georgia got up and gave her a warm hug. She closed the door behind her. "I'd offer up a tea, but I gave my private the day off. I've driven him a bit too hard lately, I think. I've driven everybody a bit hard, what with nine p.m. Saturday night meetings and we've got these . . ." She was nervous, afraid to let a sentence come to a stop. Steel finally cut her off.

"I won't need a tea. I'm sure they'll have something in the Cabinet Room and I . . ." Georgia interrupted her now.

"I'm so sorry for everything, Davina. If I've done anything. I haven't wanted to play with you, I promise. It's been hard, these days, and the circus I'm ringleading doesn't leave room for sneaking off. You understand, right?"

"Of course. Of course I do."

"I think of you. A lot." Steel smiled lightly, guardedly. She didn't want to volley back with sentiment. She wanted to stay strong. Her heart hurt too much to kick it that way. They stared at each other. Georgia reached out and moved a lock of hair from Steel's eye.

"I know, Georgia. I know."

"You know what, sweetie?"

"I know you're involved. You and others. I know it goes that high up."

The room fell and stayed silent for the longest time. Steel stirred the stillness back to life.

"I'll go in there now, give a rehash on where we are with the investigation, give the newest details that we have on where the American and his family are, and then you or someone in that room will pass it along, and before long they'll all be dead, dead like the others—murdered to keep you all safe and cushy. Here. In this house." She looked closely into Georgia's face as she spoke. She wanted some clue as to her next move. None was revealed. Georgia had been a power player too long to reveal cards so easily.

"Davina, I'm sorry, but you're off base. I'm painfully aware that I have crossed a line; a romantic involvement was . . . not smart, I'll give you that, but to come up with a story like this . . ." She paused and tried to show Davina the way it would lay. It was going to be a bravura performance. This is what she wanted Davina to register. A masterful artificial tear ran down Georgia's left cheek. "I understand if it's gotten too personal, if it's too much for you, clouded your thinking. I want you to know, I don't blame you. I've toyed with your feelings. I had no right."

Steel read between the words. Georgia would throw her against the rocks, destroy her credibility, her career. She knew it was an empty threat at best, but it still had the same wallop it would have had if it bore any honest weight to it. Once again a shock of quiet floated through the room. Neither of them was sure what the next set of words should be. Georgia finally looked at her watch.

"The sit-down is scheduled to start, love. Let's not delay it." She opened the door to the office and ushered Steel from the room. "I won't be long. I'll meet you down there." Steel looked away, marched heavily down the hall. Georgia watched her go. She knew that it was now irretrievably over for her and young Steel. If she wasn't extremely careful, the same could soon be said for her political career and maybe even her freedom.

THE MEETING WAS uneventful. Darling and his group waited in the Cabinet Room for a good twenty minutes for Georgia. She finally came in, calm, yet seemingly under the normal weight of running the business of the British people. Darling and Steel once again downloaded to the others where they were on finding Tatum, which was none too inspiring. The late-model Volvo was found in London in a parking lot of a public housing block near Wapping Gardens, just off the river. There was a dustup at the American embassy. They thought the family had been planning to go inside, but something stopped them at the last minute. There had been some shooting but no one was apprehended. The trail was cold after that, although there was some brewing evidence that the father-in-law had a cousin in Wales who had been working to get them off the island, over to Ireland, and then on to America. It was a quick meeting. Steel only spoke a bit. Darling did most of the reportage now. He was taking the reins as well as the lashing for how long this was taking to bring to conclusion.

Georgia again let it be known that she wanted to be kept close on any developments and then promptly shut the meeting down. It was Saturday night; she was aware that they all had private lives to attend to and apologized for all of the delay. As the room drained, she motioned for Darling to stay back. Once they were alone, she dropped her cool.

"Donald, we have a big problem. I'm going to need a personnel change on all this."

"Of course, ma'am. Is it me?" he half joked.

"No. Good god, no. It's Inspector Steel. I'm afraid we're going to have to replace her. It's gotten to a point where I think it's too personal, too much for her. She's too young, isn't she?"

"I suppose she is young, but she's a talent, ma'am, if you don't mind me saying. I think it's a mistake."

Georgia volleyed right back, sure in her serve. "No, it's not a mistake, Major. She's a risk. We need to set her down immediately. Bring someone else in." They stood face-to-face.

"I want it done straight off. She's out. Very important."

"Is there anything else, ma'am?"

"No, nothing else. Enjoy your Saturday—what's left of it." Darling collected his things and left the room. As he did, Georgia melted quietly away up the hall.

ONCE HE WAS gone from Downing Street, in his car headed back home to Richmond, Darling rang Steel on her mobile.

"Your trap worked. You were spot-on. She's dead center on all this. It's incredible. It's horrible is what it is. I was hoping you were way off, but you weren't."

"I knew I was right, sir. How did she handle it?"

"You're under her skin. Put it that way. She wants you off it immediately. Seems to me that you've somehow put the PM's panties into quite the bunch."

Steel nodded wistfully to herself. The good major general didn't know the half of it.

They huddled quietly in the living room of Georgia's flat at Number 11: Georgia, Heaton, and Burnlee. She was adamant that the call for a vote on this referendum had to wait. It was too damn soon, and things were in too precarious a state. She had put her foot down, called them over this late on a Saturday night to let them know she wasn't in any place or shape to be pushed on this.

"We are not in the clear here. You both need to understand that. This has become a leviathan, a landmass of its own that we're heading straight toward at a reckless speed. I'm begging you here. Not for us, not for our necks, but for the sake of country. This is a disaster. It could tear things apart at the fabric. I don't need to spell this all out to you two."

"What is it that's got you so rattled, Georgia?" Heaton had his cool and calm voice on. He was trying to remain as unruffled as he could, hoping to make her see that her agitation was unfounded. "The way I see it, things are fine. Loose ends have been tied down. Roland is healing nicely, happy in his hospital bed and planning to go home to Belgravia in a week or so. The country's moved on. A sudden referendum could be the sideshow it needs—a new story for the papers to lead with."

"People suspect. We're being watched. I have to warn you." She addressed Burnlee now, hoping for some seasoned sanity to flow. He was quietly listening, assessing as usual. "We can't thunder through, not now."

Heaton pressed back. "Who suspects, Georgia? Who has you rattled?"

"I think Darling knows. At least he suspects that I'm somehow involved. He probably assumes you are as well, David. I'm not sure who else he thinks may be on board."

Heaton rose, walked to the front window, looked out across Downing Street, over the low floating fog to the Treasury. He turned back when he was sure it was time to turn the screws.

"How about your lover? Does Inspector Steel know? Is that why Darling 'suspects'?"

Georgia's face deflated, her breath tucked in.

"Oh come on, Georgia, you think it's a big secret? Half of Whitehall knows you're eating this little thing's pussy." Georgia's eyes flared at him with a dark intensity. "If you haven't yet, you're dead set on doing it."

Georgia turned away now, no longer able to look him in the eye.

"Come down off it. You're the prime minister, for damn sakes. Nothing you do isn't good for a tongue rattle."

Burnlee averted his gaze, not enjoying this bit, in directly inverse proportion as to how much Heaton was loving it.

"Is she our problem? . . . Is she our problem? Because if you say yes, then I swear to you, Georgia, we're all going to hell in a handbag unless we fix it."

Georgia still hadn't answered the accusations. She hadn't said a word. She was embarrassed and enraged, on the verge of an implosion. She fought with all she had not to break into tears. It would be all too perfect for Heaton if she were to start crying, like dealing him a fourth ace, so she said nothing, her head bent low, like a schoolgirl who had been caught cheating on a test.

"You are in as much deep water as we are, Georgia, no less. If you think you're somehow closer to the shore, then you're sadly mistaken. You know the course, and you will goddamn stay it! I won't be back here again and hammer out this same rotted dialogue for the fifth time. Do you hear me? You push me and I will have this house tumble down with a sex scandal the likes of which has never been seen."

She wanted to bark back, tell him off, tell them both off, but to what end? What could she say? What kind of bite did she really have to deliver? She was weary. She just wanted to go to bed. She didn't want a slug-out now with Heaton. She still needed a plan to come together in her mind, something concrete, something to growl back at him when he attacked her.

She needed sleep. She needed pills.

"Fine, David. . . . Okay. Yes. Yes. We'll do it your way."

SHE WAS DEEP asleep, in her bedroom. She had the strangest dream: Jack Early was there. He led her up from and out of her bed. There was another man; she didn't know him. He was bald, with a goatee. It was all so odd. Early took her nightgown off and helped her step into a business suit. It was strange to be naked in front of Jack and a stranger like this, but she didn't mind. The other man just watched. She smiled at him in a groggy stupor. She kept telling Jack she needed to go back to sleep.

She woke up suddenly. Seated at her desk downstairs at Number 10. Jack Early was across from her. He was, it seemed, in the middle of taking notes for correspondence, staring at her. Her vision was blurred. She waited for things to come into view.

"Are you okay, ma'am? Can I get you anything?" She was startled. It had happened again—another jump cut. This time the dream seemed so real. She was sleeping in her bed, then Jack was dressing her, and now, here she was, at her desk in the course of the workday. She had fallen asleep by the look on Jack's face in the middle of writing a note. She was embarrassed and shocked, sadly bewildered. This was getting worse, not better. Was she losing her mind?

"Should we go on, ma'am?"

"Go on with what? What were we doing?"

"You were writing a letter."

"I was? To whom?"

"To the press. Telling them what had happened with the bombing. How it had all gone down. Setting the record straight."

"Setting the record straight? . . . I was writing a letter?"

"Yes, ma'am, you were going to write out the whole truth."

Adam watched from behind the thin walls of the motion picture set. It was a perfect facsimile of the prime minister's office, right down to the stationery. Early and Turnbull were seated in replicas of their chairs, while three GoPro cameras were hidden throughout the office, recording every word they said from three different angles. Adam watched on a rack of monitors with Beau.

Beau was a rock star. That's all there was to it. When he and Early arrived with their sleeping guest at the closed-down studio, just after three a.m., he had expected to be alone. They found the Number 10 office set, built and perfectly lit, just as he had asked Beau to do. All the employees had gone home for the night. It was clear sailing as they brought Georgia, still asleep from the car ride, into the stage. Then, just as they entered the blackened cavernous room, someone appeared. They weren't alone. It was Beau. He took one look at the standing, sleeping, near-comatose prime minister and just about soiled his pants.

"Good god, you've got to be kidding me."

"We have no choice. Why are you here?"

"If I had half a brain, I wouldn't be." Adam chuckled. He knew why Beau was here. He was a friend. He was here for that reason and no other. It was exactly what he needed now, too. As badly as he might crave water, or air, or food, he didn't even realize how desperate he was for just one person to be on his side, and yet here he was, this big, tall lug of an Englishman, putting everything he had at risk just for the sake of friendship. It was everything he could do not to pull him in for a hug and a cry.

Beau had set him up with the monitors and helped make sure the lights were right. Adam and Early did the rest. The PM's secretary knew what he had to do. He stayed on script like a pro, like he'd been acting in movies his whole life.

"Wait a minute. It doesn't make sense to me, Jack? Why would I write to the press with the truth? The truth? It would seal my fate, send me to prison, crumble the government. It could cause a panic."

"It didn't make sense to me, either, ma'am. But you said you wanted to write out the truth about the bombing."

"That I was involved? Was I going to write that?"

"Yes, you were. That it was Heaton's idea, but you eventually went along with it. That you had the American unknowingly place the bomb by switching the dossiers."

"Yes, yes, of course, I know that. I know what we've done . . . but why would we write this letter? I'm confused, Jack. This doesn't make any sense." She stood, shakily, reached for the edge of the desk, and hobbled over to the door. "I feel like I'm dreaming. This is all so strange. Even the office. It looks . . ." She stopped and turned to Jack in midsentence. There was a tear in each eye. After a pause, she spoke again through fractured words.

"Jack, I'm a drug addict. . . . I'm a drug addict. I'm not in control of myself. I'm lost. I fall asleep out of nowhere. Nothing seems real. I'm in trouble. I'm lost. . . ." With that she turned and walked to the closed front door to the office.

Adam and Beau, out on the floor of the stage, weren't sure what to do. That door she was about to open went to nothing. She would expect to see the rows of desk sets and then the long hallway out to the lobby of Number 10, but instead she'd see only an empty, dirty sound stage, maybe Beau and Adam at the monitors, watching. This would be a disaster. There was nothing he could do.

Early jumped up and gently grabbed her arm, just seconds before she was about to open the door.

"Ma'am, just relax. Have a seat. You need to catch your breath." She was out of it now, her eyes were rolling, her speech stammered.

"No, no, I just need to run upstairs. I need to get something." Early gently led her back to the desk set and sat her down in her chair. "Oh Lord, Jack. I am so out of sorts, aren't I?"

"It's okay. I'm here with you, ma'am. We'll get through this. You just relax." She sat back in her chair. He poured her a glass of water. She drank the whole thing, took a deep breath, appeared to calm down. Adam and Beau both simultaneously started breathing again. Early had averted a disaster.

"What have we done, Jack? How did I let this happen? We could have killed Roland, couldn't we have? We've let so much happen, let so many down. This is a disaster. It's a tragedy. I've done the unthinkable." She sat there in profound grief. Early just stared at her, not sure if there were words worth calling on. Adam and Beau watched in a stunned stupor.

"I'll resign. I'll tell everything—that I was involved in the plot, in cahoots with Heaton, helped place the bomb . . . that I've been covering it up." Then, as her face shut down, it just as quickly rebooted with another thought. "That I love her. I'll tell everyone that I love her, that I've never loved anyone. I haven't, Jack, ever, and now I have and I've lost her, I've lost me. I've lost everything. I'm pathetic." She started to cry now, uncontrollably.

It was almost unbearable to watch. She stood now, with a strength fueled by a weighty anguish. She shuffled to the office door again, this time with a purpose. She moved too fast for Early, who was overcome with his own share of the grief and regret. She beat him to the door and opened it wide, about to step out, only to realize she was stepping into nothing. Pitch-black emptiness. It stopped her cold.

"What is this? What is this?" A man suddenly, instantly, emerged from the darkness, from nowhere—the bald man with the goatee. He came close, was on her before she could even put arms up. He had a cloth in his hands as he pulled her into his long arms, put the small oily towel over her mouth and nose. He pulled his face in close to hers, their bodies in a lock so she couldn't move, and he wrapped her tight in his grasp

as she inhaled a zinc-like scent from the material he was holding over
her mouth. She knew who he was now. She saw past the shaved head
and the facial scrub, like an old photo in a chemical bath slowly coming into shape. It was him, the American, Adam Tatum. He was nodding slowly, softly, telling her to breathe deeply, and then she was gone.
Back asleep. Back into her bed at Number 11.

STEEL ▪ 5

The flat had a lingering smell of a fish dinner that had been cooked and eaten a good five hours earlier. Steel's parents' place had that ability to hold the scent of the last meal for hours at a time. No matter how much cleaning was done, it always had the downside stench of the prior meal until the new one came along with another blend of fresh scents and odors. It was late. The home was dark and muted. Steel lay in her bedroom under the blankets, fully clothed. Her gun was next to her on the side table, ready to be used.

They would come tonight. She was sure of it. She had seen them outside the shop in the afternoon. Peet and the younger one, the replacement for Harris, the one the American had killed. She felt them follow her and her mother as they left the café and made their way up the street to their building. She knew they were there. It made sense. They would come tonight. Heaton would be sending a message: a grizzly comment on her having placed the final strategic piece to her puzzle. Steel was sure of it.

Sometime after one a.m., they crept stealthily into the flat, right on schedule. They snaked in as quietly as humanly possible. If Steel weren't awake, if she weren't trained and focused on every sound, she never would have heard their muffled movements. They were that skilled, were moving with that much practiced patience. She grabbed her gun, held it tight, and waited.

The apartment was shrouded in a cloak of night. She had made sure of it. She made certain all of the lights were off, all of the curtains closed tightly, so no helpful glow could come in off the streets or from the sky. She wanted them to have to work for it, to struggle in the dark for the prize they were after. Their faint, fluid, floating footsteps piled up in count as they made their way up the hall. They came to a momentary pause as they stood outside her door.

She gripped the gun a little harder and waited. They moved on to her parents' door. She had guessed correctly. They weren't coming for her. That would be too easy, too obvious. It would be too flammable to kill a police officer. They were there for her mother and father.

She focused again on the footsteps: seven gentle sets of squeaks. Then the doorknob of her parents' bedroom slowly, achingly, turned. The hinges on their door tried to sound an alarm as the entry was breached, but the movement was laboriously slow; the creak was almost inaudible.

They were in her parents' room now. The silence took center stage. She sat up at the edge of her bed, her gun now good and ready. She waited and took a deep breath. There was a gunshot: a muffled bang, a silenced pistol. Then another shot. Then two more. For good measure, she assumed. They were pros and would have wanted to make sure her parents were both dead. With the task at hand crossed off the list, their whispering shoes gingerly made their way out of the room, back down the hallway.

Once they were past Steel's bedroom door, heading to the living room and out toward the front door, she just as silently left her room and followed them into the black. She got comfortably behind them as they fumbled their way out through the dark and then, just before they hit the door, she leaned backward and turned on a wall light and answered their earlier gunshots with a round of her own, just as quick, not as silent.

She wickedly hit Peet in the shoulder that had previously been shot. She shot the second man in the leg. They both went down to the ground. She shot again. She shot Peet in the shoulder once again. The younger man got up and went for his gun, which he had dropped in the fall. Steel came over, her gun trained on the center of his face.

"You have a choice. Your gun or the door. Pick one. Quickly."

The young man saw the iron in her eyes, turned on his bad leg, and hopped to the door and out of the flat as fast as possible. She went over to Peet, on the floor, wailing in pain. She kicked him in the stomach as hard as she could. She picked up his gun and got the other man's as well. She put them both into her belt and pulled out a set of handcuffs. She fastened Peet's good side to the radiator on the wall and then, for good measure, using everything she had, gave him another strong kick.

After dialing the Met for a backup call, she walked down to her parents' bedroom and switched on the lights. She looked at the two bundles of pillows and blankets under the oversize quilt that she had molded into her mother and father's sleeping positions and the shape of their bodies. She knew the bedding pieces were all ruined now, soiled with gunpowder and those four troublesome bullet holes, but it seemed a small price to pay.

Her mind was now on Heaton.

He wouldn't flounder the next time he wanted to lash out at her. She was sure of it. It wouldn't be as easy as hiding her parents at her uncle's place up in Biggleswade. Heaton would be coming for her with an even sharper edge in the next round. The whispering footsteps wouldn't creep past her door a second time. It was up to her now to take the fight to him.

Georgia woke up in her bed early Sunday morning. She thought instantly about her dream—about the confession she was writing out in her office, about how real it all felt. She dressed quickly and scurried down in a pair of Sunday-morning pants and late-Saturday-night hair, quickly said hello to each security officer she passed, to each of the secretaries and civil servants who had the misfortune to draw the Sunday a.m. work card, scuffled quickly into her office, and closed the door.

It was different—a different office than in the dream. She wasn't sure how, but it was. She sat down and looked across the desk where Early had been taking his notes. She got up, walked to the door, opened it, and saw the desks and the hallway out to the lobby. She assured the two young secretaries seated at the far desks that she was fine. "No, no tea. Thank you." She shut the office door, with herself alone on the inside.

She paced the room, thinking back to the dream—the American holding the cloth over her face, he and Jack Early standing resolutely as she stood naked while dressing. She turned to the door. She needed to open it again. She did. The two women looked up again, trying hard not to be too curious. She waved them off with a tight smile, then shut the door a second time. There was no doubt in her mind. It was not a dream, and it did not take place here.

It was Early. Early had betrayed her. It had been real. She had been tricked into a confession. Was it a fake version of the office? A replica of some kind? A movie set? Like in that Hugh Grant film? That had to be it. The American had somehow gotten Jack Early to assist him, to corner her. She had been recorded. That's what had happened. She was sure of it. This was a disaster.

It was all over. She would spend the rest of her life in prison. Her poor father. Her brothers. She would bring so much shame to them all. To her country. Her poor, poor country. What had she done? How had this happened? She wanted to scream, wanted to have someone to blame, but she had no one. She had done this. She had made a mess of her life, of it all, and now she would pay the price.

She walked over to the den and sat down on the far couch, the couch she had sat on so many nights while arguing across the coffee table with Roland. They had traded gallant dreams and brilliant schemes back and forth with each other here. They had the ability to change the world. They'd always come back to that one, so proud of where they'd come from, so much hope while looking to the future: a future that no longer mattered or even existed.

She poured herself a glass of room-temperature water and let the aching horror of the moment painfully settle in. Finally, she picked up the phone and dialed the only ally she had left: David Heaton.

Kate and the children had actually come to like Ryan Early. He was a nice kid. He had a pleasant, innocent disposition. He was young for his age, closer emotionally to Billy than to Trudy, it seemed. He was enthralled with Trudy, though. There was no question of it. Adam had guessed right and played it perfectly. Kate wondered if they had needed to hold the boy, tie him up somewhere if indeed his plan was going to work. Shouldn't they bind him? Gag him? She soon came to realize that wouldn't be necessary.

He and Trudy watched several movies together on her iPad. They played card games. She sang to him, sang "Across the Universe." Later he asked, and she sang it for him a second time. They talked for hours, all night long, about everything: the differences in life from London to Chicago, the kids at her school, his school. He made her laugh. The time went by, and in truth, for the last ten hours or so, he could have run out into the night anytime he wanted. Kate, quietly listening in, realized that Trudy was doing a far better job of holding the boy there than ropes or a gag could ever have done.

At the crack of dawn, Adam and Trudy took Ryan home. Adam didn't say a word on the ride down to Croydon. The two teens sat together in the backseat and played another game on his mobile, his favorite game. Trudy teased him, thought it was silly and violent, "dumb," but she played along anyway. He talked on and on about how great the game was and why, as Trudy continually teased him.

They arrived back at the Early home at around 8 a.m. Adam had called Jack when they were five minutes out. He was waiting alone on the curb, bleary-eyed and defeated. His weathered shoulders were beaten into a hunch, his wrinkled suit hanging on his paper-thin body in a way that made him look like a scarecrow posted in front of the old brick row house. The only bright moment of the long night he had endured arrived when his son climbed out of the back of the car and his father inexplicably hugged him tighter than he'd done in years.

Trudy got out of the rental alongside Adam and watched the reunion. She felt for the little British boy. She knew what it was like to be used, to be played with. Now having worked the other side of the game board, she didn't like that position any better. She knew then that she had no interest in ever hurting anyone or in breaking anybody's heart. This wasn't a game that she ever wanted to play again.

Jack asked his son to wait inside and told him how important it was not to say anything to his mother, that the story would be that he had stayed at his best friend's house last night. Ryan agreed. He wasn't sure what exactly had happened or what was still taking place, but he sensed it was best to listen to his father.

Ryan turned to Trudy before he went inside. He wanted to say so much. He couldn't summon words, so she did it for him.

"You're the first person I've ever sung in front of, Ryan."

"I like your singing."

She pulled him in for a long, fiery hug, and then, before she let go of him, kissed him sweetly on the mouth for what seemed to Ryan the longest, most fantastic amount of time that had ever been recorded. As he floated back inside, she went over to the car, sat in the front seat, and closed the door. Her father watched her for a beat, a surprise jolt of pride warming the cold morning air. Somehow, inside the dark vat of drama their family had been dropped into, Trudy had found and been reunited with her sweet side.

Early cracked the moment back open with news of the reality that he was dealing with.

"She knows, Mr. Tatum. Georgia. She knows."

"What do you mean, she knows?"

"She's not stupid. She's figured it all out. Everything we did last night. Knows it wasn't a dream. Knows I've betrayed her."

"She told you that?"

"She didn't have to. She wants me to come get her. Take her over to Heaton's place. On Hyde Park. It was in her voice. I heard it, clearly. I've been with her a long time. She knows. I'm positive of it." Adam looked at him closely. He wasn't lying. This wasn't a trap. Early was good and frightened, spooked, unsure of what would meet him once he got to Heaton's mansion.

"I'm not sure if you quite know what you're up against with Heaton." Adam thought it over. He knew he had an ace card in the hole. He knew he had Georgia's confession on file. He knew it was safely tucked up on the "cloud," in a place he could always get to it.

"Go. I know where Heaton's place is. I'll be there, too. You'll be fine. Go."

"But, he's . . . it's very dangerous, he's a man that . . ."

Adam cut him off, didn't let him finish.

"I'm not afraid of him, Jack. If anyone should be afraid, it's Heaton. Afraid of me." He turned and hobbled off up the road.

Davina, doll, are you sure you're all right, that you're going to be safe?"

"Yes, Dad, I'm gonna be fine. I just need you and Mum out of the picture for a short time. It's all going to be over very soon, I promise." She was loading her mother and father onto a train in St. Pancras railway station up to Glasgow to stay with her Auntie Laura, away from harm, out of London. She hadn't told them about the shoot-out the night before at the flat. She hadn't even told them why she had to have them spend the night up at Uncle Nigel's in Biggleswade. They just knew there was a slight, remote danger to them as a result of the investigation she was on and that she didn't want to take a chance. She promised that she couldn't tell them any more and that she was going to be all right.

"I don't like any of this, Davina." Her mother spoke through a stifled round of heavy tears. "I don't like you in this world. Never have, and now I know for sure why." Steel pulled her mother in tight.

"I know, Mummy, I know. But I'm here. I'm in this world. There's nothing I can do now but my job. Do you understand that?" Her mother regretfully answered yes. Davina kissed her soft forehead, hugged her father one more time, and helped them both up and onto the train.

She crossed the station and took the Underground to St. James Park and walked over to Met headquarters. She went upstairs, past the empty desks and the shuttered offices, and up the back elevator to the weapons lockup. She neatly signed her name in with her schoolgirl-perfect signature, scanned her credentials into the computer, and then proceeded to load herself up with a pair of her regular Glock 17s and a serious stash of additional weapons, including a small-size Browning A5 Stalker shotgun.

Down in the basement at the motor pool, she checked out a squad car. She filled the tank and drove away from the garage, slowly surfing the sleepy Sunday morning streets over to Kensington. Heading straight for Heaton's mansion.

Georgia and Jack Early drove in his Ford Focus across town to the Heaton home. Once again they had snuck away, a feat that was getting harder and harder to do with each passing day. If it wasn't a Sunday morning, it most likely would have been impossible. They didn't say a word on the way over. She was livid with him, he could tell. Maybe she was more mad at herself, he thought. She wasn't one to let all the blame and guilt be used on others. He had seen her take the whip to her own back many times and he knew she couldn't be happy that she had put herself in the middle of this execrable situation.

They pulled onto the estate, past the security, and up the drive to the long, flowing steps of the giant Georgian manor. When the car stopped, he turned the ignition off and finally broke the crushing silence.

"He took my boy, ma'am. The American. Just so you know. He took my boy. I was left with no other choice." She turned to him, her voice deep in her throat, overcome by events, by emotion.

"I figured it was something along that line, Jack. I know you too well to believe that you'd do anything like this for any other reason."

"No, ma'am. There would be no other reason." She nodded, looked up to the house, and grabbed the door handle.

"Well, we're in a world we don't traffic in now. We'll need this one's help. I don't relish that thought at all." With that, she got out and walked up the steps toward the large wooden front door. Her stride was once again in proper form, the walking cane a faded memory. Fear, contempt, anger, and rage had all banded together and given Georgia her canter back.

IN THE PARLOR, Heaton begged her to be calm. He was dressed already in one of his signature made-to-measure suits. Having politely offered drinks that had been politely refused, he poured himself a scotch.

"I'm historically not one to rev it up on a Sunday morning, but it seems like this isn't a normal one, is it?" He came back over to the couch they were both sitting on.

"So tell me, Jack, what exactly does Tatum have? What is it that has our dear prime minister so shackled in dread?" Early was afraid to tell him the truth but knew that there was no other way, so he did.

"He has a tape. A movie, I'd say."

"A movie? What kind of movie does he have?" Georgia's eyes looked away.

"A movie with the prime minister confessing. Sitting at her desk. Spelling out what it is you've all done, sir." Heaton corrected him as he reached into his maple cigar box and took out a Cohiba Behike.

"What we've all done, Jack. What *we* have all done."

"Yes, sir. Of course."

"Where was the movie taken? At her desk, you say?"

"No, sir. At a movie studio. In Gloucester. On a set. A replica of the office." Heaton took it all in as he lit his ridiculously expensive cigar.

"And you took her there? To this movie set? To make this film? That's something that you did?"

"He took my boy. He was going to kill him." Heaton took the time to puff his smoke into a rousing burn.

"Is that what he told you? He'd kill your boy?"

"Yes."

"So you in turn betrayed the prime minister? Your country? Betrayed me?" He stared at Jack, demanded with his gaze that he look him in the eye, which he hadn't been doing.

"Look at me. Answer me, Jack." His voice stayed smooth, almost

soothing, even though his words were undercut with a building, bub-
bling rage. Georgia had never seen him burn quite this way.

"You do know what it is we are trying to do here, yes? Did you somehow forget how important this all was? To England? Did you forget that,
Jack?"

"I didn't forget, sir, but I didn't know what else to do. He was going
to take my boy's life. I couldn't see another way."

Heaton set his drink and his cigar down on the coffee table. He took
a beat to let the room settle.

"Okay. We will figure this out, Georgia, trust me. Okay? I will smooth
this wrinkle. We will make a deal with Tatum. It's going to be about
money. We'll lay it all down with a figure. Have Tatum walk away. Make
a relocation arrangement with him. Like the US does with the Mafia. I'm
sure that's what he's after. We can make it all happen." He chuckled
lightly and shrugged. "It's well played on his part, I have to say."

Georgia took a deep breath. She sensed that maybe David was right.
Maybe this could all somehow be papered over.

"In the meantime, I need to have something done, Jack, an errand
run. I'll need to set the negotiations in motion with Tatum. Come with
me, won't you?" Heaton headed out of the den, motioned for Early to follow, pausing only to turn on a large-screen television. "Georgia, have a
drink. Some water's there on the table. Enjoy them taking the piss out
of you on every channel. This won't be a minute. Jack and I will just be
upstairs in the study. Give a shout if you need anything."

Jack looked for Georgia's nod to follow, which he got. By the time he
was out to the foyer, Heaton was already halfway up the grand revolving
staircase that hugged up and around the circular lobby to the second
floor. He hustled to catch up, but by the time he made the landing Heaton had already walked down the long, wide hallway and disappeared
into one of the many rooms.

"In here, Jack. Come on." He was summoned like a trained spaniel
and he followed, not sure what other recourse there was. He was just glad
to be given a way to make good on what he had done. He entered the
study, a large mahogany-paneled room crammed with books, maps, and
artifacts, plus rare hunting knives. It was a collector's den with shelves
chock-full of trinkets, coins, and curios. One wall was made up of stacks

of old steamer trunks, Victorian-era cruise ship luggage all in pristine condition, one after another, packed halfway to the ceiling. Another area had rare old hunting bugles, a good sixty of them.

"Give me a beat, Jack." Heaton was digging in a bureau at the backside of the room—a giant burl walnut thing that Jack had to believe was priceless. When he stood, he had a pair of garden gloves in his hands and a few other odd bits, along with a long, odd-looking black metal nightstick with a leather strap and a long electrical cord. He pointed easily over to one of the dome-topped steamer trunks, one of the larger ones.

"Grab this one with me, will you please?" He went over, picked up one side of the sturdy old wooden case, and waited for an extremely confused Jack to grab the other, which he did, surprised at how much the damn thing weighed. Heaton motioned for him to follow along as he headed out to the hallway again and now farther down the way toward the back of the house, going into another even larger room. This one was not as nicely furnished at all, almost empty save for another one of the old steamer boxes and a desk against the wall. He led Jack and his side of the trunk into the center of the room and then guided him as they set it down slowly.

"Carefully, please. It's a collectible. Very old. Thank you." The box safely landed, he motioned to a seat at the desk on the wall. It was a Hepplewhite Tambour from the 1800s, in perfect condition. "Have a seat, right there, Jack. I'm gonna have you take a letter down from me to Tatum. There are some supplies in the side of the desk there."

Jack sat into the elegant French-style lounge chair with a Queen Anne leg and a frilly yellow pattern, his back to Heaton. He opened the drawer and found some stationery and a few silver-cased writing pens. He took them out and placed them on the leather blotter, preparing to compose a note. He had been drowning in dread, but now the idea of a letter detailing a negotiation with Tatum was a sign that he may be okay, that he wasn't in the level of danger that he thought he was.

The strap was around his neck before he was really sure of what had happened. Heaton pulled it tight so quickly that Jack wasn't able to put up anything of a struggle, his throat cut off instantly from air. Heaton threw the gangly secretary violently backward, causing the strap to constrict even more. He guided him over to the center of the room, his suit jacket now off. The garden gloves he had grabbed were now on his hands. The dome-top cover of the large steamer box they had carted down the hall was propped open and ready as he led the suffocating Jack over and yanked him down into it, all in one violently successful movement. The cord was off of Jack's neck now as Heaton pulled him backward and down, laid him easily inside the box. The only things hanging over the edge of the trunk were his long, skinny legs.

He was suddenly punching Early now, striking him again and again. It seemed to go on for the longest time. He gave him a savage beating and finally stopped. He let his breath catch up to him.

"You're going to sit in here for a while, okay, Jack? Sit in here and think about what there is to lose. A lot more than one little snot-nosed kid! Do you understand that?" He was almost screaming now, yet controlling himself inside the shout so as not to be heard in other parts of the house. "You're going to get real strong, real fast, or you'll lose a hell of a lot more than your kid. Do you fucking understand that?"

He swung the long solid shock-stick around from the back of the strap. The cord was now plugged into an outlet on the wall. He held the prod under Jack's left arm and pushed a button on the side. An electrical shock jumped from the end of the rod, a large blue and red visible flash violently lurching Jack's whole left side into an instant spasm. It was fast and fluid and it shut down all of his ability to move or think on the entire side of his torso. The first wave was followed with a second, the end of the contraption giving off one electrical blast after another. Heaton was slamming his thumb on the button repeatedly, sending Jack into wild, rolling, speechless convulsions of shock.

Heaton finally pulled the device away, took the gloves off, wiped the sweat from his brow, and watched as Jack did everything he could to find air. Jack's face was now varnished in blood, his eyes hidden behind small mountains of tears and battered flesh. The two men said nothing for the longest time. Heaton finally spoke.

"You act like a kid, you're going to get a time-out. You won't be hurt anymore, but you are going to learn a lesson. I promise you this. We cannot afford to have anything like this happen again. We're only as strong as our weakest link. Tatum knew that. That's why he went after you, but, not to worry, we're going to toughen you up here, Jack."

Early managed to croak out a feeble response.

"I'm sorry, sir. I am." Heaton nodded, seemingly took note of the apology, struggled to get his wind right, then slammed the lid shut and buckled the latches. He picked up his suit coat, which was draped carefully over the trunk next to it, gingerly put it back on, and headed downstairs to see the prime minister.

Adam made his way into the back side of Kensington Gardens. It was Sunday morning but the park was full. Joggers, strollers, and Rollerbladers were airily whirling by in every direction. It was a clear day; the sun was just high enough to take the chill off, but not yet bright enough to share much warmth. He walked by himself, a cap over his shaved head and sunglasses on his face, his pistol tucked quietly into his back belt under his T-shirt. He had been out there for a couple of hours now, first in front of the house, getting a better sense of the security shack, then there in the back, getting a read on the movement in the park behind the mansion. His guess was that the house was staffed pretty heavily, even though it was a Sunday morning. He counted at least five men. Now he was here, once again making his way to the back, just below the large, leafy wall that separated the rear lawn at Heaton's estate from the Kensington Gardens section of Hyde Park.

He crossed the public gardens, over the small footpath, waited until there was no one in view, and then, with as much speed as he could muster, made a go at scaling the wall. The wounds on his legs weren't helping. He was climbing vines and using a small trim pipe to grab on to while trying to ignore the searing pain from the bite wounds on his legs. It took longer than he thought to scale the ten-foot wall, and he was sure one of the park patrons had seen him, but there was no going back. He thought to himself how much better this would have been at night, his original plan, but Early's boss had sped up the schedule on him.

He had made a promise to Jack that he'd be there for him and he would, but, more important, he liked the idea of having Heaton and Georgia in one place together, of confronting them both at once. He made it over the top and threw himself to the yard below, into the back of Heaton's property. He hit the ground in an awkward slant, his foot having gotten slightly wrapped in a vine on the way down.

The force of the fall knocked the wind right out of him. As he slowly pulled himself to his feet, two security men ran across the manicured yard, speeding toward him. They were coming on at full tilt. Adam woozily stood, raised his hands, and spoke in a fake drunken slur, which was not hard to imitate considering how rattled he was from the tumble he'd taken.

"Whoa, whoa, it's cool . . . it's cool. I was just trying to impress my girlfriend that I could climb the wall and fell over. I'll go back, dudes, I'm sorry. . . . Not looking for trouble." The two security men, both in cheap business suits, slowed down to listen. Adam recognized one of them. He was the shooter from up in the woods at Dorrington, the one who had murdered the young police officer with the long-range rifle. Whether they believed his drunken park-goer story or not, they both had sized him up as less of a threat, more of a nuisance. They came on him as a unit and drew close as one of them punched Adam square in the face. The other answered with a sharp kick to the midsection. One of them even laughed. They both came back in for more. Adam stood once again, doing his best not to lose consciousness. They grabbed him and were about to take the beating to a new level, both truly seeming to be enjoying the task at hand.

Neither of them saw the pistol come out. The initial shot was their first inkling of how much trouble they were in. The first bullet tore into the taller one's leg from an inch away. Adam was sure the man's femur had shattered into pieces. The second bullet pierced the second guard's hip straight on. He purposefully held the muzzle right against his body so as to dampen the sound as much as possible. Both men collapsed to the ground, rolling in pain. He saw a set of plastic restraints on one of their belts. He took it, and after a small struggle that got the Dorrington shooter pistol-whipped across the head, he managed to link them together, fastening them to the piping along the back wall. He took their radios, shattered them against the brick, then took their guns and headed up the back lawn.

He crept up the side of the lushly landscaped mansion and waited for other security staffers to follow or an alarm to go off. It didn't happen. He moved tenuously along the west wall, peeking his head carefully into each window, doing his best to be mindful of the security cameras. Finally, as he peered into the fourth window, a den on the first floor, he saw Georgia Turnbull on the couch watching a large television on the far wall. The volume was up loud enough so that Adam could hear it through the window, loud enough so that there was no way he would be able to hear what anyone in the room was saying.

Jack Early wasn't in the room. Neither was Heaton. He wanted to know that Jack was safe. He had played along well, Jack, and Adam had come to like his son, even to like Jack a bit. He pulled back slowly, needed time to figure out how best to make an entrance and confront both Heaton and Georgia with his digital file of Georgia's confession, how to start the process of forcing them to clear his name and face the police, the press, and the public for what they had done. He needed to find out where Jack was. He was inside that house someplace and Adam was pretty sure he wasn't having tea and cookies. If he were Heaton, the first thing he would do, he thought, was to shut Jack up in a permanent fashion. This poor pompous rich prick had a lot to lose.

He pulled back, not sure what to do. It might be best to wait and get a better sense of the situation, to figure out which of the big double doors would be the best way into the house.

He tucked into the safety of a large row of bushes, still trying to keep himself from being viewed on any of the security cameras. He had an idea that the two guards he had just shot had simply spotted him and weren't sent from the security shack. If they had been, more help would be coming, and none was.

There was a vine-covered latticework running from the ground floor to a second-story patio outside one of the upstairs rooms. Adam hated the idea of doing any more climbing, of wrenching open his barely healed wounds any further, but he needed to get into that house. He sucked it up and started to pull himself to the second story. He made it halfway up when his wounds demanded that he stop. His legs were on fire. He needed a short break from the pain.

Two more security guards ran into the backyard, right as he stopped climbing. They ran right beneath him and toward their cohorts at the back wall. He tried to stay silent but the latticework rung he was standing on cracked, sending him sliding down to the next one. The noise alerted the two sentries. They stopped in their tracks, turned, and saw him hanging there, blatantly exposed. The first guard bolted up to the back of the house and practically flew as he scrambled up the latticework behind Adam, grabbing him by the jacket and tossing him backward onto the grass. The guard turned around and dove down twenty feet, landing on him as the other guard grabbed Adam by the scruff of his hair and began punching him in the back in the neck.

Adam did everything he could to protect his face, his privates, and his stomach. These two punch-happy creeps were obviously cut from the same cloth as their buddies. They seemed to have been waiting for the opportunity to beat on someone like this. They reminded Adam of the dogs at Dorrington.

Sadly for them, right in the middle of their cavalcade of cheap shots, Adam pulled a knife from its sheaf on his belt. It came out fully formed and ready. He didn't even take the time to blink. He rammed it straight up into the center of the first man's chest, just off to his left side, twisted it good, twice, then pulled it out and delivered an even better lunge into the second man's neck and straight across: quick, fast, and deep, and ended it. There was no other way. One would be dead in seconds; the other would maybe have another minute to live.

Adam rose to his feet. He was covered in blood, most of it theirs, some of it his. He caught his breath as the two men on the grass groaned in agony, bled out, and died. He looked around and thought about the men at the back wall. The one whose femur Adam had shot out would most likely bleed out, too. He tried not to think too hard about any of it. They all had it coming, every last one of them.

An alarm rang out: a loud, piercing scream of electronic panic. It was raucous and earsplitting, the loudest goddamn alarm he'd ever heard. The siren was followed by a hail of gunfire coming from the front of the house. Something was going very badly in the front of the mansion. Something that for once had nothing to do with Adam.

Steel had parked her car on Bayswater Road and walked onto Kensington Palace Mews. She headed down the street dubbed "Billionaires Row" and over to Heaton's mansion. She was wearing a black rain slicker, sturdy boots, and a black cap over her dark head of hair. She walked slowly, weighed down with her favorite Glock 17, a spare Glock, her Browning shotgun, and an extensive supply of rounds for each of them. She had come because she had no choice. Her heart pounded louder and louder with each step she took toward the colossal home, yet she knew there was nothing coming that she would turn back from.

To Steel, this was simply the lesser of two evils. Between this and waiting for Heaton and his men to come and get her, which she was sure was their next move after the failed attempt to kill her parents, this was the easiest way: to confront them all head on, to take the fight to Heaton and end it one way or another in a circumstance of her own making.

Georgia and Heaton were part of a group of people that were above the law, above society's rules. For some dark, unknown reason, they had rewritten the game and had felt entitled to change it all up in some seriously sinister ways. Steel knew that anyone in their way would have to be dealt with according to new norms. The only person she could tentatively trust was Major General Darling, and even though he would have no good alternative to suggest, he would forbid this, so she moved with purpose down the sidewalk toward the house.

She had expected it to be quiet, being Sunday morning, but it was even more shut down than she had thought it would be. She strolled right into the driveway past the open gate and the guardhouse, which seemed to be empty. A small model Ford was in the driveway, parked against the main steps. She looked closely at the bottom of the windshield and saw a weathered Downing Street employee parking sticker. It made sense, she thought. Heaton was most likely some kind of shadow prime minister at this point anyway.

The first gun blast blew the side windows of the car out and into thousands of tiny pieces of glass. It had missed her by less than a few inches. She turned in time to see the young man she had shot up at her parents' house coming out at her from the front door with a handgun, firing rounds as he came. He had a gimp's gait to him, his leg bound up in a walking cast from their last encounter, but it didn't seem to have slowed him down too much. She threw herself behind the car with a wild leap, landing in a way that allowed her to roll and grab her Browning in the same instant. The shooting stopped just long enough for an alarm to sound: a loud, piercing siren.

Steel stood quickly and saw the young man prepare to fire again, so she dove back down and let him shoot up the car until he had emptied his weapon. She scurried around to the side of the vehicle and dove underneath as she grabbed the little Shetland pony version of a shotgun and let a blast out from under the car that sent a spray of munitions just wide enough to hit both of the young Heaton man's feet.

He collapsed to the ground in a broken flash. As he did, before his body fell to the surface, she fired off again. This time the discharge from the stumpy shotgun hit him everywhere: his chest, his stomach, his legs, and the side of his skull. It blew the top of his head clear off of its base as his body finally landed flat on the driveway.

There was even more shooting now. From behind, at the guard shack at the tip of the drive, someone was once again shooting up the car that Steel had now abandoned, having run over to one of the many large concrete plant pots on the front lawn. She dove behind the cement planter and waited for this round of shooting to die down. When it did, as Steel noticed that none of the bullets had even come close to hitting the row of tall, ornate pots, she poked around to see Peet comically trying to hold an automatic rifle in two hands connected to two very badly bandaged shoulders. It was laughable if not pathetic. She thought, *This old asshole has already taken two different rounds to each shoulder, and still hasn't gotten the message that his job sucks.*

She jumped up now and ran over to the shack as Peet was trying to figure out a better method to use the gun with his particular handicap. Sadly for him, there wasn't one in time. Steel got as close as she could and fired. She hit him once again in the shoulder.

He crumpled down to the ground, wildly screaming in pain. She came over quickly and took his weapon. He had been arrested at her parents' house the night before and was already out on the street in the pathetic shape he was in. That's all she needed to know about how well connected all these people were. She checked in every direction, making sure that no one else was coming. That was it: these two broken-down morons. She poked into the guard shack, rifle first. It was empty. She shut off the alarm.

The driveway fell quiet once again. She looked onto a wall of security cameras. There were two bodies lying flat on the center of the lawn at the back of the house, two other Heaton guards by the way they were dressed. Both were either dead or unconscious. Another camera showed two more men, leaning against the back wall overlooking Hyde Park. One of the men seemed dead as well. The other looked beaten, crumbled up into a painful heap.

Someone else had paid Heaton a visit. It was Adam Tatum. She was sure of it. She looked up to the house, then looked down to the old bald fucker lying on the ground, wrestling with the fact that his shoulders were never, ever going to heal. He looked up to her in agony, almost pleading for sympathy. She answered with a sharp smack to the middle of his face with the butt of her shotgun, full force. He fell back onto the driveway, out cold.

Steel trained her gaze now on the silent mansion. It wasn't going to stay that way for long. The front door was slightly ajar, inviting her to enter.

Heaton was in there. She had lost the element of surprise. He was waiting for her. Steel had no choice. She was going in.

————

SIR DAVID WAS at the top of the front hall staircase. He was at the mouth of the long hallway, about to head down to the first floor, while she was carefully coming in the front door, shotgun first, each step a wary one. She looked up, he looked down, and both saw the other in the same instant. *My god, she's dressed like a nutter*, he thought, *like one of those paramilitary wannabes in America who go around shooting up high schools.*

He turned and raced down the hall as she chased up the steps after him. He passed the room with Early locked in the steamer trunk. If Early started kicking and pounding on the trunk, she would hear it, he was sure of it. She'd hear it, and she'd open it. She wouldn't be able to resist.

She slowed down once she made the top of the stairs and walked cautiously down the hall. She knew better than to assume he wouldn't be waiting, wouldn't be ready and eager to kill her. She moved carefully, room to room, making sure she wasn't about to be jumped. She came farther down the hall and heard a struggle—someone kicking, maybe even calling for help. She carefully craned her head into the empty den. There were two steamer trunks in the center of the room. Someone was inside of one of them, kicking, calling for help in a muffled, terrified voice.

Tatum, she thought. Heaton had somehow gotten the upper hand. She got herself a good sense of the room from her perch in the hallway. It was almost barren, just the trunks and a small, old-fashioned desk and chair. She went in and stepped cautiously over to the large wooden box. She turned quickly and clocked the door. She figured there was time to open the box and release whoever was trapped inside. She lifted the lid; there was a man inside. It was Heaton.

He lunged up at her with the long, black shock-stick connected by a cord to the wall socket beside it. He pushed the button on it right as he held it against her neck. The charge raced through her body, making all of her muscles scream together in an instant, an excruciatingly symphonic chorus of pain. It was the same instant that he used to climb from the box and hit her again with the stick's electric prod, kicking the weapon from her hand.

He had caught her completely off guard and was now perfectly using his good fortune to advantage. He was fully out of the box, her gun kicked to the far side of the room, and was punching her. He was wearing garden gloves with leather flaps on the top of the fists. He zapped her again, this time between her legs, in her groin, which caused her to double over, giving him the opportunity to give her another jolt of the electrical charge under her armpit from behind, forcing her whole left side to freeze up. She fell flat to the ground.

"I can't begin to tell you how tired I've become of playing this game with you."

He started kicking her, one solid bolt of a strong leg after another. He kicked her a good four times before she could even raise her arms to deflect the punishing blows. He jumped down to her, quickly took all of the guns and the ammunition she had in her jacket, and threw them across the room as well. He took the electrical prod to her again, several times, each charge eliciting even more of a paralyzing jerk than the last. She knew she was about to pass out. She knew her body and brain would give way to the dark, seconds before it did. He was almost smiling, she thought. He knew it was over as well. He gave her one last lingering zap and then it was. She was gone.

He easily lifted her limp, battered, broken body and dropped it into the second steamer trunk next to the one that housed Early. He looked down on her in the box, so small that she fit nicely, no need to stuff her legs in like he had to do with the other one. He wanted to spit on her. Piss on her. Vomit on her. She had been the fly in the ointment, had almost ruined everything.

She made him sick to look at. He slammed the top of the trunk and locked it shut.

Georgia had become claustrophobic in the den. She was frightened, angry, and dizzy with an odd discomfort. Heaton had left the television on with the volume at a jarring level. She had no idea how to work the large over-buttoned remote panel "thingy" on the table, and when she tried to go for help with it, she found that she had been locked in the room, which infuriated her. She was forced to wait for him to return and, even worse, to watch a morning Sky News political panel drone on and on about how the government would now go to hell in a handbag under her watch. Earlier she had thought she heard some gunshots, and at one point there had been an alarm blast, but it quickly went away. She tried and failed to convince herself that maybe she'd imagined the gunfire.

She truly had no idea what to do. She was livid that she had been made a prisoner in this awful man-cave of a room. Almost in answer to her frustration, at a point when she considered using the phone to call her security chief at Downing Street, she heard a key rattling in the door lock. It was Heaton. As usual, he was calm and contained.

"Why did you lock that door, David?"

"Why? Because the fewer people that know you're here, the better. I didn't want any of the staff just wandering in." She stared at him, pretty sure he didn't even expect her to buy that line.

"Can you please turn that thing down or even off? It's beyond words how annoying it is."

"The remote is right there, love, right on the table."

"That's not a remote. That's some kind of machine. You'd need a pilot's license to operate that." He smiled, walked over, hit one button, and the room snapped into quiet.

"Now listen to me, Georgia. We need to leave. You and I. Straight off. I need to get you back to Downing Street."

"Where is Early?"

"I had one of the security staff run him out. He's doing an errand for me. I sent him with a note to Tatum. A first blush on a negotiation to buy him off."

"Do you really think that's going to be possible? Buy him off, then send him away with a new name and it's all going to be fine?"

"No. No, it's not at all possible. The press, the people, they'll need to have him. Either dead or in the docket." Georgia turned from his gaze and knew exactly what he was saying. She wanted as little to do with it as humanly possible.

"The negotiations will be a means to lure him out, nothing more. There's something else you need to know, Georgia. Your little friend, the inspector. She's here."

"Davina Steel? She's here? Where is she?"

"She's here, and she's detained for now. She came here guns blazing, Georgia. She's come unhinged. I begged you from the first to have Darling pull her back. I knew she'd be trouble, and she has been. Catastrophically so."

"I want to see her." Heaton instantly lost his signature cool in a wild flash of anger.

"She's just shot the shit out of my security staff, for Christ's sake! What do you want to say to her, Georgia? You want to tell her how much you love her perfume? Is that what you want to say? Do you have any sense of how off the rails this has all gone? I can hear the gallows being built in the square as we speak!" Georgia once again fought tears. It seemed as if it was all she did lately—suppress panic.

"Now you listen to me. We need to go; we have to get you out of here.

Get you back home. Stay here. I'm going to round up a ride for you. I'll be right back."

"And what of Steel? What will you do?"

"We don't have the time for me to answer that, for a variety of reasons. Number one because I don't know yet, and number two because you won't like any answer I come up with." He left for the front of the house. She was crying now. *The hell with him. The hell with being strong.* She wanted to die. Right there in this overdecorated, horrible, leather-clad room. She wanted it all to end. He had won. Heaton had outplayed her in every hand. He was the prime minister, not she. Events had gone from horrendous to disastrous. There was no scenario now that didn't end horribly. She was sure of it.

TATUM ∎ 8

Adam came in through the double doors off the second-story patio, having finally tackled the latticework. He was in a large, nicely done guest bedroom. He walked out of the room and then up the long hall toward the front of the house. Halfway up the way, he passed a closed door. From inside he heard someone calling for help. The voice was muffled and distant but clearly emitted by someone in extreme distress kicking something. He tried the door handle, but it was locked. He checked a little farther up the hall: no one else seemed to be up in this part of the house. He made his way into another room, an upstairs den. It was filled with memorabilia. *Rich kid collector's crap*, he thought. *This is what happens when you have more money than God; you just start buying shit up by the dozens.* Bugles. Boxes. Knifes. Maces.

Adam went back down the hall to the locked door. He used one of Heaton's fancy hunting knives to jimmy his way into the room. He saw two steamer trunks laid out on the floor. One of them had someone trapped inside it. He came over cautiously, broke the lock with the butt of his pistol, and then trained his barrel at whoever was in there as he opened it. It was Early.

Some serious roadwork had been done to his face. Adam gave him his hand and helped him stand. It was a chore, but he managed. Early was scared out of his mind, shaking like a leaf.

"Who put you in here? Heaton?" Early nodded yes, then pointed to the other trunk.

"Someone's in there, too. I heard him beating someone else." Adam went over, broke the lock in the same fashion, and found the cop from Dorrington: the little one with the badge around her neck, the one who saved him from the dogs. He turned to Early.

"Do you know this woman?" Early nodded.

"Inspector Steel. . . . Is she dead?"

"She may be, yes." He bent down; she wasn't moving. She was cute, he thought. He wondered what the hell she had gotten herself mixed up in all of this for. He lightly slapped her face. Nothing. He looked over to Early, not wanting to look at the quiet, unmoving body of the young woman any longer.

"Dead?" Adam checked under her neck, groped for a pulse, and got nothing.

"Yes. I think so." He looked out at the hallway. He turned his attention to downstairs, then looked back to Early and handed him Heaton's hunting knife.

"Hold on to this. You may need it." Early feebly took the knife.

"Be careful. Heaton's still down there."

"Good, because I'm going down to see him. I've had enough sneaking around to last a lifetime."

THE TIRED, SORE, broken, busted-up man from Michigan made his way down the ornately paneled front hall stairway, taking each step gingerly. The next face he saw was Heaton's. He was coming in from the front door, having been out on the motor court. If Jack looked like a different man, the same could be said for Sir David. His eyes were enraged, his face bright, raw, and red. It was contorted with fury. The smooth-talking, giggly game player was gone. He had no clever salutation to impart, just a large shotgun pointed up the stairway. He had been outside and had obviously found his men dead in the front and, via the security screens, in the back. Now this. Tatum. *Fine*, he thought. *Good. This has all of the players here.* He'd taken care of Steel; he'd finish up with Tatum now and end it all. He'd get Georgia back to Downing Street, come back here, and make the calls to get it all cleaned up and tucked away. But first this: first he'd kill this Tatum, do what was supposed to be done in the first place. He had him now. All he had to do was fire the shotgun and blow him back up the staircase.

Tatum kept coming. He pulled the iPad from inside his coat, turned it on, and got close enough that Heaton could see that he was playing a video of Georgia in her office, at her desk. She was talking to Early. It was nicely edited and flawlessly lit. There was no doubt what it was from the minute it unspooled. Adam moved cautiously closer so Heaton could get a good view.

"It didn't make sense to me either, ma'am. But you said you wanted to write out the truth about the bombing."

"That I was involved? Was I going to write that?"

"Yes, you were. That it was David Heaton's idea, but you eventually went along with it. You had the American unknowingly place the bomb by switching the dossiers."

Adam taunted him.

"Fat lot of good controlling the prime minister will be when this comes out. It's up on a cloud, too, Davey. Anything happens to me, it's going to a reporter at every news organization in the Western world. One pre-addressed e-mail, off to four hundred destinations."

"What have we done, Jack? How did I let this happen? We could have killed Roland, couldn't we have? We've let so much happen, let so many down. This is a disaster. It's a tragedy. I've done the unthinkable."

"What makes you think it won't be provable that this was shot on a movie sound stage, Adam? That's it's a fake?"

"Oh, I'm sure you'll be able to prove that. In a snap. You won't be able to disprove that it's Turnbull, though. It's her, the real thing. She'll go down and I'm pretty sure she'll take you with her." He winked at Heaton.

With that, Adam grabbed Heaton's shotgun from his hand in a flash. Heaton didn't even put up a fight. His enmity had taken a new form— he was furious and his mind was racing, trying to figure out how best to move forward on this newest of curves. He stared at the American, looked into his eyes. He saw that Tatum was bruised and damaged but also that he was enjoying this moment; he was euphoric. Adam almost snickered at Heaton.

Heaton lunged at him, grabbed his throat with both hands, and choked him. Adam did what he could to pull him back, but Sir David was strong, powered forward with a demonic heat—white-light anger. He had quickly gotten a two-handed solid grip around Adam's neck and was choking him as hard and as violently as he could. It was an insane, desperate, guttural reaction, but it was having an effect. Adam was struggling to breathe. He dropped the shotgun as Heaton pushed him back across the marble lobby and slammed him over the back of a large antique wooden cabinet. They struggled some more and finally Heaton had Adam up against the wall as he brutally and viciously strangled him.

Adam had been overtaken with surprise. He didn't expect the level of infuriation to come on so forcefully, didn't take into account the insane hours that the billionaire had spent in gyms, judo studios, dojos, and karate retreats around the world. He hadn't factored in how strong Heaton was. Adam reached for his knife, but Heaton was blocking his arm with his body now, not letting Adam get to it. He was trying to get him off him, but he couldn't. Heaton seemed to be picking up strength and Adam was losing it. He had been without breath long enough now to know that he was going to pass out.

Heaton choked harder and harder, his dark, vicious eyes bearing straight into Adam's withering, blinking soul. His hands clamped harder; it was the last lap and he felt it: he was going to finish this all off now, with his own hands, end the whole thing once and for all. Adam gasped, his lungs exploding in pain, the skin on his throat ablaze with the burn from Heaton's grip. His eyes went dim, his eyelids desperately struggling to stay open.

A shot rang out, a piercing blast. Heaton's eyes opened as wide as possible in utter shock as he instantly let go of his grip on Adam's battered windpipe.

STEEL ▪ 8

She was halfway down the staircase. Steel had shot Heaton in the arm. The bullet ripped through his skin and burrowed straight into his bone. He howled in pain. Adam threw him off, backward toward the center of the room. She fired off another shot, this time hitting him in the other arm. She came off the steps now, her pistol pointing straight toward him as she slowly crossed the large, marble foyer.

Georgia was there. She had come up the back hall from the den. She took it all in, speechless. Steel. The American. David. The blood. She found herself able to form only one simple word.

"Davina."

Steel didn't respond; she kept her gaze locked on Heaton. She was shaking, horrified by his image, mortified by everything he had done: to her, to her parents, to Georgia, to Britain. She raised the pistol to his numb, conquered face. Both of his arms shot through, he was in pain and beaten. It was over, he knew it now, and his creaky quiver waved his version of a flag of surrender.

Steel held the gun even closer, her face drenched with her own tears, wet with confusion, overcome by a blinding repugnance that wouldn't let up. It built up inside her brain like a steam whistle, ready now to bellow and blast. Georgia begged, once again.

"Davina. Please. Don't . . . Don't do it."

She pulled the trigger. Heaton flew back toward the far wall, with a clean gunshot hole in the center of his forehead and another straight out through the back. He dropped instantly to the ground in the same sad trajectory that Gordon's last seconds had taken, that Richard Lyle's body had traveled. He was dead before he landed flat. She turned and faced Georgia and looked over to Tatum. No one was sure what to say.

Steel and Georgia locked eyes, a view that offered both of them nothing but pain. She dropped the gun on the ground, letting Georgia know it was over. She wasn't a physical threat to her, letting Tatum know that if he was inclined to leave, now was the time to do it.

No one spoke. For a grisly length of time. The three of them stood silently together. Adam still didn't even know the name of the younger woman, the cop who had just murdered Heaton in cold blood. He knew the prime minister's name, but they, too, had never said a single word to each other. Conversely, Georgia thought she knew Steel so well, yet she obviously didn't know her at all. She had no idea what exactly led her to take the leap she had taken when deciding to end David Heaton's life.

The three of them stood there in the large, frigid foyer, standing over Heaton's dead body, with more dead bodies out in the motor court and scattered through the backyard. Yes, Steel had never said a word to the American, yet she sensed that she understood him well. She knew what it was to be used as a pawn, to be played as a game piece, to be in fear for your life once your usefulness had ended. He had saved her life—three times. She knew him better than she ever knew Georgia.

The prime minister shattered the silent daze.

"Davina, I am so sorry." She wanted to let more words fly, promises, declarations, pleas, but she couldn't summon them up, so the stillness returned. The American spoke next.

"I want my name cleared. I want my family to get home, safely." He took a deep breath and stared at Georgia across the lobby. He had more to say, but he didn't want to waste words. He wanted her to talk and

wanted her to sell him, not the other way around. He merely turned the
iPad around to her and pressed play again.

"*It didn't make sense to me either, ma'am. But you said you wanted to
write out the truth about the bombing.*"

"*That I was involved? Was I going to write that?*"

"*Yes, you were. That it was David Heaton's idea, but you eventually
went along with it. You had the American unknowingly place the bomb
by switching the dossiers.*"

Georgia nodded. The room fell silent again. Early hobbled over to the
top of the steps on the second-floor landing. He, too, was beaten and battered, on the hard end of a bad Sunday morning, as they all were. He
also said nothing. Just made a somber version of eye contact with his
boss, then looked away. Steel finally spoke.

"It's over, Georgia. It's over. I don't mean with you and me, either. I
mean with you, with this. All of this." Georgia calmly agreed.

"Yes. It is over. All of it." Her head bobbed as she took it all in. The
room sat numb, waiting for her to process it all.

"It has to be put down elegantly though. There's so, so much at
stake. I'm not talking about for me here, know that. For so many. For so
many innocents. For you, Davina. All of it, we've all lost so much of ourselves. It's all spun so wildly out of control." She looked over at Tatum.
He was bearing down on her. He wanted the answers and assurance
that she was fully ready to give him. She knew she owed him a moment
to let his shoulders drop, to know that his ordeal had truly ended.

"Mr. Tatum, I will have you and your family flown home safely to
Chicago, in quiet, first thing tomorrow morning, on a private plane." She
looked up to Early, giving him the note to have it done. Early looked over
to Adam and told him with another nod that he could trust him, that it'd
be just as she promised. "There will, of course, be no charges filed, and, in
fact, I will firmly and fully publicly declare your unbridled innocence."

"I want something else."

"What is it? Money?"

"No, fuck you lady, it isn't money." Georgia was taken aback. No one
had ever really spoken to her that way.

"What is it, then?"

"I want my father-in-law's body. I want to take him to Chicago with us." Georgia looked to Early, once again silently telling him to make it happen. She turned to address Steel.

"I will resign my office in sixty days. I will leave politics forever. I need a quick moment to drain the riverbed of those who are involved while keeping the full disclosure of what has happened under wraps for as long as possible—hopefully many years. Anything other than all of us quietly leaving right this moment and dutifully repairing whatever can be rectified in the next bit of time will only lead to both of us, Davina, in prison and an irreparable body blow to the people's psyche, the flow of government, and the very future of Great Britain. Do you see that?"

Steel swished it all around in her brilliant yet frazzled brain.

"If you don't resign, though, I promise I'll come visit, and it won't be to talk about perfume and such. You have sixty days."

"I understand. I do, Davina. I assure you that it's all over. Mr. Tatum, I'm well aware of your file, of my movie debut hanging over my head. All I ask is time to make sure that those behind all that's been done are cut off from the chance to get their hands on the tiller. Then I'll go. Sadly. Gladly. Are we all three agreed?"

Adam nodded and shrugged. All he wanted was to go home and get his family back to something close to normal. He wanted someone to have to pay for Gordon's death, for Richard Lyle, for all that was done, but that was second place to his family's safety, so he'd take this deal and run with it.

Steel agreed as well. She had lost herself, oddly in the same way that Georgia had. Heaton had gotten to both of them, and she'd known immediately, maybe just as Georgia had known in colluding with him, that she had made a disastrous decision in killing him. Something had overcome her, be it fear, rage, vengeance, or weakness: she had been lured out into waters she could never swim back from. She didn't like letting everyone else off the hook to let herself go free, but in this moment it was sound reasoning that Georgia was offering, so, soaked through in shame and regret, Steel went with Georgia's bargain. They all did.

SOMEWHERE OFF IN the distance, toward Albert Hall, there were church bells ringing twelve times. It was noon on a sleepy, now cloudy Sunday morning in London. Each of them quietly left Heaton's shattered, blood-spattered palace. Georgia and Early drove off in Jack's bullet-riddled Ford. Steel, after destroying the security camera system's computers, walked out the drive heading up the street toward her squad car. Adam was just behind her at the mouth of the motor court. She considered offering him a lift but realized that the two of them had not spoken a word to each other. They truly were strangers, she and the man she had hunted all over England.

They looked back at each other, quietly nodded one final time, then each walked the opposite way up the street.

The prime minister went back to her flat at Number 11, sadly took another pill, then a steaming hot shower. Afterward she sat buck naked in her favorite chair, clipping and polishing her toenails as she mentally prepared herself for the days to come. There would be a record-setting firestorm from the media over David Heaton's murder. She was sure Burnlee and his group would cover it up and expose some lurid criminal side of David's life that had overcome him. Some Russian mob or another would be blamed. It would be perfectly papered over and eventually die down, she was sure of that.

She would do as she said, though. In the coming months, she would figure out how to lance the government of Burnlee and the others. She would smoke them out from the places of power they were nestled into, and then she'd be done. She'd resign.

She dressed, dried her hair, and then called her father. Fighting more tears, she told him she needed "help." After her phone call, she made herself a tea. She sipped it slowly as she looked out the leaded windows onto the Horse Guards Parade grounds, trying as hard as she could to not think about Davina Steel.

Steel picked her parents up at St. Pancras station. In a taxi on the way back to their flat, she told them that not only was it all over but that she would be leaving her job. She explained to her mother and father in the best way she could that she had solved the final piece of her puzzle, that the final image, as she pulled back to view the totality, wasn't the image of a person she was looking to be. She promised them she would never go back to that world. Her mother cried with joy in the rear of the bouncing cab as it made its way down to Bloomsbury.

The next morning, she helped them both open the café for breakfast. As she and Sheena hot-mopped the linoleum floor, her mother asked innocently about Georgia Turnbull, about the possibility of working for her.

"You two seem to get on so well, Davina. Why in God's name not?" Steel stopped what she was doing. She said nothing, then finally craned back to her mother, her eyes full and worn wet with a quiet sadness.

"Georgia Turnbull is dead to me, Mother. I'm going to ask you nicely to never mention her name again, okay?" Sheena wasn't sure what to say or how to answer. She wanted to ask more, hear more, but knew it was best to let her daughter just keep on with her mopping.

"Yes. Yes, of course, doll. The name'll never come up again. I promise."

Steel went and washed her face in the sink. She soaked it in the cool water, then dried off. She walked to the counter by the window and quietly looked out onto the street, watching the cars and the people going back and forth, trying desperately not to see Georgia Turnbull's face in the crowd.

TATUM ▪ 10

On Monday morning, the Tatum family was driven to Luton Airport where they quietly boarded a Bombardier Global 5000, a private business jet that had been chartered by the prime minister's office to fly them home to Chicago. The kids were more than happy to be flying in their "very own" plane, and Kate, though still cautious, was finally settling in to the fact that the worst was behind them. She tried not to deal too much with the sharp heartache she felt every time she remembered that her father was dead, or for the loss forever of sweet Richard Lyle. She did take some small comfort knowing that Gordon's body was in a coffin in the plane's hold, that Adam had arranged for them to take him home to Chicago with them.

There was so much not to think about as she climbed the metal steps to the private jet and lumbered into the row of plush leather seats alongside Adam. They were going home and the kids were safe. She tried her best to focus on that and find whatever comfort she could.

Adam was numb as well. He was aching, beaten, bitten, and nearly broken. He was alive and free, though. Isn't that really all that mattered? What was really important? What could be walked away from? Each question raised another. Could he ever just be a normal guy with a family again? What about Kate? Had he dragged her too close to hell to ever live with her in happiness again? Would she ever just want to take a long quiet walk with him, or would every conversation forever be loaded down with pain, discomposure, and grief?

What about his children? Something told him they both would be able to recover, that they each would come to know in their hearts that their father was a victim, that he came out a victor. One day soon, he thought, they would take comfort in that and in the fact that they stood by his side through it all. It was all too soon, though. Everything was still too bitter. Everything still too raw to take much heart from. All that assessment would come along much later. There was no point in taking anyone's temperature on anything yet. There was no possible way to get any kind of an accurate reading, so he didn't. He just stared out the window at the private jet terminal's concourse.

As the plane took off, Kate instinctively took his hand. Her skin was as soft as he could ever remember it being, her fingers wrapped tightly around his. Once in the air, as the aircraft settled into the long flight east, she turned to him with a needy query.

"This is all over, right? All of it? With all of them? These people? It's done, yes?" He looked lovingly into his pretty blond wife's blue eyes. He stroked her creamy cheek while making an oath to himself that no matter what happened between the two of them, this would be the very last time in his life that he ever lied to her.

"Yes, babe. It is. It's all over."

ACKNOWLEDGMENTS

Being a first novel, this work needed more help than maybe another book would have, and so I have many people to thank. First is my wife, Diane, who is always my closest confidante and bearer of all news and views during dreaming, writing, rewriting, selling, and then even more rewriting. She was more than helpful in many early morning talks and late night walks. Then of course my truly special daughter Molly, the very first to read the book once I had written it and who gave notes along with Diane. Also, my good friend Peter Thompson, the former newspaper editor and historian who lives in London and has walked many, many of these streets with me for hours at a time, and was an early reader as well a strong sounding board. Also thanks to the American ex-pat novelist and rabble-rouser, London-based Christina Robert Thompson, who read early and gave good feedback as well.

There's a huge debt of gratitude to my good pal from Detroit, Mitch Albom, another early reader, a solid friend along the way and, in so many aspects, a bright spot on the horizon always worth heading for. The biggest debt is probably to David Gernert, my agent who picked *Keep Calm* from a pile and made it, with his support and expertise, a real book. I can't fully express what a treat it's been to have an agent with his level of experience and insight behind me.

Much thanks of course to Steve Rubin and everyone at Henry Holt who bought the book and believed in it right away, and of course the book's editor, Michael Signorelli, who taught me a lot about how much fruit can be harvested from having a first-class editor to rely on. This book went through so many changes once David, Steve, and Michael came on board that it would be unfair not to mention how much they have each added and, in fact, literally transformed the work.

Thanks are also in order for Adam Levine at Verve, my agent and friend, Alex Gartner, my longtime producing pal, and Chuck Roven at Atlas films. A shout-out as well to Toby Emmerich at New Line Cinema who was also an early reader and threw in some good threads that the story needed. Much love needs to be showered on my two best friends Clay Tatum and Dr. Kevin Sands and also my longtime buddy Max Kennedy, all who have helped and backed me in so many ways, for so many years, as have my dear friends Olugbemiga Idowu, Rachel Zimmerman Leonard, and Shauna Roberston Norton and my brothers Gary, Lee, and Jack, all who I love so much.

Finally thanks to Judy Trumbull Binder, my sweet, nutty, funny, mother, Eli and Edye Broad, my amazing godparents, who have been so warm to me for as long as I have memory. To Jeanne Binder, my wonderful and not at all wicked stepmother, who first taught me the value of a good book, and also to my sister Kristen Binder Stevens and her husband, Stan, all the above for supporting me for an entire lifetime.

And last I have to thank my mentor, brother, friend, coach, and confidant, Larry Brezner, the funniest, warmest, noblest, most talented and craziest man I ever knew. Thanks for always being my pal. I miss you so much Lar. God bless.

ABOUT THE AUTHOR

MIKE BINDER is an award-winning director, screenwriter, and producer. His latest film is *Black or White*, starring Kevin Costner. Originally from Detroit, Mike lives in Santa Monica, California, with his wife, Diane, and their two children. *Keep Calm* is his first novel.

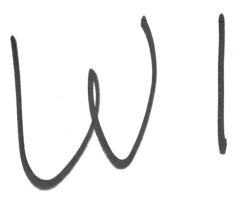

22390

F
Bin

Binder, Mike.

Keep calm

DUE DATE 28.00